Praise for
THE WEDDING SEASON

"Birchall manages to design a cheer squad of fully supportive chums and a sexy, sensitive love interest in this witty, relatable tale that doesn't fall prey to the trite rom-com formula you may be expecting."
—*USA Today*

"Birchall strikes gold with the comedic cadence of her prose and balances the humor with her winning heroine's sincere efforts to find her inner strength. This is a snappy, empowering pick for fans of Sophie Kinsella."
—*Publishers Weekly*

"A fast-paced, well-written story . . . the real HEA ending is Freya's realization that being jilted was a beginning, not an end."
—*Library Journal*

"*The Wedding Season* is the perfect antidote to recent stressful times; like a glass of prosecco, it's bubbly, fun, and over way too fast."
—Lindsay Emory, author of *The Royal Runaway*

"Fun, hilarious, and heartwarming, *The Wedding Season* is like a giant hug for anyone who has faced the challenge of a failed relationship. With a stellar cast of loyal friends, quirky family members, and a wacky plan to get through the wedding season, this book had me laughing, crying happy tears, and turning pages late into the night."
—Sara Desai, author of *The Singles Table*

"An utterly charming story about what to do when life hands you Something Blue: turn it into Something New. *The Wedding Season* is exactly what I needed to read right now."
—Julia Whelan, author of *My Oxford Year*

"I adored *The Wedding Season*! Its wit made me laugh, its relatability made me cry, and its delicious slow-burn romance had me swooning. I can't wait to read what Birchall writes next."

—Lacie Waldon, author of *The Layover*

Praise for
THE SECRET BRIDESMAID

"A pure delight."

—*BookPage* (starred review)

"A unique, hilarious spin on wedding mayhem. Birchall pays just as much attention to the complex nuances of female friendship as to the healing power of love, resulting in an entertaining romp."

—*Publishers Weekly*

"With a delightfully plucky heroine and laugh-out-loud hijinks, *The Secret Bridesmaid* gives the wedding rom-com a much-needed update: focusing on the friendships between women as much as the romance. Charming, escapist fun."

—Katharine McGee, *New York Times*
bestselling author of *American Royals*

"This laugh-out-loud funny rom-com provides the cheery escapism we all need these days. Charming, hopeful, and swoon-worthy enough to sweep even the most level-headed reader off their feet."

—Hannah Orenstein, author of *Meant to Be Mine*

"Hilarious and heartwarming—the perfect wedding season read."

—Heidi Swain, *Sunday Times* bestselling author

ALSO BY KATY BIRCHALL

The Wedding Season

The Secret Bridesmaid

Jane Austen's Emma (Awesomely Austen—Illustrated and Retold)

Morgan Charmley: Teen Witch

Hotel Royale: Dramas of a Teenage Heiress

Hotel Royale: Secrets of a Teenage Heiress

Superstar Geek

Team Awkward

Don't Tell the Bridesmaid

How to Be a Princess

The LAST WORD

KATY BIRCHALL

ST. MARTIN'S GRIFFIN
NEW YORK

First published in the United States by St. Martin's Griffin, an imprint of St. Martin's Publishing Group

THE LAST WORD. Copyright © 2023 by Katy Birchall. All rights reserved. Printed in the United States of America. For information, address St. Martin's Publishing Group, 120 Broadway, New York, NY 10271.

www.stmartins.com

Designed by Devan Norman

Library of Congress Cataloging-in-Publication Data

Names: Birchall, Katy, author.
Title: The last word / Katy Birchall.
Description: First U.S. Edition. | New York : St. Martin's Griffin, 2023.
Identifiers: LCCN 2022056749 | ISBN 9781250882752 (trade paperback) | ISBN 9781250882769 (ebook)
Classification: LCC PR6102.I724 L37 2023 | DDC 823/.92—dc23/eng/20221202
LC record available at https://lccn.loc.gov/2022056749

Our books may be purchased in bulk for promotional, educational, or business use. Please contact your local bookseller or the Macmillan Corporate and Premium Sales Department at 1-800-221-7945, extension 5442, or by email at MacmillanSpecialMarkets@macmillan.com.

First U.S. Edition: 2023

10 9 8 7 6 5 4 3 2 1

FOR BEN

The LAST WORD

PROLOGUE

The question is posed toward the end of the night, as a large box of chocolates is passed around the table and Mimi, the host, fills up wine glasses so her fridge isn't left with bottles that are two-thirds drunk. It's been a long, tiring week, so Mimi invited a few of us from the office for a much-needed Friday night boozy dinner party.

"Here's a fun conundrum for you all to consider," announces Dominic. "One that will give us an interesting insight into each other's characters, I reckon."

Mimi smiles, sitting back down at the head of the table. "Sounds intriguing."

"My thirty-one-year-old cousin works at a fashion magazine and she *loves* her job, but her boyfriend has been offered his dream job in New York. So my question to you is: Does she stay here in London, in the job she's worked hard to achieve, but potentially risk losing the man of her dreams to long distance, *or* does she hand in her notice and risk unemployment across the pond, but take the leap for love?" Dominic asks with a raised eyebrow, swilling the wine round his glass. "What do you think— should she stick or twist?"

"Hmm." Rakhee folds her arms. "Does she believe that this guy is The One?"

"She's sure of it." Dominic nods.

"Well then, it's an easy answer," Mimi says with a shrug. "She moves to New York."

"I could have guessed you'd say that." Dominic grins at her. "You've always had a romantic streak."

"I agree with Mimi," chips in Amy. "Take the leap for love. Plus, she gets to move to New York! It's a no-brainer."

"I'm not so sure; jury's out on this one," Rakhee declares, holding up her hands. "I need more time to think about it. There are advantages and disadvantages both ways you look at it."

Dominic laughs. "All right, we'll let you think on it." His eyes flash at me. "Harper?"

I take a sip of wine, as though I need more time to consider. But the truth is, before Dominic had even finished asking the question, I knew my answer.

"I'd stick," I confirm. "She's worked hard for her career. Why risk giving all of that up for . . ."

I trail off with a shrug.

"Love?" Mimi finishes for me.

"Right." I nod.

"Another answer I think we could all safely guess," Dominic sighs, giving me a knowing smile before putting on a melodramatic voice. "You're too good at your job for something as frivolous as *love* to come first."

I hold up my glass to him. "Exactly."

"Oh, I wouldn't be so sure," Mimi says. "I think if the right person came along, you might reconsider. Should she fall head over heels in love, Harper might prove to have been a secret romantic all along. If you ask me, he's out there somewhere. She just needs to give him a chance."

I laugh, shaking my head at her.

I know for a fact she's wrong, but I don't say anything.

Because then I'd have to explain why.

I'd have to tell her about how, a long time ago, I *did* give someone a chance. Someone who swept me off my feet with the kind of whirlwind, dizzying romance you read about in books and watch in movies and listen to in song lyrics. Someone who really knew me, who understood me, who made me feel as though I was all he needed to be *happy*.

It was everything I'd been told to hope for: I got lost in his eyes when he looked at me; I couldn't stop thinking about him when I was supposed to be concentrating on something else. As soon as I gave in to him, I was utterly intoxicated. I got caught up in fanciful daydreams of what we might end up being to one another, of a future together.

When I was with him, the rest of the world simply faded away.

Mimi doesn't know it, but I already met that person, the one who opened my eyes to what it was like to fall head over heels.

But I learned my lesson.

So I may not be able to say it out loud, but Mimi is wrong that someday my priorities will shift. Since him, work has always come first and will continue to do so. No one will change my mind, of that I'm quite sure.

Love won't get the better of me again.

CHAPTER ONE

FIVE MONTHS LATER

Yⁿou didn't hear this from me."

I jump at the sound of a whispery voice over my shoulder and spin round to see a young woman in her late twenties dressed in a figure-hugging black dress and towering heels, holding a half-empty champagne flute loosely in her hand.

"I'm sorry," I say. "Are you talking to me?"

She nods, glancing up and down the pavement to check that we're alone while the noise of the party rages from the building a few yards behind her. It hadn't been easy to retrieve my jacket from the cloakroom attendant, who was irritated that his celeb-spotting was being interrupted. More than a few A-listers are here to mark the release of a highly anticipated album from Mercury Prize–winning band Dark Lights.

I scrutinize the woman's face—hazel eyes framed with heavy black-kohl eyeliner, perfectly arched full eyebrows, flawless skin, delicate features, and a sharp jaw—attempting to work out which genre of celebrity she belongs to. She's gorgeous, tall and willowy, so she could easily be a model or actor, but she is so stylish and well turned out that she could also be in fashion, makeup, or hair.

I suppose there's a chance she could be a journalist, like me— although judging by her outfit she probably works for one of the high-end glossies with access to the fashion closet, as opposed to the weekend magazine supplement of a national newspaper.

"Like I said, you didn't hear this from me," she repeats in a low voice, "but Audrey Abbot has accepted the lead role in a new play. Rehearsals are about to start."

"*What?*"

"It will be directed by Gabrielle Reed," the woman continues.

"The one who directed *A Streetcar Named Desire* at The Old Vic last year?"

"That's her. She wanted Audrey to take the role from the moment she read the play. It will be Audrey's first acting role in—"

"Sixteen years." I look at her suspiciously. "Who are you? How do you know this?"

She smiles at me guiltily. "I'm Gabrielle Reed's PA. Nicole. Nice to meet you."

"Likewise," I say. "But I need to tell you that I'm a journalist. So, if you want to take any of this back, we can pretend this never happened. I don't want you getting in trouble."

"I know who you are, Harper Jenkins," she says, raising her eyebrows in amusement. "I've been waiting to get you alone all night."

I blink at her. "I . . . sorry, I'm a bit confused. I'm obviously grateful that you've approached me—"

"Audrey Abbot is a good person," Nicole says firmly. "She didn't deserve how the press portrayed her after . . . *The Incident.*"

"I'm sure she didn't." I think back to the whirlwind that surrounded Audrey in 2007.

"She deserves to have her story told by the right person."

I smile at her. "I'm flattered. But Audrey Abbot notoriously hates journalists. She hasn't spoken to one, not even to give a quote, since 'The Incident,' as you put it. If what you're saying is true and she has agreed to take a role, I doubt she'll be doing any press."

Nicole nods. "But that won't stop everything from being dragged up again, and she won't have her side of the story told." Her jaw clenches. "It's not fair."

I jump at a horn beeping behind me and realize that my Uber has arrived. I offer the driver what I hope to be a winning smile and hold up a finger to signal that I'll be just a minute, before turning back to Nicole.

"I think you should be the one to do the profile on her comeback," Nicole says hurriedly. "Not the guy at *Expression*."

"Jonathan Cliff?" I wrinkle my nose. "Does he know about this?"

"Not yet . . . this is a very well-kept secret. But I heard one of the producers saying that he'd be worth considering."

"Terrible idea. He wrote a snarky piece about Audrey at the time."

"I know. Why would they even think about asking someone like that?"

I sigh. "Because he can offer a big spread in a prominent monthly magazine. It's rare publicity, especially for a play—the glossies are usually reserved for actors promoting commercial films." I bite my lip. "Audrey Abbot is an icon. She deserves better than Jonathan Cliff."

"That's why I came to you," Nicole says. "The news that she's joined the cast will get out at some point, and I want to ensure that the person breaking the story will see her for who she is and where she's going next. Not just what happened in her past."

"It was pretty ballsy of you to tell me," I say, studying her face. "I'm impressed."

She smiles. "A good journalist wouldn't reveal her source."

"Never."

"So, you'll write the story?" she asks hopefully.

"If she lets me. It's going to be tricky getting through to her."

"If she'll speak to anyone, it'll be someone like you," Nicole says confidently. "You just need to get in there before anyone else."

My driver beeps the horn again.

"I'd better go," I say, gesturing to the car. "Thanks, Nicole."

"You didn't hear about *any* of this from me."

"Hear what?" I grin at her. "Enjoy the rest of the night."

"Thanks, Harper. Good luck."

She clacks back across the pavement and through the door to the party. I apologize to the driver for keeping him waiting before rummaging in my oversized tote for my phone. I need to Google Audrey Abbot to find who it is that represents her. When her agent's name pops up, I grin. Shamari.

Her phone goes straight to voicemail and I realize she might very well be asleep, considering it's already two in the morning. *Whoops.* I enjoyed the party more than I thought I would. There's no way I can bring this up over email, so I decide to speak to her first thing tomorrow.

Before I toss my phone back into the abyss of my handbag, I read the WhatsApps waiting for me from Liam. He messaged hours ago to say he's at my place, if that's okay, as his flatmate had a date and he wanted to get out of his hair, but he hopes the party is great fun and if there's any chance that he can join, to let him know and he will be there.

I feel a flash of regret that I gave him a key to my flat, swiftly followed by a wave of guilt. We've been seeing each other for three months and I think he is officially my "boyfriend" now. I do like him—he's ambitious, enthusiastic, and passionate about his career, which is a big turn-on for me. Not to mention, he's attractive in that sexy, scruffy musician kind of way.

It's also very sweet that he wanted to let his flatmate and his date have the place to themselves. But I'm not sure I was entirely prepared for him to make himself comfortable at my flat quite so soon, especially when I'm not even there. I suppose I've been single so long, I'm set in my ways.

Still, I'm glad I didn't see his message about joining me at the party. If he'd been there, Nicole may not have approached me.

Audrey Abbot. I was obsessed with her as a teenager. She was so elegant and brilliant in everything she did. A classically trained British actor with a dignified air, she was a master of restraint and had the ability to make you feel whatever her character was experiencing with barely any movement in her face.

Her career began in theater, then transitioned to film. She'd become famous in her late twenties and appeared in several Hollywood hits throughout her thirties, both as the lead and in supporting roles. She won an Oscar for Best Supporting Actress in a film that was so dull, I didn't even understand the ending, but she was so fantastic and convincing as the chain-smoking, hard-done-by, bitter wife of the ranch hand that it was worth sitting through two hours of men looking cross and talking about cattle.

I was a teenager when The Incident happened. I felt mortified for her and angry at the cruel headlines. In the aftermath, she withdrew from the public eye and gave up acting, even though she was only in her forties. She became a bit of a joke—The Incident cropped up again and again, alluded to mockingly by comedians and throughout pop culture. It was a lyric in a hit song a few years ago, and a podcast host described it as an "iconic" public meltdown.

By the time I arrive at my flat, I'm convinced I'm the only person who should write about Audrey's return to acting.

Carefully turning the key in my lock, I tiptoe inside and shut the door quietly behind me. A loud snore comes from the bedroom. I leave my bag on the kitchen table and quietly make my way to the bathroom.

After a futile attempt at taking off my makeup, I brush my teeth and strip off my green midi shirt dress, leaving it on the bathroom floor. I trip over one trainer and then another as I pick my way to my side of the bed. I have a vague recollection of tossing the oversized gray T-shirt I slept in last night on the duvet. I feel around and triumphantly locate it crumpled at the bottom of the bed.

I wish I was the kind of person that slept in silk lingerie or slinky posh pajamas, but there's something comforting about a T-shirt that's several sizes too big. Liam and I are surely past the point where I have to pretend I always sleep naked, which is the impression I wanted to give off at first.

I'm climbing into bed when I remember my phone and creep back out of the bedroom to retrieve it from the dreaded depths of my bag.

There's a lot swimming about in there: half-filled pocket notebooks, my digital voice recorder, loose lipsticks and eyeliner pencils, tissue packs, countless biros, stray business cards, miniature perfume samples, crumpled receipts, chewing gum packs, neglected hand moisturizer, a few sunglasses cases (unclear if there actually *are* sunglasses in them), a hairbrush, and the latest psychological thriller that I'm reading.

It's hard to find time to read for fun, so when I do, I want real page-turners with lots of twists and suspense. I don't have time for long descriptions about bleak landscapes. I want to know who murdered whom and why.

I set alarms for 5:55 A.M., 5:57 A.M., 6 A.M., 6:03 A.M., and 6:05 A.M. before placing my phone gently down on my bedside table and snuggling under the duvet. I close my eyes.

Liam emits a loud snore.

I turn my head to glare at him through the darkness.

With the knowledge of only three hours' sleep ahead of me, I will him to shut the hell up. Rudely ignoring me (due to his state of unconsciousness), he continues his nasal symphony until I'm forced to tap him on the arm.

"Liam," I whisper, "you're snoring."

Without really waking, he mutters something and turns over, falling silent.

I smugly turn away, too.

When he starts snoring again, I groan and pull the duvet over my head, accepting my fate. It's my own fault. I know Liam snores and I've been meaning to buy ear plugs, but I keep forgetting. I also really wish I hadn't given him a key. But after last week, I had to.

Liam had stayed Friday night and we'd gone on a coffee run the next morning before he planned to cook brunch back at mine. We were waiting for our drinks when I got a message from an agent that one of her supermodels was taking to Instagram to announce her retirement at twenty-eight—to start her own fruit farm in Devon, naturally—and would I like the exclusive? And if so, any chance I'd be available to speak now?

I apologetically ditched Liam at the café and dashed out with my flat white. It wasn't until after the interview that I checked my phone. Liam had left his jacket in my flat, which held his house keys and wallet, which meant he had been stranded at the café the whole time. Feeling terrible, I tried to call him, before my phone promptly died.

I gave him a key on Monday.

I'm not sure how much sleep I get, but when my first alarm goes off, it feels like maybe I've shut my eyes for thirty seconds.

Liam grunts.

I whisper a half-hearted apology, but he's already back asleep. I try to doze again, but when the third alarm goes off, I finally force myself out of bed and into the bathroom, kicking aside my rumpled dress from last night.

After showering, I begin my daily morning routine of riffling through my disorganized wardrobe, which is only more difficult in the dark.

"What time is it?" Liam mumbles into the pillow.

I don't answer because I'm busy confronting the disappointment that nothing new has miraculously appeared in my wardrobe without me having to do any shopping. Then I notice a skirt that has slipped from its hanger and excitedly recall buying it last summer—a pink-purple floral print maxi that looks great with that black blouse I know I have somewhere.

I successfully find the shirt and tuck it into the skirt, and then slip my feet into my white sneakers—comfortable shoes that I can dash about in are a necessity in my job. Checking my outfit in the mirror, I nod satisfactorily at my reflection.

I wouldn't say I spend a lot of time on my clothes, but I do take pride in my appearance. A fashion journalist once told me that I had a "playful London street style." I'm not *entirely* sure what that means, but I was extremely flattered. I wear sunglasses everywhere I go—I have several pairs, partly because I lose them a lot, but also because they are the easiest way to accessorize without making much effort.

My face is a bit of a rush job, but I make do with foundation and dabs of concealer, a lick of mascara to try to brighten my hazel eyes and disguise the tiredness, bronzer and a matte berry lipstick that the magazine's beauty editor, Amy, recommended for me. Before Amy, I used to always wear nude lipsticks or no lip color at all, preferring to draw attention to my eyes over my lips thanks to my slightly goofy, big front teeth, but I've become a bit more adventurous thanks to her encouragement—the teeth, she says, are all part of my "girl next door" appeal and I should be proud of them.

I sweep my thick wavy brown hair back and tie it in a ponytail. I cannot interview, take notes, or write with hair falling into my face. At the start of my journalism career, sometimes I'd spring for a blow-dry before a big interview, but I'd inevitably become frustrated at having to keep tucking it behind my ears and would tie it back about five minutes after I sat down to work. I know better now and tie it back first thing.

Rushing back into the bedroom, I step round to Liam's side and lean over to give him a peck on the cheek. I admire his mop of dark curly hair and his long dark lashes. He has that relaxed, sexy look and style of an indie rock star, but one that bothers to shower.

He moves as my lips brush his stubbled cheek, but doesn't open his eyes.

"Sorry, early start today," I whisper as he snuggles farther into the duvet. "Help yourself to coffee or anything you need."

"Have a good day," he mumbles, still not opening his eyes.

I'm halfway down the stairs when I remember my phone charging by the bedside. I run back up, reaching around for my keys—I really should keep them in the inside zip pouch of my bag.

"Harper?" Liam asks, squinting at me as I burst back into the bedroom.

"Sorry!" I whisper, grabbing my phone. "Forgot something."

"Dinner tonight?" he says, his voice muffled into his pillow.

"Sounds great."

I make it to the front door before I remember that my AirPods, which I'll need to do my transcribing later, are on the kitchen counter. By the time I make it outside my building, I imagine I've done a considerable amount of my goal steps today, but I'll never know because the smartwatch I bought is god-knows-where.

I speed walk to Brixton tube, hop on the Victoria line, and zip up to Oxford Circus, emerging into the sunshine and making my way to Soho.

I reach my destination at quarter past seven.

The Lark is a trendy independent café, perfectly located far away enough from Regent Street and Oxford Street that it doesn't attract too many tourists, but still central enough on a bustling side street to fuel the local office workers and the West

End artists with its top-notch coffee. I order a flat white to go before walking down the road to lean against a wall and scroll through my phone while I wait.

At half past seven, I see Shamari heading into The Lark. I smile to myself. She really is a creature of routine. Shamari is five foot four and a force of nature, one of the best agents in the business, and renowned for being fiercely protective of her clients. She's never afraid to go after what she wants on their behalf, even if it's a decidedly punchy request. With her poker-straight black hair cut in a chic bob, bold red lipstick, and a fitted black dress with heels, Shamari looks ready for battle today. As ever.

I put my phone away and saunter back toward the café, sipping my coffee and lingering to the side. A few minutes later, she marches back out. I head straight toward her.

"Shamari!" I gasp, feigning complete surprise.

"Harper Jenkins," she says, a knowing smile creeping across her lips as she comes to a stop in front of me. "What are *you* doing here?"

"Just grabbing the best coffee in London before I head to the office," I say, gesturing to The Lark. "I don't know what beans they're using, but this stuff is gold."

"Your office is in Vauxhall," she remarks. "Nowhere near Oxford Street."

"A small sacrifice for the really good stuff."

"Funny I should bump into you at the exact time and place I get my coffee every morning," she says, tilting her head at me.

"London is just one big small town, isn't it? Anyway, tell me your news! What have you been up to?"

"You can walk me to the office and tell me what you want on the way," she offers, rolling her eyes.

"How cynical of you to think I want something," I remark, falling into step with her. "Comes with being Britain's most esteemed talent agent, I guess."

"Flattery gets you everywhere. Come on, Harper, get to the point."

"I heard that Audrey Abbot is returning to acting."

She halts in her tracks to stare at me in disbelief.

"How did you find out about that?"

"So it's true, then." I brighten. "That's great news!"

She sighs before continuing toward her office. "Who told you?"

"You know I never reveal my sources."

"Don't get any ideas about Audrey, Harper, you're wasting your time," Shamari says loftily. "You know as well as I do that she does not do press. She won't go anywhere near journalists. She's made that very clear."

"She also made it clear that she wouldn't act again, but you obviously have sway there," I point out carefully.

"I didn't *sway* her to do anything."

"You have to let me do a piece on her," I plead.

"How about, instead, you interview Julian Newt?"

"Who the hell is Julian Newt?"

"My latest client and the fabulous actor playing her nephew," Shamari informs me. "I'm sure you've watched *Tell Me Again*, the Netflix rom-com he was in recently? That's right up your street."

"Oh, yes! The main guy? He's sexy," I recall.

"You want to interview him? He's *very* charming."

"Ah." I smile mischievously. "You have a *thing* for him."

She shoots me a look. "No, Harper! He's my client."

"A sexy client."

"All my clients are sexy. I represent actors and models," she reminds me.

"And I want an interview with your client Audrey Abbot."

"Harper—"

"Think about it, Shamari," I press, refusing to back down.

"A huge profile piece about her illustrious career and welcome return to the stage. It's the comeback of the year! The comeback of the decade! Maybe even the century."

"You wrote that about Craig David."

"Okay, fine, I stand by that. But still, Audrey Abbot returning will make front page of the magazine, guaranteed."

"She hates journalists, Harper. You need to let this go," she insists.

"She has every reason to hate journalists, but you *know* me— you know what kind of journalist I am. I'm not in this to tear people down; I'm all about bringing people up. With me, Audrey can tell her side of the story—or if she doesn't want to talk about what happened, we'll focus on her landing a kickass role after sixteen years out of the game, in a play written by a woman and directed by a woman. Shamari, this is her opportunity. I know it! Don't let someone else write this and screw it up. Let me reintroduce her to the public in the respectful manner she deserves."

Shamari slows down, coming to a halt outside her office door. She takes a sip of coffee and then looks at me earnestly.

"Harper, did you get much sleep last night?"

"Huh?"

"I got a call from you at two in the morning and then you're waiting for me at half seven, acting bright as a button," she remarks. "How do you do it?"

I hold up my cup. "The best coffee in London."

She laughs, shaking her head. "You still with that guy? You said there was someone new when I saw you about a month ago."

"Liam? Yes."

"He's lasted longer than most," she remarks. "Nice to see you happy."

"I'll tell you all about him if you let me chat to Audrey Abbot." She sighs. "You're like a dog with a bone."

"You know it will be excellent publicity for the play, too. The producers will love you for setting this up. They must have ideas for press in the pipeline."

"They knew Audrey wouldn't do any. They've lined up Julian Newt to do most of it."

"So a man can take all the credit for a show that wouldn't exist without the female talent on and offstage?"

Shamari closes her eyes in despair. "I'm envisioning the conversation I'll have with her when I pitch this. She'll bite my head off at the mere suggestion."

"You can vouch for me. Do you remember how you introduced me to Heather Violet at the launch of her delicious rosé? You said I was the one celebrity reporter who genuinely cared."

"I was a bottle of said delicious rosé down at that point," she recalls. "I also described her role in the film *Little Pig's Grand Adventure* as 'inspired' to a renowned director."

"I'm sure she was very good in *Little Pig's Grand Adventure*."

"She was, actually. Not easy working with a pig."

"How about this—a profile piece on Audrey Abbot's comeback, front page, *and* I'll feature that sexy Newt actor that you have a thing for in one of my regular features. He could do the 'My Little Luxuries' column."

"I do *not* have a thing for him," she emphasizes.

I smile and say nothing.

She lifts her eyes to the sky before relenting. "*Fine.* I'll see what I can do."

I beam at her. "Thank you! And when she agrees—"

"*If* she agrees," she corrects. "Let me remind you, she has refused to speak to any journalists for sixteen years."

"We can sort it quickly, yes? I want to break this before any other journos come sniffing around. We go to press in three days—I can turn it round by then and guarantee she gets the front page."

"Fine, fine. You know they haven't even started rehearsals yet?"

"Tickets will be sold out within minutes of being released. I'll have her audience primed and ready." I drain the last of my coffee. "You're the best, Shamari. Call me when you have it locked down and we can organize a time and place for the interview. I'm around all of today and tomorrow."

"You're talking as though she's already agreed to it," Shamari mutters, pushing open the door to her office building.

"If anyone can do this, it's you. Oh, before you go," I say quickly, "speaking of Heather Violet, how is she doing?"

"Why do you ask?"

"I saw that her ex, that record producer, was spotted out for dinner with someone else—when I interviewed her, she was totally smitten with him. I read about their breakup a few weeks ago, but it still feels quite soon for him to be openly dating. I've been wondering if she's all right."

Shamari looks at me curiously. "You really aren't like the other journos, are you? I haven't spoken to her about it, but when I do, I'll say you were asking after her."

"Thanks." I check the time on my phone and give her a wave. "I'm off. Let me know when Audrey wants to do the interview!"

"*If* she wants to do the interview," she calls out after me, her voice echoing down the street as I hurry away in the direction of the tube. "*If*, Harper!"

CHAPTER TWO

arper," Cosmo greets me in a strained voice as I hurry into the meeting room. "How nice of you to join us."

I somehow get the sleeve of my blouse caught on the door handle, so I have to take a couple of steps back to free my arm before entering the room properly.

"Sorry I'm late, everyone," I announce brightly, addressing the whole editorial team dotted around the long table.

"One of these days, you might just surprise us, Harper, and be on time for something," Cosmo grumbles.

"I'm late today for a very good reason," I justify, sliding into the empty seat nearest the door. "I've got a great scoop!"

"Oh?" Cosmo snorts. "Some pop star get a buttlift? Or perhaps a model has released a groundbreaking statement that she—shock, horror—drinks green juice? I seem to remember you were late last week for a 'very good reason' also, which turned out to be chasing down a B-list teenage actor involved in some ridiculous cause."

He sniggers. I fix him with a steely glare.

"You mean the nineteen-year-old Academy Award nominee leading a campaign to highlight the lack of access to clean water for billions of people across the world? Is that the cause you're referring to as *ridiculous*?"

Cosmo flushes, his jaw clenching.

I catch Mimi's eye across the table. She flashes me a winning smile before turning to observe Cosmo's reaction like the rest of the team.

"Of course not," Cosmo mumbles eventually, clearing his throat. "A very important issue in the world today. Anyway, as I was saying before I was *interrupted*, we need to discuss cover options."

As he begins his usual practice of firing questions across the table at every editor but me, I fish my notepad out of my bag in case by some miracle he's interested in any of the pieces I have lined up for the next issue.

Cosmo Chambers-Smyth: editor-in-chief of our magazine, *Narrative*, and a constant belittler of my job. He has been in his post for a year and a half and still finds my role here as celebrity editor completely baffling. Our previous editor had been supportive of my work, so it was quite the shock when during Cosmo's first editorial meeting, he burst out laughing when I introduced myself, before saying, "No, really, what is your *actual* job title?"

Cosmo used to be a features editor for *The Correspondence*, the newspaper for which *Narrative* is the weekend supplement magazine, so we'd all seen him waltzing through the open-plan office before, strutting about like he owned the place. Fifty-something, he's extremely proud of his thick mop of dark wavy hair, which he meticulously combs to one side. With his permanently smug, self-congratulatory attitude, Cosmo is unabashedly pompous and entitled. He makes snide comments about his (no doubt long-suffering) ex-wife, is much more at ease in the company of men, and seems like the type of guy who isn't afraid to say that it's a crying shame private members' clubs around London opened their doors to women.

He may be a decent writer and proofreader, but he is majorly lacking when it comes to content that he has no interest in personally. I've always believed that working at a magazine like

Narrative is a privilege—it's got an excellent reputation for reliable and well-researched journalism and it covers a huge variety of topics: culture, lifestyle, travel, fashion, food, and, best of all, it includes insightful interviews with public figures. It's the perfect magazine to curl up with over the weekend. Its editor-in-chief should be someone who values and celebrates *all* these things, not just those that interest him as an individual. But Cosmo has connections high up the ladder, so when the top job came up at *Narrative*, he was deemed the man to increase the readership and bring in more advertising revenue.

The fashion and beauty editors suffer under his leadership, too, but at least he acknowledges that luxury fashion shoots help secure big ad buys. When it comes to my work, however, he loves to offer his sneering opinion.

"Readers don't care about this *person*," he spat during his first week, as I proudly showed him the mock-up of the four-page spread I'd written about a Radio One presenter. "Let's cut this to one page."

"What? Are you serious?" I asked, flabbergasted.

"I want to make room for the piece on the new Cotswolds country club," he said simply, as though that cleared everything up. "The sort of thing our readers like to read about. Luxurious and aspirational."

"I don't understand. That's only a one-page piece at a stretch, and this one is already laid out and—"

"I don't recognize this so-called celebrity," he interrupted, waving his hand across the pages. "Why should I care how she has come to 'love herself'? Sounds like vain nonsense."

"If you read it, you'll see that she's been through a lot to get to where she is today, overcoming the kind of challenges that—"

"One page is enough on this sort of thing," he stated, cutting me off again. "Next time, bring me something that features people who are household names. What about a piece on that F1 driver? You know, someone who's actually achieved something."

I narrowed my eyes at him. "She's a top-tier radio DJ."

He shrugged before ushering me out of his office. I should have known then that getting Cosmo Chambers-Smyth to take me seriously was going to be a lost cause, but I held on to the hope that he was throwing his weight around as a new editor-in-chief and would soon settle into the role. After all, celebrity features are not only some of the most popular sections in both our print and online editions, but they usually provide the cover headline and help juice social engagement. He must recognize that my features are crucial to our numbers because he hasn't fired me. Yet.

Still, I'm proud of what I contribute to *Narrative*, and since I don't have much respect for Cosmo, I'm never afraid to snap back—which he clearly *hates*.

He's not beloved by the rest of the editorial staff, either, and they're in my corner when I need help getting my point across. Mimi, my best friend and the travel editor, is my lifesaver.

Sophisticated, smart, and demure, Mimi is amazingly observant and thoughtful. She also loves nothing better than to organize things and boss me around, which I'm the first to admit that I need, since my head tends to be all over the place. We first met years ago when we worked at *Flair*—sadly now defunct—and then eighteen months after I moved to *Narrative*, the travel editor role came up and Mimi snagged it, so we could continue the best-friend dream of working together.

She's happily married to Katya, a top surgeon who is equally as gorgeous and elegant as Mimi. On the rare and pleasurable occasion that Katya is not on shift and is at home when I go round to theirs for dinner, I feel like such a jumbled mess compared with the two of them as they glide around their immaculate Clapham house—which somehow always smells amazing—in their chic, creaseless clothes. I know that Mimi has a mild heart attack whenever she sets foot in my flat, and she keeps threatening to put in an application for me to appear on one of those shows where they declutter your home, but it would be pointless. I'd mess it up as soon as the TV crew left.

Before Liam came on the scene, Katya and Mimi loved to talk about setting me up with one of Katya's fascinating and "successful" doctor friends, but I think we all secretly knew that her colleagues wouldn't be thrilled at the prospect of being matched with someone that Katya once (affectionately) described as having a "haphazard personality."

Mimi's not the only ally I have on the team—I'm lucky to get on well with the features editor, Rakhee, who sits next to me and is, crucially, revered by Cosmo. This comes in handy when I'm fighting for a celebrity piece and Cosmo is being dismissive, because Rakhee will usually come to my rescue and help him see reason. Like everyone, Cosmo finds it difficult to say no to Rakhee. She's fiercely intelligent and intimidating, and excellent at arguing her point. When I first started at *Narrative*, I was terrified of her, but once you get to know her, you see her softer side. Without her in my corner, I don't think Cosmo would let me write half the stories I pitch.

"All right, so cover options—Rakhee, where are we at with the Don Bright piece?" Cosmo asks, clasping his hands together and leaning forward onto the table.

"The writer filed the feature this morning," she answers.

"Don is a man to watch," Cosmo declares, wagging his finger as though this is an invaluable piece of wisdom. "I've already got the headline for the cover: 'The Future's Bright.' Brilliant, eh?"

"Yeah, um, I'm not sure this should be our cover piece," Rakhee remarks.

Cosmo turns to her in surprise. "Why not? He's one of the

country's leading businessmen. Every company he touches turns to gold."

"But he's boring," she says matter-of-factly, tapping her pen against her notepad. "The writer had warned me that he didn't give her much in way of quotes. He keeps his cards close to his chest, which may make him a shrewd businessman, but a lousy subject. He didn't give her anything personal to work with at all. Mostly just profit figures. I should have sent Harper to interview him; she might have been able to draw out a personality."

"Facts and figures are interesting!" Cosmo argues.

"Not these. Look, the writer has done a fine job with what she had, but I wouldn't be drawing our readers to this piece as the main event of the edition." Rakhee's eyes flash across the table at me. "Have you got anything good this week that might make a cover story, Harper?"

"Well, funny you should ask, because—"

"I've already decided that Don Bright is our cover story," Cosmo declares in an end-of-conversation tone. "Right, on to the travel pages. Mimi, overview please."

Rakhee sighs and shrugs at me.

When Cosmo later declares the meeting has come to an end, everyone's on their feet in a flash, all of us desperate to get out of the stuffy glass box that is Meeting Room Three and return to our corner of the vast open-plan office that houses the main print newspaper, the weekend magazine, and digital. In general, we don't mingle. The digital group keeps to themselves, and the reporters on the main paper are a very serious lot.

"How does your desk not stress you out?" Rakhee asks, appearing behind me once I've plonked myself down in my office chair.

I swivel round to face her. "I'm creative."

"You're messy."

"It's organized mess."

"Sure," she replies, unconvinced, sitting down at her desk right next to mine. "So that means you know where everything is?"

I scan the contents of my desk—pages of old, scribbled notes, books (mostly celebrity memoirs) I've been sent and haven't gotten round to reading yet, ticket stubs, passes, and lanyards—and conclude it is, admittedly, a little overcrowded.

"All that matters is I can see my keyboard," I point out, pushing a file off the keys so I can type. "And everything else is within reach as soon as I need it. Thanks for your help in the meeting, by the way. I appreciate it."

"Not that it did any good." She looks pained, focusing on her screen and clicking her mouse. "That Don Bright piece almost sent me to sleep."

"Don't worry. I have someone lined up for the front page, and, when I secure the interview, she'll be impossible to turn down for a front cover," I inform her excitedly.

She turns to me, intrigued. "Do tell."

"My lips are sealed, but ask me again tomorrow. In fact, you won't have to ask. I'll be shouting it from the rooftops."

"How was the album launch last night?" Rakhee asks, suddenly remembering. "Did any of the musicians smash anything?"

"Unfortunately not," I reply, to her great disappointment. "But it was fun."

"Rock stars aren't what they used to be. Did you take Liam?"

"No, but he was at mine when I got home last night."

She raises her eyebrows. "Interesting. He's quickly become a live-in boyfriend."

"No, no," I insist, opening my inbox and watching the unread emails begin to load. "He needed somewhere to stay because his housemate had a date."

"Thanks for leaving me behind, *traitor*," Mimi hisses as she sits at her desk, directly opposite mine. "Cosmo cornered me at the end of the meeting."

"Ugh, sorry." I grimace. "What did he want?"

"He was angling for another press trip, I'll guess," Rakhee mutters.

Mimi nods and leans in between our desktops.

"I know when he hears about the trip for that French golf club, he'll want to take the spot, but I was going to offer it to Dominic. I know he's into golf." Mimi sighs, sitting back to log in, her perfectly manicured fingers tapping gently across the keys.

"Don't tell Cosmo about it until it's too late," Rakhee suggests as she types loudly, in complete contrast to Mimi, as though the keys have somehow offended her. "Say Dominic is already booked in."

"I can try." Mimi tilts her head to look at me past her screen. "How was the rave last night?"

"The *album launch* was fun."

"Why were you late this morning and what's this big cover story?" Mimi asks eagerly. "Did the lead singer offer you an exclusive on his solo career? I think he's into you."

I look at her in panic. "Solo career? Where did you hear that? Oh my god, when did it break? I can't believe it—they went to school together and started the band when they were all, like, fifteen years old in a garage at one of their parents' houses! They can't be splitting up!"

"I was *joking!*" Mimi holds up her hands. "Whoa, that was intense! And you completely skipped over the part where I said that the lead singer of a famous band has a crush on you."

"Firstly, that joke was *not funny*. Secondly, no he doesn't."

"He sent you that box of donuts."

Rakhee gasps. "Someone sent in donuts? When?"

"Last week," Mimi says. "I think you were out at your dentist appointment. No, wait . . . that was the week before. Where were you last week on donut day?"

Rakhee waves her hand. "Doesn't matter, why did he send you donuts?"

"They weren't from him, they were from the band. And it's because I wrote a piece about how wonderful they are," I laugh. "The lead singer is dating the glamorous actor from that sitcom about the Irish pub in Normandy. I saw them together last night and they looked very happy. I think she might be The One for him, you know."

"Did you bring Liam to the soirée?" Mimi asks.

"Rakhee asked, too. You're making me feel bad—what're the relationship rules on these things? Should I be asking him to work events?"

"I'm not sure anyone would enjoy being your plus-one," Mimi comments. "You flit round the room at a hundred miles per hour talking to anyone and everyone. It makes me dizzy."

"It's my *job.*"

"Liam was waiting for her when she got home last night, though," Rakhee informs Mimi without looking up from her work.

"Ooh." Mimi smiles wickedly at me. "Booty call."

"It was *not* a booty call," I tell them regretfully. "He was asleep when I got back and when I left this morning. We didn't even speak. I should check my phone actually to see if he's messaged; he said something about dinner later."

I start searching around my feet for my bag. I spin round in my swivel chair a few times, examining the floor.

"What are you doing?" Mimi asks.

I groan. "I left my bag in the meeting room."

"I'll come with you. I want a coffee anyway," Mimi says, standing. "I'm guessing you won't turn down a coffee, Rakhee?"

"You know me so well," Rakhee says, typing away furiously again.

Gabby, our editorial assistant who sits a couple of rows behind, overhears.

"I can get your coffees if you like," she sweetly offers, glancing up from her screen.

"That's okay," I say. "I need to rescue my bag from the meeting room."

"You'd lose your head if it wasn't screwed on," chuckles Dominic from the picture desk as we wander by.

"Hey! If you still want early screening tickets to the next Ryan Reynolds movie, I'd be careful about your tone," I say breezily.

"Have I told you lately how amazing you are?" he adds quickly.

"That's more like it." I grin, winking at him.

Mimi is waylaid at the picture desk about one of the hotels she's featuring in an all-inclusive round-up, so I go ahead, swiftly passing Cosmo's glass office that is situated next to Meeting Room Three. Facing away from the door, he's on the phone, leaning back in his chair with his feet on the desk. His eyes are fixed on the bookcase that runs the length of the wall.

I bet he's not listening to a word of the conversation, instead admiring that ridiculous trophy that's pride of place in the middle of the shelves.

When Cosmo first moved into his new office, it was the first thing to be unpacked, carefully positioned in the center of the bookshelves. We all assumed it was a journalism award, but when Mimi made the mistake of asking about it, she got a long-winded, blow-by-blow account of how he'd won a bowling tournament the previous year. He drops it into conversation whenever he can, which you'd think would be quite tricky, but he manages it surprisingly often.

I reach Meeting Room Three and spot my bag straightaway through the glass, on the floor under the table.

I've already entered before I realize that the room isn't empty.

A man is standing at the other end of the table, and he glances up from his phone at the sound of my footsteps.

Our eyes meet.

My cheeks burn hot under his intense gaze, his piercing blue stare seeming to look right through me. His brow furrows and his jaw clenches, as though he's cross and confused at the same time. I wonder what he's thinking. Whether he's remembering. My whole face is on fire.

"Harper?"

Mimi's voice makes me jump. He startles as well, both of us jolted from our thoughts.

"Sorry, coming," I croak, quickly crouching down.

He remains silent as I reach for my bag and pull it toward me. Mimi gives him a friendly smile and apologizes for the disturbance. Frowning, he doesn't say anything.

Without prolonging the awkwardness any further, I turn on my heel and march out, Mimi hurrying to keep up.

"What was *that?*" she asks, falling into step with me as we make our way down the side of the busy newspaper desks toward the kitchen.

I play innocent. "What do you mean?"

"Um, the *eye contact?* The tension in that room!"

"There wasn't any tension," I claim.

"Isn't that guy on the features team for the paper? He always looks cross about something, but even I can appreciate that he is *very* pretty. He's like a model masquerading as a reporter," she muses, before snapping her fingers as she remembers. "Jansson. But I can't remember his first name? It will come to me in a minute."

"Ryan."

"That's the one. Ryan Jansson. I think he's Scandinavian."

"His dad is Swedish," I say, without thinking.

As we reach the kitchen area, she stops. "Wait. Do you *know* him?"

"No, course not," I say, flustered. "He must have mentioned it in one of his articles."

"Well, he wants you," she surmises.

"You think that about everyone. A minute ago, you thought that singer was professing his love to me via donut delivery."

"I'm telling you, Harper Jenkins, that guy was undressing you with those crazy-beautiful eyes of his," she says, moving to the coffee machine. "It's a shame he works for the dark side. Did I tell you that one of the newspaper guys tried to take my meeting room last week? He tried to argue that his matter was more pressing because he has tighter deadlines. Whatever, *pal*. If you want a meeting room, then you need to book one, not try to swoop in there at the last minute and . . ."

I try to focus on Mimi, relieved she has forgotten all about Ryan Jansson.

If only it was so easy for me to get those crazy-beautiful eyes out of my head.

I arrive at exactly 8:57 A.M., which considering the delays I was up against on the Northern Line this morning, I consider a great success. I was asked to be here by nine.

I'm flustered and sweaty, having run from the tube. I throw myself into a revolving glass door, emerging into the cool, modern lobby of The Daily Bulletin Inc. offices, and hurry over to the reception desk.

I glance down my front to check my outfit and realize my skirt has already gone skew-whiff from my hectic journey, the buttons that are meant to run down the middle now aligned with my left hip. I hurry to shift it and check that my fairly crumpled white shirt doesn't have any sweat patches on it.

"Can I help you?" the woman behind the desk asks, setting down the phone.

I snap my head up and plaster a smile across my face. "I'm Harper Jenkins, the intern. It's my first day today."

"Which department?" she asks tiredly, typing into her computer.

"Editorial on the main paper, *The Daily Bulletin*."

She continues tapping away and then presses return on her

keyboard, the printer next to her coming to life and producing a tiny square of paper that she lifts with her manicured fingers and slides into a lanyard.

"This is your temporary pass for today," she says, sliding it across the desk. "You'll need to go to the first floor at some point this afternoon to have your picture taken for your full pass, which will last you the two months. Have a seat over there with the other intern and someone will be here shortly to pick you up."

"Great! Thanks so much!"

She gives me a dismissive nod, her eyes focused on her computer screen. I reach into my handbag for the travel-sized hairbrush lurking in the depths somewhere, aware that the heat of the tube and the race to the office will have caused a certain amount of frizz that I'd like to tame before meeting my (hopefully) future employer.

All the seats in the waiting area are empty bar one: the "other intern," I take it. He's wearing a suit and tie and it's obvious he's nervous because he's sitting bolt upright and he keeps glancing hopefully at the elevators whenever one pings and the doors open.

As I join him, unsuccessfully tugging my brush through the bird's nest that is my hair, he looks up and our eyes meet.

Two things are immediately obvious:

1. He has the most beautiful blue eyes I've ever seen.
2. I utterly baffle him.

His brow furrows in confusion, his eyes narrowing as I breeze over, and I suddenly feel a wave of both anxiety and indignation under such intense and shameless scrutiny. He is gorgeous, with his defined jawline, combed fair hair, and striking eyes, but there's something standoffish about him.

He tenses as I approach.

Deciding to give him the benefit of the doubt, I offer a warm smile, making a beeline for the chair next to his.

"Hi," I say brightly. "I'm Harper. I'm an intern, too. It's really nice to . . . uh . . . oh . . . hang on . . ."

I trail off as I battle with my hairbrush that seems to have become entangled with a preexisting knot. Struggling to release it, I attempt humor, dropping my hands to my waist and leaving the hairbrush dangling from my head.

"You think they'll notice?" I quip.

He looks bewildered, the lines on his forehead deepening as he stares at me. When he doesn't answer, I shrug, then proceed to wrench the brush from my hair.

"I suppose I should learn from this," I say to him. "I was standing on the tube, right at the end of the carriage and the window was open. Great spot for getting a breeze when you're slammed in like sardines, but *terrible* for your hair, right?"

He hesitates, before saying quietly, "Okay."

"So, what's your name?"

"Ryan."

"I didn't realize there were two of us."

"Excuse me?"

"Two interns on *The Daily Bulletin*."

His eyes widen in horror. "You're an intern at *The Daily Bulletin*, too?"

"That's right. Here for two months. You?"

"Same."

"Looks like we'll be working together, then!"

He turns his head away from me, staring straight on before muttering, "Maybe we'll be in different departments."

My smile drops; I'm stunned at his overt rudeness. Fine. Ryan is an absolute dickhead, and he *better* hope we're in different departments.

After fifteen minutes of silence, a woman in her twenties dressed head to toe in black walks toward us, typing something into her phone. She continues to tap away for a minute before tearing her eyes away from her screen and letting out a sigh as though we're disturbing her.

"Ryan and Harper?"

"Yes, hi!" I say, jumping to my feet.

Ryan stands, too, silent.

She does a double take at Ryan, but then thinks better of ogling him and clears her throat.

"I'm Celia," she says. "I'm the editorial assistant, and I'll be showing you the ropes. You've got your temporary passes?"

Remaining mute, Ryan gestures to the pass hanging round his neck.

"Me too," I say, "I've got it right . . . uh . . ."

I realize it's not round my neck, so I check the top of my handbag, but it's not there, either. It's not on the chairs in the waiting area, nor does it appear to be on the floor. I can practically *hear* Ryan rolling his eyes as I look around frantically.

"Excuse me, Harper Jenkins?"

I turn to see the receptionist tapping the counter. I must have forgotten to take it in the first place.

I scurry over and grab it with an apologetic smile. "Whoops! Thanks so much!"

"Great," Celia says dryly, "let's go."

Blushing, I follow them toward the elevator, my stomach fluttering. I take a deep breath and remind myself that this is my chance to work with real journalists—and that if I work hard enough, maybe there will be a job for me at the end of the summer. I want that *so badly*.

The lift doors ping open and I shuffle in behind aloof, uptight Ryan.

I *really* hope he's right and they're not going to make us work together.

With any luck, I won't have anything to do with him.

CHAPTER THREE

After Mimi and I return to our desks, I reluctantly start trawling through my emails, replying to contacts at various PR companies—I accept an invitation for a screening of an upcoming romantic comedy, but decline one for an animation about a cello-playing octopus, and read through a press release about a footballer who's launching a range of colorful children's football boots.

I hear the journalists filing out of Meeting Room Three and look up to see Ryan walking out at the back of the group. I quickly duck my head behind my screen.

We may technically work on separate publications, but it hasn't been easy avoiding him in an open-plan office since he got the job at *The Correspondence* a little over a year ago. When Cosmo moved over to *Narrative*, someone on his team was promoted to features editor, and they hired Ryan to fill the empty reporter spot.

When I first saw him lurking about the place last year and realized with horror that he'd left the business magazine I'd last heard he worked at, I made it *very* clear that it would be better for us to pretend we'd never met before. When I accidentally caught his eye as I strolled past his desk during his first week, he noticeably straightened and looked as though he might say something, but I quickly looked away as though I didn't recognize him.

Just seeing Ryan Jansson puts me in a bad mood. I hate that he has that effect on me after all this time.

A reminder suddenly pops up on my screen that I am due at Claridge's for a press junket in half an hour.

Bollocks. I forgot.

As I'm rushing past his office, Cosmo wearily calls out, "Where are you off to this time, Harper?" and I'm forced to poke my head round his door.

"Press junket for the new Isabella Blossom film."

"I always thought Bella Blossom sounds like an air freshener," he remarks, wrinkling his nose in disapproval.

I force a laugh. "I probably won't mention that in our interview."

"No." He strokes his chin. "She's pregnant, isn't she? She did that *Vogue* photoshoot."

"Yep, she's due in a few weeks."

"She's a big name these days—a big Hollywood draw. She'd make a good candidate for the magazine, actually."

"Yes." I grit my teeth. "That's why I'm off to speak to her."

"I know you don't get much time at junkets, but do try to build a rapport," he instructs pompously. "Then we can get her lined up for a feature in the future, once she's back from maternity."

"Yes," I repeat. "I'm aware that building a rapport is always a good idea. I've actually met her briefly before, so I'll—"

"Oh, and word of advice: don't be late," he says, turning back to his screen. "People lose respect for journalists when they don't show up on time."

It takes every bit of willpower not to shout "WHY DO YOU THINK I WAS RUSHING OUT OF HERE?!" and instead say, "Gotcha," before scuttling off as though he's only just given me the idea.

After a few stops on the tube, I'm back to where I was this morning, rushing out of Oxford Circus, and reaching for my phone in my bag as I head toward the junket.

I decide to call Liam, and he answers on the third ring.

"Hey, how are you?" he says, and as soon as I've heard his

voice, I forgive him for the snoring, because he sounds so pleased to hear from me.

"Busy, but good! I wanted to say sorry for coming in so late last night and then dashing out this morning."

"Don't worry, I wasn't expecting you to be around. I knew you had a work thing."

"I'm sorry I didn't see your messages about coming until it was too late."

"I was worried you were ignoring me and I'd made a fool out of myself." He laughs nervously.

"No, of course not!" I assure him. "You know what I'm like with my phone."

"Yeah," he says, and I hear a bit of irritation in his voice. "Did it go well? Did you meet lots of interesting people? Get some good gossip?"

I flinch. Most people assume that my job is all about showbiz rumors, breaking scandalous stories, and dishing dirt. But that's not what I do.

I interview some of the most interesting and talented people in the arts, discussing their careers but also trying to understand them as individuals, so that I can craft a well-written, engaging interview that's going to captivate readers.

I don't do gossip. I don't shame anyone or speculate on the ups and downs of their love lives. Mimi's right that I have a habit of becoming too invested. My job is to immediately establish rapport with someone who is inclined to be wary around me, and while some journalists might be able to fake their warmth or interest, I can't. I genuinely care about the joys of their work, their heartbreaking moments, how they found the strength to go through difficult periods, and what they're hoping for the future.

I told Liam before that I don't like being seen as a gossipmonger, but it was after we'd had at least three espresso martinis on our second date, so I shouldn't expect him to remember.

"I spoke to a lot of people," I reply instead. "How was your night?"

"Very productive actually. I sent a lot of emails to potential clients. Some of them were probably at that party last night with you."

"Really?"

"I reckon so. Makes you think, it would be easier for me to come along with you next time."

"Oh," I say, a bit taken aback.

"So, next event—you can show me off to everyone?" he presses, going from a business voice to a cute one.

I laugh. "I'll see if I can wrangle a plus-one."

"You're the best, Harper. And hey, I can cook for you tonight, if you don't have plans. You like Thai green curry, right? I make a mean one."

"Sounds great, thank you. I'm just at Claridge's, so I'd better go. It's a press junket."

"Cool! If you see any hot new actors there looking for representation, put in a good word for me, yeah? I should give you a stack of my cards."

Liam is a talent agent, namely for musicians and actors. He worked at an agency, but he didn't like the management style (aka, he didn't like being managed) and didn't feel like he was going to move up any time soon. They didn't value his potential. So, about a month ago, he broke out to set up his own agency, taking two clients with him: a singer-songwriter, who has recently done some jingles for commercials, and a musical-theater actor.

Personally, I thought it was a bit soon for Liam to branch out on his own. Most talent agents wait until they've made a name for themselves and have huge clients to poach. But Liam has an incredible confidence and self-belief—just shy of cocky—and when he talks about his career, it's with the utmost certainty.

I met him at an industry event a few months ago when he

was still at his old agency. We got chatting and I was instantly drawn to his passion for his work. He *loves* helping musicians find their audience and talked about that vocation so zealously, I couldn't help but feel a sense of camaraderie. So many people discuss their work like it's a chore, and it was gratifying to speak to someone who also genuinely loves what they do. He didn't just talk about himself, either, unlike the last few dates I'd attempted. He was genuinely fascinated with me and my job. When he found me at the end of the event to ask for my number, I was happy to give it to him.

I hastily end the call and scurry past the porter at the entrance to Claridge's, who taps his hat as he holds open the door.

"Harper!"

I smile as I spot Rachael Walker gliding across the shiny lobby. She's one of my favorite film publicists to work with—she's great at her job, and she's also a *lot* of fun. We've had some wild nights together over the years.

"Why do you always look so gorgeous?" I ask.

She gives me a kiss on each cheek, her expensive perfume reminding me that I forgot to spritz myself this morning. When I get a chance, I can put those Jo Malone samples swimming about in my bag to use.

Rachael is about my height, around five foot five, but lives in heels so she always seems taller. With long wavy golden blond hair that looks freshly highlighted, she's sporting perfectly winged bold black eyeliner and a matte dark berry lipstick. Today, she's in a yellow blazer over a crisp white shirt, with high-waisted, wide-leg black trousers—she can be anywhere with a smart dress code at the drop of a hat.

"I get an excellent deal on Botox with the best in the business, thanks to my celebrity referrals," she says quietly, taking a step back. "You look fabulous, too."

"You're just buttering me up for a front page feature."

"Always on the clock, babe." She grins, gesturing for me to follow her toward the elevators. "I've been meaning to thank you for all that space you gave to the period drama—I told you it was going to be a hit."

"I had to fight Cosmo tooth and nail for that spread," I tell her as she presses the button and we wait side by side. "So, how long do I get with everyone today?"

"Ten minutes."

"Or fifteen?" I counter hopefully.

She gives me a stern look. "*Ten.*"

I try my luck. "How about fifteen minutes with Isabella Blossom and then just eight minutes with everyone else? That seems fair."

She can't help but smile at my attempt. "You know we're on a schedule, Harper. You're not the only journalist here, today. Although you are the latest."

"I'm perfectly on time!" I check my phone screen as the lift pings its arrival. "Sort of. Blame my editor. He insisted on giving me advice about celebrity interviews before I left."

"That buffoon gave *you* advice? Go on, I could do with a laugh. What did he say?" she asks, following me into the elevator.

"That I shouldn't be late." I groan, leaning against the mirror while she presses the button. "Why do you need a laugh today?"

She sighs heavily. "Have you got your journalist hat on?"

"I'll whip it right off. You're off the record."

She smiles gratefully, watching the numbers on the elevator go up. "Isabella Blossom's boyfriend is here."

"The indie-film director?"

"Yeah, Elijah." She frowns. "He's a thorn in my side. They've been arguing all day. She's told him to make himself scarce for the junket—he's not involved in this movie at all—but he's insisting on hanging around. He's putting her in a bad mood."

I grimace. "Uh-oh. Press junket and actors in a bad mood . . . never a good combination."

"Never," she confirms.

"Isn't he new on the scene? He's not the father of the baby, is he?"

"They've been together three months," she confirms. "This should be the honeymoon period."

"Promoting a film is a stressful time," I reason. "It's probably putting a bit of strain on the relationship with her being so busy. It will get easier once this bit is over."

"Let's hope so," she says as the doors open onto the top floor.

We step into the throng of journalists chatting as they wait to be shown to the next actor, while publicists and assistants dart around with iPads, trying to find whoever they've been sent to locate.

An hour at a press junket can feel like a lifetime as you're shepherded from room to room to ask the same questions as every other journalist there, the actors forced to repeat why they were drawn to this role, this script, this director, this setting, when they likely finished filming it a year ago and can't remember the answers to any of those questions.

To give the actors a bit of a break and in an attempt to stand out from other journalists, I've discovered that it's best to throw in some kooky questions to try to make them laugh, which consequently leads them to answer questions with a little more ease and enthusiasm. Although, I have to admit that method doesn't *always* work—I once joked with a particularly straightlaced actor about ditching the junket and flying together to the Bahamas and, without cracking even a hint of a smile, he said, "I don't think that would be appropriate," and promptly cut the interview short.

Today I get some nice quotes from the other actors in the film, but, like everyone else, I'm here to get time with Isabella Blossom, the star who will draw in the crowds. She's a talented actor but she's also got a *huge* social media following, and lots of endorsement deals. Her face seems to be everywhere at the moment, from promoting makeup brands to maternity items. She's young, powerful, and aspirational, which could make her a difficult interview subject.

Celebrities with a big social following tend to know what sells and what doesn't, what engages an audience and what turns them off. They can create the perfect persona and rarely put a toe out of line—it's why I try to avoid interviewing "influencers." They reel off well-rehearsed sound bites and aren't very forthcoming on their opinions, avoiding any topics that might put their brand endorsements at risk. I completely understand, but it doesn't make for the most engaging read. But Isabella is an actor first and foremost, so I'm hoping she'll give me some good stuff about her creative process at the very least.

When I'm finally ushered into her suite by Rachael (who reminds me under her breath that I have "*ten* minutes, not fifteen"), I find Isabella in a comfortable armchair by the window, a large vase of flowers on the table next to her.

There are some people in this world who just *look* like movie stars, and Isabella Blossom is one of them, with the name to match, as though her parents knew that one day it would be emblazoned across movie posters. She's strikingly beautiful, with big, dark eyes, razor-sharp cheekbones, and plump, full lips, and her long, black curls are impossibly glossy.

She's in a bold red maxi summer dress with a flowing skirt and a tied waist that shows off her bump.

"Hi!" I say, heading over. "I'm not sure if you'll remember me, I'm Harper, from—"

"It's nice to see you again, Harper," she smiles, about to get up.

"Sit down, please," I insist, plonking myself on the chair opposite her while Rachael lurks in the background, there to monitor proceedings and make sure nothing gets untoward, like a

Regency chaperone. "You look great. Not long now until your due date, how are you feeling? And I'm asking that off the record."

"Like a beached whale," she says, slumping back in her seat. "Everyone talks about the glow of pregnancy. No one mentions the constipation."

"Prune juice," I recommend, placing my digital voice recorder on the table and flicking through the pages on my notepad to find my prepared list of questions that I jotted down on the tube on the way here. "A celebrity nutritionist told me she had stockpiled the stuff when she was pregnant."

"Yeah, I've tried that. It's gross." She wrinkles her nose. "The beautiful journey of pregnancy. What a load of bollocks."

I laugh. "Now, if only you'd said that on the record—that would make a great cover line. Are you ready for me to press Record? I know we're on a tight schedule."

"Please," she says, nodding, while Rachael checks her watch.

I press the button on my digital voice recorder.

"So, Isabella Blossom, why—"

The adjoining doors of her suite suddenly burst open and a man marches in with a thunderous expression on his face.

"Did you tell that Jonathan Cliff guy from *Expression* that I didn't write the lighthouse movie?" he seethes, striding across the room toward us.

Rachael tenses, widening her eyes at me. I take this to be the charming new film-director boyfriend, Elijah.

"Honey," Isabella says with a fixed smile, "this is Harper; she's a journalist from—"

"Yeah, hi, I don't have time for introductions," he says, dismissing me with a wave of his hand before addressing her again. "Did you say that to the *Expression* journo? You know he writes scathing articles about everyone!"

"We can talk about this in a minute. I'm in the middle of an interview," she says, her smile wobbling.

"I can't believe you!" He runs his hands through his shoulder-length brown hair, pacing back and forth. "I *wrote* that movie!"

"You're *directing* the movie," Isabella says, frowning at him. "You didn't write it. It's adapted from a novel and the author has written the script."

"Yes, but I have had *major* influence on the screenplay!" he argues. "You know that!"

"Elijah," Rachael interjects calmly, "perhaps you could find another time to—"

"I'm so fed up with this bullshit!" Elijah rages to Isabella, ignoring Rachael's attempt to diffuse the situation. "It's like you go out of your way to bring me down."

"It was an honest mistake!" Isabella says, looking hurt. "I wasn't trying to upset you or make you look bad. He asked who wrote the script, so I told him. I didn't realize you were getting a writing credit, too. I'm sure you can speak to the journalist and correct him?"

"You don't think I tried that?" he says, his eyes flashing with anger. "It doesn't matter now, anyway. He's just going to think I consulted on the script, but that I didn't write it."

"But . . . you *didn't* write it," Isabella points out, confused.

He stops pacing, turns to her, and puts his hands on his hips before inhaling dramatically through his nose, the three of us watching in silence. He finally speaks, slowly and steadily, as though he's trying to stop himself from imploding.

"*That's not the point,*" he hisses.

"Okay, you know what? You're not making any sense," Isabella tells him crossly. "And I'm in the middle of the interview. We can discuss this later."

"So, as always, I have to work around you and your commitments?" he replies, his eyes narrowed to slits. "No, thanks. I'm out of here."

He turns on his heel and struts out of the suite, slamming the door behind him. The room falls into silence. Isabella closes her eyes in despair.

Rachael clears her throat. "Isabella, would you like a glass of water?"

"No, I'm fine," she states, rubbing her forehead with her fingertips.

"I can give you a minute," I offer, half standing.

"No, wait," Isabella says, her head snapping up as she looks at me, panicked. "I know there's not much point in me asking this, but if there was any way that you could . . . omit that exchange from your interview, I would be so grateful."

"Isabella, you don't need to worry," I say, sitting back down, "none of that happened in front of me. I wasn't here."

She hesitates. "I'm not sure I understand."

"You can trust Harper," Rachael says quietly, putting a hand on Isabella's shoulder and giving me a warm, appreciative smile. "She won't print a word about any of that."

"It's none of my business, and it's none of the public's, either. I'm here to talk about you and your movie. Not Elijah."

Isabella looks unconvinced. "You . . . you won't comment on my relationship in your article?"

I reach over to my digital voice recorder and stop the recording, then delete it. I put it back down on the table and shrug.

"You can let me know when you're ready to begin the interview," I say.

"Thank you," she says, her eyes gleaming with tears. "It's been a long day."

"Days like this always are."

"We're both under a lot of pressure and with the baby . . ." Isabella trails off, gently stroking her belly. "I'm not sure Elijah was really prepared for what he was taking on." She sighs, glancing up at me again. "I'm sorry you witnessed that. I'm embarrassed."

"Oh god, don't be," I insist with a wave of my hand. "I've

had full-on arguments with boyfriends before in public places. One of them was in a lobster restaurant and I decided to storm out, but I had one of those bibs tied round my neck and I could not get the bloody thing off. I was there trying to yank it from my neck while shuffling on my bottom to the end of the booth we were in, and he just sat there, along with anyone else who'd overheard the argument, watching me struggle with the bib in silence. It was not at all dignified."

She chuckles. "Did you manage to get it off?"

"No, I did not. In the end, I stormed out of the restaurant and walked all the way home with the bib on."

She bursts out laughing.

"Was that the guy you told me about who was obsessed with balloon animals?" Rachael asks, pouring Isabella a glass of water from a jug on the side, despite her objections.

"No, that was someone from school," I correct. "The guy I dated in sixth form wanted to be a clown," I explain to Isabella.

"*What?*" She looks at me in disbelief.

"He signed up for clown college and everything. Such a nice guy, but any time we hung out, he would make me a balloon animal. My room was filled with them."

"Wow." Isabella nods. "That is quite a hobby. Do you have a boyfriend now? Sorry—" she frowns "—that's none of my business."

"Don't be sorry! It's okay to ask questions during a chat," I assure her. "Yeah, I do. It's early days, but he's great. He's actually cooking for me tonight."

"He's a good chef?"

"He's better than I am. You any good in the kitchen?"

"I like cooking," Isabella says. "But I really *love* baking."

"Ah, so you're an enthusiastic baker. A good one, too?"

"Excellent," she tells me confidently. "I make the best cookies in the country."

I nod to her bump. "That is one lucky baby—their mummy bakes the best cookies in the world."

"Country," she corrects, chuckling. "World might be a step too far."

"Nah," I say. "Your child will think they're the best in the world. That's the only opinion that matters."

A warm smile spreads across Isabella's face. She gazes down at her bump, rubbing it in circles with her right hand. Eventually, she looks up, taking a deep breath.

"Thanks, Harper, I think I'm ready for our interview now."

"Yeah? Great. How long have we got according to your schedule, Rachael?"

Rachael checks her watch. "Your slot finished eight minutes ago."

"Plenty of time, then," I declare, before addressing Isabella in a serious voice. "I hope you're ready for some groundbreaking questions."

She grins at me. "I'm on the edge of my seat."

"You should be. The first one is going to blow you away. Bet no one's asked you this today."

She chuckles, shifting in her seat to get comfortable and placing her clasped hands in her lap. I reach over to the digital voice recorder and press Record, clearing my throat.

"So, Isabella Blossom, why did you feel drawn to this role?"

⌐───────

"Harper, wait!" Rachael calls out after me, her voice echoing off the walls of Claridge's reception.

I turn round to see her rushing over to me, which is quite the feat in heels.

"What did I forget?" I instinctively ask, double-checking I have my bag on my shoulder.

"No, nothing," she says. "I just wanted to say thank you for that interview. You really put her at ease and, regarding that whole Elijah thing—"

"Rachael, you do not need to worry. I promise."

"I know that, but I wanted to thank you anyway," she insists. "And so does Isabella."

"She already did. Tell her she gave a great interview. And don't worry about the shortened time. I understand you still have people to get through."

Rachael holds up her hands to stop me.

"She wants to give you the exclusive about the baby."

I blink at her. "What?"

"Isabella Blossom wants to give you the exclusive when her baby comes along," she emphasizes. "You can be the first to let the world know the sex, the name, print the first photos, everything. She's going to give you exclusive rights. Nothing will go up on social media or be released until your piece has gone out."

"You're . . . you're joking."

"I'm not."

"But . . . doesn't she want to give that to a magazine that will pay her a huge sum of money for it? Or one of the monthly glossies that will do a big shoot with some famous photographer flown in from LA?"

Rachael shakes her head. "She doesn't want any of that. She wants you, Harper Jenkins, to have the exclusive. She's adamant."

I stare at her. "Wow. I don't know what to say! I'm so honored."

"Thanks again for today, Harper, and let me know when this piece about the film will be appearing. You'll send me the PDF?"

"Sure." I nod.

She checks her watch. "I have to get back. We are so behind. I'll be in touch and see you soon!"

Giving me a kiss on the cheek goodbye, she hurries back to the elevator.

"Rachael," I call out, causing her to turn round after she's hit the button. "Thank you."

"Nothing to do with me, Harper," she replies, stepping into the lift. "It's all down to you."

CHAPTER FOUR

M y dad calls during dinner.

I don't pick up, but Liam notices my face when I see the caller's name flashing on the phone.

"Sorry," I say, turning the phone facedown on the table and pushing it away. "I needed to check, just in case it was Shamari. You know, Audrey Abbot's agent? I'm still waiting to hear if I've landed that interview with her. Fingers crossed!"

"No problem." Liam watches me curiously as he chews his mouthful. "You don't really talk about your parents."

I shrug, pushing my rice around my plate. "Not much to say."

"You haven't told me anything about them, or your sister," he comments, swallowing. "You know about my whole family."

"You know enough. I have two parents and an older sister, Juliet. There you go."

He picks up his glass of white wine, swirling it thoughtfully. "Yes, but what are they like? All I know is they're lawyers and that's it. Any time I ask you something about them, you change the subject."

I feign surprise. "Do I?"

He tilts his head. "You don't want to talk about them."

"It's not that I don't want to talk about them," I say, sighing. "It's just . . . I don't know. Okay, maybe I don't want to talk about them."

"Have you told them about me?" he asks expectantly.

I hesitate, thinking about lying, but decide to be honest so as not to get caught out later on. "No. But it's nothing to do with you. My family . . . I don't really speak to them that often, so I haven't had the opportunity." I pick up my glass and take two large gulps of wine. "Let's talk about something else."

"All right." He scoops some rice onto his fork. "So, what's Isabella Blossom like in person? Is she happy with her current representation? Oh, that reminds me, I need to give you some of my cards. I had a very promising email today from a musician who is starting to get some attention on TikTok . . ."

I try to focus on what Liam is saying, nodding in all the right places and doing my best to look interested, but my dad's call hangs over me. I'll have to call him back at some point, and the idea of how awkward and stilted our conversation will be fills me with dread. I wish he'd send a WhatsApp or text like a normal person, but he's old fashioned when it comes to communication, and on the rare occasion that he makes contact, it's usually a phone call about meeting for dinner, which is then followed by a formal email in which he confirms the date we've just discussed to meet.

When I think about it, my dad and I have a relationship similar to that of mutually disapproving colleagues forced to keep each other in the loop.

"So, what do you think?"

Liam's question takes me by surprise. I haven't been listening to a thing he's been saying.

"About . . . ?"

"Writing a feature on my company," he prompts eagerly. "That kind of publicity would be invaluable; I think I'd get a lot of clients with a plug like that."

"I don't feature talent agencies. I feature . . . talent."

"Yeah, but weren't you listening? It would be a 'behind the scenes' piece!" he explains, his eyes wide with enthusiasm as he envisions it. "You could do, like, a whole thing on the hot new agencies propping up these artists, the legs beneath the water, paddling madly."

I stare at him. "What?"

"You know! On the surface of the water, ducks look all calm and chilled, but underneath the water, those webbed feet are working like crazy. Talent agencies are just like that. We're the webbed feet. The artists are the ducks." He looks thoughtful for a moment. "I like that analogy. I might put that on my website."

I'm too bewildered to speak.

"So, will you at least think about the feature?"

"Uh. Yes. Okay," I lie, too tired to explain that it will never happen.

"Great," he says, finishing his wine and gesturing to my glass. "Want a top-up?"

"No, thanks. I have a busy day tomorrow."

"That's why you want to be working for yourself, babe. I get to pick my own hours," he says, winking at me.

He opens the fridge to retrieve the wine bottle. I quickly check my phone on the off chance that Dad has sent a text to explain why he called, but there are no new messages.

While the phone is in my hand, it vibrates. I pick up as soon as I see the name, my heart leaping into my throat.

"Shamari, hi," I say as breezily as I can muster. "How's your evening?"

"Audrey Abbot will do the interview."

I inhale sharply.

"It will have to be before her rehearsal tomorrow morning. I'll send you the address of the theater," Shamari continues. "I'm just finalizing a time with her, so I'll confirm when I can. I told her the focus would be on her career, not on . . . what happened. And it will be a celebration of her work. I mentioned that the journalist in question could be trusted. You should have heard what she replied to that."

I smile to myself. "Was it something along the lines of how no journalists could be trusted?"

"Plus a few choice words, yes," she says briskly.

"Shamari, this is . . . this is brilliant news," I gush, hardly daring to believe that this is happening. "Her first interview in sixteen years! I knew you could persuade her. You are a wonder."

"Front page of the magazine, yes?"

"You have my word," I promise.

"I'll see you tomorrow morning, then."

"See you tomorrow."

"Oh, and Harper?"

"Yes?"

"Don't fuck this up."

I would not like to play Audrey Abbot at poker.

From the moment I walk in the room, I know she's going to be a tough nut to crack. I'd expected to be greeted with a scowl or, at the very least, a look of mistrust, but she's impossible to read, giving nothing away, her expression blank.

The interview is being held in a studio in central London where they're conducting rehearsals for the upcoming play. I've arranged to meet her forty-five minutes before she's needed for her scenes, which sounds like forever, but when you factor in the greetings and how long it takes to draw an actor out of themselves, it isn't much time at all.

Shamari met me outside the door to the studio before guiding me through to the room in which Audrey was waiting, sitting at a desk reading through a script. Poised, elegant, immaculate, Audrey Abbot is as mesmerizing and commanding in person as I'd imagined. She has a short, stylish pixie haircut, hazel-green

eyes, delicate features, and thin lips—she was always best at playing misunderstood, prickly characters that the audience would
slowly warm to as she carefully exposed their vulnerabilities and
humanity.

"Audrey, this is Harper Jenkins," Shamari introduces. "Harper,
this is Audrey Abbot."

"It's a pleasure to meet you, Miss Abbot," I say, holding out
my hand.

Closing her script, she takes my hand in hers and shakes it
firmly, but remains silent, studying me as I pull up a chair opposite her and begin pulling my things from my bag.

I accept Shamari's offer of a coffee and Audrey requests a
green tea. I notice Shamari hesitate before she leaves the room,
as though she's suddenly unsure whether she should be leaving
us alone for any amount of time.

"We won't start until you get back," I assure her.

She gives me a grateful smile before hurrying out, the door
swinging shut behind her.

"Are you happy for me to use this?" I ask, showing my digital
voice recorder.

"Yes, that's fine," she replies, her voice clear and controlled.

"Great, thank you. I won't press Record until Shamari is back
and you feel absolutely ready and comfortable," I inform her.

"All right," she says.

We fall into silence and, under her scrutinizing gaze, I cross
my legs, then uncross them, then cross them again.

"I have to thank you for agreeing to speak to me today," I say
eventually. "I'm honored that I get to be the person to celebrate
your return to the stage."

She arches an eyebrow. "You think that should be celebrated?"

"Are you kidding? People are going to lose their heads with
excitement!"

It's perhaps a little too casual an expression to use in a

professional setting, but she seems to find it mildly amusing, so perhaps casual is the way to go here.

"Shamari tells me you're a 'kindhearted' journalist." She leans back and folds her arms. "Seems like a paradox to me."

I smile. I was ready for this.

"You think journalists who write about public figures are evil?" I ask.

"I think journalists who write about public figures have a flair for sadism," she explains. "That's what sells."

"Something the movie industry knows all about," I reason.

The corners of her lips twitch, but she suppresses the smile. She inhales deeply, juts out her chin, and then speaks.

"Are you going to ask me about what happened?" she says coldly, as though daring me to do it. "Where it all went wrong? That's what your readers want to know, don't they? My downfall makes them feel better about themselves."

"Sounds like your problem lies with readers rather than journalists?"

She purses her lips at my quick reply. I shrug and continue.

"It's up to you. We all know what happened sixteen years ago—if you want to talk about why it happened, what led you there, how you felt, then you're welcome to. Shamari told me that you wanted to focus on your acting career, so that's what I'm here for."

"You won't be disappointed if you leave here today without the *inside scoop*?" she spits out the words. "You'll be perfectly happy to write the article without a mention of it?"

"Yes."

"I don't believe you."

I know she's trying to get a rise out of me, but I refuse to crack. "You can believe what you want."

"You're *really* saying you'd write an article about me with no mention of such an infamous and defining incident?"

"Is that incident the only thing that defines you?" I retort. "I strongly suspect it isn't, so I'm sure I'll have a lot of other material to focus on."

"It's a scandal. And journalists like to tell a good story."

"Only if it's a truthful one, otherwise we'd write fiction. Or maybe go into film."

She pauses. "Nothing much fazes you, does it, Harper?"

"You're wrong there. A while ago, I had to do a feature on Madame Tussauds. Have you been there? Terrified the crap out of me. I don't know why anyone in their right mind would agree to have a wax replica made of themselves."

"*I'm* in Madame Tussauds."

"I know."

She laughs despite herself, lines forming satisfactorily around the corners of her mouth, her eyes brightening. Her whole face changes. I start laughing along with her.

Shamari comes bustling into the room, carrying a tray of hot drinks. "I'm sorry I was so long! The kettle wasn't working in the kitchen here, so I had to pop across the road to get these. Here you are." She hands me a coffee and passes Audrey a tea, before perching on a chair to the side of the room with her own coffee. "All right, we can get started now, if you're both ready?"

"I am, if you are?" I ask Audrey.

"Yes," she says warmly, giving me an easy, relaxed smile that I can tell takes Shamari by surprise. "After all this time, I'm finally ready."

The Incident involving Audrey Abbot happened at a restaurant in Mayfair.

She was a famous Hollywood star, an established, dignified, and highly regarded actor, whom nobody expected to put a foot wrong, so when she did, it was documented and analyzed in an unsympathetic, almost offended way. As though she'd let down all of us, not just herself.

And as with any woman in her position, the tabloids relished her fall from grace.

It all started when she fell in love with Hank Lane, famous punk rocker and son of an LA real estate billionaire. She married him after four months of dating. It was her third marriage—first, there was her childhood sweetheart, followed by a film director, who left her for the lead in his newest film—and while she was quite a lot older than Hank, she was head over heels. He was adventurous, spontaneous, outrageous, the opposite of anyone else she'd publicly dated.

Audrey began making headlines when she was caught drunkenly emerging from a club; rumors started circulating that "a source close to the star" had seen her "sniffing a suspicious substance at a party" (of course, there wasn't any evidence). She started wearing louder and brasher clothes, and experimenting more with her makeup; soon, reporters wrote that "her friends said" she married Hank too fast; their public arguments were "embarrassingly loud, according to onlookers"; she was "spiraling out of control."

Increasingly hunted by the paparazzi, she was reportedly "paranoid and anxious," and Hank began to lose interest. When she accused him of cheating, he told her she was deluded and controlling. A photo emerged of him kissing another woman in a Battersea nightclub, an actor who had played Audrey's daughter in her latest film. Then another rumor began circulating that he was dating the model who had opened the Versace show at that year's London Fashion Week.

One day, after drinking too much while on some prescription medication, Audrey Abbot showed up at a fancy Mayfair restaurant, having learned that Hank was inside enjoying scones and having the cream licked off his fingers by the dancer who'd starred in his latest music video.

The paparazzi were already waiting outside.

First, there was a huge screaming match between Audrey and Hank. Then, according to witnesses, she picked up a champagne bottle and brandished it at Hank, prompting the waiting staff to yell out for everyone to get down just in case. She burst into tears and dropped it, smashing it across the floor and causing all the guests to gasp in horror and excitement.

When Hank yelled out that he was going to "divorce the crazy bitch," she tried to slap him, but he dodged, grabbing her arm. She grabbed a fistful of the tablecloth and pulled it. The contents went flying: the cake stand, the scones, the macaroons, the finger sandwiches, the teapot, the cups and saucers, the crockery and cutlery.

The noise, according to onlookers, "was deafening."

Audrey then went marching out of the restaurant, flipped off the paparazzi, and when one photographer put his camera so close to her face that it nudged her sunglasses farther up her nose, she pushed him aside and his camera was knocked out of his hands, the lens cracking as it hit the ground. (The photographer accused her of "viciously attacking" him, and she settled out of court for a rumored six-figure sum.)

The paparazzi followed her home that day, where she proceeded to grab a golf club and smash up Hank's Ferrari. Those pictures have gained a sort of legendary status in pop culture: the scorned, blurry-eyed older woman smashing up the young, philandering heartthrob's car.

Hank wrote a song about The Incident and it went straight to number one. *The Correspondence* called him a "lyrical, musical genius." Jonathan Cliff at *Expression* said the song was "inspired." Hank released several more successful albums over the following years, cleaned up his act, and appeared on a *Bachelor*-type TV show in the USA, dating the winner briefly but marrying the runner-up instead and having two children with her. He launched an alcohol-free gin alternative and released a children's book about a young boy who dreams of being a rock star. It was a bestseller.

Meanwhile, Audrey Abbot disappeared from the public eye.

As social media became a thing, the photo of her smashing the car with her mascara running down her cheeks transformed from an iconic image to a readily adaptable meme. But in recent years, she's been reconsidered as one of the victims of an era that didn't forgive women when they acted out.

Off the record, Audrey tells me that in the immediate aftermath, she was in so much pain, so humiliated, so lost, and so small, that she wanted to disappear. There is nothing like that feeling, she says, when you're made to think everyone in the world despises you. It makes you afraid to leave the house, to go into a shop, to speak to anyone without hiding your face.

She eventually got help and began to feel whole again. The friendships that lasted through that period of her life became stronger. That overpowering feeling of shame began to fade. She invested in businesses, becoming a silent partner in a best-selling health, wellness, and beauty brand. She started writing her memoir. Depending on how this foray back into the world of theater goes, she's considering taking a stab at directing a play, which she's always wanted to try. She is happier now, more accepting, more loving—she forgives Hank. She forgives herself.

"I wish I could go back, wrap my arms around that woman I was then, and protect her," she says, before adding thoughtfully, "I'm not afraid of what happened anymore. Looking back reminds me how far I've come."

On the record, Audrey tells me that she decided to take the role in this play because it is about a passionate, reckless, haunted woman with sinful secrets, a character she can understand and hopes to do justice. Determined to live in the here and now, Audrey Abbot won't dwell on regrets.

"Everyone has bad days," she says with an impish smile. "Like everything else I do, mine was particularly spectacular."

"Cosmo, you have *got* to listen to me," I plead, exasperated. "It's Audrey Abbot. *The* Audrey Abbot. She has to be front page."

Cosmo puts his hands behind his head and leans back in his office chair. "I've already decided that Don Bright is our cover story, Harper."

"If you decide to bury the comeback story of Audrey Abbot behind a cover story on a boring businessman, the whole industry will think you have lost your mind." I rub my temples, taking a deep breath. "Cosmo, this is a very important story and sixty-one percent of our audience is made up of women."

"Exactly." He shrugs. "They'll want a bit of eye candy on the front. Don Bright is a good-looking chap."

"Eye candy is great, but they'd rather read about a woman who they looked up to and who, after being torn down by the press, has come back to the stage stronger than ever! You have to trust me on this, Cosmo, this is *the* story."

His brow furrows, as though he might be considering it, and I press on with a glimmer of hope.

"This is the first time she's spoken to a journalist since 2007. People will talk about this; it will trend on social media. Audrey Abbot is *back*."

Cosmo rubs his chin and then lets out a long sigh.

"Sorry, Harper, the answer is no. I've got the clever 'Future Is Bright' cover line. That piece is a surefire hit, ready to go to press, and I'm not willing to brush—"

"Cosmo, we have a problem!"

Rakhee comes rushing into Cosmo's office, her eyebrows knitted together in concern.

"I'm so sorry to disturb your meeting, Harper, but this couldn't wait," she says breathlessly, before turning to Cosmo. "We can't run the Don Bright piece this week."

"What?" he splutters.

"It looks like he may have lied to us."

"Who?" Cosmo demands to know. "Who lied to us?"

"Don Bright! His quotes and statistics about some of his business ventures don't quite match up," Rakhee explains. "We're going to need more time for our fact checkers to run it past his lawyers. They've said they're flat out with a case at the moment—I think he's being sued by a disgruntled employee?—but they can have a look over it this weekend."

Cosmo bangs his fist on the table. "This weekend! We go to press tomorrow!"

"I've told them that."

"Well, we'll just have to publish it how it is," he says, his expression thunderous.

"We can't risk it," Rakhee says simply. "If we publish incorrect details, it will cause embarrassment for us *and* Don Bright. And it will open us up for legal repercussions."

"Let me speak to these lawyers," Cosmo huffs. "If they hear from the editor himself, they might make some time in their hectic schedules to run some bloody numbers."

Rakhee grimaces. "I already said that you'd be calling them, and they said it didn't matter—they're up to their neck in this other lawsuit and this article is not a priority in comparison. It can wait until next week or we can pull it altogether, they said. I said we'd wait until next week. We don't want to lose Don Bright altogether, do we?"

Cosmo's jaw clenches.

"No," he seethes. "I suppose not."

"The only thing is, we need to find a good cover story to go to press tomorrow," Rakhee says, biting her lip.

I turn to Cosmo triumphantly.

Rubbing his forehead with his right hand, he glances up at me through the cracks in his fingers.

"All right, Harper," he mutters. "Audrey Abbot is our cover story. Make it happen."

"*Yes!* Thank you!" I cry ecstatically, skipping out of his office feeling like I could burst with happiness, followed by Rakhee.

When we get back to our seats, I let out a squeal of excitement and then lean over to Rakhee to say, "I know it's probably caused you a lot of stress, but I am so pleased that Don Bright mucked up his interview."

"He didn't," she whispers back calmly, opening an email on her screen.

I stare at her. "*What?*"

"Do you think I was going to let anyone but Audrey Abbot grace our front cover?" She turns to look at me with a sly smile. "Not on my watch."

CHAPTER FIVE

I would like to propose a toast," Mimi declares, holding her glass of Prosecco aloft. "To my two astounding colleagues: Harper, for landing a fabulous scoop, and Rakhee, for fooling our idiot of an editor and making sure the right person is gracing our cover this weekend. To teamwork!"

Rakhee and I laugh, leaning over to clink our glasses. The Old Oak is just down the road from the office and is the unofficial *Correspondence* newspaper hangout. No matter how good our intentions are to try somewhere else, we always end up here. The pub is familiar and cozy and has hosted many a memorable night for us, from the evenings when we've needed to drown our sorrows to those when we've required a celebration. Happily, tonight is the latter.

"I still can't believe you made up that story about Don Bright," I say to Rakhee, shaking my head. "I didn't doubt you for a moment!"

"I had to be convincing," she says.

"What if he phones the lawyers? I don't want you getting in trouble."

"Firstly, he won't, because he knows deep down that he wouldn't be able to change their minds. He knows if anyone could, it's me," Rakhee says confidently.

Mimi nods. "She makes a good point."

"Secondly, I don't care about getting in trouble. Audrey Abbot had to be the cover story, there was no question about it. I'd have brought the matter to our publishers if I had to—they'd agree, I know it."

"You are so badass," I say, impressed.

"Says the woman who landed Audrey Abbot's first interview in sixteen years. I take it you've finished writing the piece, otherwise you wouldn't be here?" Mimi adds.

I grimace. "Uh. Sort of."

She rolls her eyes. "The subs are going to kill you. You need to give them time to fact check and do the layout!"

"I'm going to finish it on my laptop when I get home," I insist. "It's almost there. It just needs polishing. And I have to go out tonight anyway, so I might as well squeeze in a drink with you two."

"Where are you going tonight?" Rakhee asks.

"A book launch. A member of Parliament has written his autobiography."

"Juicy," Mimi comments sarcastically.

"He came runner-up in a reality TV show last year, so I'm sure the book is not without its glitz and glamour," I inform her. "He could be a good subject for a feature."

Mimi shoots me a concerned look. "Shouldn't you be giving yourself a night off sometime soon? You haven't stopped in a while."

"I have nights off," I argue. "Yesterday, I was at home and Liam cooked for me. It was very pleasant."

"*Pleasant*," she says, unconvinced. "I meant more like a night for yourself, where you just . . . stop. There's a great press trip coming up that you should take—a beautiful boutique hotel in the Kent countryside that you could review. You can get away from everything and relax."

"I don't *need* to relax," I insist. "I like being busy. You know that."

Rakhee laughs. "You must be a nightmare on holiday. One of

those people who always wants to be doing activities rather than lazing about on the beach."

"You're wrong," I tell her proudly. "I'm very relaxed on holiday. I read all the books I've been sent to review."

"Holidays aren't for catching up on work, Harper!" Rakhee points out. "Honestly, I hope Liam is the kind of person who likes to be busy; otherwise he's in for a rude awakening on your first couples trip."

"Ooh, speaking of Liam," Mimi says. "Will you bring him to my birthday party? It would be nice to spend more time with him, since I've only met him once. Rakhee, you're coming too, right?"

"Yes, thank you for inviting me."

"Quite a lot of the *Narrative* team are coming," Mimi tells me.

"Tell me you didn't invite Cosmo," I check.

She balks at the suggestion. "Don't be stupid."

"Okay, I'll ask if Liam's free. Although, I'm not sure your birthday party is the best occasion to introduce someone new."

Mimi grins. "If he can't handle a spot of rounders and some silly games, he's not The One. It's the ultimate test."

Every year, Mimi spends her birthday in Brockwell Park, in South London, where she splits the group into two teams and we play rounders, before taking part in ridiculous drinking games. It's always a lot of fun and gets quite rowdy and competitive.

"Let's hope we're still together by the end of the day," I laugh, before checking the time. "Right, I better go, or I'll miss the start of the reading."

Rakhee looks disappointed. "You're leaving already?"

"I might actually be on time if I go now," I say proudly.

"Before you go, I actually . . . I need to tell you both something," Rakhee announces, setting down her glass, her tone serious and urgent.

I share a concerned look with Mimi. "Is everything okay?"

She nods. "Yes, yes. Well. In some ways, it's great. In other ways . . ." She trails off and then takes a deep breath. "I've got a new job."

Mimi gasps. "*What?*"

"Those doctor and dentist appointments I've been going to? They've been interviews," Rakhee admits with a nervous smile. "I've been offered the job of deputy editor at *Sleek* magazine."

"Rakhee!" I gasp. "That's amazing! Congratulations!"

"Wow, I love *Sleek!*" Mimi enthuses. "Well done, you!"

"Thank you," she says, smiling modestly. "I'm really excited, although I'll be sad to leave the *Narrative* team."

In my first flush of happiness for her landing such a brilliant new job, I hadn't actually considered that Rakhee won't be sitting next to me every day. I can't believe I'll lose my partner-in-crime when it comes to standing up to Cosmo.

"We'll miss you, but huge congratulations!" Mimi says quickly, reading my mind. She stands to give Rakhee a hug. "You deserve this. *Sleek* is one of the best. They couldn't have hired a better person for the job."

"I second that," I say, getting up to throw my arms round her, too.

Rakhee is not a natural hugger, all angles and awkwardness, but I hold her close anyway. I really will miss her.

"When do you start?" Mimi asks, sitting back down.

"In a month. I handed in my notice to Cosmo yesterday," she tells us. "You should have seen his face. He had to act happy for me, but he looked furious."

"What did he say?" I laugh, curious.

"Something along the lines of, 'I guess this means I'll have extra work on my plate as I'll have to start interviewing for your replacement.'"

"Oh god, please tell me you'll be helping out with the interview process," I plead. "You have to make sure I end up sitting next to someone good! Not one of Cosmo's golfing buddies."

Having a good relationship with the features editor at *Narrative* is very important to my job as celebrity editor—although the two roles are distinct and both report to the editor-in-chief, they're fairly intertwined and can even overlap, depending on who my subject is.

Rakhee has never made me feel like she is superior to me (despite Cosmo's clear personal feelings on the hierarchy of our jobs), and it's extremely helpful to have a features editor who respects my position. A lot of magazines have scrapped celebrity editors, whereas the features editor is long established at all publications and undoubtedly a safe title to hold. I just hope I'll be able to work in tandem rather than in competition with whoever replaces Rakhee.

"I will be conducting the interviews along with Cosmo," she assures me. "I promise to hire the perfect person for the job."

"The office won't be the same without you," Mimi sighs, and I nod in forlorn agreement.

"I'll miss working with you. I hope I'll get on well with the *Sleek* team. I'm pretty nervous about the move, to be honest."

"It's an exciting new adventure," I emphasize. "And one we should celebrate with a round of drinks! I'll get another bottle of Prosecco. No! Strike that. Champagne."

Mimi claps her hands excitedly.

"But won't you be late for the book launch?" Rakhee asks, checking her watch.

"That's okay," I tell her with a smile, slipping away in the direction of the bar. "I do have a reputation to uphold."

On my way from the tube to Waterstones, I get a phone call. It's my dad again. I didn't message him after the missed call yesterday, so I decide to answer, grateful that I have an excuse to rush off. I'm also tipsy from Rakhee's celebratory champagne and I'd rather not handle a phone call with my dad sober.

"Hi, Dad."

"Harper, finally," he says, already sounding annoyed, even though I missed *one* call from him. "I've been trying to get through to you."

"Sorry," I say, doing my best not to be irked by his tone before our conversation has even really started. "How are you and Mum?"

"Well, thank you," he says snippily.

"Good. Look, I can't be long, Dad, I'm about to head into an event."

"I don't intend to keep you long, Harper," he grumbles. "Since we haven't seen you since Easter, we thought we should get a dinner in the diary. Your sister's idea."

"Okay," I say, dreading it already. "When were you thinking?"

"I'll send across some suitable dates," he states, in the same way that he'd book a meeting with one of his clients. I am fully used to this formal manner. He's always like this with me, as though I'm essentially a burden to him, someone he has a duty toward, rather than someone he'd like to spend time with.

"Great. Anyway, I have this event so I'd better—"

"Some celebrity bash, is it?"

The disdain oozes from every word.

"It's a book launch, actually," I reply, annoyed at myself for feeling like I have to justify anything.

He sighs. "I suppose that is a little better than your usual occupations."

"You know what, Dad, I don't have time for you to talk shit about my career tonight, okay? You can save that for our dinner."

"Don't swear, Harper," he scolds.

"I have to go."

"All right, we're perfectly used to you running off," he snaps. "I'll send you those dates."

"Great. Bye, then."

"Goodbye."

I hang up, throw my phone in my bag, and try to shake the conversation off as I walk into the warm, welcoming bookshop.

Clearly, my relationship with my parents is . . . strained.

We've never got on. Actually, that's a lie. I have nice memories of my childhood, but they faded at some point in my teens when I slowly became a repeat disappointment to them while my older sister, Juliet, became the golden child who could do no wrong.

My mum and dad are partners in different law firms—both brilliantly successful, highly driven, tough-as-nails workaholics. One of the worst things about us not seeing eye to eye is that I still remain weirdly proud of their success, even with the knowledge that they see me as a total letdown.

I think they thought I was joking when I first told them I wanted to apply for journalism courses after school. They had always assumed I'd complete a law degree, like Juliet. They made no attempt to hide their disapproval and disappointment.

With her perfect grades, Cambridge degree, and a job at a top London law firm straight out of university, Juliet was, and still is, our parents' pride and joy. She and I are very different people and have never been close, despite only being two years apart in age. She's quiet, straightlaced, and standoffish, looking down on me as much as our parents do. She never paid much attention to me when we were growing up, and she had absolutely no time for me once she was a hotshot lawyer in London. I never hear from her and we only speak at family gatherings, and those conversations are painful and dry, sharing no personal information whatsoever. She is completely uninterested in anything going on in my life, so I've learned to feel the same way about her.

When I started interning as a journalist, my mum said I was being irresponsible because the entry-level jobs paid so little. When I got my first journalism job, as junior celebrity writer at *Flair* magazine, my dad said he hadn't imagined my education would surmount to writing sleazy stories about cocaine-fueled wannabes. And when I landed my current celebrity editor job at *Narrative*, I sent them a message saying I would now be writing sleazy stories about cocaine-fueled wannabes for more money.

They didn't reply.

Every now and then we have these dinners where Juliet sits in silence and my parents ask me where I think my life is going and whether I've realized yet that I made a huge mistake.

But I love my job. I'm *happy.*

I just wish that was enough for my parents.

By the time I've made it up the stairs of Waterstones to the first floor, there's a round of applause for the end of the reading, so I loiter at the back and join in the clapping. The publicist spots me and gives me a warm smile when I introduce myself, before encouraging me to help myself to a drink if I'd like and to be sure to speak to her or the MP if I have any questions, as they'll both be doing the rounds.

Making my way through the mingling crowds to the drinks table, I reach out for the last paper cup of warm white wine at the same time as someone else does. We both retract our hands quickly and glance at each other to apologize.

I look up into the blue eyes of Ryan Jansson.

At least he looks as shocked to see me as I am to see him. I'm not the only one caught off guard here.

"Sorry," he mutters.

"You have it," I tell him brusquely, gesturing to the cup.

"You can have it," he replies.

"I insist."

"*I* insist."

I glare at him, inhaling deeply. *God*, he's annoying.

"Fine. I'll have it, then." Taking the cup while he reaches for a red wine, I'm ready to leave his vicinity as soon as is humanly possible when he decides to make conversation.

"I didn't think you'd be here," he says, putting his spare hand in his pocket and turning to scan the room of journalists.

"Why?" I reply defensively. "Because it's too high-brow for the magazine?"

He frowns. "No. Because I thought it would be covered by the books editor."

Ryan Jansson is very good at being condescending and trying to conceal it with his charm and sex appeal, but I know better.

"We don't have a books editor, as you know," I say pointedly.

"I didn't know that, actually."

"Why isn't the newspaper's books editor here?" I retort.

"She is here." He points at a woman across the room.

"Oh. Well, why are you here, too?"

"Because he's had some colorful experiences," he claims, nodding to the MP, who is chatting away cheerily to a circle of people. "I think it will make a nice feature—the book release and an interview with him."

"Yes, well, it's the type of feature that suits the magazine rather than the newspaper, in my opinion," I point out.

"I heard there's a change coming up on your editorial team," he says breezily.

I narrow my eyes at him. "Excuse me?"

"Rakhee, your features editor. She's leaving, right?"

"How do *you* know about that?"

He shrugs. "Word spreads. Did *you* know about it?"

"Of course! I've known for ages."

I can't help it. How does *he* know about Rakhee? I've only just found out!

"She's going to *Sleek* magazine. She's going to be deputy editor there," I continue. "They're lucky to have her."

He nods. "So, what did you think of the reading?"

"Sorry?"

"The chapter we just heard," Ryan explains. "What did you think?"

"Oh . . . I thought . . . I thought it was interesting."

"Really."

"Yes," I say firmly. "Very interesting."

The corners of his mouth twitch up into a knowing smile. "You were late, weren't you?"

"No!"

"What was the chapter about, then?" he challenges.

"I'm sorry, I didn't realize that attending a book launch involves a spontaneous quiz to see if you were paying attention," I snarl.

"You were late," he confirms, smiling into his cup, his eyes twinkling with triumph.

"I was a *tiny* bit late, not that it's any of your business." I scowl at his smug expression. "Anyway, as much as I'd love to hang around, I've already reached my quota of talking to pompous assholes today, so I'm going now."

He looks amused at this, which only serves to make me even more infuriated.

He has no right to be *amused*. He's supposed to be *insulted*.

He opens his mouth to reply, but I stalk off before he can. I will *not* let Ryan Jansson have the last word. The very idea of him thinking that he has one up on me makes my blood boil.

I avoid him as much as possible throughout the evening, managing to keep tabs on where he is at all times and ensure that I am always on the opposite side of the room, talking to a different set of people. By the time I leave, I'm proud of myself for steering clear of him and, consequently, having had a very nice time enjoying interesting conversations with clever people.

I step out into the evening air and take a moment to get my bearings before I start walking in the direction of the tube. This momentary pause is a grave mistake.

Ryan Jansson walks out, too.

He frowns at me. I scowl at him.

I start walking away from the bookshop and toward the tube station. I can hear his footsteps behind me. I keep going for a bit before I call out over my shoulder, "Are you following me?"

"No."

"Then why are you walking right behind me?"

"I'm walking to the tube," he says irritably.

"Fine."

"Fine."

"*Fine!*" I huff, pulling my jacket closer around me and marching on determinedly.

But his footsteps only get closer. I glance up to see him striding along next to me, trying to overtake me on the pavement. I walk even faster, refusing to let him win. His brow furrowed in concentration, he speeds up, taking the lead. I almost go into a light jog to pace just ahead of him and he huffs in annoyance.

The sign comes into view and we're both full-on running at this point. We sprint down the steps underground and, feeling more determined to win than ever, I manage to take the lead by a nose, reaching the barriers just before him. I start rummaging in my bag for my phone so I can use it to get through the barrier.

"Damn it!" I hiss.

Ryan Jansson swans past me through the barrier next to mine.

He stops on the other side to give me a victorious smile, his hands in his pockets.

"You weren't racing me, were you, Harper?" he says, tilting his head to one side. "Because if you were, then looks like you lost."

"I was not racing you, Ryan," I say, still searching for my phone. "I'm not a *child*."

He shrugs smugly before sauntering away toward the escalator.

"But if I was racing you," I quickly call out after him, "I would have won because the race was to the barrier, which I reached first!"

He doesn't respond, stepping onto the top of the escalator that carries him out of sight.

During the interview for *The Daily Bulletin* internship, there was an implication that there could be a job at the end of it. The chance to become a junior reporter at a national newspaper is the dream. I'll work my way up and one day be a features editor or a columnist. I want that more than anything. And I'll work harder than anyone to get it.

After all, I need to prove to my parents that I can make it as a writer.

When I first graduated in early June, I took a job at a bar near my parents' house while applying for journalism positions, realizing very quickly I was desperately underqualified for any writing jobs. Publications wanted experience, and for that I'd have to land some kind of internship. It was supposed to be an incredible summer to be in London: the Olympics were looming at the end of the month and the atmosphere in the city was buzzing—the bar was packed every night—but I couldn't enjoy any of the excitement, weighed down by the pressure of getting a foot in the door.

At the end of the *Daily Bulletin* interview, the editor said he could see I *really* wanted this, and he kind of chuckled as though maybe I'd come across a bit too strong. I wasn't embarrassed by that, though. I wanted them to know that if they chose me I would be so grateful that I wouldn't let them down. I screamed when I read the email saying I'd been accepted, the excitement bubbling through me so furiously that I couldn't stand still, jumping up and down and punching the air with both fists. Okay, so it wasn't a swish, fancy job in the city, it wasn't a writing gig, but it was a start. Finally, I could see it. I *allowed* myself to see it: a career in journalism.

Of course, I didn't realize they were taking on *two* interns, which means there's obviously an extra hurdle for landing a job here. But a bit of healthy competition is fine by me. I'm not going to let this Ryan guy get in my way. If there's a job waiting at the end of this, I'm going to be the one who gets it.

In the elevator that first morning, editorial assistant Celia runs through the types of tasks we can expect to be getting over the next few weeks.

"Coffee and tea runs are par for the course, I'm afraid, as well as some admin tasks, like taking notes, photocopying, transcribing recorded interviews, but it isn't all bleak," she promises, scrolling through her phone. "You'll be doing some interesting research, and once you're settled in, you can help with interviews and maybe do some writing."

"For the paper?" I ask hopefully.

"Maybe for the website. We'll see how you go."

The doors ping open and we step into the hustle and bustle of the newsroom, where we're led to two tiny desks in the back corner, with stacks of messy files piled on top of them next to the computers.

These are ours for the two months, Celia tells us, swiftly destroying my and Ryan's mutual hope that we wouldn't be working together.

She writes our login details on a Post-it note and sticks it on top of the nearest folder. After pointing out where the kitchen and toilets are, she says she'll let us get ourselves sorted and then will be back in a while to run through some things, including the intern binder—she points at the black file in the middle of the two desks. It has everything we need to know, compiled by previous interns as they went along.

"Do you have a preference of desk?" Ryan asks me once she's left, finding his voice.

"Do *you?*"

The corner of his mouth twitches, as though he's suppressing a smile.

"I'll take the one by the window," I say before he can answer, his secretive smile pissing me off enough to decide that politeness is wasted on someone like him.

"You sure?" he says, shrugging and pulling out the chair of the other. "Okay."

"This one is clearly the best one," I point out, sitting down. "Who doesn't want to be next to the window?"

"Someone who doesn't want the glare of the sun on their screen."

"There's no glare."

"Not today, but on a nice day, it will be very annoying," he warns.

"Today is a nice day. It's boiling out there."

"It's humid," he agrees, "but not sunny."

I press my lips together, irritated. "The sun is coming out in intervals," I say.

I don't know when I became a meteorologist, but this guy is really pushing my buttons, and I feel the need to one-up him.

I type in the login details and wait for the desktop to load. As I do, I can't help but observe Ryan tackling the mess on his desk with a fierce determination, his expression serious and focused as he begins the painstaking process of gathering the various pens scattered everywhere and slotting them into a knocked-over stationery holder, then reading the names of the files and stacking them to the side of his screen in alphabetical order.

"What are you doing?" I ask, unable to hide the note of ridicule to my tone.

"Tidying."

"Yeah, but why are you doing it so inefficiently?"

That makes him stop abruptly and look up at me. "You think there's a more efficient way of doing this?"

"Watch and learn," I announce, before sweeping everything on my desk to one side.

It doesn't go as smoothly as I'd like: lots of items topple onto the floor and the various pieces of paper dispersed about the desk crumple together or even rip. But I have the outcome I was hoping for, a nice clear bit of space right in front of my keyboard.

Ryan looks appalled. "That's not tidying!"

"It is. Kind of." I shrug, peering at the screen and examining the folders dotted around the desktop.

"You can't seriously work like that," he says, aghast.

"Work like what?"

"Surrounded by mess."

"I prefer things to be a little chaotic," I inform him, delighted at his disapproval. "You want a bit of character when it comes to a writing space."

He shakes his head and gets back to his organizing until his desk is perfectly neat, a stark contrast to the bombsite that is mine. Acknowledging that he's obviously one of those neat freaks, I take great pleasure in his side glances, knowing that the state of my surroundings must be killing him.

"Shame we're not working in different departments like you wanted," I say innocently, reaching for the intern folder and plonking it on top of a stack of files, some of their contents flitting down onto the floor. "Then you wouldn't have to put up with my mess. Oh well! It's only eight weeks."

He doesn't say anything, but I see the muscle in his jaw twitch. I smile to myself, flicking open the folder triumphantly.

CHAPTER SIX

The Audrey Abbot issue was a hit.

Almost two weeks later, her comeback is still being widely discussed on social media. The weekend it hit the newsstands, the interview sparked a reexamination of how she was treated all those years ago in comparison with Hank, and she received an overwhelming wave of support. A bouquet of flowers arrived for me the following Monday from Shamari, and then another from the producers of the play—they brought the ticket release forward and sold out the whole run in three minutes. Our social media and digital director, Roman, has been rushed off his feet trying to keep up with the interaction.

To absolutely no one's surprise, Cosmo is taking the credit.

In front of the publishers, he's acting as though it was all his idea. Thank goodness I have the byline on the interview so he can't claim to have written the piece himself, which I'm sure he would if he could. The Don Bright cover story the following week was barely noticed. I'm waiting for Cosmo to congratulate me on the interview but he's yet to bring it up. In the editorial meeting that followed the issue, he acknowledged how well it had gone down without even looking at me.

On our way out of that meeting last week, Rakhee whispered encouragingly, "Maybe next week when people are still talking about it, he'll give you the credit you deserve."

But I have a feeling that that won't be the case today, because I'm going to be late to the meeting again.

However, I do have a good reason *and* I'm standing right outside the office, so I'm very close by, but I'm on hold to get through to a music agent who used to look after Artistry. The band split up years ago but, if the Twitter rumor mill this morning is to be believed, the members are in discussions for a reunion tour.

"Miss Jenkins?" A voice finally says after I've had to listen to a crackly version of "Pachelbel's Canon" on repeat for ten minutes.

"Yes! I'm still here!"

"Oh, hi, I'm afraid he won't be able to make it to the phone now," the agent's PA tells me regretfully. "But I'll let him know you called."

"I just need a confirmation on the tour," I say, trying not to sound too impatient. "If it's happening, then—"

"I'm afraid I can't comment, but as I said, I'll pass on the message you called."

I sigh, knowing I'm fighting a losing battle. "All right, thanks so much."

After hanging up, I open my emails and ping a quick message across to the agent to ask him to call me back, casually reminding him that the last time I saw him, I put those espresso martinis on my company card, so technically he owes me a drink but I'll happily accept a phone call as replacement.

Then I push through the doors of the office and hurry to Meeting Room Three, steeling myself for some kind of snarky comment from Cosmo. He doesn't disappoint. As I slide into the room, he's in the middle of talking about expanding the luxury travel section and pauses to say, "Tell me, Harper, are you late for everything in your life, or is it just for work-related appointments?"

"Sorry!" I say cheerily. "But it was for a good reason."

"I'm sure," he mutters.

"I'll remind you that last time I said that, it was because I was securing the Audrey Abbot interview, which has been our most successful issue of the year."

He clears his throat. "Editorial meetings are extremely important, and I expect you to respect them enough to arrive on time."

"Of course, Cosmo," I reply sweetly with a bow of my head. "But as you've never once required me to speak in an editorial meeting before, I thought that my presence here might not be as important as speaking to the agent of the much-loved band Artistry, who might be getting back together for a tour."

Mimi gasps loudly. "Are you *serious?* I *love* them!!"

"Are tickets on sale?" Rakhee asks urgently, whipping out her phone and prompting a lot of other people in the room to do the same.

I smile smugly as Cosmo's eyes bulge out of his head in fury.

"Can we get back to our meeting, *please?*" he demands.

Everyone reluctantly puts their phones down.

"Don't worry," I whisper audibly for everyone to hear, "there hasn't been a tour announcement yet."

They all gratefully relax. Cosmo raps his knuckles impatiently on the table.

"*Right.* As I was saying," he grumbles, "we're going to expand the luxury travel section as it draws in more advertising. Thank you, Mimi, for your overview on how that's going to look. Now, on to another very important matter—as you know, Rakhee is leaving us in two weeks, and we've been looking for her replacement."

My heart sinks, as it has done every time her move is brought up in conversation. She catches my eye and gives me an it's-going-to-be-okay smile.

"I'm pleased to announce we have already found the person who is going to step into her role, and I'm delighted to say that he is in fact here today."

He's here?! Who comes into an office two weeks before their start date? I can't believe Rakhee didn't give me the heads-up on who was replacing her. I have to sit next to this person!

"Please give a warm welcome to our new features editor," Cosmo continues, gesturing toward the back of the room. "Ryan Jansson!"

My blood turns to ice.

I spin round to see him sitting in the back corner of the room. My mouth drops open as he acknowledges Cosmo's introduction with a curt nod to the team.

This has to be some sort of joke.

"Ryan currently works on the features team on the paper, so he knows the brand inside out, and he's a dab hand at commissioning, writing, and editing. We're delighted to have you join us, Ryan."

"Thank you," he replies quietly.

"Marvelous," Cosmo says, before clapping his hands. "Right, then. I don't think there's anything else to address . . ."

As Cosmo rounds off the meeting, Ryan glances over to me. I quickly look away, my cheeks burning. There's the sound of chairs scraping back as everyone gets up to go, and I trip over my feet on the way out, still in shock at the announcement.

Rakhee finds me leaning on my desk, trying to make sense of the impending doom that I'll be forced to sit next to Ryan Jansson *every single day.*

"Harper?" she asks, plonking herself down in her chair and swiveling it to face me. "Are you okay?"

"Ryan Jansson?" I whisper, checking he's nowhere near. Thankfully, he's still in the meeting room, talking to Cosmo. "*That's* who you've chosen to be the features editor?"

"He's going to be a great addition," she says, completely oblivious. "He's knowledgeable, driven, and an excellent editor. Great experience, too—before *The Correspondence*, he worked as a lifestyle reporter for *Venture*, you know, the business magazine. He has a few other big names on his CV, too. He's impressive."

"Does he ever smile?" Mimi asks, leaning forward on her desk.

"Admittedly, he's a bit . . . reserved," Rakhee acknowledges. "He's the quiet type. Very focused. But I'm sure he'll relax and lighten up a bit once he's settled into the role."

I run a hand through my hair. "This is . . . unbelievable."

"Why are you so upset?" Rakhee asks.

Mimi gasps. "Oh my god! That's the guy you had eye-sex with the other day!"

"You had eye-sex with Ryan Jansson?" Rakhee wants to know, startled.

"*No!*" I hiss, horrified that someone might overhear.

"They definitely did," Mimi tells Rakhee gleefully. "The chemistry was *very* intense."

"No, there's no chemistry! The opposite, if anything. If you must know . . . we don't get on," I say quietly through gritted teeth.

"You said you didn't know him," Mimi recalls.

"I don't! We met . . . recently. At a book launch. He was arrogant and obnoxious and patronizing. We can't work together."

Emerging from the meeting room with Cosmo, Ryan continues toward us as Cosmo splits off into his office, and I quickly sit down, ducking my head behind my monitor.

"Thanks again, Rakhee, for the opportunity," he says, appearing at her side.

I busy myself with my notebook, angling my chair away from them, toward the wall.

"Don't thank me! You got the job on your own merits," she says brightly.

"Big shoes to fill," he remarks.

"Nah," she chuckles. "Hey, I hear you've met our wonderful celebrity editor, Harper."

What have I ever done to you, Rakhee?

I reluctantly turn my chair to face him.

"I was telling Rakhee we met at that book launch recently," I explain before he can jump to any conclusions.

"Right," he says, his brow furrowed.

"I'm sure you two will get on well," Rakhee adds nervously, noting his grave expression that likely matches mine.

His eyes flicker toward the scattered papers and heaped books across my desk, and he suddenly looks pained.

"Are you a neat-desk person or someone who prefers a busy workspace?" Rakhee continues gallantly.

"Neat," he replies without hesitation.

"Apparently, Harper's messy desk reflects her creativity," Mimi pipes up.

"Studies have shown that messiness and creativity are strongly correlated," I explain, lifting my chin.

"Studies have also shown that messiness is a significant contributing factor to stress," he retorts.

"Albert Einstein once said, 'If a cluttered desk is a sign of a cluttered mind, of what, then, is an empty desk a sign?'" I quote, delighted with myself for remembering that one.

"Science has proven that our brains thrive in an orderly environment," he says.

"Research has also proven that those in cluttered settings are more likely to break the mold, while those in neat, orderly ones simply follow social convention," I declare.

He lifts his eyebrows at me, as though accepting an unspoken challenge.

"In some cases, disorganization is a sign of laziness," he snaps back.

"Neat and empty spaces often belong to sterile, bland, and uninspiring personalities."

"Messiness can signal a deeper underlying issue of feeling overwhelmed."

"Tidiness is usually a sign of a Type A personality."

He hesitates, frowning. "That's a good thing."

"Is it?" I counter.

He narrows his eyes at me. "Type A personalities are associated with high achievement, strong motivation, and being meticulous."

"As well as impatience, hostility, and stress."

"And you'd describe yourself as Type B, would you, Harper?" he asks.

"I'd say I have a more casual and carefree approach."

"So you wouldn't describe yourself as, say, a workaholic?" he suggests, watching me carefully.

"No, I wouldn't."

Mimi snorts. I glare at her. Ryan looks satisfied.

"Ryan! Good, you're still here," Cosmo calls out, sticking his head out of his office door. "I want to go over a few things with you."

"I'll be right there," he replies before turning back to address us. "I look forward to working with you, Mimi and . . . Harper. Rakhee, good luck with everything."

"Thanks," she smiles. "You'll come to my goodbye drinks, though, right?"

"See you then."

He sticks his hands in his pockets and slopes off to Cosmo's office. Taking a deep breath, I bring up my emails. After clicking angrily at a couple of them, I notice Rakhee and Mimi staring at me.

"What?" I ask, frowning at them.

"Nothing," Mimi says innocently, before looking to Rakhee. "You see what I mean, though, right?"

"It was out of control," Rakhee agrees.

"What was?" I ask.

"The chemistry," she replies breezily.

"And the eye-sex," Mimi adds.

"Yes, there was a lot of that." Rakhee nods.

"What!? Have you both lost your minds?" I say, unable to keep my voice down. "He's *infuriating!* I told you, we don't get on! I can't believe you hired him, Rakhee. This is going to be a complete disaster."

"For you maybe. But for me," Mimi says, grinning at Rakhee, "it's going to be *very* entertaining."

There's no hope of avoiding Ryan at Rakhee's goodbye drinks.

I try my best, but the pub area that she's reserved isn't huge, so I know I'm going to be forced to see him at some point tonight. And starting Monday, I have to sit next to him every day. I'm two gin and tonics down and aiming for at least three before I have to acknowledge him.

"This sucks," Mimi sighs.

I watch Ryan as he looks interested in whatever Cosmo is saying. Nothing Cosmo says is interesting, so Ryan is either a giant suck-up or just as insufferable as Cosmo.

"Yeah," I reply, shaking my head at him. "It does."

"I'm going to really miss having Rakhee in the office," Mimi says glumly.

You know something else about Ryan Jansson? He's not quiet. Not really. Everyone always thinks he's reserved, but when he wants to, he'll talk and talk, usually disagreeing with whatever point you're making. I've witnessed this side to him on many occasions. The sexy, brooding, tight-lipped persona he has around everyone else is a façade.

"I don't know what we're going to do," I say, watching him as he continues to listen to Cosmo's rambling.

"At least we always have each other," Mimi says, gripping my arm. "You can never leave me."

"Oh, I won't be the one to go," I assure her.

She follows my eye line and then gives me a strange look. "Are you still obsessing over how much you dislike Ryan?"

"I'm not *obsessing* over it."

"You don't need to worry, Harper. I know you're nervous about him sitting next to you, but you still have me right across! And once he gets to know you, I know you'll win him over."

"I don't *want* to win him over. If anything, he needs to win *me* over."

She laughs. "I'm not sure I've ever seen you this stubborn about anything. He must really push your buttons, huh?"

"He'll push everyone's buttons soon enough," I inform her haughtily. "Trust me. Ryan Jansson may seem harmless, but I know the truth."

She gives me a strange look. "You've met him, what, twice?"

I shake my head, forgetting my white lie. "Oh, I've got the measure of him all right."

He suddenly glances up and catches my eye. I look away, but it's too late. He excuses himself from Cosmo's company and makes his way toward us.

"He's coming over," Mimi warns me through her smile, before saying brightly, "Hi, Ryan! Excited to join the team?"

"Yes," he replies, greeting me with a curt nod.

"We're looking forward to having you," she says warmly. "If you need anything, you can let us know." Her phone starts vibrating in her pocket and she checks the screen. "It's my better half—I should take this."

She gives him an apologetic smile and then ducks out of our

conversation as she answers the phone, leaving Ryan and me alone together. Traitor.

"So," he begins.

"So," I reply.

"We need to make this work," he says, lowering his voice so no one can hear.

I wrinkle my nose at him. "Make *what* work?"

"Us. Together. Sitting next to each other. Being on the same team." He lets out a long sigh. "Clearly, you're still upset about what happened, even though it was a long time ago and I think that—"

"Excuse you," I hiss, "I am *not* still upset about what happened."

He snorts. "Oh, really."

"Really."

"Because from what I can tell from our recent interactions, you still have a lot of hostility toward me," he says, scowling.

"That's not because of what happened, Ryan," I say crossly.

"Then why is it?"

"Perhaps your general personality annoys me."

He rolls his eyes. "Okay. That's mature."

"You know, you've hardly been lovely and sweet toward me in our recent interactions," I point out. "Maybe *you're* the one who bears a grudge."

"Why would *I* bear a grudge?"

"I don't know. I won't pretend to understand how your scheming mind works."

"Harper," he says quietly, pinching the top of his nose as though he's trying to keep his temper, "can we at least be *civil*? So that both of us don't dread going into the office every day? Can you forget about what happened and—"

"As far as I'm concerned, nothing ever happened," I snap, looking him right in the eye.

A flash of emotion crosses his expression, but I can't quite work out what it is. Hurt perhaps, or regret? Maybe confusion. It's gone as quickly as it came.

"Great," he says matter-of-factly.

"Fine."

"Fine."

"*Fine*."

"Why do you keep doing that?" he growls impatiently.

"Doing what?"

"You *have* to have the last word whenever I speak to you."

"Maybe it's *you* who always has to have the last word and that's why *my* having the last word pisses you off so much," I observe smugly.

He rolls his eyes, taking a swig of his beer. "You're unbelievable. Is it always going to be like this between us?"

"There's nothing between us."

"And you claim that you're not still angry, ten or so years on."

"I told you to forget about it!" I snap.

"I wish *you* would forget about it. I wish . . ."

He trails off, his expression softening as I glare at him.

I notice his eyes flicker down to my lips. My throat tightens and my heart begins to thud against my chest. Suddenly, my thoughts are clouded by how close I am to him. My cheeks flushing under his gaze, I exhale shakily and swallow. His forehead creases and then, out of the corner of my eye, I see his fingers twitch. I think about what would happen if I reached out and pulled him toward me and—

"Jansson! There you are."

Cosmo appears next to us and we jolt apart. My face is on fire.

"I'd like your opinion on something," Cosmo continues, clapping him on the back. He notices me and adds impatiently, "Unless I'm interrupting, of course."

"No," I assure him. "I was going to go get another drink anyway."

I move toward the bar, eager to erase what just happened. I can't let myself think that way about Ryan. I focus on steadying my breathing as I lean against the counter and wait for my drink, closing my eyes in the hope of shutting out the memories.

CHAPTER SEVEN

It's official: Ryan Jansson is impossible.

I don't know how long I'll be able to work in these conditions. He's only been here a couple of weeks and already he's driving me crazy. His first day, he waltzed in with a box of—get this—*homemade cookies*. What kind of person does that? A sneaky, arrogant, manipulative one, that's who. Of course, the whole team flocked around him and his stupid cookies, praising his baking skills and saying he *must* share the recipe.

Please.

I wasn't fooled for one moment. I saw him nervously take out the Tupperware and slide it onto the treat shelf, where we put out edible items sent in for the food and drink review pages. Then he stalked back to his desk without announcing the cookies to anyone, obviously waiting for Mimi to call out, "Hey, where did these cookies come from?" when she passed a little later, so that he could look modest as he admitted that he baked them over the weekend.

What a performance.

I did not fawn over his cookies, no matter how delicious they smelled. I would never give him that kind of satisfaction. When he noticed me staring at them, an amused smile played on his lips and he casually said, "You can help yourself, Harper."

"No, thank you," I replied *civilly*, as was required.

"They've got extra chocolate chips."

"I'll pass," I said, cool as a cucumber. "I don't like cookies."

Mimi then had to ruin everything by saying, "What? You *love* cookies! Last Thursday you ate four of those Millie's Cookies that were sent in. Wow, Ryan, these are delicious!"

"Thanks," he said, before leaning toward me and muttering, "I promise you they're not poisonous."

"I never said they were."

"You shouldn't not eat them just because I made them."

"I told you, I don't like cookies."

"Suit yourself," he grumbled.

I ignored him and got on with my day, successfully avoiding the temptation to eat any of those cookies, despite having to walk past the treat shelf several times.

If only it was as easy to avoid Ryan.

All week he's made snide comments about the state of my desk and how my "mess" is encroaching on his character-less space. He started small, passive-aggressively pushing back any papers that slid over onto his desk, but on the third or fourth time, he began clearing his throat pointedly as he did so. I decided not to acknowledge him at all. If anything, I might have ensured that a couple of things made it over to his side.

A few days later, I arrived to discover that three piles of books had been neatly stacked along the line between our desks, creating a makeshift divider.

"Hope this doesn't bother you," he said breezily as he marked up a layout and I sat in my chair. "I appreciate it gives you less space to *spread out.*"

"I'm very happy with this arrangement," I replied, before noticing that he had cunningly snaffled my multicolored biro before erecting his book fortress. "Although, that pen you're using is on the wrong side of the barrier."

He had the audacity to look confused. "Excuse me?"

"That's *my* pen. And if you're so intent on making sure there's no cross-contamination of our things, then please give it back."

"This is not your pen," he said, twirling it round in his fingers.

"I think you'll find it is."

"Harper," he said wearily, "I got this from the stationery cupboard."

"They don't stock those kind of pens in the stationery cupboard. You plucked it from my desk and hoped I wouldn't notice."

"I wouldn't have been able to find anything on your desk, even if I'd wanted to!"

"Uh, Harper?" Mimi squeaked from across the way, holding up a biro. "I have a spare pen if you need one."

"I don't need one, thanks Mimi, I already have one. Ryan is using it."

"Maybe if you tidied up, you'd find the pen you're referring to buried underneath all the stuff strewn across your desk," he said haughtily.

"Don't you think it's a bit odd that you're so bothered by a few bits of paper on someone else's desk?" I remarked, crossing my arms. "I'm not bothered by anyone else's desk. Mimi isn't bothered by anyone else's desk—"

"Don't bring me into this," Mimi muttered.

"Maybe there's an underlying issue here that you need to address, Ryan," I continued brazenly. "I think your obsession with the state of my desk has something to do with feeling out of control in other areas of your life."

He narrowed his eyes at me before standing up and holding out the pen.

"Here," he said with a heavy sigh. "Just take it."

"Thank you," I said crisply as he placed it in my hand and marched away toward the stationery cupboard. "If you want to borrow anything, Ryan, next time just ask. We're very pleasant this side of the book fort."

It was a deeply satisfying conclusion to the discussion.

When I later found my multicolored retractable biro folded

into an old issue of the magazine lying next to my computer, while simultaneously holding the one I'd demanded back from Ryan, I quickly closed the magazine, determined to get rid of the evidence when no one was looking.

Listen, I get that if you're an organized neat freak, I'm not going to be your number one desk buddy. But apart from that, I am an excellent colleague. I'm cheerful and enthusiastic in the office, and supportive and thoughtful toward other people's work.

Ryan, on the other hand, may be neat and occasionally bring in baked goods, but he brings down the mood with his aloof, unapproachable demeanor. He also seems to go out of his way to piss me off.

First, he gave Gabby, the editorial assistant, some transcriptions to do for him, and when she mentioned that she was doing one for me, I overheard him saying that his was more important. I jumped to my feet and called out across the office, "Excuse me, but why are your transcriptions more important than mine? You're not being dismissive of celebrity pieces, are you, Ryan?"

"No, of course not, Harper," he replied with a fixed smile, blushing furiously as the rest of the office jerked their heads up to pay attention. Poor Gabby looked panicked. "I was merely suggesting to Gabby that she prioritize my task as my deadline is tomorrow and I know that the interview she's transcribing for you isn't due until the end of next week."

"Actually, I'm planning on writing up that interview this afternoon because the art desk needs to start working on the layout tomorrow," I informed him, not missing the opportunity to add bitterly, "and *the reason* art wants to get started on it is because it's going to be a difficult one to fit in, now that it's gone from a three-pager to a double spread, thanks to your insistence that your piece celebrating con artists needs more pages."

"It's not a piece *celebrating* con artists. It's a psychological exploration of why we seem to have an obsession with watching TV series and films about them," he said impatiently. "Which I already explained to you this morning. And while the art desk may need to start working on your piece soon, they need to mock up my article first to meet the deadline, so I think it's more important that my transcriptions are done as soon as possible. Wouldn't you agree?"

Before I could answer, he continued: "Or is there an underlying issue that you need to address here, Harper? Maybe your need to go first here has something to do with *feeling out of control in other areas of your life.*"

How *dare* he use my own excellent words against me?!

I was furious and I'd have liked to have told him where to go, but instead I had to smile sweetly (because everyone was looking) and say, "All right, then. Gabby, please do go ahead and transcribe Ryan's interviews. Of course, if you'd have come to me first, Ryan, and asked whether it was okay for your transcription to take priority with your reasonable explanation, I wouldn't have minded in the least. That's usually how we do it around here."

"My apologies. I'll know for next time," he said.

I sat back down and glanced across at Mimi, who whispered, "*Awkward,*" and then quickly pretended to be working when Ryan came back to his desk.

That was Strike One. (I haven't included the book fort in the strikes because I'm feeling generous.)

Strike Two occurred during the editorial meeting when Cosmo casually dropped the bomb that Ryan would be writing up a profile piece on the MP whose book launch we both attended.

"Excuse me," I said, raising my hand as Cosmo waffled on about how it was sure to be a thrilling article.

"Yes, Harper, we're all aware that you're here on time today," Cosmo said with a chuckle to himself. "You don't need to draw attention to the fact."

"Ha, no," I said impatiently, causing Cosmo to scowl. "I wanted to ask why Ryan is writing that piece and not me?"

Cosmo raised his eyebrows, heartily amused at the question. "You think *you* should be writing that article?"

"Yes, you may remember I mentioned to you that I'd been to that book launch and thought that it would make an interesting profile piece. You said you weren't sure it was a good fit but that you'd think about it."

Ryan shifted in his seat, as though he was embarrassed. I wasn't buying it. He saw me at that book launch, so he must have known I'd already pitched this idea. He was playing dumb in the knowledge that if it's between him and me, Cosmo is always going to pick a fellow member of the "lads' club."

"I'm afraid I don't remember that conversation," Cosmo said. "Ryan came to me with a fully formed pitch and, though I'm sure you'd do a nice job of it, he has experience writing articles of this nature, so I think he's probably the best person to take this one on."

"I've written articles about politicians," I reminded Cosmo.

"Yes, you did that piece last year on the former education secretary," Ryan recalled.

I waited for him to add something dismissive, but he didn't expand, and instead looked surprised that everyone was staring at him, as though he hadn't realized he'd been speaking out loud.

"Yes, but this pitch is a little more specific than speaking to a politician about their lifestyle," Cosmo continued. "As Ryan has prior knowledge of the issue, since he's written about it for the main paper in the past, it makes sense for him to write this."

"Cosmo, I should be the one writing this piece! We both went to the same book launch—I know as much about this issue as Ryan does!"

"You know a lot about land mines?" Cosmo asked, surprised.

I blinked at him in confusion. "*Land mines?*"

Ryan's expression shifted to pure delight.

"Yes, Harper," he said, watching me curiously. "I was planning on talking to the politician about his fierce and passionate campaigning to raise awareness of the humanitarian crisis caused by leftover land mines. You remember, he read a chapter regarding the issue at his launch."

"Right." I nodded. "Of course. I knew that."

"And you were saying that you know a lot about the issue?"

"Yes," I lied, my face growing even hotter than before.

"Well, then you should write the piece," Ryan offered, causing Cosmo to look alarmed. "As you know so much about land mines."

"I do know a lot about land mines," I said, with no idea why I was digging myself into a bigger hole except that I wasn't about to lose face in front of my work nemesis. "Princess Diana walked through that minefield, for example."

That secretive, amused, mocking smile of Ryan's appeared on his lips. The one he seems to always reserve for me.

God, he's the worst.

I cleared my throat. "But actually, I have a lot on this week, so if you've already assigned it to Ryan, Cosmo, then I'm happy to let him write that one."

Cosmo looked relieved.

"Thanks, Harper, that's really good of you," Ryan said graciously.

Mimi's shoulders were shaking with silent laughter.

Strike Number Three happens on a dreary Tuesday morning after an evening spent at a Leicester Square premiere, at which I managed to make many excellent notes in my notebook about the film and the stars attending it, but then lost said notebook by Wednesday morning.

While I'm busy excavating the contents of my bag, Ryan appears with a carrot cake he whipped up last night.

I don't know why this impresses everyone.

Carrot cake isn't even the best sponge.

"Harper, is Liam looking forward to taking part in my annual birthday sports day?" Mimi says, taking a small bite of Ryan's cake and swooning. "I hope he's been practicing his beer-pong skills because I will be entirely judging his character on those."

I pause, looking at her guiltily. "Liam can't come."

"Oh no! I thought you said he could?"

That's because he had *told* me he could. But we'd spoken about it over the weekend and things had changed. We were at a restaurant near my place and I had been ranting about Ryan while Liam nodded loyally, saying "hmm" in all the right places. Then I'd mentioned a charity ball that was coming up in my diary.

"I don't understand why Ryan, of all people, got an invite too," I huffed, tearing off a chunk of sourdough bread as we waited to order. "He's not interested in stuff like that. It will be full of celebrities, and it's not like he even bothers to talk to people at these events. He stands in the corner, acting all high and mighty."

"Do you remember we talked about me accompanying you to a work event?" Liam asked, leaning forward across the table.

"Yeah, course."

"How about this ball you're talking about?"

I hesitated. "You want to come?"

"Harper," he said, looking at me in disbelief, "of course I want to come! It would be so fun to be your plus-one. It would be nice to spend time together at a posh event. And I could meet your friends in the business."

I paused to consider. "I guess. Although I'm not sure how many people going are my *friends* per se. Some of them are, but others are really just work—"

"I want to be a part of your life, Harper, and this stuff is important to you, I know it is. So I'd really like to go with you to this event." His eyes were expectant.

I smiled at him. "That's really sweet. Okay, I'll ask for a plus-one."

"Amazing!" He sat back and slapped his knee. "Man, this is going to be so cool. Is it black tie?"

"Yes, but don't get too excited. I have to get you an invitation first."

"You'll get one," he said confidently, beaming at me. "If anyone can, you can. This will be such a great opportunity to meet clients. And I get to be your arm candy. Win-win!"

I laughed. "Speaking of being my arm candy, are you excited to meet everyone at Mimi's birthday? It's next weekend."

"Oh, right," he nodded, looking pensive. "Mimi's birthday party."

"Don't worry, I know I've made a big deal out of these games, but they're really just silly ones. It doesn't matter if you're not very good at them."

Liam grimaced. "I don't think I'll be able to make it anymore."

"What? Really?"

"I have so much work to do. I really need to focus on expanding the business at the moment. It's all very exciting, but it means that my weekends are taken up with work unfortunately."

"But . . . if you wanted to get to know my friends, then Mimi's party is better than the charity ball."

"I know it's a shame, but I can meet them another time. There will be other weekends."

I felt slightly taken aback but said, "Oh. Okay. Well, I'm sad you won't be able to come."

"Me too," he said, perusing the menu. "Ooh—" he glanced up excitedly "—shall we get the arancini balls and buffalo mozzarella to start?"

I feel guilty that I didn't message Mimi then to let her know that Liam could no longer come, rather than dropping it on her now in the office, but I had been putting it off. I don't want her thinking that he's not making an effort with my friends. I'm sure he will when he has the time.

Still, I can't help but compare his lack of enthusiasm for Mimi's birthday with his intense eagerness for networking at the charity ball. Liam's ambition is what attracted me to him in the first place, but it does make me doubt his intentions a little. To be fair, it's not like I've prioritized getting to know his friends, either.

I'm not sure that's a good sign.

"I'm really sorry, Mimi, he did want to come and was hoping he'd be able to make it," I tell her hurriedly. "But he's got so much work on at the moment, and it's taking over his weekends, too. I hope this hasn't ruined the rounders teams. I feel awful."

"Don't feel bad," she tells me, brightening. "This actually works out quite nicely."

I look at her in surprise. "It does?"

"Obviously, I'm sorry that Liam can't come," she says, taking another bite of the carrot cake. "But I was going to invite Ryan, too, which would have made the teams uneven numbers, but now without Liam, they'll be the same."

"I . . . *sorry?*"

Before she can address my baffled reaction, she calls out Ryan's name, stopping him in his tracks as he returns to his desk.

"I wanted to invite you to my birthday party this Saturday," Mimi says cheerily.

He looks puzzled. "Really?"

"Yeah, course! If you're free?"

"Yes, I am. Thanks," he says, his forehead creasing as though he's trying to work out why she would possibly want him to come. He glances at me suspiciously.

"Great! It's going to be a day of fun games in the park, so get your competitive hat on and pray for sunshine."

He allows himself a small smile. "I definitely have a competitive streak."

"I thought you might," Mimi comments. "I'll message you the details, but it's Brockwell Park around lunchtime."

"Brockwell—is that the one near Brixton?"

She nods. "Where do you live?"

"Finsbury Park."

"Literally the other end of London. Bit of a pain for you, then," Mimi remarks with a sympathetic look. "Although, it's straight down the Victoria Line, which is nice and speedy."

"I'll be there, thanks for the invite," he assures her.

"So pleased you can make it! And feel free to bake something for the occasion. That cake was incredible." She pauses, adding, "Oh and you're very welcome to bring your other half, too . . . if you have one?"

He blushes, shaking his head. "Just me at the moment."

"Oh good," she says, brightening. "I didn't want to be rude, but it would have ruined the even numbers of the teams if you'd brought a plus-one, to be honest."

"Mimi," I say calmly, as Ryan sits down next to me and starts typing away, "would you mind accompanying me to the bathroom?"

"Sure," she says, dropping her napkin in the paper basket next to her desk. "Let's go."

Once we're in the safe haven of the toilets, I round on her.

"Why did you invite *him* to your party?" I demand.

She puts her hands on her hips. "Harper. Why are you so against this guy? I know there are a few things you don't see eye to eye on in the office, but I've got to know him a bit and I want to give him a chance. He's obviously a guarded person, and I think his baking is his way of making an effort with the team. It's quite sweet."

"Sweet? *Ha!*"

"Look, my party is a good way to chat to him outside of the office—a nice relaxed, informal setting where you won't need to squabble over who's in charge of what," she says, leaning against the sinks. "If you gave him a chance, you might like him."

"I doubt it."

She hesitates. "You know he talks to you more than he talks to anyone else in the office."

"That's because he argues with me all the time."

"True," she acknowledges, "but he also seems different around you. When you're in the conversation, he's less reserved. You bring him out of his shell."

"Mimi, what are you talking about? Him disagreeing with everything I say is not coming out of his shell!"

"I'm just saying that around everyone else he has a bit of a wall up, but he seems a lot more at ease around you. Like he forgets to be in his own head all the time. Sometimes I catch him looking at you. And, I don't know, there's something about the way he . . ."

"*What?*" I feel my cheeks growing hot as she scrutinizes my reaction. "Mimi, please do not make up ridiculous scenarios in your head. Ryan and I have nothing in common, and the only reason he may seem to talk to me more is because we both cover features in the magazine."

"If you say so," she sighs. "Just promise me you'll play nice at my party. I'm the birthday girl, so you can't say no."

I roll my eyes. "Fine."

"Thank you, and don't worry," she says with a grin, "I'll make sure you're on opposite teams."

CHAPTER EIGHT

The sun is shining on the day of Mimi's birthday party.

It's an easy walk from my flat to the park, so I have all morning to get ready, which I'm grateful for because I have no idea what to wear.

And it's not because *Ryan's* going.

Okay, fine. It's because Ryan's going.

It's not that I want to look nice for *him*. It's more that I need to feel confident, and it's also very important I look like a winner. Because there is no way in hell that I am letting Ryan Jansson's team beat mine. I wouldn't be able to stand that stupid little smile of his that he saves for when he gets one up on me.

The other day in the office, the art team put up two potential cover designs on the wall and asked for our thoughts because Cosmo couldn't decide which was more striking.

"The orange," I said instantly, tapping the printout with my finger. "It's bold and eye-catching. Plus, it looks really good with the white and pink cover lines."

"The blue," Ryan countered, stroking his chin and nodding to the other one. "It's softer, warmer. More inviting."

I glared at him.

"Mimi, what do you think?" I asked, lifting my chin as she examined the two.

"I think—" she paused, her eyes darting between the two covers and then anxiously between me and Ryan "—the blue. It works better. Sorry," she added for my benefit.

The smug smile on Ryan's face.

It made my blood boil.

I swear he looked so pleased with himself for the rest of the day. At one point he started *humming*.

"I'm not allowed to hum?" he questioned when I told him off.

"People are trying to concentrate," I snapped back.

"Mimi was just talking about that song, and I literally hummed the chorus for about five seconds."

"Yes, well, it was five seconds too long," I said, scowling at him. "Would you like it if I casually started singing while you were trying to write an important journalistic piece?"

He glanced at my screen. "You're Googling *bald eagles.*"

"And?"

"It doesn't look like you're in the middle of writing an important journalistic piece."

"I'm still trying to concentrate."

He frowned in confusion. "While looking at pictures of bald eagles?"

"Yes!"

He raised his eyebrows. By now, a few colleagues had swiveled slightly to listen. I've noticed it becoming a theme—whenever Ryan and I start bickering over something, the rest of the office becomes eerily silent.

"Are you looking at pictures of bald eagles for a piece you're writing?" he asked breezily. "Are you interviewing . . . a celebrity bald eagle?"

Mimi sniggered. I glared at her. She quickly pretended to focus on her screen.

"It's none of your business why I'm Googling bald eagles," I pointed out.

"Then it's none of your business that I'm humming."

"It is my business when it affects me, which your humming does."

"You Googling bald eagles on office time when it's not work related could be affecting *me*. If you're wasting time and falling behind, then I'll be the one to pick up the slack."

Ugh.

I'd been listening to a comedy podcast on the way into work that morning and one of the hosts had mentioned bald eagles, which made me wonder if they were *actually* bald? I couldn't Google it because I was on the tube with no signal, and I'd just now remembered to look it up.

But I could hardly explain that to him, could I?

"You know that's a ridiculous argument," I hissed at him.

"Harper, I think this isn't about bald eagles or my humming. I think you're annoyed that everyone agreed with my opinion on the blue cover over the orange cover."

"Please!" I guffawed. "This is *not* about that."

"So you don't care that I was right?"

"You weren't *right*. It was a subjective opinion." I shifted in my seat. "It just so happens that in the end, the art desk and the editor decided to go with the one you *personally* preferred."

He nodded. "So, I was right."

"No."

"Yes," he insisted.

"No, you . . ." I exhaled, trying to stay calm. "You know what? It doesn't matter."

"That I was right?"

"That we had *differing opinions*," I clarified. "And I was telling you to stop humming because it's distracting, not because I was annoyed the blue cover was decided on."

He shrugged. "Okay."

"Good, then. Humming is banned."

We fell into silence and didn't speak to each other for the rest of the day.

It's very clear that I cannot let Ryan win today, because if he does, he will lord it over me forever. A winning outfit is *key* to the operation: it needs to be sporty enough for me to move in for the competitive activities, but it can't be gym gear because it's Mimi's birthday and I need to make an effort.

I'm actually quite glad Liam isn't here, because I need to practically empty my entire wardrobe onto the bed and bedroom floor to see what my options are. I'm surprised to come across clothes that I'd forgotten I owned, including high-waisted gray denim shorts that I had bought last summer on a whim after watching a slew of Taylor Swift music videos.

I slip those on and then start rooting around for a clean T-shirt. Once I've found one, pulled it over my head, and tucked it into my shorts, I start working out what to wear if it gets cold and land on a roll-sleeved blazer jacket. After putting some effort into my makeup (but trying to make it look as though I've spent hardly any time at all), I rummage through my bedside table looking for my new sunglasses. They're an *essential* accessory for the outfit.

I tear the flat apart, getting angrier and less merciful with my belongings as I go, chucking items over my shoulder out of drawers as I search for them.

My bedroom looks like it's been hit by a tornado, and I groan as I realize I'm going to be late. And then I perk up when I remember that I wore those sunglasses earlier this week! They're in one of the cases in my bag!

I slide them up my nose happily and head out of the flat in a rush, returning once for my phone, which is still in my bedroom playing a summer day playlist, and a second time for Mimi's present, a pretty gold bracelet that I left in its box on the kitchen counter.

After stopping briefly on the way to buy a couple of bottles, I make my way through Brockwell Park, spotting from a mile off the long outdoor table with pink, white, and silver balloons tied all along the side and picnic food platters and bottle coolers laid out on the top. Mimi picks the same spot every year for her birthday, right beneath one of the huge old oak trees in the park, so the food table is safely in the shade.

I smile as I stroll past the clusters of people sitting cross-legged in circles laughing and chatting as they swig from cans of cider. When the sun is shining, the whole mood of London is lifted.

I spot Rakhee chatting to one of Mimi's school friends. She sees me approaching and her expression brightens.

"Have I missed you!" I say, giving her a kiss on the cheek. "Please tell me you hate your new magazine and you're going to come crawling back to us."

"I'm afraid not." She laughs. "I'm sort of loving the new job. But I'm glad to see that nothing has changed and you're still rocking up late to everything."

"Blame that on my sunglasses. I couldn't find them anywhere."

"Let me guess, they were in your bag the whole time?"

"You see? This is why I need you to come back to *Narrative* and look after me!"

She chuckles. "How is it working with Ryan?"

"Don't ask her opinion on Ryan," Mimi butts in, appearing next to me and giving me a hug. "She'll tell you how much she doesn't want to speak about him before speaking about him a *lot*."

"Oi!" I nudge her in the ribs. "I can't get mad at you because it's your birthday. Everything looks amazing, of course. The food looks delicious. Is it all homemade? Maybe I should have baked something."

"A very sweet thought, but we all know you and baking don't mix, Harper. Besides, everything you see was provided by my dear friend Marks & Spencer," Mimi tells us, hitching up her white high-waisted trousers that she's wearing with a bright orange top.

I wouldn't *dream* of wearing white trousers to a day at the park where I know I'll be playing games and lounging around on the grass, but of course Mimi wouldn't blink before throwing them on. She's the kind of person who always looks neat as a pin—like she's just arrived from sitting front row of Victoria Beckham's latest show, but she's ready to kick off her shoes and play rounders.

"When do the games start?" Rakhee asks.

"Soon," Mimi promises. "You two are on the same team. I'm on the other team, but don't worry, I'm not expecting you to let me win just because I'm the birthday girl. I'll beat you fair and square."

"Oh, here we go," I say with a grin. "The rivalry begins now, does it?"

"Never too early to rile the spirits with a bit of healthy competition," Mimi declares. She glances over my shoulder and smiles. "Speaking of competition, Ryan is here."

I look round and see him sauntering over.

"Remember to play nice, Harper," Mimi says sternly.

"You were just talking about healthy competition."

"*Healthy* being the optimum word," she insists. "Everything has to be aboveboard. I don't want to have to break you two up after you attack each other with bats."

"If that scenario did happen, I would so win. You can tell he has a weak swing."

"Hey," Ryan says as he approaches, carrying a bag that clinks loudly. "Happy birthday, Mimi. I wasn't sure what drinks you'd like, so I brought a selection." In his other hand, he holds out a Tupperware. "And I made some millionaire's shortbread. I think I remember you saying you liked it."

"I *love* it! Thank you so much, that's so lovely of you." She gratefully takes the Tupperware and peers inside. "These look amazing."

"I hope they taste good."

"Knowing your baking talent, I'm sure they'll be delicious."

"Oh, I brought some ice, too. I thought that might be help-ful," he says, pulling out a bag of ice cubes. "Do you have a cooler box or anything?"

"I have three!" Mimi cries excitedly, while Rakhee and I hide our smiles at how happy she is to show off her organizational skills. "No one ever remembers to bring ice. I'm impressed."

"It's nice to see you again," Rakhee begins, offering him a wave as Mimi totters off with the bag of ice. "Mimi's been tell-ing me about your baking—you've definitely one-upped me by bringing that angle to the job."

He blushes. "I bribe people to like me through cake."

Rakhee chuckles. "So, how are you finding the office? Every-one keeping you on your toes?"

"Some more than others," he remarks, his eyes flicking to me.

"I'm sure you're well able to rise to the challenge," she com-ments, giving me a sly smile as I pretend to ignore the conver-sation.

"What about you?" he asks her. "How's your new role?"

As Rakhee fills him in on *Sleek*, I take in Ryan's appearance. He looks annoyingly good, wearing blue jeans and a white T-shirt underneath an unbuttoned khaki shirt with the sleeves rolled up. He really suits those Ray-Bans, too. His head angles toward me slightly as Rakhee is talking, as though he can tell I'm studying him, and I quickly drop my eyes to the ground.

Rakhee excuses herself when she is waved over by some of our *Narrative* colleagues who haven't had the chance to say hello yet. I glance around, searching for someone else to speak to so I'm not stuck making awkward small talk with Ryan, when he cracks open a can of beer, making me jump.

"Feeling on edge today, Harper?" he asks, taking a sip of his drink. "Perhaps you're nervous about the competitive games."

"Please. I could not be more ready to take you down."

"How do you know we're not on the same team?"

"Because Mimi told me."

He raises his eyebrows. "Ah, you were asking about me, then."

"What? No!" I immediately feel my cheeks flush.

"You must have been, for Mimi to inform you that we were on opposite teams."

"Don't flatter yourself. She mentioned it in passing."

He nods to the rounders bat and ball lying on the grass near the table. "You any good?"

"At rounders? Yes, very good."

"Really?"

"You sound surprised. For your information, I am very good at sports with balls."

He looks delighted. "*Excuse me?*"

"Oh, don't make it dirty," I scold. "You know what I meant. Netball, tennis, rounders. I wasn't one for the running track at school, but team sports I excelled at. My PE teacher told me I have excellent hand-eye coordination."

"As impressive a compliment as that is, you do realize you were at school quite a long time ago," he points out.

"Hand-eye coordination doesn't disappear. It's a lifelong skill."

"That's true. In case you're interested, I am also very good at sports with balls."

"Good for you."

"Never enjoyed sprinting or long-distance running. Seemed . . . pointless."

I nod. "I'll run to catch a ball or to win a point after hitting it, but I won't sprint for no reason."

"Exactly. I need to be distracted from the running part." He pauses. "Did I ever tell you about the catch I made that was reported in the paper?"

I snort. "Sure, okay."

"No, I'm being serious," he insists. "We were playing a cricket match against a rival school on this local green and I was a fielder, really far out, not really paying attention. The batter thwacks the ball right up in the air and it soared in my direction. I ran as fast as I could, caught the ball, and then *splosh!* Fell backward into the lake."

I laugh. "No, you didn't."

"I swear I did," he says, grinning. "I rose from the water, clutching the ball in my hand. Everyone went wild. It was the best catch I ever made."

"You really fell backward into the lake?"

"No word of a lie, it was the peak of my career."

"Your extensive cricket career?"

"The peak of my career *period*. There's no way I can top that moment. Not even if I won a Pulitzer. The photo of me in the lake holding the ball made the front page of the local paper. Guess what the caption was?"

"Give me a moment," I say, concentrating. "Something like 'Quite the catch'?"

"If only they'd been so creative. But no," he laughs, "the caption read: *Local boy, Ronan, goes for a dip during cricket match.*"

"Ronan!"

"They got my name wrong *and* they didn't even mention how good the catch was! They made it seem as though I was going for a casual swim during a game."

"Hey, at least you were in the paper. That's pretty cool."

"It's still framed on my parents' mantelpiece."

"Guess I'll try not to hit the ball in your direction today, then."

"Likewise, since you're so good at sports with balls," he remarks, smiling into his beer.

Catching his eye, I can't help but giggle.

Then I remember I'm not supposed to enjoy his company and quickly look away.

"All right, everyone!" Mimi cries out, clapping her hands and getting our attention. "The annual games are about to begin. Anyone who has brought a jumper, throw it this way so we can use them to mark the posts of the rounders pitch."

Ryan turns to me. "Let the best team win."

"Oh, we will," I assure him.

He smiles, tiny little crinkles forming around the corners of his mouth, his striking eyes fixed on me intently. It's a different smile to the smug, superior one I've grown so used to over the past few weeks. It's warm and sincere and inviting.

He wanders off and, while Mimi yells instructions at those holding up jumpers, Rakhee sidles up next to me.

"Did I just witness you and Ryan laughing?" she asks curiously.

"No," I say defensively, suddenly feeling flustered. "I was laughing *at* him."

"Maybe he's not as bad as you think."

"You're wrong." I frown, watching his back as he walks away and desperately trying to fight off memories prompted by his smile. "He's exactly as bad as I think."

During our internship, it becomes obvious that Ryan and I are very different people who work in completely different ways. Everything we do seems to be at odds with the other one— even the coffee run. I know the journalists prefer that Ryan gets their coffee order correct (I should really note it down before I leave), *but* I also know that they prefer me delivering it, because we have a good chat, whereas Ryan simply hands it over in nervous silence.

At our desks, we have very little to talk about unless we're mocking each other. He likes to tease me about my obsession with reality TV shows, but the joke's on him because Celia is a huge *Made in Chelsea* fan, so we end up bonding over that, and I can see him giving us jealous glances whenever she perches on my desk and we chat away happily. I have to admit that I get a bit envious when Ryan *purposefully* leaves whatever dull war book he's reading out on his desk so that when one of the senior reporters comes over to ask us to do some photocopying, she just so happens to see it and asks him his thoughts.

Ryan isn't naturally at ease in conversation, but when you

get him on something he's interested in—like the author Ben Macintyre and his book about the D-Day spies—he suddenly opens up. Until he realizes that he's been talking and then quickly falls silent again, his forehead furrowing, as though embarrassed to have gotten carried away. If he wasn't such an asshole, I'd think it was endearing.

As the days go by we both catch on to the fact that it's easier if we split the jobs equally between us, rather than attempt to work on a task together, and we work out which tasks might be better suited for the other, passing them on if necessary. And we do have our moments of cease-fire and, even, courtesy. Ryan is an enthusiastic baker and shares some of his delicious creations with me. I introduce him to putting honey in his tea, and sometimes, if one of us is feeling in a generous mood, we might go so far as to make honey tea for each other in the afternoons.

But things go south very quickly when a few weeks in Celia confirms that her job is up for grabs—she's giving her notice and taking a features assistant job at *Flair*, a women's glossy magazine. She says if Ryan and I would like to apply, one of us would have a strong chance of getting it, since we're learning the ropes already.

And just like that, it's war.

Ryan and I go into overdrive to impress the team and outdo the other one. We squabble over who gets to do stupid everyday tasks and race to produce research notes, each trying to ensure our bullet points are thorough but first on the desk of the reporter who requested them. A low point is on one of these occasions when we're both waiting by the printer, each hoping we pressed Print first, and then we realize the ink cartridge needs replacing— we almost break the machine, arguing over how best to put the cartridge in and causing a scene as others notice us yelling at each other about being too slow or doing it wrong.

And then, just when I think I can't stand him, something happens that makes me question that completely.

It begins when Celia comes over late one afternoon to announce the exciting news that she would like us to work on a piece together for the paper.

"Wait, are you serious?" I ask, sitting up straight. "As in, it will be published?"

"You'll get your first byline and everything," she says, laughing at both our elated expressions. "It's pretty cool the first time you see your name in print, I have to admit."

"What's the piece?" I ask eagerly.

"It's a round-up, so not too taxing: 'The Best Picnic Spots in London.' Adorable, right? My idea," she says proudly. "But I don't have time to write it, so I thought you could take it on. As it's a summer piece, it needs to be published pretty soon, so we need it by end of play Monday. I know it's Thursday, so it's a tight deadline, but good experience. Choose five or six places and write about fifty words on each. And you may not like this, but I really want you to work on it *together*. As in, no splitting it down the middle, otherwise the writing style will be different or repetitive and it won't work. Got it?"

"No problem," I say with a fixed smile.

"Excellent," Ryan mumbles, his voice strained.

She shakes her head at us. "Jesus. What is it with you two? Anyway, good luck."

Straight off the bat, we're at loggerheads. Ryan thinks we should research picnic spots online—I'm of the opinion that we should make the time to actually go to these places and then decide.

"How are we going to visit all the places in London we can have a picnic?" he argues.

"We don't have to go to *all* of them, that would be ridiculous. Just famous ones," I explain.

"And the only way we'll find out the famous ones is to research online."

"Fine, we'll do that."

He nods. "Great."

"Then this weekend, we'll go visit them," I add smugly.

He sighs.

"Ryan," I begin calmly, "don't you want to be honest with your readers? How are they supposed to trust that these are the best picnic spots in London if the writers haven't even visited themselves?"

"I suppose you're right," he grumbles.

"I usually am, and the sooner you realize that, the better. So we'll compile a list of spots tomorrow and then are you free Saturday?"

"Unfortunately."

"We'll have an adventure," I assure him, adding, "Don't worry, we'll bring wine."

"I think that's a necessity," he says, his mouth twitching into a smile.

Once we've got a satisfactory list of ideas, we spend Saturday traipsing round London to see which ones make our top six. It sounds like a chore, but it's a nice day and it's surprisingly fun, largely because Ryan seems much more relaxed outside of the office. We both arrive with backpacks filled with wine and snacks, and consequently end up having mini picnics at each spot, sitting on Primrose Hill or in the middle of Holland Park discussing the advantages and disadvantages of each view point.

By the time we reach our final destination—Greenwich Park—I'm feeling very tipsy. It's fairly busy, but as there's only two of us, we manage to squeeze into a good spot in the middle of the hill, right at the top. Pouring some more wine, we forget to review the merits of the park and instead start discussing why we wanted to become journalists and what our ambitions are for the future. He tells me he wants to write a book someday.

"What about?" I ask.

"I don't know, something important," he answers vaguely. "Maybe I'll write an investigative report into some kind of awful injustice and blow it wide open, so I bring about real change, and then I can turn that into a book. That's why I wanted to be a journalist in the first place."

"To get a book deal off the back of an article?"

He laughs. "No, to give people a voice who might not have one."

I tell him I think that's very noble and that I want to be a journalist simply because I like telling people's stories. He says he thinks that's noble, too.

We somehow end up talking about family and he tells me about his parents, his Swedish heritage, and his one true love, Cracker, his parents' Irish setter. He asks me about my family and I tiptoe round the subject, but regale him with a couple of funny stories from university, like how I auditioned for the pantomime and landed the role of a nonspeaking duck.

He roars with laughter and I think how nice it is to see him really let loose, and how I wish he laughed like that more often. He catches me staring at him and I blush, looking away.

Remembering why we're here in the first place, I gesture at the view and declare this to be my favorite picnic spot in London.

"Nah," he says, shaking his head, "I prefer Battersea Park."

"But you can see the whole city from here!"

He smiles at my enthusiasm. "Yeah, but I like picnicking by a lake or something."

"Oh, I see," I say, rolling my eyes and putting on a posh voice. "Ryan enjoys a water feature, don't you know."

"Nothing wrong with a good water feature."

I take a sip of wine, chewing on the edge of the cup.

"Did you get the email last night about . . . the application?" he asks carefully.

"Yeah. I got an interview. You?"

He nods. "Yep. It's on Friday the twenty-seventh of August."

"Same. Pretty harsh that it's the week before we leave."

"Probably a good thing. Less awkwardness if we don't get it," he reasons.

"That's true."

"What time is yours?" he asks.

"Four P.M."

"Mine's at three."

"You can give me tips."

He snorts in response, instantly irritating me.

"I was obviously joking," I grumble into my wine. "I appreciate you would never in a million years help me out."

He starts. "That's not what I was laughing at!"

"Yeah, sure."

"I'm being honest." He frowns, shuffling closer to me and giving me a nudge on the arm with his elbow, so I'm forced to look directly into his earnest eyes. "The reason I laughed at the idea of giving you tips is because it's obvious you don't need any."

"Oh, please," I sigh, putting my cup down on the grass, where it topples over. "I know today has been all right, but you don't need to pretend to be nice to me."

"I'm not pretending, I mean it, Harper," he insists. "You're so good at chatting to anyone; it comes so naturally to you to put people at ease. I wish I could be like that."

I blink at him. "Are you being serious?"

"Yes," he says without hesitation. "I can work as hard as I like, but I don't have your—" he waves his hand up and down at me "—likability."

I shift, thrown by the compliment. "Oh. Uh . . . thanks."

He nods.

"Okay, fine, I suppose I need to say something nice about you now," I blurt out.

That makes him chuckle, his shoulders relaxing.

"You're much more well-read than I am," I admit reluctantly. "You know all this stuff about the world off the top of your head."

"I don't think I know any more than you do."

"Well, maybe not about who's dating who—a subject you really need to brush up on, by the way—but you have a better grasp on economics and history and politics. Stuff like that."

"Eloquently put."

"I am a writer."

He smiles warmly, and my stomach flips. We're so close in proximity that it makes my breath catch in my throat. And the way he's looking at me suddenly shifts—the moment has become charged under his intense gaze. Instinctively, I lift my chin, inviting him to make the move. He leans closer and I can smell the wine on his breath.

"Heads!"

We spring back from each other at someone's shout, a football hurtling over our heads, missing us by inches and bouncing just in front of our feet. A couple of boys stumble after it, apologizing to us as they go.

Flustered, I glance at Ryan, who looks as bewildered as I feel by what the hell just happened.

"We should . . . uh . . . get back," I say, running a hand through my hair.

"Yeah, it's getting late."

We gather our cups and scramble to our feet, brushing grass off our clothes before making our way back toward the station, my head swirling with confusion and excitement. I find myself hoping that on our way home he'll suggest going for another drink somewhere or maybe try kissing me again. But he only gives me an awkward goodbye as he gets off the tube at his stop.

The next day, I wake up with a hangover and an unwelcome bout of anxiety.

I almost *kissed* Ryan Jansson. *What was I thinking?*

CHAPTER NINE

Mimi's team is up to bat first, so our team gathers in a huddle to discuss fielding tactics while Mimi finishes setting out the jumpers to mark the pitch.

"Harper, you okay to bowl again this year?" Katya suggests, after she's finished explaining to a new yoga friend of Mimi's, who hails from New York, that rounders is essentially the same as baseball except with a small bat and there's no such thing as strikes—you get one shot to hit the ball and then you have to run.

"As long as no one else wants to give it a go," I reply, glancing round the circle as everyone shakes their heads, refusing the responsibility.

Katya is on second base while Rakhee, who mentions she has pretty good throwing skills, is elected as a deep fielder. The others on our team decide among themselves who's taking the other positions, and then we all put our hands in the middle and, on Katya's instruction, cry out in chorus, "WINNERS!"

As our huddle disperses and the other team begins to line up at the batting jumper, I hunt down the tennis ball that we use instead of a rounders one—since the park is always fairly busy, a softer ball is deemed more appropriate should a stray one be sent careening in the direction of an oblivious family enjoying a picnic nearby.

I do a few practice throws with the backstop before Mimi steps up to bat first.

"Ready, birthday girl?" I ask with a grin.

"Born ready," she replies, holding up the bat.

The game begins, Mimi scoring half a rounder on her first hit. I always forget how fun rounders is until I'm playing it in a London park on a sunny day. The competitive spirit is running high, the batters yelling instructions at each other about when to run to the next post, while cheering each other on after a great hit. The fielding team is just as enthusiastic, their shouting and screaming gathering interest from passersby who look in our direction and smile.

By the time it's Ryan's turn to bat, there's been a real mix of ability on his team and no one has managed to score a full rounder on their own. Mimi claps him on the back as he bends down to pick up the bat from where the last teammate dropped it as they ran to the first post.

"You've got this, Ryan," she says. "Don't let Harper bait you and put you off your game."

"Hey!" I cry out, tossing the tennis ball from hand to hand. "You really think I'd stoop so low as to bait someone right before they bat?"

"I wouldn't put anything past you, Harper Jenkins," Ryan declares as he strolls toward the batting jumper.

Flicking my hair back behind my shoulder, I wait for him to position himself and then, with full concentration, I bowl the ball. There's a loud crack as the bat makes forceful contact, sending the ball soaring overhead, way out beyond third base. Dropping the bat to an eruption of cheers from his team, Ryan starts sprinting.

"*Come on, Rakhee!*" I shout encouragingly as she races toward the tennis ball and then, finding it, throws it with all her might back toward us as Ryan clears second and heads to third. Katya jumps into the air to catch the ball, before spinning and lobbing it to our teammate on fourth base, but Ryan has already swept past into the arms of his team, who congratulate him ecstatically.

"Damn it," I mutter under my breath, catching the tennis ball as it's thrown back to me for the next batter. I was really hoping he wouldn't be good at this.

"You lot were so cocky with your 'winners' chant!" Mimi announces, picking up the bat and doing a victory dance on the spot. "But we're going to be difficult to beat! Our points are ticking up and no one is out."

"Yet," Katya yells from behind me.

Tearing my eyes from Ryan, who is still receiving highfives from his teammates, I prepare to bowl to Mimi. She hits it straight up in the air and I run forward, catching it as it falls right into my outstretched hands.

"Noooooo!" Mimi cries, burying her head in her hands, as it becomes my team's turn to cheer.

Katya runs over to lift me up in celebration, before plonking me down and saying to Mimi, "You tempted fate, babe! Rookie error!"

As the game continues, their team gradually begins to deplete until Ryan is the last man standing.

"Okay everyone," I say, turning to address the fielders. "Whatever happens, we can't let him get all the way round. If he gets a rounder, he can keep batting, but if we stop him from reaching that fourth post, then his team is out. Look alert, people!"

"Let's do this!" Katya shouts, clapping her hands above her head.

Accepting words of encouragement from his team, who are standing around the table, drinking and crunching on crisps, Ryan acknowledges that it's getting serious and peels off his over-shirt to wolf whistles. In his T-shirt, he rolls his arms back and forth.

I try not to be distracted by his muscled arms, now on show, as he picks up the bat and tosses it in the air so it spins, like a drummer showing off with a drumstick. It takes a lot of self-control not to stare at his bicep when it flexes as he catches the grip of the bat.

His blue eyes flash at me.

"Ready when you are, Harper," he says, a hint of a smile appearing.

Swallowing the lump in my throat, I take a step forward and bowl a terrible ball that goes right over his head.

"No ball!" Mimi calls out.

As the backstop chucks it back to me, I catch Ryan tilting his head at me curiously.

"Something put you off your game, Harper?"

"I was merely luring you into a false sense of security."

"Try not to buckle under the pressure," he advises.

I narrow my eyes at him. "I'm not the last man standing."

He grins, getting into position again. This time, I push any thoughts about his sexy arms out of my head and *focus*. It's a perfect bowl, but it's also a very good bat. He runs as fast as he can to the screams of his team, while I shout myself hoarse yelling at Rakhee to throw it back as quickly as possible, my whole team now congregating around the third and fourth bases, all of us on hand to stop him.

Just as he rounds the third, the ball is neatly caught by one of Mimi's school friends, who taps it on the fourth-base jumper and Ryan is declared out.

Our team now gets ready to bat, knowing how many points we need to score to win. Mimi decides to bowl, while Ryan ends up in the space between third and fourth base, manning both of them, no doubt having regaled his team with the story of his famous pond catch.

My team gets off to a rocky start, but soon we're into the swing of things and scoring some rounders. My first go at batting is a success, and I hit it far enough to make it the whole way round and score, which prompts Ryan to shout to his fellow fielders to "get back" when it's my turn again, something that gives me a huge thrill of satisfaction.

As I rejoin my team's queue after my second turn batting, my phone buzzes in my back pocket and I reach for it, expecting it to be Liam, whom I haven't heard from today. I know he's working, so I can't be annoyed, but it would have been nice for him to message this morning to say he was sorry he couldn't make it.

Checking the screen, I see it's not a message but a showbiz notification.

IT'S OVER! Pregnant star Isabella Blossom splits with film director boyfriend the day after tearful public fight in Hyde Park!

Judging from the horrible way that Elijah behaved during those few minutes I was in his company during the press junket, I imagine she's better off without him, but I still feel a wave of sadness for Isabella. She seemed like a really decent person, and she must have found some comfort in knowing she had a partner at her side while going through pregnancy and for when the baby arrives.

Ignoring the cheers and shouts from my team as someone legs it round the rounders pitch, I begin typing out a message to Rachael, from the press junket, saying I've seen the story and if there's any truth to it, I hope Isabella is okay.

Her reply comes back moments later:

She's not great, to be honest. It's all very overwhelming for her and think she feels quite alone.
I'll let her know that you messaged, she'll appreciate
it xx

I frown reading the message, my heart sinking.

"Harper!" Katya says, nudging my arm. "You're up!"

I'd been so engrossed in the news, I hadn't realized it was my turn to bat again.

"Come on, Harper, just one rounder and we've beat them!" Katya informs me.

"Oh! Uh . . . sorry, I was distracted. Hang on, does this mean the whole of the game rests on my shoulders?"

She nods solemnly. "It's all down to you, my friend."

To a round of applause from my team, I make my way to the jumper crumpled on the ground marking the batting spot. I catch Ryan's eye as I prepare myself.

"Not too long ago I was in your position, Harper," he says. "You think you have what it takes to make it all the way round?"

"You certainly didn't make the grade as far as I can remember."

He flashes me a grin. "You need the rounder to win. Not half a rounder, a full one."

"Yes, thank you, Ryan, for explaining that really complicated point system to me."

"I was emphasizing for dramatic effect, not explaining."

"If you two stop bickering, then we can actually play," Mimi says bossily, her hands on her hips. "Ready, Harper?"

I scowl at Ryan as he winks at me, before turning my focus to Mimi and lifting my bat.

"Ready."

As the ball is tossed in my direction, I swing with all my might. There's a loud *thwack* as it collides with the bat, before it soars through the air.

"*Run, Harper! Run!*" Katya shouts at the top of her lungs.

Dropping the bat, I begin sprinting, the eruption of noise from both teams roaring in my ears as I keep going round first, then second base. The ball is sent flying back overhead as I make it to third and is caught by Ryan as I near the fourth base.

Both of us launch ourselves at the final base at the same time, skidding across the grass and colliding as we land on the fourth jumper, me on the flat of my back and he on his front, the ball clutched in his hand.

Both teams start cheering and clapping, until Katya stops and says, "Wait, why are you celebrating?" to Mimi, who replies, "Hello! We won!"

"No, we won," Katya retorts.

"No," Mimi says, giving her a strange look. "*We* won!"

"Harper got the rounder!"

"Ryan got her out!"

"She's in!"

"She's out!"

As the two teams launch into an argument over what happened, I push myself up on my elbows to look at Ryan, whose face is level with my knees.

"You okay?" he asks.

"I think I've bruised my bum," I admit. "You?"

"I'm going to have a few grass stains," he says, getting to his feet.

He holds out his hand to help me up, and I take it. His hand is warm as it clasps mine, his grip strong and firm. I stumble a little as he pulls me up, steadying myself by grabbing his forearms. He's so close, it makes me a little light-headed.

"All right?" he says. His voice is suddenly softer.

"Yeah. Thanks." I drop my hands, stepping back from him and collecting myself. "Sorry you lost, but good game."

He blinks at me. "Excuse me? *You* lost."

"Are you joking?" I look him up and down. "My feet hit the jumper before you did!"

"No," he says slowly, "I got you out."

"I can't believe you're doing this!"

He frowns. "Doing what? Telling the truth?"

"You're lying just so you can win!" I say accusingly.

"I'm not the liar here, Harper. You know as well as I do that I got to the jumper first."

"I was *in*!" I insist.

"You were *out*!"

I turn to appeal to everyone else, who have come to gather around the birthday girl. "What's the final verdict?"

Katya throws her arm around Mimi. "How about we call it a draw?"

"That's a bit boring," she responds.

"It's only the first round of the day. There are still a few more games to get through," Katya reasons. "We can beat you at everything else and win overall."

"You wish," Mimi says, her eyes twinkling at her wife. "Fine, since no one can impartially call that final point, we'll say it's a draw."

Anyone else who still cares nods, accepting the judgment, while others amble over to the table to refill their drinks, energized after the game.

"Um, no, it was not a draw," I maintain stubbornly, folding my arms. "I was in and Ryan knows it; he just can't admit that he lost to me."

"I would happily admit if I did lose fair and square, but I didn't," he says. "You know I got you out. I reached that jumper before you did."

"Oh, come off it, Ryan!" I sigh impatiently. "You just can't accept that I beat you."

"It's not about you, this is a team game," he says, rolling his eyes. Mimi and Katya share a look before mutually agreeing to leave us to it, wandering away to join everyone else round the table. "Your team didn't get that final rounder because I got you out."

"You know, losing does not make you a loser. But lying does."

He doesn't look impressed. "Spouting inspirational quotes at me won't make me give in and pretend that you won. You need to stop thinking about this personally."

"How am I thinking about this personally, Ryan?"

"Maybe because I'm the one who got you out, you're refusing to accept it," he says and my face flushes with heat.

"I'm refusing because *it didn't happen*," I affirm. "God, you're annoying. You really think that—"

"Wait, Harper—"

"No, don't interrupt. I'll have you know that I am a very fair and reasonable person, and there is no way that just because it's *you* who happened to be the person to attempt to get me out—"

"Harper, if you—"

"It's genuinely insulting that you think I would lie about winning simply to get one up on you personally. I know we don't—"

"Harper . . . cake!" he cries in exasperation.

I blink at him.

"They've brought the cake out and they're singing 'Happy Birthday,'" he explains, pointing over at the table. "I'd be very happy to stand here listening to you rant afterward, but we should probably go join in."

"Oh. Right. Yeah."

We hurry over to the rest of the group, who are singing while Katya holds up a chocolate cake with one lit candle on the top. Ryan and I manage to join in on the last line and dutifully clap when Mimi blows out the candle.

"Time to set up for beer pong!" Katya announces. "The tournament will resume in ten minutes."

I stand awkwardly next to Ryan, wondering if it's appropriate to go back to our disagreement. He knows deep down that I'm the victor here, and that's really all that matters. He's just lied to save face, whereas I can hold my head up high and—

"Why do you look so pleased with yourself?" he asks me suddenly.

I glance up to see he's watching me intently with a bemused expression.

"I was thinking that there's no point in arguing over the rounders game."

"I agree. Would you like a drink?"

"Sorry?"

"I brought some gin along. I was going to make myself a gin and tonic. Would you like one?"

"Oh. Yes, please. Thanks."

I follow him as he grabs a couple of cups and fills them with ice from one of the cooler boxes before looking round for the bottle of gin.

"Was it bad news?" he asks, locating the gin and splashing it into the cups.

"What?"

"The message you got on your phone during the game. You've got an open-book face," he says, opening a bottle of tonic and letting it fizz. "I noticed you looked upset. I don't mean to be nosy, I just hope it wasn't anything too bad, whatever it was."

"It's okay, you're not being nosy. I mean, it was bad news. Not for me, for someone else. But if I tell you, you'll laugh at me."

He glances up, intrigued. "Try me."

I exhale. "Fine. I got a notification that an actor I interviewed recently broke up with her boyfriend. She seemed like a really nice person and now she's going to have to deal with all these reporters prying into her business, trying to get a photo of her crying or something. And she's having a baby any minute, so you know, she's got a lot on her plate, and . . . I don't know. It made me sad."

He passes me my drink.

"Go on, then," I say, taking the cup from him. "You're thinking I'm too invested in celebrities who I don't even know. You and Cosmo both think my job is ridiculous."

He recoils, lines forming on his forehead. "No, I don't think that."

"The celebrity world is silly in your lofty opinion, I'm sure."

"I'm not going to pretend I am as invested in the . . . uh . . . celebrity world, as you put it. But I'd never make fun of you for caring about someone who is hurting. It says a lot about what kind of a person you are."

I'm so taken aback by the compliment, I'm lost for words.

"What? Why are you looking at me like that?" he asks, confused.

"I was expecting you to say something snarky."

"About you being upset because someone is going through a tough time?"

"Well . . . yeah."

He takes a sip of his drink. "So, that's what you think of me."

"What you think of my job," I remind him.

"Not being particularly interested in something isn't the same as looking down on it. Besides, you haven't asked my opinion on your job, so how would you know?"

"All right, then. Ryan, what do you think about the celebrity angle of the magazine?"

He smiles into his drink. "Fluffy nonsense."

"I knew it!"

"I'm joking!" He laughs, shaking his head. "Okay, you want my honest opinion?"

I sigh. "This should be interesting."

"I think . . . I think you write insightful, clever features about people who lead extraordinary lives, and even though they might be so famous that everyone *thinks* they know everything about them, somehow you manage to show them in a light that makes it seem as though we didn't really know them at all— until we read your piece. You really care, and because of that, your readers care. It's brilliant and powerful journalism. Oh, and you're quite funny sometimes, too," he adds as an afterthought.

Once again, in a matter of minutes, I'm stunned into silence by Ryan Jansson.

"You look confused," he observes after a while of me standing there staring at him with my mouth open.

"I . . . what do you mean by '*quite* funny'?"

He rolls his eyes. "I say all of those things about your writing talents and that's the comment you pick up on."

"I'm genuinely shocked you've read any of my articles."

"Have you read any of mine?"

"A few," I admit coyly.

He seems impressed. "What do you think?"

"Are you still planning on writing a book?"

He looks surprised at my question. "I told you about that?"

"A long time ago."

He nods. "Right. Yes, like a lot of journalists, I'm working on my first novel."

"You're writing fiction. Huh." I pause, before admitting, "I always thought you'd write nonfiction, some kind of big exposé or something."

He sighs at my assumption. "Because I'm so serious and boring."

"No," I say. "You told me you wanted to use your journalism to do something good. To give people a voice who might not have one."

He gives the smallest hint of a smile, as though I've just proved him right about something.

"Why are you looking so smug?" I ask, frowning at him.

He laughs. "I'm not. I . . . never mind."

Rakhee appears at my side. "Are you two still arguing about who won? The beer pong is about to start, so you can forget about the rounders and try to beat each other at this instead."

"Excellent," Ryan declares, unhooking his sunglasses from the front of his shirt and putting them on. "There'll be no mistaking the winner in this one. Your team has no chance."

He wanders off to the end of the table where Mimi is busy lining up the cups for the game, while I follow Rakhee to join my team at the other end, who are discussing tactics such as whether it's worth bouncing the Ping-Pong ball first or if it's easier just to aim for a clean throw into the cups.

I pretend to listen, but really I'm distracted by two things that Ryan said to me today that, when I think back on how he said them, make me feel strangely giddy.

One, he called my journalism brilliant and powerful.

And two, he declared he would be very happy to stand and listen to me rant after singing Mimi a happy birthday.

Which, when you think about it, is really a very sweet thing to say.

CHAPTER TEN

U h-oh. I've only got one shoe.

I can't believe I left the house without checking I had *both* shoes in my bag. Who only packs *one shoe*?! I knew I had the charity ball tonight and that I'd be going straight from work, so *why* didn't I get myself organized last night?!

Now I'm in the toilet at work wearing the gorgeous new emerald-green plunge-neck dress I bought especially for the occasion, with my hair fabulously blow-dried, for which I stepped out at lunch, prompting a stink eye and sarcastic comment about work ethic from Cosmo, and all my makeup carefully reapplied . . . *and only one shoe.*

I don't have time to go home before the event, so I'm going to have to hope that someone in the office has a spare pair of heels lying around that just so happen to be my size. Shoving my lone heel back in my bag, I exit the cubicle, check my appearance, and, satisfied except for the footwear situation, make my way through the open-plan office to the magazine corner.

"Wow!" Mimi gasps, swiveling in her office chair to take in my new dress as I approach her. "You look *hot*. That *dress!*" She lowers her voice. "Your boobs look amazing."

"It's a push-up bra."

"Liam is a lucky guy. Is he coming here first?"

"No, I said I'd meet him there. Hey, do you have any shoes I can borrow?"

"Sorry?"

"I only brought one shoe to wear tonight."

She laughs. "Of course you did."

"Any chance you have a pair of heels lurking in one of these drawers?"

"I actually do."

I brighten. "Really?"

"Yes, for emergencies."

"You have a pair of heels in your desk drawer for *emergencies*?" I tease.

She sighs. "What would you call your current predicament, Harper?"

I hesitate before glumly admitting, "An emergency."

"Unfortunately, I can't help you, because I'm pretty sure you're a size five and I'm a size four."

"Oh yeah, I forgot you had freakishly small feet."

"Dainty feet," she corrects. "Maybe someone else here will have a spare pair."

I turn to address the rest of the team. "Does anyone have a pair of heels I could borrow? Preferably in a size five so they fit?"

My colleagues glance up from their screens and shake their heads apologetically.

"Fashion team, please say we have some in the cupboard yet to be returned from a shoot?"

"Afraid not," comes the reply. "We packaged and returned everything yesterday."

Cosmo emerges from his office studying a travel layout and slowly makes his way over to Mimi's desk wearing a confused expression.

"Mimi, talk me through why anyone would want to go on a . . . literary trail for an entire week? Is this appealing to our readers?" he asks.

"Absolutely," she replies confidently. "I think a lot of people would be interested in seeing sights and country houses that are linked to celebrated authors."

"Hmm," he says, unconvinced, passing the layout back to her. "All right, keep it in, but make it much shorter and let's give that leading story to something a bit sexier. A picture of a nice turquoise sea or something, rather than all these fields."

"I thought it might be nice to mix it up a bit, though. The picture on this page always seems to be a sparkling blue sea. Don't you think it would be a good idea to try something different?" she says hopefully.

"I think readers dream of escaping to a beach, not the English countryside that a lot of them live in already," he insists. "Let's keep to the ocean, please."

She mutters, "Sure," through gritted teeth.

He suddenly notices me.

"Oh yes, it's that cancer research charity ball this evening," he says, his eyes running down my outfit and landing on my bare feet. "You're not wearing any shoes."

"Not right now, no."

"I assume you intend to."

"Eventually, yes. But unfortunately, I've only got the one on me."

"One what?"

"Shoe."

"You only have one shoe." He lets out a long, weary sigh. "Why does that not surprise me, Harper?"

"I can only apologize for being so predictable. You don't have any spare heels lurking in your office, do you, Cosmo?"

He looks appalled. "I beg your pardon."

"Worth a shot. If you—"

I stop midsentence on seeing Ryan approaching our corner. He's wearing a full-on tux and is busy fiddling with one of the cuffs of his shirt, sorting his cuff links, I think, before bringing his eyes up to meet mine. His eyebrows lift in surprise before the corner of his mouth twitches into a smile.

"Nice dress," he comments.

"Nice tux," I reply. "I forgot you were going tonight."

"Wouldn't miss it."

I snort. "You hate black tie."

"I can put up with it for one night."

"Great to have you attending tonight, Jansson," Cosmo declares, patting him on the arm. "The crowd will be a real mix of who's who. Lucky we have someone like you there to bag us some good interviews, eh? I best be off, I have a dinner reservation."

I glare as he bustles away, while Ryan has the decency to look embarrassed. When he's gone, Ryan puts his hands in his pockets and looks at me expectantly.

"If you want to put your shoes on, Harper, we can share a taxi."

"I can't put my shoes on. I only have one."

He blinks at me. "What?"

"You can go on ahead and I'll see you there," I sigh, pulling my trainers back out from my bag. "I need to stop by a shoe shop on the way to buy some heels."

"Okay, well, if you're quick, I might as well come with you," Ryan offers, checking his watch. "We have time, and it's not so fun showing up alone to these things. I'll just grab my things from my desk."

He strolls away, and as I slip on my trainers, I notice Mimi giving me a funny look.

"What?" I ask.

"How do you know he doesn't like black tie events?" she whispers.

"I don't know." I shrug, feeling the heat rise in my cheeks. "He must have mentioned it when I was talking about going to this thing tonight."

She doesn't look convinced, eyeing me suspiciously.

"Harper," Ryan says from the end of our station of desks, having retrieved his wallet and phone. "Ready?"

Ignoring Mimi's prying eyes, I walk over, feeling ridiculous in this dress with my trainers on. We make our way through the open-plan office toward the exit, and he waits until we're out of earshot of everyone to say he actually thinks I can pull off the trainers with the black-tie dress look.

"If you're trying to persuade me not to bother with the shoe shopping, I'm afraid it won't work," I inform him haughtily. "It's essential that we stop for some appropriate shoes on the way. Don't worry, though. I won't take long. I can be very decisive when I want to be."

"I don't doubt it. And I wasn't trying to put you off shoe shopping," he insists. "I was genuinely trying to pay you a compliment."

"That I can pull off trainers?"

"That you look good in that dress."

Looking bemused by my stunned reaction, he pulls the door open and gestures outside.

"Shall we?"

By the time we arrive at the charity ball, Ryan is in a slightly worse mood than when we left, having had to put up with me trying on almost every pair of heels in the shop and then deciding to go with the first pair I selected. I'm in a much better mood myself, because I now have two shoes, which is great, *and* Ryan said my legs look good in these shoes. I mean, I sort of forced him to say it, but it still counts.

"Like I told you the first time you tried that pair on *half an hour ago*, yes, your legs look good," he had groaned, lifting his head from his hands.

"You are such a drama queen, Ryan; it was not half an hour ago. It was, like, twenty minutes ago. And are you *sure* these look good? You're not just saying that?" I checked, pointing my toes at him. "Because if you think a chunkier heel might be more flattering—"

"Harper, you're killing me," he said, scrunching up his eyes, before opening them and letting out a long sigh. "Okay, if my honest opinion will help move this along faster, then here you go: those shoes look sexy. You have great legs. Okay? I mean it. Can we go now? Please?"

I grinned at him. "I'll take them. But to be sure, I might try on—"

"Harper!"

"I'm *kidding!*" I laughed, before quickly paying for them at the till.

When we pull up to the grand entrance of The Langham hotel, there is the usual horde of paparazzi waiting for any celebrities to make an appearance. They look at us with interest as we step out of the car, but then quickly go back to chatting among themselves.

"Are you going to wait for your boyfriend?" Ryan asks as we pass through the magnificent columns of the hotel entrance and head through the door into reception.

"He's already inside," I reply. "He messaged me earlier."

Ryan nods, gesturing for me to go first into the ballroom after we've had our names checked off the list. The room looks spectacular, twinkling pink and white lights all over the black drapes hanging across the ceiling and stunning displays of pink roses. The event is raising money for breast cancer research, and there are stands dotted around the room, filled with items that are being sold off at auction. A waiter holding a tray of champagne glasses approaches as we step into the room, and we both take one gratefully.

"A lot of glamorous people here," Ryan observes, scanning

the sea of people mingling as a jazz band plays at the other end of the space.

"Don't tell me you're intimidated by this situation," I say, raising my eyebrows. "The guy who has covered political scandals and given pep talks to Olympians with stage fright right before their record-breaking race."

He looks pleased. "You read that piece."

"*Everyone* read that piece," I point out. "It got picked up by every national paper. I'm surprised you didn't get a book deal out of it."

"Actually, I was offered a deal off the back of it," he says, "but I turned it down."

I look at him in surprise. "Seriously?"

He shrugs. "I'm not sure how I'd write an entire book about a five-minute conversation. Also, I'm not even a sports journalist, so I'd have nothing interesting to say to that audience—I was really just in the right place at the right time. I was actually covering for someone. Pure luck."

"But you obviously said the right things to him. That wasn't luck, was it? That was . . . you."

He gives me a strange look. "I think that might be the nicest thing you've ever said to me."

"Don't get used to it. I'm still annoyed that you're here."

"How can you say that when I've just willingly accompanied you through a torturous shopping excursion?"

I roll my eyes. "I'm annoyed that Cosmo implied your presence here was more important than mine. He completely ignored me! What do you think he's up to?"

He takes a sip of his champagne. "You think he's up to something?"

"You don't?"

"Not really. I think he can be clueless and ignorant, especially when it comes to your people skills. But he was right that it's handy having us both here to do some networking," he says, gesturing to the room. "Not that we've spoken to one other person yet."

"I just think it's offensive that he doesn't trust me to get the stories, despite me continuing to land them. He only trusts you, his best pal."

"Please stop implying that Cosmo and I are in any way friends," he pleads, wincing. "We really are not. He has similar journalistic interests to mine, so that's probably why he's a bit warmer to my ideas."

"That, and you have a penis, which helps," I mutter, just as he takes another drink. He splutters at my comment, so I give him a pat on the back as he coughs and collects himself.

"So, can you see your boyfriend anywhere?" Ryan asks, his eyes still watering.

I crane my neck over the crowd to check. "Nope, but he's in here somewhere. Eager to meet him, are you?"

He frowns as he takes a gulp of his drink.

My stomach twists—a strange mix of irritation that he's being dismissive of Liam and unwelcome pleasure that his reaction *could* be read as a touch of jealousy. I quickly tell myself not to be so ridiculous.

"You didn't want to bring a date?" I ask, swirling my glass.

He shakes his head. "It's bad enough I have to suffer such an event for work, let alone drag some innocent bystander along."

"So, no one special on the scene at the moment."

He raises his eyebrows at me, looking intrigued. "Are you prying into my private life?"

"I was simply making polite conversation with a colleague," I say irritably, rolling my eyes. "But if it makes you uncomfortable, feel free to change the subject."

A small, triumphant smile creeps across his lips that immediately makes me incensed.

"I'm not seeing anyone right now," he informs me breezily. "I haven't really been looking for anything serious since I broke up with my ex-girlfriend. We were together almost four years."

"Sorry to hear that," I say, keeping my tone neutral and professional. "When did you break up?"

He pauses at that question, lines forming on his forehead.

"Just over a year ago," he states, keeping his eyes looking straight ahead.

"Around the time you started working at *The Correspondence*?"

He takes another swig of his drink, polishing off his glass before he answers. "Exactly."

I realize that this line of questioning is making him uncomfortable, which is fair enough—it's not like chatting about ex-partners is a typically fun conversation at any occasion—so I'm about to change the subject when I spot Shamari coming over to me with her arms outstretched.

"Harper, hi!"

We greet each other with a kiss on each cheek, and then she turns to Ryan.

"Shamari, this is Ryan, he's our new features editor," I introduce. "Ryan, Shamari is a brilliant talent agent—she was the one who set up the interview with Audrey Abbot."

"That was an amazing feature. Nice to meet you," he says, shaking her hand.

"It was all Harper, really. She stalked me until I gave in," she says with a sly smile.

"Stalked is a strong word," I retort.

"You usually get your morning coffee next to my office in Vauxhall, then?" she asks.

"It's the best in the city."

She laughs, giving a wave of her hand. "All's well that ends well. Audrey loved you, no surprises there. The interview was a hit and the theater company adore me even more thanks to the ticket sales that went through the roof. Not to mention my other client in the same play has now got a fantastic start to his career—he really is the next big thing, Harper."

"Oh yeah, I remember you telling me about him. The good-looking one. Julian Frog?"

"Julian Newt."

"That's the one. I'll keep an eye on him."

"Won't we all." She grins. "Talking of good looking, I had a chat with your boyfriend earlier. Liam."

"Oh, you've seen him!"

"Yes, he's charming. He told me about the feature you're doing on hot talent agencies. I know we're established, but any chance of a mention would be welcomed. We've got lots of exciting things coming up and—"

"Hang on," I interrupt, holding up my hand. "He told you what?"

"About the piece you're writing on talent agencies," she repeats. "I'm surprised you haven't already approached me for a quote."

Ryan turns to me, confused. "I didn't know we were doing a piece on talent agencies."

"We're not."

"You're not?" Shamari says. "I could have sworn that Liam mentioned—"

"It came up as an idea," I explain hurriedly. "But I can tell you this: *if* we were to do one on talent agencies, you would of course be one of the first people I contacted."

"I should hope so. Ah," she says, glancing to her right and giving a wave, "I've just seen someone I absolutely detest but have to butter up on behalf of a client. Excuse me."

As she swans off, I spot Liam talking animatedly to a Tik-Tok influencer turned pop star. He laughs at something she says, touching her arm, and then catches my eye. I wave him over, and in response he holds up his finger and mouths, *One minute.* I frown at him, but he doesn't seem to notice.

"Who's that?" Ryan asks, watching the exchange.

"That's Liam."

"Oh. He seems . . . busy."

"He's sociable," I say, bristling. "That's how you're supposed to be at parties."

"He's giving her his card. Bit weird."

I glare up at Ryan. "As you were saying a moment ago, it's important to network at these events. Don't be so judgmental, you haven't even met him."

"Sorry, you're right," he says, blushing slightly. "I'm just surprised he hasn't rushed over yet to—at the very least—say hi to you when the only reason he's invited is because he's your plus-one."

"What is your problem, Ryan?" I snap defensively, putting my hand on my hip. "Do you enjoy putting other people down? You like to feel superior?"

"What? No!" He scowls, recoiling. "I was making an observation."

"Well, don't!"

"Fine, I won't!"

"Fine."

"Fine!"

We fall into silence. He shakes his head.

"I'm going to mingle," he grumbles eventually.

"You go do that."

He drifts into the crowd. I clench my jaw, furious at him. Who does he think he is? I mean, yes, I see his point, it would have been nice if Liam had come over to say hello to me, but he's in the middle of an important conversation, and it would be rude of him to break away from it, especially if he's hoping to take her on as a client and—

Oh, okay, he's now introducing himself to a guy standing next to her. And another influencer I sort of recognize standing next to him. He's now completely turned his back to me and has launched into that conversation.

He doesn't need to greet me as soon as I walk through the door. But I have been standing over here waiting for him to finish up for a while. You know what, what am I doing? Usually I'd have worked the entire room by now. Ryan distracted me and now I'm lingering like a loser waiting for Liam while everyone else is busy chatting.

I pull myself together and leave Liam to it—he can find me later.

I soon bump into a glossy-magazine editor I love, before I'm pulled into another conversation with the two leads of a hit crime drama that's been renewed for a second season. I make a note of their agents, after pitching the idea of doing a joint interview.

I'm having such a good time, I've forgotten about how annoyed I am at Liam. At one point I spot Ryan in conversation with a reality TV star renowned for her eccentricity and notice he looks particularly pained as she tells him they *must* go for drinks to discuss her new fly-on-the-wall TV show about her "bonkers life." He notices me watching and I quickly look away so he doesn't get any ideas about me rescuing him from the situation. If he hadn't been so obnoxious earlier, I might have considered it.

"Harper, there you are," Liam says in my ear a few minutes later, interrupting my conversation with a producer. "I've been looking for you."

I excuse myself to the producer and turn to him as he gives me a kiss on the cheek.

"You disappeared earlier," he notes.

"You seemed busy," I reply sharply, but he doesn't seem to notice my tone.

"Hasn't this been a great night? I have met so many people,

definitely got some potential clients!" he says enthusiastically, grabbing my hand and giving it a squeeze. "Did I see you chatting with that actor from *Don't Give Up Hope,* or whatever that Netflix show was called? You can introduce us, right?"

"He already has an agent."

"Yeah, but no harm in a chat to make sure he's got the right person representing him," Liam tells me, swigging his champagne. "I won't have the chance to meet him tonight, but if you chat with him again, pass on my details, yeah?"

"Why won't you have a chance tonight?"

"I'm going to shoot off because, get this—you know Halo Skewed?"

I stare at him blankly.

"They're this fantastic up-and-coming band," he gushes. "I was talking to them earlier, and they're about to go play a gig in Soho. They've invited me to come watch, with potential for me to represent them!"

"But Liam, what about . . . this?" I say, gesturing around us.

"I know, I'm so sad to leave, because it's been so great, but I think I've talked to enough people and I've officially run out of business cards," he says gleefully, his eyes twinkling. "What a success! Better get some more printed. Watch this space, am I right?"

"Liam," I begin, trying to remain calm, "have you been telling people that I'm writing a feature on talent agencies and I'm including you in it?"

"I mentioned it to a couple of people. Good to get the buzz going."

I stare at him in disbelief. "But I never said I'd write that piece!"

He looks confused. "We talked about it."

"I said I'd consider it, but I didn't say it was a done deal," I explain, trying to keep my cool but feeling really quite irritated.

"Someone brought it up in front of Ryan and it was really embarrassing. He's our features editor. It can't look like I'm writing features without his knowledge."

Liam wrinkles his nose. "Since when do you care about what Ryan thinks? I thought you didn't like the guy. And it's not like he's your boss or anything."

"It's nothing to do with personal feelings. It's about being professional. Look, you can't assume I'm writing something and then go around telling people about it just because it makes you look good, okay?"

"Got it," he says coolly, pulling his phone out of his pocket. "Right, I better shoot."

He leans down to give me a kiss on the cheek, before he hesitates and adds, "You're okay getting home, right? Because I really should go to this gig, it's an excellent opportunity and—"

"It's fine," I snap.

"Great!" he beams, either too stupid to read my tone or deciding to ignore it. "I'll call you in the morning, babe."

As he turns round, he bumps into a striking raven-haired woman wearing an incredible black figure-hugging dress, heavy dark eye shadow, and bright red lipstick. I assume she is part of this Halo Skewed band he was talking about because her eyes light up on seeing him and she quickly ushers him to follow her through the crowd to where a group of guys are waiting by the door. Moving to the side of the room where I have a clear view, I watch as they clap him on the back and then exit together.

I sigh heavily, snatching a drink from a passing waiter's tray, before Ryan appears out of nowhere.

"Is your boyfriend leaving?" he asks, raising his eyebrows.

"Yes," I say breezily, as though I'm on board with it all. "He's got a meeting with a client now, so he had to go."

He nods slowly. "Late meeting."

"They're a rock band," I explain through gritted teeth.

"Ah, makes sense." He hesitates. "I actually met him earlier."

"Liam?"

"He barged into my chat with a photographer, who he mistook for one of the *Bridgerton* cast members. As soon as he realized his mistake, he disappeared again into the night. I didn't get to talk to him much, but he seems like a catch," he notes sarcastically.

"Did you come over here just to be horrible about Liam?" I bristle.

"No. I just . . . I don't understand why you're with *him*."

I look at him in disbelief. "Oh my god. Are you actually being *serious?*"

I see some guests glance our way, and I realize I can't have it out with Ryan here in the ballroom. There's a fire exit door to my right that's slightly ajar, so I push it open and demand that he follow me. We step out into an empty corridor and, confirming there's no one in either direction, I round on him.

"How dare you talk to me like that about Liam? You have no right!"

"I know it's none of my business—"

"That's right. It is none of your business!"

"—but he doesn't seem like . . . your type," he says, holding up his hands as though he feels obliged to tell me his opinion. As though it's *important.*

He makes my blood *boil.*

"How would you even know what my type is?" I snap furiously. "You don't get to have an opinion on who I date. You met him for all of five seconds!"

"Five seconds was all I needed to work out exactly what kind of person he is," he seethes. "You shouldn't be with someone who treats you like that."

"You have no idea how he treats me!"

"I know that he didn't even bother saying hi to you because

he was too busy chatting up all your contacts! He barely acknowledged you. It was rude," he argues.

"Liam is smart and he's ambitious, and I respect that," I tell
him proudly.

Ryan snorts. "Well, I'm glad you respect his ambition, because I'm not sure he has much else to recommend him."

"You are so out of order," I cry, my whole face on fire with
rage. "We're not even friends! Why should I care about your
opinion?"

"Fine! Then *don't* care about my opinion!"

"I *don't!*"

Ryan takes a deep breath and lowers his voice. "I'm only trying to look out for you, Harper, and that guy is—"

"Don't look out for me, Ryan," I snap. "I can look after myself! Liam is a wonderful, thoughtful person who just had a bad
night . . ." I hear myself faltering.

"Oh, come on! You can't *really* think that!"

"Don't tell me what to think!"

"For god's sake, Harper," he says impatiently, throwing his
hands up in exasperation, "you're so determined to argue with
me all the time, you're not even bothering to listen to what I'm
saying!"

"You're saying that Liam is using me!"

"I'm saying that he doesn't deserve you! No one does!"

I stare at him. His eyes bore into mine, his chest rising up and
down with his heavy breathing. We stand in utter silence, both
refusing to back down and drop eye contact.

And I have a sudden overwhelming and uncontrollable urge
to kiss him.

CHAPTER ELEVEN

I take a step toward him. Ryan's gaze softens as I do, the anger in his expression fading into something else. Something hopeful.

"Ryan," I whisper.

"Yes?" he replies without hesitating, moving closer, his hand twitching.

The fire door from the ballroom suddenly swings open and the two of us spring apart as Isabella Blossom appears. She slams the door shut behind her, before leaning against it and shutting her eyes in despair, rubbing a hand in circular motions around her bump.

"Isabella, hi!" I begin, my cheeks still burning from my interaction with Ryan.

She opens one eye to look at me. "Oh, hey, Harper. How are you?"

"Good. Are you doing okay? I didn't realize you were here."

"Yeah, well, maybe I shouldn't have come," she admits with a heavy sigh. "I was determined to save face by showing up tonight. You know, make sure the world knows that I'm not a big mess after the breakup and—"

She pauses, opening both eyes this time to study Ryan suspiciously.

"Don't worry, I can vouch for him," I assure her. "He works with me."

"So he's a journalist," she surmises grumpily.

"Yeah, but anything you say here is completely off the record. He's not interested in that kind of journalism anyway, isn't that right, Ryan?" I say, tapping his arm.

"Yes," he says quickly, nodding.

"I like your dress," I comment, admiring the pale pink tulle skirt.

"Thanks. It's Versace."

"I didn't realize Versace did maternity wear."

She chuckles, wiping her forehead. I can see that she's sweating and she doesn't look too steady on her feet.

"Are you okay?" I ask again, watching her with some concern.

"Yeah, fine. Sort of. Everyone's being so nosy and fake in there. I kept trying to smile my way through it, but it got a bit much," she admits, before suddenly grimacing and adding in a strained voice, "Also, I think I might be having contractions."

Ryan turns to me in alarm.

"Y-you what?" I ask, my eyes widening at her.

She can't answer, instead letting out an "argh!" and shutting her eyes tight.

"Isabella, oh my god," I say, rushing over to her. "You're having contractions?"

"I know. I've been having them a while now. Such bad timing." She winces. "I need to put a pause on them."

"You can't put a pause on contractions!"

"I have to, Harper!" she cries, her eyes filled with anguish. "I need to show all those people in there that I'm over Elijah! They all think I'm falling apart. That's why I had to come tonight, despite the fact my water broke this morning. I had to show them I'm *fine*."

"Isabella," I say slowly, taking her hand, "if your water broke, you are having your *baby*. We need to get you to the hospital."

"The baby won't come for a while yet, don't worry," she says, shaking her head. "It can take hours after the water breaks for anything to really begin. And anyway, we can't go to the hospital. Not right now."

"*What?*"

"If we go out the front, all the paparazzi will see and they'll crowd the hospital, and I don't want them knowing because I can't handle the stress of that and . . . ahhhhhh!"

"Just breathe. That's it, you're doing great."

"I know I'm doing great," she says, her forehead creased in pain. "That's why I think we have a few hours before this baby is coming, so I can just walk right back in there with my head held high and show them all."

"You've already shown them all!" I say urgently, looking to Ryan for help.

"Uh, yes, you've shown them that you're fine," he says, coming to stand behind me.

She looks up at him hopefully. "Really? They don't think I'm a big horrible mess after the breakup?"

"Oh, well," he says nervously, glancing at me as I give him encouraging eyes. "I . . . um . . . overheard someone saying that this breakup was clearly the best thing to happen to you because you look so good."

She smiles in relief.

"Okay, so now we need to get you to the hospital," I say in as soothing a tone as I can muster. "How can I contact your driver?"

"I need my phone. It has his number in there."

"Where's your phone?"

"In my bag."

"Where's your bag?"

She looks around herself and then groans. "I don't know. I think I gave it to someone."

"Your PA? Your manager? The cloakroom?"

"I don't know, *someone!*" she whines.

"Okay, no worries, I can go ask around," I assure her.

She grips my hand so tight, I squeak in pain. "You are *not* leaving me," she says sternly. "I need you right now, Harper."

"I can go look for the bag," Ryan offers.

"No! If you go asking around about my bag, people will get suspicious," Isabella growls at him. "They'll ask you questions about where I am and then everyone will know! Neither of you is leaving me!"

"Who did you come with?" Ryan asks. "I can at least find them to come help."

"I didn't come with anyone," she growls. "I came alone. I just went through a breakup, remember?"

"Right, that's absolutely fine, we're here," I say calmly as Ryan looks panicked at her fierce tone. "We can go out the back way of the hotel and get a taxi. Yeah? I'm sure whoever has your bag can look after it. Okay, let's get moving, shall we?"

"Fine," she says, pushing herself away from the door and then pointing her finger at both of us. "I cannot handle press attention right now. So if we see anyone, act *normal*. Got it?"

Ryan nods. "Got it."

"Got it," I echo.

"Good. Now, do either of you know how to get out of here the back way?"

"That's a very good question," Ryan comments. "Harper?"

"Actually, yes I do."

The two of them look at me in pleasant surprise.

"How?" Isabella asks, intrigued.

"Thanks to directions from a very helpful waiter, I once came to the rescue of a very well-known chat show host who needed to sneak out."

"He was escaping the press, too?"

"His ex was lurking around, actually. He didn't want to risk bumping into her. Anyway"—I gesture one way down the corridor—"we should probably get going."

"Right." Isabella nods, moving forward.

Unfortunately, my memory of the back corridors of The Langham proves somewhat hazy, due in part to the several mojitos I'd enjoyed that evening, and we get lost more than once. This doesn't go down too well with Isabella, whose contractions seem to be getting closer together and more painful.

At one point, Ryan takes her hand, chanting, "Breathe, breathe," before yelping in pain as she grips his fingers and goes, *"You fucking breathe."*

"I think my thumb is broken," he whispers to me as she bumbles on ahead down the stairs.

"Oh, poor thing, we all feel very sorry for you," she calls back, overhearing him. "Because that sounds just as painful as pushing a basketball out of your vagina."

"To be fair, she has a point," I tell him, stifling a laugh. "But don't worry; we can have your hand checked out at the hospital, too, if you like."

"I'm fine," he grumbles.

We make it to a corridor I recognize, knowing that the outside world is just a few steps away. A couple of the kitchen staff look a bit puzzled as we pass, but as soon as I say I need fresh air because I feel I'm going to be sick, they quickly point toward the correct door, no questions asked.

We finally burst outside. Ryan and I check a couple of taxi apps, but all of them are coming up with drivers unavailable. It's a busy night, and we're in the heart of Central London.

"We should call an ambulance," Ryan suggests.

"No! You don't call an ambulance when you go into labor!" Isabella balks. "I just need a bloody car to get me to the hospital."

"I really think an ambulance is a good idea," he insists gently.

"No ambulance," she seethes.

"Okay, I'll try the main road for a black cab," Ryan says, his voice much higher-pitched than usual as he shudders under her glare. "You going to be okay here for a bit?"

"Sure, take your time," Isabella replies, "it's not like I'm having a baby or anything."

I give him a thumbs-up as he scuttles away.

"Poor guy. It's not his fault. I'm just pissed off at men not having to go through any of this. Oh god," she says, trying to steady her breathing and pushing her hair out of her face, "this is not how this was supposed to go."

"It's going to be fine, I promise," I assure her. "We'll get you to the hospital."

"No, I mean—" she throws her hands up in the air "—having a baby on my own. I thought Elijah would be here. I thought that I'd have someone to face all this with. The baby's father doesn't want anything to do with me, and now I've messed up a relationship with someone who was happy to help raise the baby even though it wasn't his. I'm all alone. This baby is coming and . . . it's just me." She looks at me, her eyes glistening as tears threaten to spill down her cheeks. "It wasn't supposed to be like this."

She starts having another contraction, and I put my arm around her as she cries out in pain, before she begins steadying her breathing again. I watch her in admiration, waiting until the contraction is over to speak.

"Isabella, you can't plan everything out in life. No one can. Nothing is supposed to be a certain way. It is what it is and we make the best of it."

"I know, but this baby doesn't have a family."

"Are you kidding? This baby has *you!*" I say, squeezing her arm. "You're their family. Trust me, this baby doesn't need anyone else."

"I don't know if I can do this," she whimpers.

"Of course you can do this. I know you can do this."

Tears stream down her cheeks. "I'm not so sure."

"Isabella, look at me," I demand, staring her right in the eye. "You've got this. All this baby needs is you, their loving and wonderful mum. That's it. They need you. So, you can do this because you have to. Yes?"

Her lip quivering, she nods slowly. "Yes. You're right."

"I am right. I'm always right. Feel free to mention that in front of Ryan when he comes back."

She laughs, wiping her face with the back of her hand. "Thanks, Harper."

"You don't need to thank me. You already knew all that before I said it."

"I mean it," she croaks, grabbing my hands in hers. "Thank you."

I smile at her.

She sighs. "Where the fuck is Ryan?"

"He'll be here any minute, I'm sure." I bite my lip and check my phone. "Let me just give him a call."

"Tell him if he's not here in two minutes with a taxi, I'm going to break all his other fingers," she grumbles.

"I'll pass that right on," I say, taking a few paces away from her with the phone up to my ear. As soon as he picks up, I hiss, "*Where are you?*"

"I'm trying to flag down a taxi," he snaps.

"Any luck?"

"If I'd had any luck, I'd be with you, wouldn't I?"

"For god's sake, Ryan, there must be *one* taxi somewhere!"

"Hang on," he gasps. "Is that . . . I think I see . . . a yellow light. A *yellow light!*"

"Oh good! Get it quick!"

"I'm running out into the middle of the road to make sure it stops."

"You're what?"

"I'm in the road!" he cries.

"Oh my god, hail it down with your hand like a normal person!"

"I will take no such risk! He can't miss me." His voice grows faint as he yells, "Taxi, taxi!" and I assume he's waving his arms around. "Harper, he's stopped!"

"*Yes!*"

"I'll be with you in one second! Stay where you are!"

"Trust me," I say, glancing over my shoulder at Isabella, who is now almost bent double leaning against the wall of the hotel. "We're not moving."

As I hang up, Isabella raises her head. "Harper, I think . . . I think this baby is coming soon!" she says, looking much sweatier than before.

"It's okay. Ryan's got the taxi." I gulp. "Although maybe we really should call an ambulance?"

"No. No, just get me to the hospital."

"I promise we will."

She experiences a long, painful contraction. I rub her back and then hear the beep of the taxi pull up next to us, Ryan swinging open the door and jumping out.

"We need to get you into the car," I tell her as she turns huffing and puffing to face Ryan.

He puts his arm around her and gently guides her toward the taxi, saying, "It's okay, Isabella, you're doing really well. Almost there, in you go."

"You're both coming with me, right?" she asks nervously as she climbs in.

"Yeah, of course," I assure her, hopping in opposite her as she lies across the back seats.

Ryan pulls down the seat next to me, slams the door, and, over his shoulder, tells the driver to go, go, go.

"Where?" the driver asks.

"The hospital! Where do you think? Ahhhhhh!" Isabella shrieks, hunching in pain.

"I think the closest is St. Thomas' Hospital," Ryan says frantically. "Let's go, let's go!"

"She better not have a baby in my cab," the driver grumbles, putting his foot down. "I had someone in here only last night being sick everywhere. I don't want to have to clean those floors again!"

As we set off, Ryan and I share frequent looks of panic as Isabella's contractions seem to be getting closer and closer together.

"I need you to come sit over here, Harper, and comfort me," she says, puffing out breaths as she continues to shift positions throughout the journey, sometimes perching on the edge of the seat then moving to kneel on the floor of the taxi, resting her forehead and arms on the seat. "You're going to be my birthing partner."

"It's an honor," I tell her, determined to do a good job.

I launch myself from one side of the taxi to the other, offering my hand. She reaches for it and grips it tight.

"I've got this. I've got this," she says repeatedly through breaths.

"You've got this," I echo, Ryan nodding in solidarity.

"Please say we're nearly there!" she squeals, just as we come to the stop in some heavy traffic on Westminster Bridge, before crying out at a contraction.

"Almost there! We're so close!"

"Oh god, this is bad," she croaks. "I don't know if we're going to make it. I'm feeling an urge to push. We *need* to get to the hospital!"

"We're going to make it," Ryan assures her, glancing back over his shoulder at the long queue of traffic across the bridge. "Any minute and we'll be moving again."

There are beeps and angry shouts up ahead, and I see the cabdriver look at us in his rearview mirror, his forehead creased in panic. After a while of standstill traffic, our cabdriver starts honking the horn constantly, especially when Isabella shrieks in pain at another contraction.

"*Move it!*" the driver yells out his window. "LADY HAVING A BABY HERE!"

"Harper," Isabella says, tightening her grip on my hand, beads of sweat appearing on her forehead as she moves her position again, "you need to phone the ambulance. I'm feeling the urge to push."

I feel like all the breath has been knocked out of me. "Are you s-sure?"

She nods.

"Okay, don't worry, it's going to be all right, it's going to be fine," I say, convincing myself as well as everyone else as I grapple with my phone and dial 999.

"You have got to be kidding me," the driver groans, slamming his hand on the horn. "You should have called an ambulance in the first place, not a cab!"

Ryan opens his mouth, but Isabella shoots him the evilest of glares. "If you dare say anything along the lines of 'I told you so' . . ."

"I wasn't going to, I swear," he says, his eyes wide with fear.

I explain the situation to the emergency call handler, as Isabella instinctively moves into a squatting position, shouting, "Do any of you have a towel? We're going to need a towel! This baby is coming! It's not supposed to be coming yet! This is too soon! This pushing part is supposed to take ages! Tell them, Ryan!"

"I . . . uh . . . if you can hear me in there, little baby, you're not s-supposed to come yet," Ryan stammers dutifully.

"I DIDN'T MEAN TELL THE BABY! I MEANT, TELL THE DOCTORS!" Isabella bellows.

"Right, of course," he whispers fearfully.

"We think the baby is coming now," I say urgently into the phone. "But apparently it's not supposed to be happening this quickly."

"Every birth is different. Do you have a clean towel?" the calm woman echoes on the other end of the phone.

Quick as a flash, Ryan whips off his tux jacket and holds it ready.

"We have a tux jacket," I respond, helping Isabella to balance.

"You need to ask the driver to pull over and put on the hazard lights," she instructs.

I repeat the instruction and he says, "We're in the middle of standstill traffic!" before putting on the hazard lights and opening his car door. I watch out the window as he starts yelling, "Is anyone in this traffic jam a doctor?" at the top of his lungs.

"Oh my god, the baby is coming!" Isabella shrieks. "Ryan, I can feel its head! ITS HEAD IS COMING!"

"I'm ready, Isabella," Ryan says, holding his dinner jacket under her legs and looking at her with an encouraging smile. He suddenly doesn't look panicked at all, as though a switch has gone off in his brain and he knows he needs to step up. "Don't worry, we can do this. We're right here with you. You can do this! Keep breathing. You're doing brilliantly."

Her eyes fixed on his, she nods.

"An ambulance is on its way to you," the caller promises as I tell her the head is coming out. "It will be with you any minute. She needs to push."

"Isabella, you need to push," I inform her.

"NO SHIT."

"That's it, Isabella," Ryan says in this steady, calm voice that's so convincing. He's making me feel much better, too, as though he might actually know what he's doing. "Big push, you can do it. It's going to be okay."

I hear sirens in the distance as Isabella howls, gripping my hand until my fingers no longer have any feeling left in them. Ryan has positioned his jacket right underneath her, ready for the baby to come, so when the woman on the phone tells me to make sure the baby won't fall on the floor, I can assure her that we have that covered.

"More pushing, Isabella, you're doing so brilliantly," Ryan says, a great big smile on his face.

"You've got this, another push, you can do it," I say, Ryan nodding along.

Above Isabella's groans, I hear the cabdriver yell, "It's here! The ambulance is here! Cars are parting to let them through! Why didn't you do that for us when I was saying we were having a baby, eh? You load of *wankers*!"

"Almost there, Isabella, almost there!" Ryan says soothingly, and I watch in disbelief as after a few more pushes from Isabella, he wraps his jacket around a baby whose cries pierce the air and send a wave of relief through all of us. As he passes the baby to her to hold on her chest, the door behind swings open and paramedics appear.

"It's a boy," Ryan whispers.

Tears are streaming down all three of our faces. Ryan and I tell Isabella that we have to step out to let the paramedics into the cab and, as the fresh air hits my damp cheeks, I notice the driver is also crying, beaming down through the window at the little baby. Other drivers have gotten out of their cars and are squinting at us to see what's happening, the blue lights of the ambulance flashing across their faces.

Ryan and I look at each other, big dopey smiles on our faces.

"I can't believe that just happened. Ryan, you were . . . incredible. I would hug you, but you are covered in blood."

He laughs, looking down at his shirt. "This is going to be a fun story to tell the dry cleaners."

"You delivered a baby," I whisper in amazement.

"It was a team effort. You were so great with her, Harper, she really trusts you."

As a paramedic steps out of the cab to speak to his colleague, I ask him if everything is okay.

"Everything is great. You did really well; well done. We're going to get them both to the hospital now. We can take one of you with us if you'd like? I think she wants you there."

"You go," Ryan says, gesturing to his shirt.

"No, you should come, too. Please," I plead.

Having just gone through such an event together, I suddenly feel bereft at the idea of him leaving me.

"I'll meet you there. I can walk, it's really not far."

We look on as Isabella is transported out of the cab to the ambulance, and I nod toward our driver, who is dabbing at his eyes with a tissue that a fellow motorist has offered him.

"We need to tip heavily on this fare," I whisper to Ryan.

"Don't worry. I'll expense it. Cosmo will love this story," Ryan laughs. "Go on, don't let her be alone in the ambulance."

"I'll see you at the hospital?"

"Promise."

Tearing myself away from him, I hurry to climb into the ambulance and we set off, meandering through the traffic. I sit at the side, trying not to get in the way of the paramedic while beaming down at Isabella and her baby.

"Can you believe it?" she says to me, her eyes filled with joy and wonder. "Can you believe that that just happened?"

"No," I laugh as tears start spilling down my cheeks again. "I guess it's proof of what we talked about—when it comes down to it, you really can't plan everything."

"That's true," she says, gazing at her little boy, now wrapped in a proper towel. "I wouldn't change a thing. It was absolutely perfect."

"I'll say," I nod. "Very Hollywood."

She tilts her head up at me. "How so?"

"It was outrageous and extraordinary," I say, before flashing her a grin. "And you gave birth wearing Versace."

After my interview, I plan to head home but find Ryan waiting in reception. He jumps up when he sees me, coming over with an apprehensive smile on his face.

"How was it?" he asks, shoving his hands in his pockets.

"Terrifying. What are you still doing here?"

"I thought we could go for a drink, maybe," he says quickly. "It's been a pretty stressful day, so we've earned it. Only if you don't have any plans."

It has been a *very* stressful week, really, trying to focus on our usual intern tasks but secretly prepping for the interviews that were cruelly scheduled for Friday afternoon.

The interview was conducted by one of the senior editors, Martha, and Celia was in there, too, mostly making notes, but every now and then asking a less grueling question than the ones Martha was firing at me. I have no idea how I did, but Celia whispered, "Well done," as she opened the door for me at the end, and right now I'm just so relieved it's over. I spent the last two weeks practicing interview questions and studying *The Daily Bulletin*. At least I can rest assured there was nothing more I could have done.

"A drink sounds great," I say, and his expression brightens.

He suggests a pub in North London, since we're both heading that way home anyway. We get the tube together, talking about the interviews and what questions came up, before we both agree we shouldn't discuss it any further because it's boring work chat and we deserve a night of fun.

It's busy at the pub Ryan chooses—the only rule I had was that we don't go to the bar I work at—as there's a large group of smartly dressed friends who must be going on to a fancy black-tie event. We manage to bag a couple of chairs and a small table inside, which I'm grateful for because I've been wearing smart heels all day for the interview and, even though it's late August, it's threatening to rain. As soon as I sit down, I cause Ryan to wrinkle his nose with disapproval as I use the sleeve of my jacket to give the table a quick wipe.

"What?" I sigh. "It's *fine*."

"I'll get some napkins from the bar. White wine?"

"Yes, please."

His phone starts vibrating with a call, and he tells me he'll be back in a moment, answering and ducking back outside the pub. I shrug off my jacket, leaving it on the table before heading to the bar myself and ordering the drinks, just in case his call takes a while. When he reappears, he makes a beeline for the bar, but I call him over and gesture to the bottle already waiting in a wine chiller with two glasses.

"Sorry about that," he says, taking a seat on the stool next to me.

"I'm making them a large, I hope that's okay," I say, pouring the wine into our glasses.

"Fine by me." His cheeks are flushed. "It's been a day."

"You can say that again. I can't believe they pushed our picnic piece back, too. Do you think they'll still publish it?"

"I reckon so. Cheers."

"Cheers," I respond glumly, clinking my glass against his.

"Why do you look so upset?" he asks, concerned.

"Oh, I just really want to have an article published so I can show my parents."

He smiles. "They'd be really proud, huh?"

"Ha!" I say, throwing him off guard. "It's complicated," I hurry to explain. "Anyway, sorry, we said we wouldn't talk about work, didn't we? Let's focus on something else."

There's an eruption of guffaws and laughter from the fancily clad group on the other side of the pub. I nod toward them.

"Where do you think they're going?" I ask him. "Maybe we could make friends and try to wrangle an invite."

"No, thanks," Ryan says, glancing at them. "I'm not a fan of black tie."

"What? I love it! It's so fun dressing up for posh events!"

"They're the worst kind of events," Ryan groans. "You have to stand there in an uncomfortable suit and make small talk and worst of all, *dance*."

"All of that sounds great!" I laugh.

"Yeah, for people like you, who find those situations easy. For me, they're excruciating," he admits shyly, shrugging. "I feel so out of place, like I don't belong and everyone knows it."

Has he looked in the mirror? Does he not know how *beautiful* he is? If he wanted to, he'd have people falling over themselves to dance with him. Bet he looks good in a tux, too.

I haven't drunk enough wine to say any of that to him, though.

"I'd rather just go to the pub with a friend," he concludes.

"Like right now?"

He smiles. "Like right now."

"I'm glad you're happy, then. But for the record, black-tie events would be absolutely fine if you threw yourself into them. It's about attitude. You've got to forget what everyone else thinks, believe you belong, and shimmy about."

He laughs, shaking his head. "I will never have that confidence. You have this amazing aura about you, Harper, like you can just walk into any room and be completely comfortable. You can talk to anyone."

"So can you."

"We both know that's not true," he says, giving me a pointed look. "I've never been . . . brave in that way. I'm so self-conscious."

"Everyone feels that way."

He smiles at me. "My brother used to say that to try to make me feel better, too."

"You have a brother?"

He nods, a sadness shrouding his eyes as he turns the stem of his wine glass round and round. "Yeah. Adam. He died when we were younger. He had leukemia."

My heart sinks. "Ryan, I'm so sorry."

"It's okay, it's been a while now. I mean, I miss him all the time, but . . . you know." He shrugs. "He was always the confident one."

"You say that like every family has one."

He chuckles. "Mine certainly does. You have any siblings?"

"Yes. I have an older sister, Juliet. We don't really speak. She's a lawyer here in the city, but I never see her. I try to be out of the house when she comes home to visit. Sorry, that sounds ungrateful when you've lost your brother," I add guiltily.

"Don't be silly. Families are complicated." He hesitates. "I get the feeling you're not close to your parents, either."

I let out a long sigh. "An understatement."

He grimaces. "I'm sorry. That can't be easy."

"It is what it is. You close to yours?"

"Yeah. Although they weren't thrilled about me moving to London. They live in Manchester."

"Who do you live with here, then?"

"I have a flatmate, a friend from uni." He pauses. "He's actually away this weekend, though, so I've got the place to myself."

The atmosphere feels instantly charged. I have no idea if it's just me. He likely said that as a throw-away comment; *of course* he just said that as a throwaway comment, Harper, you think he was saying it so that you would know you could go back to his tonight, no problem?! Don't be stupid.

Although.

It's kind of a weird throwaway comment, isn't it? I didn't ask if his housemate was there or not. He voluntarily offered that information. Was it a hint? But why would he do that? We don't get on! We can barely have a conversation without it becoming a full-on argument! I think he's an irritating know-it-all! He thinks I'm a vapid, reality-TV-show-loving, hideous mess of a person! There's *no way* he wants to sleep with me!

Although.

He did hang around for ages after his interview to wait for me to invite me for a drink. We did have that moment in Greenwich. And we're currently having a very pleasant conversation without any arguing whatsoever, so it's not like we're *always* at each other's throats. Maybe we do get on after all. Maybe there's some kind of . . . spark here.

I feel overly excited and terrifyingly nervous at the same time. My hands are getting all sweaty.

You know what I blame?

His *eyes*. They're earnest and gentle and piercing, all at the same time. How does he get away with them? They don't belong to someone like him, they belong to Claudia Schiffer! He has no right to have such eyes!

"Are you okay?" Ryan asks suddenly. "You look . . . vexed."

"Me? I'm fine! Absolutely fine," I repeat, picking up my glass and draining it. "I'm going to go wee."

I hop off my stool and scurry away from him toward the loo, instantly regretting saying the word "wee" in front of him. When I finish washing my hands, I lean on the basin to stare at my reflection. Thankfully, none of my makeup has smudged (yet). I'm glad I took particular care over my appearance for my interview today.

"Sleeping with him would be a bad idea," I tell my reflection.

"Sex is never a bad idea!" replies a drunken voice from another cubicle, giving me a fright. I dash out of the toilets, absolutely mortified. Thank god whoever it is didn't see me come into the bathroom and won't be able to identify me in the pub.

As I make my way back over to Ryan, he glances up from his phone and smiles at me. It's that secretive one he does sometimes, like he knows something I don't. It usually annoys me in the office, but now it brings me to a swift realization.

It's like the phantom girl in the cubicle said: sex is never a bad idea.

CHAPTER TWELVE

R yan and I appear to have formed a truce.

When you go through something as momentous as delivering a baby in the back of a London cab together, a bond inevitably forms, and on Monday morning when I arrive at the office, he looks up from his desk as I approach and smiles. I smile back.

"Good weekend?" he asks.

"Pretty uneventful," I reply breezily, taking my seat next to him. "You?"

"Oh, same old."

We both turn to our screens, equally amused, and I spot Mimi arch her eyebrows at us across the way. She is the only one in the office who knows what happened at the party—we agreed with Isabella not to tell anyone because it would make such a great story for the exclusive she'd already agreed to give me about the baby. Once she's settled at home, we'll interview her and can work the drama of the birth into the story. It will have a much bigger impact if we keep the details to ourselves until the piece is published. We were worried the cabdriver might spill the beans, but there's been no whiff of the story anywhere, so we're confident he had no idea who Isabella Blossom was.

"Cosmo is going to lose his mind when he reads it," Ryan had chuckled while we sipped the terrible coffee from the machine in the hospital. "Two of his journalists delivering a world-famous actor's baby? What a scoop."

"Remember, this is Cosmo we're talking about," I reminded

him. "He'll probably bump it from the front page for a piece on why bowling is making a comeback among young successful businessmen."

"You think so little of him?"

"He thinks so little of me."

"That can't be true," he claimed, frowning. "It's obvious that he doesn't appreciate celebrity culture in the same way you might, but he must know how lucky he is to have you. You're one of the best journalists out there."

"If he thinks so, he has a funny way of showing it. You must have noticed how he treats you compared with how he talks to me," I sighed, before giving him a suspicious look. "One of the best journalists out there, huh?"

He shrugged. "I've always thought so."

He seemed genuine, but I think he was still high on adrenaline from delivering a baby, so I probably shouldn't look into it too much.

Still, our bickering and snide remarks have noticeably decreased. We're almost pleasant to one another. For example, when Dominic comes over from the art desk late Monday morning to consult Ryan about a layout for a piece on village cricket, Ryan examines it with his brow furrowed before turning to me.

"I'm not sure about this lead picture," he says. "Harper, what do you think?"

I tear my eyes away from a press release about a TV presenter's new clothing line.

"Sorry?"

"What are your thoughts on this picture?" Ryan asks, gesturing to his screen. "I'm not sure it's quite right."

Attempting to hide my shock at being asked, I move closer to his desk to have a look.

"Yeah, I agree with you. I don't think it should focus on one cricketer bowling."

"Right." Ryan nods. "It needs a bit more . . ."

"Green?" I suggest when he trails off.

"Exactly. We need to see the bigger picture. Set the scene. Give it a bit more of a . . ."

"An English-country-village feel."

"Yes!" Ryan beams at me. "Thanks, Harper. That okay, Dominic?"

"No problem," Dominic says, glancing at the two of us in confusion. He walks away, looking back at us as though trying to work out what just happened.

Later that day, Ryan wanders into the kitchen while I'm making a cup of tea and looks surprised when I add half a sachet of sugar. I catch his expression and roll my eyes.

"I only allow myself sugar in my tea as a treat sometimes," I explain, although I don't know why I feel the need to justify it. "Don't worry, I'm aware of how bad it is for me."

"Actually, I was confused at you using sugar rather than honey," he muses, going about making himself a coffee. "I thought you were a fan of honey tea."

I stare at him. "You . . . you remember that?"

"Sure." He shrugs. "You were the person who introduced it to me. I'd never had honey in my tea before. I think you said it was your mum who used to make it for you?"

"Only when I was ill," I confirm, before grimacing. "The rare occasion that Mum would bother to show she cared. Guess that's why I find it so comforting."

He looks sad and I feel bad for making the conversation so deep all of a sudden, so I brightly add, "I'm glad that I passed on honey tea to someone else. I hope you still dabble?"

"I certainly do. It's great on a hangover." He gestures to my mug. "But you don't have it at work anymore?"

"No, just at home. Only because I'm so lazy and never remember to bring honey into the office with me," I say, picking up my tea from the side once his coffee is done and strolling back to our desks together.

The next day, by the time I come in—which, Cosmo gleefully announces so that everyone can hear, is twenty minutes after my contracted hours (and he doesn't care if I was on a work call)—Ryan is already typing away on his keyboard and looks up momentarily to say hi before focusing on his writing again. I throw my bag down on the floor and then notice something waiting for me among all my belongings scattered across my desk: a jar of honey.

I pick it up in wonder.

"So you can have your honey tea here," Ryan explains simply, standing up and wandering over to the printer to collect something before being called into Cosmo's office.

Stunned, I watch him go.

"What's that all about?" Mimi asks, resting her chin in her hands and smiling coyly.

"Nothing," I say with a wave of my hand, lowering myself into my chair.

She leans back. "Doesn't look like nothing to me."

Ignoring her, I log on and start going through my emails, every now and then stealing a glance at the jar of honey, unable to stop a smile spreading across my face.

I have to admit that work is a lot more pleasant without constantly arguing over everything with Ryan, but it's slightly unnerving, him being so nice and me enjoying it so much. I've started *looking forward* to seeing him every morning, a flutter of butterflies hitting my stomach at the sight of those amazing blue eyes and the crinkles around the corners of his mouth when he smiles hello. And Mimi is right—he definitely does seem to pay more attention to me than to anyone else in the office. He's quiet in group conversations, but when we're together, it's easy to get him talking.

This is bad. I have a *boyfriend*. I shouldn't be getting excited about someone else's smile, especially when it's a person with whom I have history. Not just any history. Checkered history.

But I'm starting to have doubts over Liam.

I thought it was going to be hard to keep the story about Isabella's baby secret from him, but it turns out to have been unbelievably easy because he hasn't asked me one question about the party. Instead, he went on about how proud he is that he put himself out there, bravely approaching people to introduce himself, and how he's pretty much signed that band Halo Skewed, some of the best performers he'd ever seen play live.

"You have to come to their gig next Friday," he said on Tuesday night when I met him at the sushi restaurant near his flat. "They'd be perfect for a big article in the magazine."

"In my magazine?"

"Yeah, course," he said, chuckling. "A piece all about the hottest new band about to go skyrocketing into the charts. Trust me, when you come to the gig, you'll be blown away. So, you'll come?"

"Uh . . ."

I hesitated, selecting a spicy tuna roll with my chopsticks. I knew nothing about this band. And I couldn't shake Ryan's implication at the party that Liam was much more interested in networking than he was in . . . well . . . me.

"I'm so excited for you to see them live," he'd continued, taking my pause in answering to be a resounding yes. I couldn't be bothered to correct him, so I'd left it.

Part of my uncertainty about Liam is that I know very well that I have a tendency to put work before anything else. It's the reason none of my previous relationships have worked out. I'm not an easy person to date, so maybe I shouldn't give up on Liam quite yet. He's gorgeous, smart, driven . . .

But he didn't buy me honey for my tea.

"Penny for your thoughts?"

I jump at Ryan's voice, having been fretting over Liam while waiting for an iced coffee in Roasted, the café closest to the office.

"Oh hi," I say, blushing. "I was . . . uh . . . thinking about work stuff."

He puts his hands in his pockets. "Something that's vexing you."

"How do you know I was vexed?"

"You got the crinkle in between your eyebrows," he admits.

"Excuse me?"

He runs the tip of his forefinger down the middle of his eyebrows. "You get a crinkle here when something is stressing you out."

"No, I don't."

He nods. "You do. It's an obvious tell. You're usually pretty relaxed, but when something is bothering you, the crinkle appears."

"I have an iced coffee here for Parker?" the barista yells out from behind the counter, reading the scribbled name on the side of the cup. "Is Parker here? Iced coffee for Parker!"

When no one else steps forward, I raise my hand. "I think I'm Parker."

"Here you go," she beams, handing it over. "Enjoy!"

"Thank you," I reply, turning to see Ryan looking amused. "What's so funny?"

"Nothing, Parker." He grins. "Enjoy your iced coffee."

"What are you waiting on?"

"A mocha."

I wrinkle my nose. "A *mocha*?"

"What's wrong with a mocha?" he asks defensively, folding his arms.

"I don't know." I look him up and down. "You write about land mines but you like chocolate in your coffee."

He tilts his head. "I'm a man of many layers."

"Clearly."

"I have a mocha here for Brian!" the barista calls out, and it's like music to my ears. "Mocha for Brian!"

He sighs, shuffling forward as he says, "I'm Brian," while I wait with an *extremely* smug smile plastered across my face.

"All right, Parker, no need to look so pleased with yourself," he grumbles as we fall into step with each other after leaving Roasted, making our way back to the office.

"I hope that mocha is up to scratch, Brian."

"The really sad thing is, I get my coffee here almost every morning before work around quarter to eight. Literally same time, every day. You'd think they would recognize me by now." He shrugs. "So, you're not going to tell me what was stressing you out and causing the crinkle before I disturbed your train of thought?"

"It's all very *When Harry Met Sally*, this crinkle nonsense."

He looks confused. "What do you mean?"

"You know, at the end of the movie when he runs to find her at the party and he does that amazing speech, and he says that he loves the crinkle above her nose," I explain.

He shrugs. "I've never seen it. But it sounds like you just spoiled the ending."

I gasp, stopping suddenly and gripping his arm. "You've never seen *When Harry Met Sally*?"

He shakes his head. "Is that bad?"

"*Yes!* It's the greatest rom-com of all time. No. Wait. Maybe tied with *Notting Hill*."

"*Notting Hill* always bothered me."

"Ryan, please don't tell me that you don't like *Notting Hill*, because we're only just starting to see eye to eye again, and I don't want to go back to hating on you all the time."

He bursts out laughing. "Wow, Harper, say it how it is."

"Well, it's true, isn't it?"

"Yeah, I guess so," he says as we start walking again. "Delivering a baby really breaks down barriers."

"So, put me out of my misery. What is it about *Notting Hill* that bothers you?"

He takes a deep breath. "Okay, I like the movie, so don't panic. But isn't she kind of mean to him the whole time? She doesn't tell him she has a boyfriend and then she picks him up and drops him whenever she likes. She treats him terribly. I don't get it."

"She does not! She's . . . aloof," I tell him, frowning. "It's not easy for her, being a Hollywood star. She doesn't trust anyone around her."

"Of course you're on the side of the movie star," he says with a knowing smile. "Has there ever been anyone you've interviewed who you didn't like?"

"A journalist does not reveal her secrets."

"Aha! That's a yes, then."

"There have been a couple who have been difficult to warm to maybe, but I always try to see things from their point of view. I mean, we're journalists, Ryan. We're the enemy."

"The enemy who gives them the publicity they need to be famous and successful," he remarks. "They act as though they hate us, but the truth is, they need us."

"The complex truth." I nod. "Which is why I make sure that I'm the good guy. What's the point in dragging people down? Where does that get you?"

"Valid, but you have to be honest with your audience," he says as we reach our building and he opens the doors for me. "If you only write good things, they're not going to think you mean it. As Mr. Darcy said, 'Your good opinion is rarely bestowed and therefore more worth the earning.' There's something to that, I think."

Once again, he causes me to halt in my tracks.

"Did you just quote Jane Austen at me?"

"My mum is obsessed with Colin Firth," he replies breezily, continuing on past the main paper desks and giving some of his former colleagues a wave as he passes. "It's my secret talent, quoting the BBC adaptation of *Pride and Prejudice*. We used to watch it every Christmas."

Catching up with him again, I'm completely bowled over by this new information. Sometimes I think I know Ryan through and through, and then other times I realize I don't know him at all.

"There," he says suddenly, glancing at me and waggling his finger at my face.

"What?"

"There's the crinkle." He grins as he sits at his desk, placing down his mocha. "My Jane Austen knowledge is vexing you."

Shaking my head and concentrating on making my forehead as un-crinkled as possible, I log back into my computer. Forcing myself not to look at him, I consider his theory. He's wrong, of course. It's not his Jane Austen knowledge that's getting to me.

It's him.

⌐⎯⎯⎯

Our truce doesn't last long.

It should come as no surprise that the crack in our newfound peace is caused by Cosmo, who calls us both into his office that Thursday afternoon.

"Harper, I've seen your email about interviewing Max Sjöberg tomorrow in Manchester—"

"It's going to be amazing," I say enthusiastically. "They're currently filming series two of his detective drama there, *Blue Lights*, and his publicist has promised that I can have at least half an hour, maybe an hour, and then we can send a photographer next week to do a shoot. We've never had the chance to interview him before; he's a hard man to pin down. Totally iconic, obviously. He put woolly jumpers on the map."

"I thought the detective from *The Killing* put woolly jumpers on the map," Ryan interjects.

"She definitely shined a light on them, but Max has been sporting woolly jumpers in Scandinavian detective dramas for two decades. Plus, it's a pretty big deal that he was asked to be in the English version of the original Swedish show, playing the same detective. I mean, when does that ever happen?"

"True." Ryan nods.

"He's *that* good. They couldn't possibly ask anyone else to play that role."

Cosmo clears his throat pointedly. "I'm going to ask Ryan to do the interview."

I blink at him. "*What?*"

"It's a good interview for the magazine, but Ryan will write it," Cosmo emphasizes, clasping his hands together across his lap and leaning back in his chair. "It makes sense."

I glance at Ryan, who, in his defense, looks like this has been sprung on him, too.

"Cosmo, this is my interview. I know the publicist, I made the contact," I tell him as calmly as possible. "I've been pestering her to let me talk to Max Sjöberg for a long time."

"I know," Cosmo replies, shifting in his seat. "But I would like Ryan to take it from here."

"But . . . *why?*" I ask, my voice going a little more high-pitched than I'd have liked, like a put-out child.

"Ryan is Swedish," Cosmo says, as if it's obvious. "Max Sjöberg is Swedish."

I put my hands on my hips. "What does that have to do with anything?"

"It's likely they'll have more of a connection," Cosmo explains, getting irritated now. "Ryan will understand him better, his heritage and background."

"Ryan is *half* Swedish," I point out. "He grew up in England."

"I did spend my holidays in Stockholm with my dad's family," Ryan comments, but quickly cowers under my glare.

"Cosmo," I begin, attempting to keep my rage under control, "I don't connect well with the people I interview because we're the same nationality. That has nothing to do with getting actors to open up."

"Ryan is our features editor, an excellent writer, a brilliant interviewer, *and* he's Swedish," Cosmo lists, jutting his chin out. "If you had to pick one person in this office to interview Max Sjöberg, who would you pick?"

"I would pick me!" I argue.

Cosmo sighs. "I've made my decision, Harper. Ryan is doing the interview."

I turn to Ryan to appeal to him. "You agree with this?"

"I . . . look," he says, holding up his hands, "I think you should do the interview, you're the one who set it up."

"Thank you!"

"But I do think the Swedish angle might be helpful in putting him at ease during the interview and getting him to chat more openly. He's been known to be prickly, and it's always helpful to have something in common to break the ice."

"Are you *serious?*" I cry, throwing my hands up. "I didn't get Audrey Abbot to relax by starting the conversation about how we both grew up in London! *Really*, Ryan? You think Max Sjöberg will be more forthcoming if you open by asking him what his favorite . . . ABBA song is?"

Ryan offers me an amused smile, which I do *not* appreciate right now.

"Is ABBA the most Swedish thing you could think of?"

"That and schnapps," I admit grumpily.

"Harper—" Cosmo begins, but Ryan interrupts him.

"I might have a solution," he says optimistically. "We could both go."

Cosmo looks as confused as I feel. "I'm sorry?"

"Why don't Harper and I both go to Manchester tomorrow? We could interview him together."

"What?" I shake my head. "That wouldn't work."

"Yes, it would. You're the best interviewer on the team and, as Cosmo says, it would be helpful for me to be there, too, if he discusses growing up in Stockholm," Ryan suggests, before giving me a look. "It's not like it would be the first time we've worked on a feature together, Harper."

I blush at the memory, but before I can speak, Cosmo interjects.

"I'm not sure how I feel about expensing two of you traveling to Manchester for an interview that can easily be conducted by one journalist," he says with a frown.

"My parents live in Didsbury, and I was planning on driving up to see them this weekend anyway, so I'm happy not to expense my travel," Ryan informs him. "I think this is going to be great. Between the two of us, we'll be able to get the best out of one of Sweden's best actors. I really think this is a smart idea, Cosmo. Trust me."

Cosmo hesitates, then begins to nod slowly. "All right. Problem solved."

"But . . . but . . ." I flail around, trying to say something, but feeling too thrown to know what I'm trying to convey.

"Harper, Cosmo has agreed that you can interview *Max Sjöberg*," Ryan points out. "Everyone's happy, right?"

I stare at him and realize that he's probably right. Cosmo

wasn't going to back down, so as much as I want to do this myself, I don't think I have much of a choice. But as I follow Ryan back to our desks, my frustration gets the better of me.

"I can't believe you just did that," I hiss.

"You mean, helped you get what you want?" he replies, confused.

"You stole my interview!"

He gives me a strange look, slowly replying, "No, I was offered your interview and worked out a solution so that you could keep it."

"You should have refused."

"Oh, because that's always a good move when your editor asks you to do something?" he says sarcastically.

"You are unbelievable."

"So are you!" he huffs. "You're doing the interview you wanted!"

"I'm doing the interview I *deserve* to do because it's *my interview*," I say, raising my voice and causing people to look our way.

"Just because you set it up doesn't automatically mean you're the best person for the job," Ryan argues. "And I never said it wasn't your interview! I'm saying that this way, it's the best of both worlds!"

I jab my finger at him. "For you, not for me. If you had any integrity, you would stand down!"

"Well, I think it will be better if we're both there!"

"You have to stick your nose into *everything*, don't you? You just have to show that you can do it better!"

"And you don't know when to drop things!" He shakes his head in disbelief. "Why can't you accept that this is a smart move that makes perfect sense?"

"Why can't you stop stealing my features?" I snap, my face growing hot in anger.

"I haven't stolen your feature! I'm helping you!"

"I don't need your help!" I cry.

He lets out a heavy sigh, glancing around at our colleagues trying not to obviously stare at us.

"Let's discuss this later, Harper," he whispers, turning to his screen.

I sit stewing for a moment before I blurt out, "We both know you *stole* my feature."

"And we also both know that you just *have* to have the last word," he snaps.

I scowl at him. "No, I don't."

He lifts his eyes to the ceiling and then starts furiously typing.

In response, I start angrily tapping away, too, even though I'm actually writing a very pleasant email to a publicist I like a lot.

After a few moments of tense silence, Mimi sighs and says, "Peacetime was nice while it lasted."

CHAPTER THIRTEEN

Max Sjöberg's publicist, Mae, is very nice about her client now being interviewed by not one, but two journalists, and sitting on the train to Manchester the next day, I wonder whether I overreacted a bit. It wasn't Ryan's fault he was put in that position by Cosmo.

He actually messaged this morning to ask if I wanted to join him on the drive, but I tersely replied that I'd bought a ticket *when I scheduled the interview* and wanted to do some work on the train. But I think his message was an olive branch, so I added, "Thanks for asking."

And anyway, something good came out of yesterday's chaos, because Mimi insisted that we go for a drink after work—according to her, I looked like I needed a large glass of rosé—and once we were in the pub, she had the perfect news to cheer me up.

"I'm sending you on a press trip next week," she announced.

"What are you talking about?"

"You, my friend, are going to Florence, Italy, from Friday morning until Sunday. You are very welcome."

I looked at her in bewilderment. "I'm not following."

"There's a press trip to a luxury hotel in Florence next Friday, a hotel that I'd very much like you to review for me. I already emailed the publicist, Sadie, giving her your name and details. She'll be in contact with you for your passport, so she can book your tickets. It is going to be fabulous—Sadie is a good friend of mine, you'll adore her."

"Mimi! That sounds amazing, but I can't go to Florence next weekend."

"Why not? Do you have better plans?"

"No, but I can't drop everything and go to Florence!"

"Yes, you can," she insisted. "You never go on press trips and you work too hard. You deserve this, Harper. I want you to go and have a nice relaxing weekend. It's *Florence*. You can't say no."

"But don't you want to go?"

"Harper, I go on loads of press trips. It's about time that you take advantage of having the travel editor as your best friend. You're always turning me down, but I refuse to let you this time. Everyone needs a holiday, and you are no exception."

"Are you sure? You don't want to offer it to someone else?"

"I want *you* to go," she laughed. "I figured that since it's over a weekend, you'd be more inclined to accept. You won't miss any work. This will be good for you, Harper. You're not allowed to think about who you should be interviewing or what piece will be the next hit or how Cosmo has slighted you—you need to get away and *relax*. That's all I ask."

So this time next week I'll be on my way to Italy for the weekend. Mimi is right. I haven't taken time for myself for . . . well . . . ever, and I could do with a break.

My shoulders feel very tense all the time lately—largely because of work, but also because of Liam. When I apologetically told him I couldn't make the Halo Skewed gig next Friday because I'd be on a work trip to Florence, his reply was:

Oh, that's a shame but you can come to their gig the following week, right?? Florence would be amazing. Any chance you can get me a cheeky place on the trip, too?? Could use a holiday!

I wasn't sure if he was joking, so I replied:

Haha, I wish! But think it's journalists only. I'll be
sure to bring you back a cheesy keyring, though!

He didn't respond and I haven't heard anything from him
this morning, either. Is he actually mad at me for not getting
him a spot on a press trip?! Even if I could, I'm not sure I'd want
him there. I'd really love some time to myself.

I know, I know. I should want my boyfriend to be there,
shouldn't I?

Ugh, my head hurts.

It aches even more when my phone starts vibrating on the
tray table in front of me, and I see it's Dad calling.

He'll only keep calling until I pick up. Might as well get it
over with now.

"Hello, Dad."

"You haven't been in touch at all about dinner dates," he says
gruffly.

"I'm fine, thank you for asking, and how are you?"

"Harper, I've had a bad morning and I'm not in the mood,"
he warns. "I sent you an email with a list of dates convenient
for us and Juliet, but you didn't reply and some of those may be
filled now."

"Sorry, I've been busy."

"Well, it would be polite of you to get back to me," he snaps.
"Juliet works much longer days and still finds the time to message her parents."

I sigh, lifting my eyes to the ceiling. "Dad, I'll reply to your
email, okay? Thanks for the reminder."

"Where are you? Why does it sound so loud?"

"I'm on a train."

"You're not in the office on a weekday?" he asks with great disapproval.

I rub my forehead, closing my eyes. "My job sometimes involves travel. I'm going to Manchester to interview Max Sjöberg."

"Who?"

"The Swedish actor. Have you seen *Blue Lights*?"

"I don't have time to watch soaps," he says dismissively. "Send me the dates that suit when you find the time in your hectic schedule."

I bite my tongue, not letting myself snap back at his heavily sarcastic tone.

"Okay, will do. Anyway, I might lose you at any moment because of the train signal, so thanks for the call and I'll message you with those dates."

I hang up and slump back in my seat, tossing my phone onto the tray table and trying to take deep breaths, as a therapist once advised me to do. I booked a couple of sessions after attending my parents' greatly challenging anniversary dinner where, after listing Juliet's many achievements to their fawning friends, my parents breezed past me saying I was "still experimenting career-wise."

No one spoke to me the whole night. I drank too much vodka and left before dessert without saying goodbye, stealthily tipping the spoon from my place setting into my handbag before I went. The next morning I pondered why stealing from my own parents felt like a small victory, but it did. I couldn't explain it.

By the time the train pulls into Manchester station, I've gone through my questions for Max and rechecked my makeup and general appearance, feeling a little nervous. I don't know how this is going to play out with Ryan, but I have to stand firm and make sure I lead this interview, not him. I head to the taxi rank and send Ryan a message once I'm in a car to let him know I'm on my way.

He replies:

Great, I just arrived so see you soon.

Of *course* he's early. He's probably done that on purpose, trying to get in there with Max so that when I show up, they're already best buddies. I hope Max's publicist, Mae, wouldn't allow anything to go ahead without me being there, too.

We reach the set location—a cobbled road called Little David Street, which has been closed off for filming. I spot Mae standing in a corner behind the camera crew; she's talking to Ryan, who is holding two coffee cups.

I scowl instinctively.

Ryan is probably filling her in on his Swedish heritage and trying to suck up to her by bringing her a delicious coffee. I hope Mae isn't falling for it, although by the way she's fluttering her eyelashes up at him, I may have already lost her allegiance.

I've worked with Mae before and we get on well. She's very smart and has a cool, trendy edge to her, always dressed like she's heading to an exclusive house party hosted by a DJ in an abandoned warehouse in Hackney. Today she's in high-waisted black-and-white checkered trousers with a loose white collared shirt tucked in and buttoned up to the top and heeled black ankle boots. She's wearing little to no makeup because she has that kind of effortless beauty that people like me can only dream of: long, dark, impossibly glossy curls; strikingly large dark-brown doe eyes; full, plump lips.

Slinging my bag over my shoulder, I march toward them determinedly.

"Harper, you're here!" Mae says, brightening and giving me a kiss on the cheek. "It's been ages. How was your journey?"

"Not too bad, thanks," I say, plastering on a smile and greeting Ryan with a curt nod. "The train wasn't as busy as I thought."

"Good. Well, I've been telling Ryan that, as usual, we're a

teensy bit behind so I'm not sure you're going to be able to speak to Max for a while."

"And I was telling Mae that we're happy to wait around so long as we get one of those cool chairs that say WRITER across the back," Ryan says with more animation than he usually exhibits around a stranger.

I'm hit by an unwelcome and unreasonable wave of jealousy.

Mae giggles. "I'll see what I can do. You two wait here and I'll go get an update."

"All right, then," Ryan begins once she's hurried off. "What's wrong?"

"Nothing."

"I can tell that something is wrong."

I roll my eyes. "Don't give me any of that 'crinkle between the eyebrows' crap."

"It's not just the crinkle between the eyebrows, Harper, it's your entire aura. Something has really upset you this morning and I just wanted to check that you're okay, but I'm sorry for prying." He sighs before holding out one of the coffees for me. "Here—I got you a flat white. It might not be as hot as it should be, but I wasn't sure you'd have time to get one after the train."

Damn it. Why does he have to be so nice when I'm in such a bad mood?! Now I feel bad, and it's all his fault. He is *infuriating.*

"Thanks," I say sheepishly, taking the coffee. "Sorry, it's not you I'm mad at."

"For once," he teases.

His comment allows me to crack a smile. "True." I let out a heavy sigh. "My dad phoned on the way here and I made the mistake of picking up."

"Ah." He nods in understanding. "Are things still difficult between you and your parents?"

"Some things never change."

"I'm sorry," he says quietly.

I shrug. "I don't know why I let him get to me."

"Because he's your dad," Ryan says simply. "But you shouldn't let him ruin today. This is an amazing interview that you've worked hard to get."

"You're right. I just wish . . ." I trail off. "Never mind."

Ryan's expression is earnest. "Listen, Harper, I've never understood why your parents treat you the way they do, but if they're blind to their daughter's happiness and achievements, then what does that say about them? It's a shame they're so narrow-minded. I feel sorry for them, personally. Your sister, too. Imagine only caring about how far someone gets in *one* kind of career? Think how much they must miss out on. It's sad."

I stare at him.

"What?" he asks. "Did I say something weird?"

"No, you said something . . . really nice. Thank you. It's strange that you remember so much about my family."

His blue eyes bore into mine, and he adds quietly, "I remember everything."

My cheeks burn under his gaze.

In that moment, I know that as soon as I get back to London, I need to break up with Liam.

It's not because Ryan has the kind of blue eyes that would make anyone go weak at the knees, and it's not even because there appears to be . . . *something* between us, some kind of inexplicable spark that's getting harder and harder to ignore.

No, the reason I need to break up with Liam is because I've never told him the truth about my family. I've never shared the shame I carry, knowing that I'm a failure in my parents' eyes and a loser in my sister's. He doesn't know how horrible I feel when he says he's told his family all about me, the unbearable humiliation of knowing that I can't tell my parents about him—simply because they don't care about my personal life.

It's not just Liam. I haven't told anyone about my family, really.

But eleven years ago, I told Ryan.

I blurted out my most painful secrets when those gorgeous eyes were locked on mine—but also, I told Ryan because I trusted him. And in turn, he told me about his brother Adam.

"Can I say something that's going to annoy you?" Ryan asks suddenly.

"You have just said something really nice, so, sure, throw in something to piss me off. The universe will be balanced again."

He grins at me. "You have the crinkle."

"Oh, for fuck's sake."

He laughs as Mae comes bustling over wearing a pained expression, and I brace myself for bad news.

"It's not good, I'm afraid," she says, confirming my suspicions. "The producer says they are *very* behind and they can't possibly spare Max, at least not for a few hours. You are welcome to stay here and watch the action—I'll be sure to find you one of those cool chairs—or if you'd rather go find somewhere quiet to do some work, I can phone you when things are looking hopeful."

"Are you kidding? Leave and miss Max Sjöberg doing his thing? I'll stay put, thank you very much," I declare, craning my neck to try to spot him among the huddle of actors down the street listening to instructions from the director.

"I actually have a bit of editing I could get done," Ryan says, seeming amused at my enthusiasm. "Harper, will you give me a call before the interview?"

"Sure."

He gives me a suspicious look.

"Oh, come on," I say, rolling my eyes. "I wouldn't *not* call you. I'm not that petty."

"Thanks," he says, laughing. "See you in a bit."

Mae and I watch him walk away, and then she turns to me, her eyes wide with excitement.

"Um *hello*, why didn't you give me the heads-up that your colleague was an *Adonis?!* I would have paid a little more attention to my outfit if I'd known," she says.

"Ryan? Oh. Yeah, he's . . . uh . . ."

"*Hot*. You know if he's single?"

I blink at her, taken off guard. "I . . . yeah, I think he is."

"Amazing. I don't know how you get any work done with him wandering around your office."

"Says the woman who works alongside Hollywood actors all day long."

"I don't date actors, Harper," she says proudly, lifting up her chin. "I couldn't handle their delicate egos."

I snort. "If you can't handle delicate egos, then you might want to avoid writers, too."

"Fair point," she says with a smile. "But I'll take my chances. Let me go find you a chair, and put in a good word with Ryan for me, would you? Do it stealthily, though."

I find myself nodding as she hurries off, and I'm left trying to work out how I feel about her crush on Ryan and wondering why I may be *furious* about it. An assistant comes over with a chair and I sit down, reminding myself that I have no right to be annoyed because, firstly, Ryan is single and Mae is single; secondly, Ryan probably doesn't see me in that way considering we fight over absolutely everything; and, thirdly, I have a boyfriend. Even if not for much longer.

But I *still* don't want Ryan and Mae to get together.

I can't think about that. I get out my notepad, jotting down details about the set and the general atmosphere around me, useful observations that I can include in the feature. I get really excited when I see the intimidatingly-tall-in-real-life Max

Sjöberg appear in his character's iconic look, at least in the British version: a three-piece suit and a dark trench coat. (The woolly jumpers made sense for a detective examining dead bodies in the vast, icy landscape of Sweden, but for a British cop peering down at a victim on a cobbled street in rainy Manchester, it would probably look a bit odd.)

Anyway, when I see him walk down the cobbled street chatting to the director, I feel incredibly privileged to watch the scene play out. This feeling gets old quite quickly when the same scene has to be reshot several times over. By the tenth take, I begin to wonder how anyone in television has this kind of patience and how the guy holding up the boom mic doesn't have a dead arm.

When the producer announces that we are breaking for lunch, I look to Mae hopefully, but she shakes her head and I deflate. She informs me that Max needs to eat and he doesn't want to be disturbed in the precious moments he has off. We move to a different street for another scene, and I send Ryan the new location. When he arrives, he looks as excited as I'd been when offered one of those "cool" chairs.

His excitement inevitably wanes after watching Max declare—for the twelfth time—his theory on why the man who was stabbed in the cobbled street was there to begin with.

By late afternoon, Mae profusely apologizes and says it isn't looking likely to happen today.

"However," she says brightly, "there is always tomorrow! I can definitely squeeze in some time then, I promise."

"Tomorrow? You mean stay in Manchester tonight?"

My heart sinks as I consider finding a hotel at the last minute and how I have nothing on me for an overnight stay, not even a toothbrush.

"We could do that," Ryan considers. "Harper, have you got anything tomorrow you need to be back for?"

"No, I don't have plans, but I'd have to find a hotel and—"

"We can sort all that," Ryan says confidently with a wave of his hand. "Are you sure we can get the time tomorrow, Mae?"

"Absolutely! I would offer to buy you dinner as an apology, but it looks like I'm going to be here a long time," she sighs. "I can recommend some great places if you need."

"Don't worry, I know the area; my parents live in Didsbury," Ryan informs her. "Leave it with me."

"Great! I'll send you the details for tomorrow. Thanks for being so understanding and I'm *so* sorry again," she says, offering Ryan a winning smile before leaving us.

"What a disaster," I mutter.

"It's not a disaster."

I cross my arms. "Oh really?"

"Well, I've been shopping with you once before, and it was only mildly torturous, so I'm willing to accompany you to get a toothbrush and other stuff you may need for tomorrow, like . . ."

He trails off, his eyebrows knitted together.

"Like underwear?" I prompt.

"Yes. Right." He clears his throat. "Underwear and other . . . garments."

I squint at him. "Did you just say 'garments'?"

"Yeah," he says, slowly nodding. "I have no idea why. I think the underwear topic made my brain go into awkward mode."

"Indeed, it did," I say, greatly amused. "Anyway, I know I can buy *garments*, but Cosmo is going to lose his head when I tell him I need to expense a hotel."

"I've already got that sorted!" Ryan proclaims, reaching for his phone in his pocket. "You can stay at my parents' house."

"*What?*"

"They have a spare room. Problem solved."

My jaw drops. "Ryan! I can't stay at your parents' house!"

"Why not?"

"Because that would be *totally* inappropriate!"

He tilts his head at me. "Why?"

"I'm your colleague!" I cry, throwing my hands up in the air.

"And?"

"And colleagues don't turn up at parents' houses and stay in their spare rooms!"

"I reckon you may be overthinking this, Harper," he replies, looking unfazed by my reaction. "It's not that big a deal. You need somewhere to stay. I have somewhere you can stay. What's left to discuss?"

He lifts his phone to his ear.

"What are you doing?" I ask.

His expression brightens as he says, "Hi Mum!"

"Oh my God, Ryan, *hang up!*" I hiss at him. "You better not be about to—"

"Yeah, we've finished up now. Listen, bit of a situation here. We didn't get the interview, but they've said we can do it tomorrow instead—only thing is, Harper doesn't have anywhere booked to stay," he says, batting my hand away as I desperately try to grab his phone.

Why is he so tall?!

"Yeah," he continues, "so I wondered . . . Exactly what I was thinking! Thanks Mum . . . yeah . . . yeah sounds great. Thanks, you're the best. I'll tell her. All right, see you soon." He hangs up. "You see? I didn't even have to ask her; she said you're very welcome to stay with them, she won't hear of you staying in some terrible hotel. She's going to make up the spare room now, and there's plenty of food for you to join us for dinner, too."

I bury my head in my hands. "Ryan, no! No, no, no!"

"You don't want a delicious home-cooked meal and free accommodation?"

"Look, it's really kind of them to offer, but I can't stay at your parents' house. I will find a hotel and then—"

"Harper," he says gently, placing a hand on my arm, "I insist. And you know what? You get to laugh at all the baby photos of me dotted around the house. Doesn't that sound fun?"

I hesitate. That does sound quite fun.

"*Fine*," I say, because I don't want his mum to think I'm rude and, also, his warm hand clasping my arm is making it hard to think straight.

"Come on, let's go get you toiletries and garments." He grins. "And then you get to meet the parents."

Bloody hell.

Yep. It's confirmed. This is *very* weird.

CHAPTER FOURTEEN

I t's a strange thing witnessing someone you know as an adult returning to their childhood home, especially when it's someone you see in a professional capacity. You get glimpses of what they were like growing up through small moments, like how Ryan had barely stepped through the door before he was down on his knees ruffling the hair of an Irish setter, which had come lolloping down the hall to greet him and was spinning round in circles, then resting its paws on Ryan's shoulders to lick his ears.

Through raucous laughter, Ryan glances up at me with a boyish grin across his face. "This is Sullivan. But his friends call him Sully."

I've never seen Ryan more comfortable and happy than in that moment with his dog.

"Oh, Ryan, you're going to get his hairs all over your trousers," his mum, Emily, says, smiling fondly at her son as she emerges into the hall. "Just step around him, Harper, and come on in. He'll be down there getting Sully overexcited for a while."

Slender and petite, Emily has strikingly sharp cheekbones and delicate features with gray-blue eyes and honey-blond highlighted hair. She is dressed in a dusty-blue shirt tucked into beige linen trousers and has a calm aura about her, with a small, secretive smile as though she knows something you don't—similar to the one I've caught Ryan sporting from time to time. On her, though, it's not annoying.

When Ryan finally gets to his feet, she wraps her arms around his shoulders as he bends down to her level and then pulls back to admire him, patting his cheek lightly with her hand and telling him she's missed him. He looks mildly embarrassed at her attention, but softens, too, and I can see from their embrace that they have a close bond.

I feel a pang of regret that I don't ever get such a welcome from my family.

"Ryan! You're home!" comes a booming voice from the end of the hall. Ryan's dad appears with oven gloves and an apron on. He comes striding toward us, a wide smile across his face.

"And you must be Harper," he says with a slight Swedish accent. He shakes off the oven gloves to hold his hand out to me. "Welcome! I'm Fredrik. Pleasure to have you, make yourself at home. Ryan, don't leave your bag on the ground there for everyone to trip over, yes?"

Ryan says, "Give me a moment to breathe, Dad, before you start telling me off for nonexistent mess," and then they give each other one of those man-hugs that involves just one arm wrapped round the other person and some rough pats on the back.

Fredrik must be where Ryan gets his height from—he's imposingly tall and broad with light brown hair, speckled with gray, and sparkling blue eyes that could rival his son's. He chuckles as he instructs Ryan to take our bags upstairs where they're "out of the way."

"And there you were thinking I was a neat freak," Ryan mumbles to me. "You'll soon see I didn't have a choice living in this house. I'll be back down in a minute."

Sully dances around his legs and then looks distraught when Ryan heads up the stairs, somewhere he must not be allowed. I crouch down to pat his head and he spins around excitedly, then licks my hands as I give him a good scratch behind the ears.

"You're a dog person, then," Emily observes as Fredrik heads back into the kitchen.

"I love them, but we weren't allowed one growing up," I tell her, smiling at how soft Sully's head is. "My parents aren't big on animals."

"Sully rules the house here," she admits, laughing at his dopey expression as his tongue lolls out the side of his mouth when I get back to scratching his ears.

"Have you always had setters?"

"Yes, we got the first one a couple of years after we were married. And then, of course, we had Cracker—the love of Ryan's life when he was a teenager. They were inseparable."

"I remember him telling me about Cracker," I say absent-mindedly.

Emily nods as though she wouldn't expect anything less. "She supported Ryan through . . . well . . . everything."

A lump forms in my throat. I know she's talking about Adam, Ryan's older brother.

"Dogs are amazing," Emily continues as I hold Sully a little bit closer. "They can get us through anything. And they're goof-balls, which helps when you need a laugh."

On cue, Sully gives me a big slobbery lick across the cheek, taking me by surprise and causing me to topple over backward as Ryan appears at the top of the stairs. He breaks into a grin as Sully stands over me, attacking me with licks.

"Come on through and let's get you a drink," Emily offers, pulling Sully back and holding out her hand to help me up. "It sounds like you've had quite a day."

"A very unsuccessful one," I confess.

"I wouldn't say that," Ryan contends, coming down the steps. "We did get to sit in one of those cool movie director chairs."

"What is your obsession with those chairs?" I ask, following

Emily into the kitchen, Ryan bringing up the rear. "Surely, watching Max Sjöberg in action beats sitting in a chair."

"Did you at least get to speak to the great man at all?" Fredrik asks, having removed his oven gloves to put the finishing touches on a huge bowl of salad.

"Sadly no, but we'll get the interview tomorrow," Ryan says confidently.

Emily grimaces. "I hope they don't let you down. It would be awful for you to have come all this way and not get any time with him."

"Don't worry, Mum, Harper would never let that happen," he assures her. "I don't want to know her methods, but it's a well-known fact in the industry that Harper Jenkins gets whatever interview she wants."

"A slight exaggeration," I say, flushing and looking down at my feet.

"Ryan never exaggerates," Fredrik insists. "If anything, he's much too keen to play things down, always leaning toward the cynical. He gets that from his mother's side—the Brits."

"Would you like wine, Harper?" Emily asks, rolling her eyes at her husband. "White or red?"

"Whatever's open." I smile politely.

"She prefers white," Ryan jumps in, opening the fridge and finding a bottle.

Emily shoots him a small smile, and I wonder how much his parents know about me.

"Thank you so much for having me this evening," I say. "It's so kind of you when it's so last minute. I told Ryan I could easily find a hotel . . ."

"Nonsense," Fredrik insists with a wave of his hand, Emily nodding in agreement as she passes me a glass. "It's a pleasure to have you. Take a seat, anywhere you fancy."

I move to the table at the far end of the kitchen, next to the open French windows that look out onto a beautifully kept garden, which has a footpath winding down the middle, surrounded by various colorful flowers. At the bottom of the garden, next to a small wooden shed, is a blossoming cherry tree.

"Wow, your garden is stunning," I observe, setting my glass down at one of the places nearest to the windows. "Are you both gardeners?"

"That would be me," Emily says, ordering Sully to sit in his bed in the corner, before gesturing for me to sit down as she pulls out the chair on the opposite side of the table. "Fredrik is better in the kitchen. He doesn't have the patience for plants. Do you have a garden in London?"

I shake my head. "No, but I did have some herb plants on my windowsill. They didn't last very long. I wouldn't say I'm a natural. I kept forgetting about them, to be honest."

"Ryan's very green-fingered," Emily tells me.

"Mum always says this, despite the fact that the last time I helped out in the garden was when I was fifteen," Ryan sighs, carrying the salad over to the table and then coming to sit next to me. "I think she hopes that if she tells me I'm a good gardener, I might find some interest in it. So far her tactic hasn't worked, but she admirably persists."

"I'm telling you, he had a knack for it," she says, prompting Ryan to give me an I-told-you-so look and making me laugh. "We used to plant things together, turning the soil and weeding while he practiced his speeches for debate club."

"You were in debate club?" I ask, impressed.

"He was *captain* of debate club," Fredrik informs me, bringing over a steaming chicken dish, fresh from the oven, that he sets down on a mat in the middle of the table.

"Great, thanks, Mum and Dad," Ryan mumbles. "We've been here all of half an hour and you're already spilling childhood secrets to Harper. Since it's now common knowledge, I just want to be clear that being captain of the debate club at school was considered very cool by all my peers."

"Oh, I can imagine," I say with a teasing smile. "You know, it makes complete sense to me that you would be captain of the debate club." I turn to address his parents, now that Fredrik has taken his seat at the table, too. "Ryan is very good at arguing his point when it comes to a heated discussion in the office."

"That's code for 'Ryan is a pain in the arse,'" Ryan translates.

"Not what I meant."

"Ah, but he *is* a pain, because he's stubborn," Fredrik says, gesturing for my plate so he can serve. "Always has to have the last word in a fight. It's maddening."

I turn to look at Ryan accusingly. "Hey! You always say that about me!"

He shrugs. "Takes one to know one."

"You could never win with Ryan, but he used that power wisely," Fredrik says, passing my plate back once he's loaded it up. "You know, he founded his school newspaper? When he proposed it, the head teacher refused. He was worried it would encourage anarchy, I think. Well, as you can imagine, Ryan wasn't going to take no for an answer."

"Dad," Ryan groans, "Harper isn't interested in hearing about—"

"Um, Harper is very interested, thank you very much," I interrupt. "Please carry on."

"He rallied support from the other students, proposed a debate for and against a school paper to take place in an assembly and be judged by a panel made up of teachers and students— clever, right? The vote was unanimous. Ryan got his way and became the very first editor. It's still running at the school today, and it's great experience for the students who want to go on to study journalism at university."

"Wow!" I say, genuinely impressed. "That's really cool, Ryan. You never told me that."

"Debate club, gardening, school newspapers—why bother filling you in on such sexy achievements when I can just bring you back to my parents and let them do the honors?" he mutters, taking a drink in between mouthfuls.

"To be fair, you do quite a good job of that yourself. Let's not forget you telling me that story about your famous cricket ball catch in the lake."

Fredrik lets out a gruff laugh. "Still boasting about that one, eh, Ryan?"

"It came up naturally in conversation!" Ryan justifies.

I grin. "He did mention it's still up on your mantelpiece."

"At his insistence," Fredrik says. "I'm sure he'll point it out to you later."

"It really was the pinnacle of my career," Ryan sighs, sitting back in his chair. "Harper got the scoop on Audrey Abbot after sixteen years; I caught a cricket ball mid-fall backward into a lake. You tell me which is more impressive?"

"Speaking of, I loved that interview," Emily tells me, her eyes widening with interest. "What was she like in person? You must get to speak to the most amazing people as celebrity editor."

"Audrey was as incredible as you'd expect," I confirm, much to her delight. "She was guarded at first—no surprises there—but once she got talking, she really was fascinating."

"Did she approach you for the interview?"

"Not exactly. I had to bring her round to the idea, but it wasn't as painful as I was expecting."

"Have you always been interested in the arts?" Fredrik asks, swallowing his mouthful.

"Yeah, I always leaned more toward the arts at school. I loved reading and film, too."

"And did you always want to be a journalist?" Emily asks.

"Okay, Mum and Dad, chill out on the questions," Ryan says, blushing.

"What?" Fredrik says innocently.

"You're interrogating her!"

"No, it's fine," I say, laughing. "It's actually really nice that anyone is interested."

His parents look a bit confused by my comment, which I let slip without thinking. I try to gloss it over. "My parents aren't fans of my chosen career path, so I'm not used to being asked about it."

I take a mouthful, and as I'm chewing I notice a flicker of sympathy cross Emily's face, so I quickly swallow in order to change the subject.

"So, did Ryan tell you about the rounders match we played at my friend's birthday party? The one where I beat him but he was such a sore loser, he wouldn't admit to it?"

Fredrik throws back his head to laugh, while Emily smiles into her glass.

"This sounds all too familiar," Fredrik tells me. "We rarely play board games because *someone* doesn't take kindly to losing."

"Whoa, whoa, whoa!" Ryan holds up his hands. "Firstly, we don't play board games because Mum always cheats"—Emily gives him a mock-indignant look—"and secondly, Harper, I think you'll find that I got you out fair and square, and if anyone had been watching closely, there would have been no contest over the result."

I gesture to him. "You see what I have to put up with in the office?"

"I don't know how you do it, Harper," Emily says.

"You're a saint." Fredrik nods.

"This is outrageous," Ryan says, as I can't help but giggle. "My team won that rounders match, no question about it."

"If you tell enough people that, Ronan, maybe your local

newspaper will run a story on it," I muse, swirling the wine around my glass.

Ryan sighs, burying his head in his hands.

"I like her," Fredrik laughs, pointing his glass at me. "You can come again."

After dinner, Ryan and I insist on clearing the table and washing up, allowing Fredrik and Emily to head into the sitting room. I laugh as we battle with Sully trying desperately to get to the plates as we load them in the dishwasher, and then Ryan takes charge of washing any pots that won't fit in, while I head up drying duty.

"Sorry about them pelting questions at you," he says quietly when we hear music on in the other room. "I hope it didn't make you uncomfortable."

"Not at all. They're great."

He smiles, passing me a soapy casserole dish. "Yeah, they're all right."

"I feel like I learned a lot about you tonight. The gardening talent came as the biggest surprise." He laughs, and I glance out the windows at the garden now bathed in a dusk blue as the sun sets. "That blossom tree is so beautiful."

"We planted that for Adam," he says.

I turn to look at him. "I'm so sorry, Ryan."

"There's some photos of him in the sitting room, I'll show you."

"Was he similar to you? If you don't mind me asking."

"No, it's nice to talk about him. We were both competitive, but we had very different personalities. He was much sportier than I was, and things came so easy to him. He beat me at everything but books."

"Books?" I ask, putting down the casserole dish.

"Yeah, he wasn't big on reading. Too easily distracted. He preferred being outside, always had to be doing something. That's why when he got sick . . . well, it was just particularly hard seeing him in bed all the time, you know?"

I nod.

"I used to bring him books when he was going through his treatment; I picked ones about sports usually. Sometimes I'd read to him and do all the voices to make him laugh," he says, smiling at the memory. "Even when he was sick, he still managed to remind me that I was a dork."

"He wouldn't have been surprised, then, that you became a dorky journalist."

He laughs. "Not at all."

We share a smile and he passes me the final pot. My fingers brush over his as he hands it to me. Sully gives a loud bark, making us both jump.

When we're finished in the kitchen, we join Emily and Fredrik, who lets me ask him a bunch of questions about his life in Sweden before he moved to England, where he met Emily.

He roars with laughter when I tell him that Ryan pulled the "but I'm Swedish" card to get in on the interview with Max Sjöberg, happily informing me about the time Ryan's cousins, who live in Stockholm, taught Ryan a bunch of very rude Swedish words when he was little. Apparently, Ryan repeated them in front of everyone over dinner, not knowing what he was saying, taking his paternal grandmother by such surprise that the wine she was drinking went right up her nose, prompting her to repeat the very rude words herself.

It gets late and we head upstairs to bed after Fredrik and Emily give me a very warm hug good night. Ryan shows me to the spare room, which is at the end of the landing, right next to his and opposite the bathroom.

"There's a towel there for the morning, and if you need anything else, just say," he tells me, putting his hands in his pockets.

"I think I've got it all, thanks to our handy trip to Boots."

"Good. Oh, I got one of my old T-shirts out for you," he says, nodding to the gray one folded on my pillow. "I know earlier you said there was no point in buying pajamas for one night, but I figured you might want something to sleep in."

"Thanks, Ryan, that's so . . . thoughtful," I say, beaming at him. "And thanks again for letting me stay the night."

"And to think you could have had a lovely evening all to yourself without hearing about tales of my youth. Bet you're glad you took me up on the offer."

"I am, actually."

His expression changes then, his amused smile dropping away into something more serious as our eyes meet. I feel my heart beating faster as silence engulfs the room and we stand in front of one another, trying to work out what's going on.

I suddenly remember something.

"Mae wanted me to put in a good word about her," I blurt out.

He looks confused. "What?"

"Mae, the publicist today? I think she likes you and she's really great, so if you're interested, you should ask for her number tomorrow or whatever, because I think she'd say yes to going on a date," I babble away hurriedly.

He nods slowly. I drop my eyes to the floor.

"Okay, thanks," he says eventually. "Well . . . good night."

"Good night."

Turning to go, he hovers for a moment in the doorway, turning his head to the side slightly, as though he's going to say something, but then thinks better of it.

He shuts the bedroom door firmly behind him.

S everal glasses of wine down on an empty stomach, I suggest that we go back to Ryan's for our next drink.

It's bold and presumptuous, but I'm worried he'll be too shy to make the move, and I've got my mind made up that this is happening. A huge weight has been lifted now that the interview is over and I reckon I deserve a night of fun. We both do. His jaw tenses at my suggestion, and then he nods, croaking that it sounds like a good idea. His nervousness makes me happy, as though it's confirmation he likes me, too.

He had picked a pub that was nearer my parents' than his flat because he was being polite, so we have to take a taxi to his place. We sit in the backseat in silence—both of us just giving ourselves a moment to take in what's happening—until I feel his hand brush against mine. I don't move my hand away, instead threading my fingers through his, and suddenly I'm holding hands with Ryan in the back of a taxi and it's *so cringe*, but because we're drunk, it's okay I guess?

He lives in a big apartment block of flats, and we have to suffer the excruciating bright lights of the shared corridors before getting to his front door, where he fumbles with the key in the lock. He pushes the door open and gestures for me to step in first. It's a small flat but nice, with a spacious lounge and the kitchen area tucked away at the back. It's very obvious that two men live here, as there's not much in way of decoration, but the black IKEA bookcase next to the TV stand has Ryan written all over it—the books are arranged in alphabetical order by author surname.

He offers me a drink, and I ask for a white wine. While he pours a glass, I perch on his sofa, tapping my knees with my hands. He puts on some music and then comes over with the drinks, handing me mine before sitting down next to me. Our knees are angled toward each other, almost touching. Being this close is exhilarating. Which is strange, because I sit next to him every day in the office.

But something has changed now. I fight the ache of wanting to be closer.

"I'm surprised at your choice of music," I admit. "This is actually quite a good song."

He shakes his head in amusement. "I'll try not to be insulted. What kind of music did you think I was into?"

"I don't know. I always pictured you reading serious books and listening to something grown-up, like old jazz, while drinking a Scotch. Maybe smoking a pipe."

He bursts out laughing, that lovely free laugh of his when he forgets to restrain it.

"Basically, what you're saying is, you think of me as someone who hangs out in gentlemen's clubs in the 1950s."

"More like a cool spy, like the ones in those books you like."

He gives me a look. "Are you just trying to make me feel better?"

"I bet my estimation of you is better than how you think of me."

"Really?" He raises his eyebrows.

"You think I'm an airhead who is obsessed with celebrities."

"Wrong," he states simply.

"Fine. You think I'm a smart person who is obsessed with celebrities."

He smiles into his glass.

"Well, I don't care what you think, Ryan Jansson," I continue brazenly. "If you ask me, you need a little more celebrity culture in your life. It's worrying how little you know about anyone in the public eye. I'm *proud* of my cultural knowledge. Ask me any film and I'll be able to tell you which actor starred in it."

"I don't feel the need to test you, Harper, I know that you're—"

"Aaaaaany film! Come on! Any one! The first one you think of!" I insist.

"Okay, okay! Uh . . . um . . . I can't think of any. My mind has gone blank!"

"You can't think of *one* film?"

"It's too much pressure!"

"The first one that pops into your head! Just say it!"

"*Shakespeare in Love!*" he blurts out.

I stare at him. He looks upset with himself.

"Did you say . . . *Shakespeare in Love*?" I check, and press my lips together so as not to laugh in his face.

"You put me under too much pressure and it was the first film that came to mind."

"Uh-huh."

"My mind went blank."

"Nothing to be ashamed of, Ryan. I'm a big fan myself."

"I didn't say I was a *big fan* of it. It was the only film I could think of."

"Excellent performances by Joseph and Gwyneth."

"You're judging me."

"I swear I'm not."

"I can tell when you're lying."

"No, you can't."

"I can," he insists, before letting out a sigh. "Anyway, your point is proven: you have excellent cultural knowledge."

"And you have proven you have a . . . fascinating taste in film."

"Here we go." He shakes his head, before offering me a small smile. "Just so you know, I don't think of you how you think I think of you."

I frown at him. "I've had too many drinks to decipher that sentence. Start again."

"You're wrong about how I think of you."

"Yeah? Then tell me, Ryan, how do you think of me?" I ask innocently, taking a sip of my wine.

He doesn't say anything. He just looks at me.

I freeze, completely under the spell of his unflinching gaze.

He puts his drink down on the coffee table and then reaches over to take my glass before setting that down next to his. It's such a simple but sexy move, him taking control of the situation. Up until now—the suggestion to go back to his, the fingers entwining in the taxi—I've been leading the charge. But now, the way he's looking at me, it's different than before. There's a *want* there.

I smile so he knows. *I want you, too.*

He leans forward and I close my eyes as he presses his lips against mine, kissing him back hungrily. We fall back onto the cushions and I wrap my arms around his neck as his hands drift down my sides to my waist. My heart is pounding as I move my hands to the front of his chest, fumbling at his shirt buttons, desperate to feel his bare skin underneath.

He stops my hands with his, lifting his face to hover over mine and smiling, before rolling off the sofa onto his feet, straightening and holding his hand out to me. A little confused at the pause in proceedings, I take his hand and he pulls me up to stand with him, steadying me as I stumble, before leading me through a door off the lounge and into a bedroom.

I want to look around his room properly, but I want him more.

As soon as Ryan turns to face me again, I step toward him, tugging at his shirt as his hand brushes my hair out of my face. He kisses me again, crushing our lips together, and I'm so turned on I can barely breathe. His hands lower to my waist and then slide to the top of my back where he finds the zip of my dress, pulling it down so I can slip out of it as it crumples onto the floor. I frantically attempt to undo the buttons of his shirt, but they seem impossible, my fingers are shaking from exhilaration. I feel Ryan smile against my lips as his fingers take over from mine, whipping his shirt off in a matter of seconds.

As we hastily remove the rest of our clothes, we move unsteadily toward the bed, and when the back of my knees hit the mattress, I fall back onto the navy duvet, pulling Ryan down on top of me. As he presses his body against mine, I lift my hips up into his, and he pauses. For a moment I feel frozen with fear that he's realized this is a mistake.

Instead, he whispers against my lips, "I've wanted this since the moment I saw you," and kisses me so deeply, I shudder in frenzied anticipation.

We spend the weekend in a bubble of blissful happiness. I don't know what's gotten into me, but I devote myself to the role of heroine in a rom-com, walking around his flat in just my knickers and his shirt, nuzzling into his neck while he strokes my hair and kisses my forehead, spontaneously having sex at three o'clock in the afternoon without a care in the world for anything else but each other.

It's surreal, a fleeting fantasy that I know has to end come Monday morning when we're obligated to go to work, but for now it's perfect. When I first woke up on Saturday morning, naked and slightly hungover, I got the classic wave of anxiety and fear, terrified that it might be awkward, but as soon as Ryan stirred and kissed all the way along my shoulder, I relaxed.

It was he who suggested we stay together for the weekend,

and when I mentioned that I had no spare clothes, he said no problem, we could go back to my parents' in a taxi and he'd wait in the car while I ran up and packed a bag.

"Unless that sounds much too intense, which I totally understand if it does," he had said hurriedly, trying to read my expression.

It *was* intense. To sleep with a colleague after a boozy night was one thing, but to then pop back home to pack a *weekend bag* sounded utterly absurd and the actions of a love-drunk, horny teenager. But to be honest, that's how I felt. Ryan had somehow opened this Pandora's Box of suppressed feelings—I'd spent two months fighting with this guy and going out of my way to annoy him, and now, I couldn't get enough of him.

So I went with it: he waited downstairs while I packed a bag and told Mum I was spending the weekend at a friend's, not that she seemed to care. She hadn't even noticed I'd been gone all night, assuming I'd gotten back late after they went to bed. When I shut the front door of the house and hopped into the backseat of the taxi, his eyes lit up and he leaned over and kissed me, as though he'd been wondering whether I really was going to return.

It's a magical weekend; too perfect to be true. I lie next to him under the duvet, studying his face, his long eyelashes, his faint stubble, the way his throat moves as he answers all the questions I ask about him, wondering how I've spent two months next to this man and not really appreciated how mesmerizing he is.

"By the way, what did you mean last night when you said you'd wanted this since you saw me?" I press when we get onto the topic of the office, laughing at our spats.

"I meant exactly that," he replies, turning on his side to face me.

"But how? I mean, it's hard to believe. I got my hairbrush stuck in my hair in the first five minutes of meeting you."

He chuckles, reaching over to run his thumb along my cheek-bone. "I promise you, it's true."

"Why didn't you say anything?"

"Because it was obvious you didn't like me."

"I didn't *not* like you!"

He looks at me skeptically.

"Okay, maybe I *thought* I didn't like you, but only because you were so rude to me at first. I thought I was just making the feeling mutual."

"How was I rude?" he asks, confused.

"You looked so disappointed that I was interning with you, and then you said something about us maybe being in different departments. I knew straightaway you thought I didn't deserve to be there."

His brow furrows. "Okay, I can see how that could be mis-leading, but I promise that's not what I was thinking. I was worried that I'd be working with someone so distractingly pretty," he explains.

"Yeah right!"

"I swear!"

"Ryan, there is no way that you were thinking that."

"Harper, look where we are now," he says, moving his face closer to mine so our noses are almost touching. "Like I said, I've wanted this from that first moment. Which wasn't ideal when I knew I had to focus and do really well at this internship if I was going to get a job at the end of it. Trust me, trying to keep my distance from you has been torture."

I want to believe him because it's so lovely.

"Well, you managed it up until now," I say with a smile, ex-haling and turning onto my back to stare up at the ceiling. "And I guess we'll find out soon enough if that focus landed you the job. It's going to be weird, isn't it?"

"What do you mean?"

"Going back to the office after this weekend. Finding out whether one of us got the job; the other one having to pack up and leave when the internship ends on Wednesday."

"Yeah," he says, his voice low and sad.

"My parents are going to be so smug if I don't get the job. I'm not sure I'll be able to face them. They'll be unbearable."

"What are your parents like?" he asks curiously.

I hesitate. I was ready to change the topic, like I always do, but something stops me and for the first time in forever, I feel like telling the truth. Maybe it's because he's already been so vulnerable: he told me about his brother and that he wanted me from the moment we met.

Maybe it was his excited expression when I got back in the taxi at my parents' house.

Maybe it's the way he's looking at me now.

Whatever it is, it makes me trust him. So, I tell him everything. He patiently listens, his brow furrowed, first in concentration, and then sadness and sympathy. When I conclude, telling him that I want this job so that I can show them that they're wrong, he doesn't do that annoying thing that people have done before and say he's sure my parents are secretly proud of me deep down or anything like that.

Instead, he props his head up on his elbow.

"Screw your parents," he says. "Want this job for yourself. Not for them. They don't deserve any credit for what you achieve."

In that moment, I'm glad I told him the truth.

And I don't tell Ryan this, but I feel a wave of excitement for what might happen between us; what the future might hold. Because I know that this man is special and I'm not sure I'll ever want to give him up.

CHAPTER FIFTEEN

I hardly sleep a wink that night at Ryan's parents' house. I can't stop thinking about kissing him, the idea sending such a thrill through me that I toss and turn. I wish I could forget how he was looking at me before we said good night, or the fact that he's just on the other side of this wall. At the same time, all I want to do is think about him, my stomach churning with butterflies.

I let myself remember what it was like, lying next to him in bed, feeling his strong arms wrapped around me, nuzzling his neck and smelling his skin as he held me close, safe and warm in our perfect bubble. I remember his face so close to mine on the pillow that our noses were touching and how he'd looked at me so intensely before cracking a smile, the crinkles appearing around the corners of his lips.

It may have been a long time ago, but those are details I've never forgotten, no matter how hard I've tried to.

Then the guilt sets in: Liam. I didn't even text him good night after climbing into bed. I haven't spoken to him all day and he's my *boyfriend*. We didn't make plans for the evening—I wasn't sure what time I'd be back in London from the interview, and I didn't want him hanging around waiting—but I probably should have at least messaged to say I was staying in Manchester until tomorrow. I feel like a terrible person until I consider that he hasn't messaged me all day, either. In fact, he never replied after I said he couldn't come on my work trip to Florence, which seems a little odd. But it's still no excuse for fantasizing about another guy—and not just any guy, but someone I work with. Someone I have history with. It's not fair to Liam.

I'm suddenly hit with anxiety at the idea of falling for Ryan *again*. I can try with all my might to pretend that that I don't have feelings for him, but I do. I know I do. Even though we fight all the time, even though he pisses me off to no end, even though we're so different, I'm drawn to him. *Again.* Having a crush on a colleague is never a good idea, not to mention the fact you'd think I'd avoid making the same mistakes, but here I am, under the spell of those eyes eleven years down the line.

He seems different now, though, I tell myself. Maybe I can forgive him for what happened and move on. It's a little embarrassing that I haven't already.

I mean, he bought me honey for my tea.

Bad people don't do that, do they?

God, I feel *sick* when I think about him asking Mae for her number tomorrow. I have no right to care about Ryan's dating life! But I do, I do, I do.

And you know what doesn't help the situation? That I'm wearing Ryan's T-shirt. I clutch the material in my fingers like a teenager wearing their boyfriend's hoodie at a house party.

He belongs to me.

But the truth is, he doesn't. He never has.

⌐━━━━━

The minute my alarm goes off in the morning, I send Liam a message asking how his day was yesterday and apologizing for being MIA. I explain that I had to stay in Manchester last minute and then ask if we can meet tonight for dinner.

We can have the talk then. I'm geared up for it, confident in my decision and only sorry to hurt Liam, who I'm worried will be caught off guard. When he sends a cheery reply back that he can't do tonight as he's working on some things with Halo Skewed, I'm deflated and disappointed that I'll have to wait any longer to break things off.

Grabbing the towel folded on top of the stool of the dressing table, I open my bedroom door at the same time as Ryan opens his. We both freeze. He's only wearing his boxers, his broad shoulders, toned arms, and sculpted abs on full display.

Why is this guy in a job where he has to wear clothes?!

What a bloody waste.

I feel incensed on behalf of swimwear brands everywhere.

His hair ruffled from sleep, he blinks at me with tired eyes before his lips twist up into a dozy smile.

"Morning," he says.

I try to say "Hi," but his appearance has made my mouth incredibly dry, so it sort of comes out as some kind of croak, like that of a toad.

Sexy.

I quickly clear my throat. "Sorry, hi. Hello. Morning."

"You use the bathroom first. I'll go in after you."

"No, you can use it first. I'm happy to wait."

He gestures to the bathroom door. "I insist. Let me know if you have any trouble with working the shower. It's pretty straight-forward, though."

"Great, thanks."

He turns round to go back into his room, and I find myself admiring his back, his smooth muscled shoulders, the indent of his spine. As his door shuts, I give myself a shake and try to Get. A. Grip.

Once I'm ready, wearing my newly purchased red Zara shirt and the same tapered trousers I was wearing yesterday, I head downstairs, where Sully jumps up all over me and Fredrik greets me so jovially I can't help but laugh, taken aback at how welcoming this house is. He desperately tries to get me to eat breakfast, and I have to repeat several times that I'm really just a coffee person in the mornings. When it's time to go, I crouch down on the floor to say goodbye to Sully and promptly receive a scolding from Emily that I'm going to get hair all over my trousers. Before Ryan and I head out the door to the car, Fredrik hugs me and tells me to look after myself.

"I hope we'll see you again soon," Emily says as she gives me a kiss on the cheek, and something about her voice makes me think she really does mean it.

But maybe that's just twisted wishful thinking this morning, because I'm still affected from wearing Ryan's T-shirt and seeing him topless?

As we drive to the set, I sit nervously in the passenger seat, trying my best to act normally, but irrationally terrified that Ryan can read my mind. He seems fine, pointing out things about Manchester that might interest me and wondering aloud what time we'll get to speak to Max this morning.

"I've also been thinking—do you want to come back with me afterward?"

I spin my head round so fast I almost give myself a neck injury.

"As in, I could drive you back to London if you wanted," he explains. "Rather than you getting the train. I'm heading to Finsbury Park, so you'll be able to get on the Victoria Line train all the way down to Brixton. I'd feel guilty having you wait around to get the train when I'm driving that way anyway. And I'll let you choose one or two songs we can listen to on the journey, if you like."

I smile down at my hands in my lap. "Very generous. Uh . . . okay then, I guess it would be handy just to jump in the car with you when we finish up. As long as you're sure."

Of course, I should have said no. I don't know why I'm putting myself through more torture, accepting an invitation like this. Plus, if he does end up getting Mae's number, he might want to talk about that on the journey home, and I'll have to listen. I need to go back to thinking about him as my irritating work nemesis.

"Are you okay?" he asks as we pull into a parking space.

"Yes," I reply, flustered. "Why wouldn't I be?"

"You have the . . . you look tense."

"You were going to say I have the crinkle, weren't you?"

He laughs, putting on the handbrake and turning the engine off. "Seriously, are you all right? You've been very quiet. My parents didn't freak you out, did they? I know they can be a lot."

"No! No, they're wonderful," I tell him sincerely. "You have an amazing family."

"Good. Are you worried about the feature?"

I blink at him. "Huh?"

"Max Sjöberg."

"Oh! Yes, that's it. I'm worried about the interview."

"No need to be," he assures me, undoing his seatbelt and opening the car door. "You take the lead on it. I won't get in your way."

I lean back on the headrest and close my eyes for a moment, wishing my head and heart weren't such a mess, before forcing myself into work mode, hopping out of the car ready to sit down with a brilliant actor.

Unfortunately, my zest for the interview is a tad premature— Max has another busy day of filming lined up, and Mae is doing her best to work out a time to squeeze us in. We don't get our hands on him until the afternoon, and by then he's exhausted and grouchy. Sitting in a trailer in costume, he leans back, his elbows resting on the arms of his chair. He watches me suspiciously while I press the Record button on my digital voice recorder and flip through my notebook to a blank page.

"How long will this take?" he asks gruffly, looking toward

Mae, who is lingering in the doorway. Next to me, Ryan shifts his weight uncomfortably.

But I'm not fazed by his attitude. I get this all the time.

"We won't take up much of your time," I promise confidently. "These filming days get long, don't they? But they can't be as long as the ones you had to do on the set of *Ambition*."

He raises his eyebrows in pleasant surprise. "Now, that was a long time ago."

"Didn't you have to film all through the night, like three days in a row?"

"Four days in a row," he corrects, stroking his chin as he thinks back on it. "Not easy for a kid of ten years old."

"I read that you fell asleep under a pile of coats waiting for your scene."

"And got sat on by the late, great Bill Olin," he chuckles, his expression softening. "He was a fine actor, but I still wouldn't recommend getting sat on by your heroes."

"Sage advice."

He smiles warmly at me. "I haven't thought about that film in a while."

"I watched it recently."

"Yes?"

"It's still so relevant."

"Hmm." He nods. "Well, when you get a great writer like Margit, then the work tends to resonate through generations; the themes about heartbreak and how cruel it can feel that life simply goes on after losing someone . . . the world around us may change, but these experiences are common ground for all. You can go back centuries and the art then, it reflects the same emotions of the art produced now. It's amazing, really, how little people have changed. We are all connected."

"*Blue Lights* plays on that, doesn't it? The past connecting with the present."

"Yes, I think you're right. But again, it's the writing of the show that is its strength—the investigation drives the plot, but surrounding it you have these compelling narratives: the families affected by the murders, their grief and desperation for answers, the tangled relationships, and the wider repercussions of each individual decision. I think so many projects now are too heavily wrapped up in CGI and special effects, and some of them are very good, but really, what still resonates with an audience is a story that focuses on people."

I glance up as I scribble notes. "The writing is very important to you, then."

"Unbelievably so. I have the luxury of being able to choose which projects I want to do, and I only accept the ones where the writing grips me. That's the bare bones."

"And your own writing?"

He looks at me suspiciously. "My own writing?"

"I'm just curious as to whether you'd be tempted to write something yourself. You have mentioned before that it's something you've thought about."

He breaks into a small smile. "You've done your research. I can't remember talking about that to the press recently."

"I remember things that interest me—you said it in an interview with GQ once."

"Did I? Well, I suppose I can admit that I've done a bit more than think about it. I'm currently writing a drama set in Stockholm."

"And I can mention that in the piece?" I ask excitedly.

"Yes, although the reaction to it terrifies me."

I'm surprised at this admission. "Really?"

"There's something more vulnerable about writing than acting, I find," he explains. "There's no pretense. You're putting your soul laid bare on the page. But I've enjoyed the process.

The research around Stockholm was interesting, and I learned a lot about my hometown."

"Ah, well, I have never been to Stockholm, but my colleague here is half-Swedish, and his family lives there," I say, gesturing to Ryan.

"Is that so?" Max says, his eyes lighting up as he turns his attention to Ryan. "You should have said! Tell me, whereabouts do they live?"

The journey home is nowhere near as excruciating as I imagined because both Ryan and I are on a high over how well the interview went. We got way more content than we're going to need—Mae even had to politely interrupt to say our time was up and Max was needed back on set, which he actually looked a little disappointed about. We parted ways with him telling me it was an absolute pleasure and reminding Ryan to pass along those Stockholm restaurant recommendations he gave him.

"I can't believe how long you talked about Stockholm," I laugh as we zip down the M6 back toward London. "I thought we'd be there all day."

"Time flies when you're having fun." He grins. "When Max Sjöberg is animated, you do not cut him off."

"Totally agree. And anyway, it's brilliant for the piece. He was so passionate. I have to admit, I'm glad you were there—he came alive when he was speaking to you about home."

"Hang on. Are you admitting that my suggestion that we write the piece together was a good one? Is that what you're saying, Harper Jenkins?"

"I'm saying it *might* be. Don't get all cocky about it."

"I wouldn't dream of it." He smiles mischievously, glancing at me before returning his eyes to the road ahead. "Anyway, I can't take credit for his good mood. That was all you. The way you put him at ease right away, without him even realizing what you were doing? Masterful."

"I was simply having a conversation."

"Seriously, Harper, it's amazing. I feel honored I got to see you in action."

"Likewise," I say warmly.

He seems pleased. "So, do you want to plot the structure of the article and then you could maybe send that document over and we can work out how to get writing—"

"Whoa, whoa," I interrupt. "What do you mean 'plot the structure'? What document are you talking about?"

He gives me a strange look. "You know, you plot out an article before you write it."

I snort. "Who does that?"

"*Everyone?*" he answers, baffled.

"I don't," I inform him proudly.

"How can you possibly write a piece without working out the structure first?"

"Easy. You start writing and go from there."

I enjoy watching him struggle to comprehend this approach, his mouth opening and closing, his eyebrows knitted together.

"Hang on," he says, tapping a finger on the steering wheel. "You just launch into writing? Without planning it out . . . *at all?*"

"It's not that big of a deal," I laugh, resting my elbow on the side of the door.

"How do you know where all the quotes are going to go?" he asks, sounding almost panicked. "How do you know it will flow nicely? How do you make sure you don't repeat yourself? How do you know where it will start and how it will end?"

I shrug. "I don't know. I start writing and . . . go with it."

"*Go with it*," he repeats, bewildered. "But your first draft must be . . . a complete jumble!"

"Usually, yes," I admit. "It's all over the shop. But then I re-write it."

"So wouldn't it save you a lot of time and hassle if you plotted it out first?"

"It would stifle the creativity of my writing," I insist with a flourish of my hands. "If I structured it first, my sentences would be all forced and stilted. Better to let it flow onto the page and then sort it out later."

He shakes his head, looking completely thrown by this revelation.

"We all have a different process, Ryan," I remind him, chuckling at his expression.

"I guess we do," he admits.

"You should already be well-versed with mine. As you said, it's not the first time we've written a piece together."

He runs a hand through his hair before cracking a smile. "I must have forced myself to forget the trauma of witnessing your process the last time."

I laugh and we fall into comfortable silence. I check my phone, scrolling through some work emails that I missed yesterday and replying to Mimi's WhatsApps asking me how the interview went and whether Ryan and I have killed each other yet.

"Do you want to have a drink at mine?" Ryan suddenly asks.

I jerk my head up from my phone. "Sorry?"

"When we get back to London," he says, looking straight ahead, his brow furrowed. "It's been a long couple of days for both of us, and I don't know about you, but I could really use a drink. I think we've earned it."

I feel my heart soar. "I guess we have."

"I have a really nice wine in the fridge that one of my pretentious friends bought me last time he came for dinner. We could crack that open, if you fancy it," he says hurriedly, looking a little flustered. "My flat is near to the station, so easy for you to get home. Or we could go to the pub if you'd rather? Or, you may actually have plans because it's a Saturday night and why wouldn't you? You can tell me to shut up at any point."

"I don't have any plans," I say, laughing. "And a pretentious bottle of wine sounds right up my street. Thanks."

He nods, smiling at my response, the lines on his forehead fading, and a flurry of tingles runs through my entire body. I turn away to look out the window, my jaw aching from trying not to grin ear to ear.

God, I'm having that dizzying rush of adrenaline you get when the person you like shows signs of liking you back and you let your imagination run wild, picturing them pulling you close and kissing you. My face grows hot, and I rub the back of my neck, forcing myself to remember that this is just a drink. It doesn't mean anything.

It's quite a long drive back to London, and by the time Ryan parks near his flat, I'm happy to jump out and stretch, thanking him for the lift. He notices my look of surprise when he leads me to a Victorian house, getting out his keys.

"What?" he says, pushing through the gate and holding it open for me.

"It sounds stupid, but I pictured you in a big apartment block."

He hesitates before offering a shy smile. "That's not stupid—I used to live in one, back when we . . . first met. Remember?"

"Yes," I say, blushing. "I remember."

"I moved here a couple of years ago."

He slides the key into the front door and heads into a shared hallway, ushering me in and picking up some of the post on the floor addressed to him, before unlocking the door on the right. There's one other door straight ahead.

"This is just two flats, then?" I ask.

"Yeah, I'm the ground floor and then a guy in his twenties lives in the flat above. He's great—a real computer geek. He works for Apple. Very handy whenever I have any technical problems."

He swings open the door and gestures for me to go in ahead. I step inside and am immediately struck by how spacious and tidy it is. Considering the traditional Victorian exterior, it's very modern, renovated so that the kitchen and living room are open plan, with smart wooden flooring and amazing floor-to-ceiling windows at the back that look onto a small garden.

A light gray corner sofa faces a wide flat-screen TV hanging on the wall above a fireplace that's been painted dark gray, and there's a glass coffee table in the middle with an unused three-wick white candle set perfectly in the center of it. Either side of the TV, the walls are lined with shelves of books—and on closer inspection I notice that the books are in alphabetical order according to the author's surname.

"Some things don't change," I murmur under my breath as Ryan goes straight to the fridge.

"What was that?"

"Nothing!" I reply, scanning the shelves. "This place is amazing."

"Yeah, I got lucky. It belongs to a friend of mine from uni, who moved to New York to set up a new office for his company. He lets me pay mate rates. There's no way I could afford this on a journalist's salary. The location is great, too."

"It really is. And you keep it *very* tidy."

He chuckles. "You've met my dad, so you know where I get it from now. Let me guess, your flat is a little more . . . chaotic?"

"It's *creative*."

"Much like your desk."

I tear my eyes away from the books with the intention of following him into the kitchen, where he's pouring the wine, when something catches my eye: a framed newspaper article hanging on the opposite wall near the door. I don't know how I missed it when I first came in; I was distracted by the big open space, I suppose. But I recognize it straightaway.

"Oh my god!" I exclaim, breaking into a grin as I get up close to admire it. "Ryan!"

"Oh yeah. That," he says sheepishly, strolling over and placing the two glasses of wine down on the coffee table before coming to stand next to me.

"I can't believe you still have this. And you got it framed!"

He shrugs. "Yeah, well. It was my first-ever article in a paper. My first-ever byline."

"Mine too."

"I know."

Side by side, we gaze at the framed *Daily Bulletin* article that was published in 2012. It's been a long time since I've seen it, but there it is, the first time Ryan and I ever had our names in print:

THE BEST PICNIC SPOTS IN LONDON
Compiled by Harper Jenkins and Ryan Jansson

The day this article was published was, I suppose, the day Ryan and I officially became journalists. And it was the day that everything between us fell apart.

The last day of the internship is Wednesday and that's the day I'm called to Martha's office. We only interviewed on Friday, but it's felt like a *very* long wait to find out whether or not we've got the job, which Martha acknowledges as soon as she's told me that I didn't get it.

"And I'm sorry that it's taken this long to tell you, but I wanted to do it in person because you've been such a great intern and I've been away on a press trip. An email seemed too impersonal," she says, her hands clasped together in front of her on the desk. "I want to reiterate, Harper, that you have been a fantastic addition to the team and I have no doubt that you will make it in this industry. But in this instance, we felt Ryan was just that bit better suited to the role."

I nod. "I understand."

"I promise you I will give you a glowing reference. We're going to miss your sunshiny personality around here!"

"Thanks," I say, managing a smile. "And thank you for the opportunity."

I leave her office, distraught but determined to be happy for Ryan. I know that if it was the other way round, he'd do the same for me. He deserves this job, maybe more than I do, and he's going to be brilliant at it. I can't resent him for that. I don't want to resent him for that. I don't know what we are yet, but we seem to be *something*. For the last couple of days, he's been grabbing me for secret kisses in the kitchen when no one's looking, sending me flirtatious messages while sitting right next to me, and making me honey tea each afternoon at exactly three o'clock. Every morning I've been waking up excited to see him.

It's both strange and wonderful how quickly and easily I've allowed myself to be completely consumed by my feelings for him.

I decide to go straight over to congratulate him. He was called to Martha's office right before me, so he'll know I didn't get the job, and, no matter how happy he is that he's got it, I'm sure he'll be worrying about my reaction.

Before I get over to our desks, Celia catches me on her way to the kitchen and insists I join her, looping her arm through mine.

"I'm so sorry, Harper, I really was rooting for you," she says, stopping by the kettle and giving me a hug. "If it was up to me, you would have been the clear winner."

"Thanks, Celia. That means a lot."

"If anything comes up at *Flair*, I'll be in touch, okay?"

I smile, reaching for her hand and squeezing it. "That's so kind of you, thanks."

She sighs. "If you want my personal opinion—and I'm only saying this because we're both leaving—I think Martha should have taken a bit more time with the decision-making process, you know? It's like she made a snap decision, and I'm sure it will bite her in the arse. She's going to regret not keeping you on."

"Thanks, but it wasn't exactly a snap decision," I point out. "It took her almost five days to tell us."

"No, she told Ryan on Friday evening, like half an hour after your interview," she informs me, rolling her eyes. "Although, I do have some good news for you. Have you seen the paper today? Your picnic piece is in there! So that's something. Your first by-line! Exciting, right?"

I freeze. She must be mistaken. Ryan couldn't have known this whole time. He couldn't have. It would be too . . . *humiliating.* She must have gotten that wrong.

Leaving Celia in the kitchen, I walk toward our desks, slowly at first, but then I break into a determined march, desperate to hear Ryan deny what she's just told me. He looks up from his screen as I appear next to him and looks pained.

"Harper—"

"Did you find out on Friday?"

He blinks at me, taken by surprise. "W-what?"

"Did you find out about the job on Friday, Ryan?"

His eyes drop to the floor. He doesn't say anything. He doesn't have to. I know what that means. I turn on my heel and walk away from him, overwhelmed by the need to get out of that building.

"Harper, wait," he says, hurrying to keep up with me as we pass the reporters too busy with their stories to notice another spat between the interns. I don't bother to wait for the elevator, not wanting to be in such close quarters with him, so I race down the stairs, bursting into the lobby and through the swivel doors out into the cold where it's started to drizzle.

"Harper," I hear him call out behind me as I quickly wipe the tears from my cheeks, "please listen to me. I couldn't tell you—"

"You lied to me. This whole time, you lied. Do you know how mortifying this is? How embarrassed I feel right now? I was lying in your bed talking about how much the job meant to me and . . . the whole time you *knew.*"

"I'm so sorry," he says, desperately trying to grab my hand as I recoil from him. "I'm sorry. She called me on Friday night, and I knew if I told you, you wouldn't want to spend time with me. And we were finally having fun together. If I'd said anything, you would have left that pub straightaway, I know it."

"Oh my god, that phone call you got at the pub." I push my damp hair away from my eyes as it starts sticking to my forehead from the rain. "You knew then, before we'd even ordered our drinks."

"Please forgive me, Harper, she told me not to say anything, that she wanted to tell you herself. It was horrible keeping this from you, but I—"

"You spent the whole weekend lying."

"No!"

"I told you things that I . . . oh my god, I'm such an idiot."

"No, Harper, please," he says, his voice cracking. "I didn't want to ruin everything."

"Everything *is* ruined, Ryan. I trusted you. I was wrong."

I leave him outside in the rain and go back inside. It's almost the end of the day, so I pull myself together in the loos to say my goodbyes to the team, laughing at and apologizing for my bedraggled look as I explain I was caught in the rain on the hunt for a decent coffee. Then, without looking Ryan in the eye, I pack up my things at my desk. He lurks miserably nearby the whole time, any attempt to talk to me ignored. But with everyone watching, I muster the spoonful of professionalism I have left to hold out my hand to him.

"Good luck, Ryan. The team is lucky to have someone so hardworking and *honest* joining them permanently. Exactly what a good journalist should be."

Visibly stung, he shakes my hand dismally.

With a final wave, I walk out of *The Daily Bulletin* for the last time. As soon as I'm alone in the elevator, I get out my phone and block Ryan's number.

With any luck, I'll never see him again.

CHAPTER SIXTEEN

I stare at the article on Ryan's wall, lost in a haze of memories. I've spent the last eleven years convinced that Ryan's betrayal proved that he was sneaky and conniving. But standing here, I'm realizing that we were just kids. Both of us were stumbling through the murky bit of real life that comes straight at you the minute you leave school or university—the moment where, suddenly, you're on your own. We were trying to find our footing. When I think about it, I loved my experience at *The Daily Bulletin,* and I'm grateful that I eventually ended up at *Flair,* where I met Mimi and discovered that my interest in pop culture and celebrity could actually become my calling card. I'm glad things happened how they did.

I don't want to be mad at Ryan anymore. I want . . .

"You're smiling," Ryan remarks, interrupting my thoughts. I realize that he's been watching me with an expression of concern.

"I'm remembering," I inform him, nodding to the article.

"I wouldn't have thought that would make you smile."

"You thought wrong, then. Who wouldn't have fond memories of photocopying and hours of transcribing?"

He relaxes, a small laugh emitting from his lips. "God, the transcribing. It really is one of the worst parts of our job."

"Which is why you'll be doing it for our Max Sjöberg interview," I say, prompting him to give me a look that says, *Nice try.* "Do you remember visiting all the picnic spots?"

"I'll never forget it. I was so nervous."

"Why?"

"Because I was going to be spending a whole day with you outside of work, and I didn't really know how to be around you," he admits coolly. "You weren't my biggest fan."

"We were in competition with each other for the job, and you were infuriating in the office." I pause, adding with a mischievous smile, "Which hasn't really changed."

"*I'm* the infuriating one? Have you *seen* your desk?"

"Ryan, you're a broken record. You have got to care less about the state of my desk."

"I have to look on it every single day. You have no idea how much it stresses me out."

"I know *exactly* how much it stresses you out," I retort cheerily. "It's written all over your face whenever you sit down."

"And here I was thinking I was hard to read."

"Not to me."

He pauses, those ocean-blue eyes fixed on me, his expression softening and making a swarm of butterflies flutter in my stomach. I swallow, nervous under his intense gaze, the heat rising in my cheeks.

"What was it like in the office after I left?" I manage to ask, trying to keep things light. "It must have been nice for everyone to get the coffees they actually ordered."

"It would have been, but the interns who came in after us were shit."

I burst out laughing at his bluntness.

"Neither of them had anything like our drive," he continues, a playful smile on his lips as he enjoys my reaction. "The problem was they actually got on well, so there was no motivation for them to beat the other one. They were slow with the research I assigned to them, took their time on the coffee runs, and talk about sloppy transcribing. The number of typos was laughable."

"I suppose we did motivate each other. I should thank you for that—Celia never would have contacted me later to offer me the interview at *Flair* if I'd been a half-assed intern under her watch at *The Daily Bulletin*."

"I don't think you have it in you to be half-assed at anything," Ryan comments. "Except punctuality, which you fully dedicate yourself to being terrible at, so I suppose that doesn't count."

I chuckle. "I mean it, though, Ryan. I know us going up against each other for that job wasn't ideal, but in the end it was for the best that I didn't get it. I wasn't meant to be a reporter at *The Daily Bulletin*. I was much more at home at a magazine like *Flair*."

He nods, saying quietly, "I felt so terrible when you left."

I get a stab of guilt at his sincerity.

"You must have hated me," he adds.

"I was angry at the situation," I say quickly, not wanting to linger on the topic, because in all honesty, I did hate him at the time. "Maybe if I'd had a better relationship with my parents . . . Going home to them after was painful. Those next few weeks were pretty bad—I was so desperate to move out, but the job at the bar paid so little, and I knew I was lucky to have parents living in a house in London where I could stay. When Celia called, I cried with happiness. As soon as I was on the payroll, I moved to the other side of London, away from them. It all worked out in the end!" I smile up at him.

"I went to your parents' house," he says quietly.

"When?"

"A couple of days after you left *The Daily Bulletin*. I thought I'd give you some time to cool off, then try to get you to talk to me," he admits. "But I couldn't bring myself to ring that bloody doorbell. As usual, I didn't have the confidence."

His throat bobs as he swallows.

I stare at him, stunned by this admission. "I can't believe you came to the house."

"I didn't linger like a weird stalker or anything, I promise."

"No, it's not . . . I wasn't thinking that," I stammer. "I'm just surprised you bothered."

He frowns. "What makes you say that?"

"I don't know. I assumed you forgot all about me the second I was gone."

He blinks at me. "Harper, are you being serious?"

"Well, you got the job we both wanted and what happened between us . . . it was a fling," I say with a wave of my hand. "I figured that you were focused on your career and that weekend was a blip. God, I was so panicked when you got that job at *The Correspondence*. Did you know when you started there that I was the celebrity editor at *Narrative*?"

He nods, his eyes fixed on me. "Yeah, I did."

"Well, at least you were prepared to bump into me, then. Must have been nice to have some warning," I laugh nervously. "When I spotted you in the newsroom, I didn't know what to do with myself. At first, I wasn't sure if you'd remember me, and then when I realized you did, I thought it was easier to pretend we'd never met. Save ourselves the embarrassment of . . . well, thinking back to that time and everything that had happened."

"Harper," he groans, running a hand through his hair, "when you say stuff like that, it makes me . . . you thought that I might not *remember* you?"

"I suppose we did sit next to each other for eight weeks," I admit.

His jaw tenses and he doesn't say anything, breathing in deeply through his nose as though he's steadying himself. He turns, taking a few paces away from me deep in thought before stopping still and spinning back to address me, his brow furrowed in what looks like a mixture of confusion and frustration.

"You honestly thought there was a chance I would have . . . *forgotten*?" he asks in disbelief, his cheeks flushed in anger.

I'm taken aback by the sudden change in his demeanor, staring at him, startled.

"It was a long time ago," I stammer. "Okay, so maybe I knew that you'd probably recognize me, but it wasn't like it was a big thing that happened between us. It was just one weekend, it's not like it was—" I search for the words, waving my hands through the air "—a *grand* affair. You know, I was just a fellow intern with you. A lot's happened since then; you might not have been able to place me."

He throws his head back and lets out a *"Ha,"* exasperation flooding his features.

"A fellow intern," he repeats breathlessly, shaking his head as he paces back and forth in front of me, as though I'm not even there and he's talking to himself. "That's what you thought I saw you as. Just a fellow intern."

"Ryan," I begin, baffled by his agitated behavior, "what's—"

"I was crazy about you," he interrupts, his eyes flashing at me as he stops short.

My breath catches in my throat.

"I was *crazy about you,*" he emphasizes again, loudly and urgently, as though he can't hold it in any longer. "I told you. Right from the moment we met, I was—" He throws his hands up, flustered as he searches for the right words. He sighs, lowering his voice. "That weekend eleven years ago, what happened between us, it was what I'd been waiting for that whole summer. I was such an idiot to lie to you, Harper. But I wanted you so badly and I knew that you wouldn't go for that drink with me . . . not if you knew I had the job."

He pauses, eyes closing, as if the memory pains him. "God, it was so shit. I tried to explain it to you the day you left, but you didn't want to hear it. You have no idea what it was like without you in that office once you'd left. I couldn't bear the idea that you were out there, hating me. I kept trying to call and message you—"

"I blocked you," I whisper.

"I knew that." He looks dejected. "I knew how much I'd fucked up. I'd lost the only person I'd ever really . . ."

I wait for him to finish his sentence, but he doesn't, his eyes moving back to the framed article on the wall. He looks lost for a moment.

"You'd ever really what?" I prompt gently.

He sighs, but doesn't say anything.

I can't help myself. I reach out and brush my fingers against his so that he'll look at me again, and when he does, his forehead creases and his eyes search mine.

Ever so slightly, I tilt my head up toward his.

It's the permission he needs.

His fingers sweep softly along my cheekbone before cupping my face as he moves to close the gap between us, bowing his head, his eyelashes lowering as his nose softly nudges the side of mine. My lips part and as he brushes his lips against mine, I close my eyes, my hands reaching round the back of his neck as his slide down to my waist, pulling me closer to him. He presses his mouth to mine, soft and tentative at first as though to savor it, but I kiss him back harder, and he immediately reciprocates, deepening the kiss, moving me back against the wall. I inhale sharply as he moves his mouth to my neck, running his lips down to my collarbone, his warm hands finding their way beneath the fabric of my top, warm against my bare skin. I don't want him to stop. I don't want *this* to stop.

But the tiniest niggle at the back of my brain makes me reach down and wrap my fingers around his wrists.

"We can't," I hear myself whispering.

"Harper," he growls, his warm breath tickling my neck.

"I can't," I say, firmer this time. "I have a boyfriend."

Ryan exhales shakily and then abruptly pulls away, leaving me flat against the wall and feeling suddenly vulnerable. I cross my arms, watching as he turns from me. He goes to the table by the sofa, where the two glasses of wine have been left untouched. He picks one up and swigs from it before daring to look at me.

"You want to be with him," he states coldly.

"No!" I exclaim, my eyes widening in horror at him mistaking my meaning. "No, but cheating isn't my style. I'm pretty sure it isn't yours, either. I need to go see him and . . . talk."

Ryan shakes his head. "Please don't go to him tonight, Harper."

"I have to. This isn't fair."

He doesn't say anything, his jaw clenching, and after a moment he takes another large gulp of wine. My head spinning from the whirlwind of tonight, I go to pick up my bag.

"Let me sort everything with him and then . . ."

"And then?" he asks, as I falter.

"Then we'll go from there," is all I can think of to say.

He gives a sharp nod, his lips pressing together into a thin line until they've all but disappeared. I walk over to him and reach up to give him a kiss on the cheek. I linger there and he angles his face toward mine as though daring me to make a move.

While I still have any willpower left, I break away from him and walk over to his door, opening it and stepping out into the evening air without looking back.

<hr />

Everything is pulling me toward Ryan, every inch of my body screaming to return to his arms. But my moral compass has clawed its way back to lead the charge, and I know that as terrible as I feel about leaving this way, I'm doing the right thing. I've already kissed someone else and—worse than that—I know I have feelings for him. Strong feelings that I can't suppress. Not after that kiss, anyway.

Bloody hell, what a kiss.

Sitting on the tube, I can't stop thinking about Ryan, almost missing the stop where I change onto the Northern Line to get to Liam's flat. That kiss was amazing. It was more than that. It was *mind-blowing*. No one has ever kissed me like that before. I'm not sure I've ever felt that wanted. That *needed*.

Everything about Ryan makes me dizzy with excitement: the way he smiles; the clean, fresh masculine scent of his cologne; his broad shoulders and strong arms; those dazzling blue eyes. But also the way he makes me feel; the way he notices things about me; the way he looks at me . . .

I can't believe he came to my parents' house after our fight. I'd felt so humiliated and betrayed that it was easier to write those few days off as a stupid mistake—I had lost myself for a weekend in a silly fairytale romance that wasn't real. As far as I was concerned, Ryan had played his part as the devilishly handsome adversary-turned-lover with perfect finesse. He had said all the right things to have his fun for a weekend, and then he was right back to focusing on his own ends come Monday morning. I'd told myself I was stupid for being so naïve as to think that a guy like him would put a girl like me first.

It was easier to think that way because I was so angry and embarrassed. And it was plausible, too—Ryan is the sort of handsome that makes people do a double take. The only reason anyone would look twice at me is if I fell over because I was in a rush, late for wherever I needed to be.

But now, as I walk to Liam's flat from the tube station, I consider what I'd have done if I had been in Ryan's shoes—if we'd gone for that drink and then it had been me who got the phone call to say I'd got the job. Would I have told him, knowing I'd ruin the night? Especially if, as he claims, there were feelings already there in the mix? Would it even be my place to tell him he hadn't gotten the job?

Turning the corner onto Liam's road, I force myself to focus on what's coming next.

I'll break up with Liam, kindly and respectfully, and then I will go home and have a bath and get my head sorted. Once I've worked out exactly what I want to say to Ryan, I'll pop him a message and go round to see him to talk things through.

It's a sensible, grown-up plan.

Nearing Liam's building, I start to feel sick with nerves. Breakups are horrible and I hate the idea of hurting him. None of this is his fault, it's completely on me, and I can only hope that he realizes sooner rather than later that we're not meant to be. Even if Ryan hadn't come into my life, Liam and I would not have worked out. The charity ball had been an eye-opener, and honestly, I really didn't like the way he kept trying to mix our business lives. This breakup is for the best.

Someone is exiting his block of flats as I arrive, and I catch the door, so there's no need for me to ring the bell for him to let me up. I start climbing the stairs apprehensively, wondering if he'll even be home. He did say he was working on something with Halo Skewed tonight, but he might be back from his meeting with them by now. And if not, his flatmate might be in, so I can always wait until he's back.

I reach his floor and walk slowly along the landing, my heart pounding against my chest as I try to focus on what I'm going to say exactly. There's no easy way to break up with someone. I just have to keep it simple and calm.

Approaching his door, I hear music coming from inside and instantly feel awash with dread. He's probably home. *That's what I want*, I tell myself, *it's a good thing he's home.* It's like pulling off a Band-Aid. It's unpleasant and painful, but it's a necessity.

I lift my hand to knock on the door but pause when I hear a voice in there floating above the music. It's someone laughing, but not Liam, nor his male flatmate.

It's a woman.

Her shrill giggles are soon accompanied by Liam's booming laugh that I recognize immediately. I wait for a bit longer to knock, turning my head and pressing my ear up against the door. Listening to their muffled conversation, largely obscured by the guitar-led crooning music, I'm almost certain that there's just the two of them in there. Their voices stop after a while and all I can hear is the music, their conversation obviously coming to an end for one reason or another.

Interesting.

Taking a deep breath, I knock on the door.

There are footsteps and then it swings open. Liam stands in the doorway wearing nothing but pajama bottoms. His hair is tousled, sticking up in an unruly manner, and he has a telltale tint of pink across his lips, the kind left behind from lipstick. His eyes widen in horror when he sees me standing there.

"H-Harper," he stutters.

He begins to say something else, but I push past him into the flat to find a raven-haired woman sitting on his sofa in a gorgeous set of lacy teal underwear and one of his shirts thrown over the top. She's clutching a half-drunk bottle of beer and sits bolt upright as I march in, wrapping the shirt across her chest as quickly as possible. I recognize her from the charity ball—she was the woman that Liam left with that night.

"Harper, it's not what it looks like," Liam claims, appearing next to me, his bare feet sliding across the floor. "This is Bianca, the lead singer of Halo Skewed. Like I told you, we were working tonight on band stuff and then . . . uh . . . we thought . . . we thought we would—"

"Have sex?" I finish for him.

He winces. "No! No, no, no, no, *no*."

"Yes," Bianca corrects with a sigh. I turn to her, impressed.

"*Bianca!*" he hisses.

"Liam, she's not an idiot," she reasons before looking up at me. "Are you an idiot?"

"No, I'm not."

"There you go." Bianca shrugs. "I'm in my underwear, Liam. Might as well be honest."

"Yes, Liam, might as well be honest," I say, crossing my arms.

He deflates, scrunching up his eyes and burying his face in his hands. After emitting an irritated groan, he jerks his head back up and drops his arms, inhaling deeply.

"I'm so sorry, Harper. I'm so, so sorry."

"Was it just tonight?" I ask.

"Yes," he replies firmly.

"No," Bianca says.

"*Seriously!*" Liam cries, looking at her aghast.

"Sorry, but I've been cheated on before and the truth always comes out anyway, so it's better she knows the whole story!"

"Thank you, Bianca, I'd appreciate that," I say, really warming to her despite the circumstances. "Liam, could you expand?"

"Fine," he says through gritted teeth, before looking at me pleadingly. "I didn't mean for this to happen, I promise, Harper. When Bianca and I met at the charity ball, it was completely innocent, and I went to see the band play and then we went for drinks afterward and . . . there was an undeniable spark between us. I'm *so* sorry."

"So it was that night and then tonight?" I ask.

"And a few other nights in between," he mumbles.

"Ah."

"Harper," he begins, "I really like you! I'm confused! I'm completely torn about this!"

"That wasn't what you were saying to me earlier," Bianca seethes, her expression darkening.

"My head is all over the place," Liam says, appealing to both of us.

I hold up my hand. "Let me stop you there, Liam. As horrible as it is to walk in on this . . . scenario, I appreciate your honesty. Even if it was really Bianca's candor that aided yours. But I need to be honest myself—I came here tonight to break up with you."

He recoils, looking insulted. "You did?"

"Yes. For a while now I haven't felt quite right about us, and I don't think we . . . mesh well."

"We mesh perfectly!" he claims, and I wonder if Bianca is as stumped as I am about why he's bothering to defend our shattered relationship.

"Liam, we went to a black-tie ball together and barely acknowledged each other. Don't you think that says quite a lot? And on top of all that—" I hesitate, taking a breath "—I've had feelings for someone else. Tonight, we kissed."

Liam gasps. "You kissed? Who?"

"Ryan."

He wrinkles his nose in disgust. "That guy you hate?"

"It's complicated. Anyway, we kissed—only kissed—but then I stopped him because I said it was wrong when I had a boyfriend, so I came straight here to end things with you." I gesture to Bianca. "But I realize now that I'm not the worst person in this relationship—*you've* earned that particular accolade, Liam."

"I thought it was one mistake with Bianca," he says hurriedly, "but then it happened again and again and . . . I should have told you."

"Yeah." I nod, putting my hands on my hips. "Clearly we're not meant to be."

We fall into silence, the music still playing in the background. I clear my throat.

"Right, I should go. This has been . . . enlightening. For everyone involved. Bianca, I don't love that you were sleeping with a guy that you knew had a girlfriend, but I want to thank you for encouraging Liam to be honest and for telling me the truth."

"No problem," she says, with a nod in solidarity. "And if it helps, I think you're a wicked writer, with a very entertaining style."

"That shouldn't help, but it really does. Thank you. Liam, you've been a total dickhead, but saying that, I think this relationship was fizzling out anyway, and I did kiss someone else behind your back. That was wrong and I'm sorry. Anyway, please could I have my key back?"

He plods off toward the bedroom and Bianca and I wait in silence until he returns, placing my flat key into the palm of my hand.

"Great, well, I should go."

"Wait, Harper," Liam says, grabbing my arm, "are you sure you don't want to talk things through? It feels sad to break up in this way."

"I'm not sure there's much to talk about, Liam, because there's a half-naked girl on your sofa. I think we can agree this is over and the best thing to do is to wish each other luck and move on."

He looks downcast. "Can I call or message you? I have things I want to say."

I glance at Bianca. She shrugs, looking as bewildered as I feel.

"Um . . . maybe message, if you'd really like."

"Thank you," he says in a gratingly austere manner.

He holds his arms out to me, and I realize he wants a hug, which I guess is appropriate if we want to end this amicably. And even though I'm disgusted that he's been shagging Bianca, I want out of this relationship, and there's no need to make this even more excruciatingly awkward than it already is. I hug him back and he holds me tighter than I was expecting, causing me to stumble as he pulls me closer.

"Thanks for everything," he whispers into my hair. "I'm so sorry this didn't work out."

"Me too," I reply, hoping he'll release me soon. "Goodbye, Liam."

He squeezes me once more, before giving me a forceful kiss on the cheek and then letting me go from his grasp. I step back, smile at him, and then head toward the door, desperate to get the hell out of there as quickly as possible.

I'm moments from freedom when he calls out, "Harper, wait!" causing me to stop in the doorway, forced to turn around again.

"Yes?"

"I just want to check," he says, his expression brightening, "you'll still write a profile piece on Halo Skewed, right? They really are fantastic. I think they're a great fit for the magazine. Oh, and don't forget about that hot new talent agencies article I pitched."

I stare at him. "I . . . I'll keep it in mind."

"Great." He gives me a thumbs-up.

And on that note, I leave, never more grateful to hear a door slam shut behind me.

CHAPTER SEVENTEEN

When I message Mimi to tell her about the breakup the next morning, she is over at my flat in a flash with some kind of gross green juice that she forces me to drink because, according to her, it is important that I look after myself "during this tumultuous time."

She doesn't know the half of it.

Once she's sat down on my sofa and I've had a few gulps of the green sludge, I decide to tell her about the kiss with Ryan, too. I hold back on revealing our history—I'm not ready to go into all of that now, I don't have the energy—but I tell her about the trip to Manchester and what happened when we got back to his London flat.

"What kind of kiss was it?" she asks, her eyes wide with excitement. "Was it like a tentative peck? Or was it passionate?"

"Wait," I say, surprised by her reaction. "You're not shocked that Ryan and I kissed in the first place?"

She shakes her head. "Not at all. I *told* you there was chemistry there. I called it as soon as I saw the way you two looked at each other in Meeting Room Three! Now . . . I ask again, what kind of kiss are we talking about here?"

"I was up against the wall."

She exhales. "Sounds hot."

"It *was* hot. It was the best kiss of my life."

Which is the absolute truth.

I tell Mimi about showing up at Liam's place unannounced,

and she swiftly agrees that it was a good thing I met the surprisingly delightful Bianca, because otherwise I might have never heard the truth. Knowing that Liam cheated has spared me excessive guilt over my kiss with Ryan.

"Have you told him?" Mimi asks when I conclude the saga.

"Told who what?"

"Have you told Ryan about the breakup?" Mimi says, looking at me as though I've lost my mind.

"Oh. No, not yet."

She gasps. "Why the hell not?"

I bury my head in my hands. When I got home from Liam's last night, I spent a long time drafting and redrafting a message to Ryan, but no matter how hard I tried, nothing sounded right and it looked too formal and stilted in writing. Then I realized what the problem was: I had no idea what I *wanted* to say. Was it enough to say I'd broken up with Liam? Or should I acknowledge what happened between *us*? And if I did, should I then say what I *want* to happen going forward? What *do* I want to happen going forward?!

It was all too overwhelming, and I got a terrible headache, so in the end I gave up and decided I'd message him in the morning. But today nothing seems clearer.

"What am I supposed to say?" I moan. "Send him a casual WhatsApp informing him I've broken up with my boyfriend?"

"Um. *Yes?*" She stares at me wide-eyed.

"Wouldn't it be better to just . . . drop it into conversation when I see him? It doesn't seem right putting anything in a message."

"You left him *mid-kiss*," Mimi says accusingly. "And now he hasn't heard from you? Come on, he deserves more than that. We're doing it now. I'll help you compose it."

She's right. I know she's right. So, together, we craft the following message, and I press Send before I can overthink it:

Hey Ryan, sorry again about yesterday. It would be
great to chat everything through in person if that's
okay? X

I check my phone every thirty seconds until he *finally* replies a few minutes later: **Sounds good x**

I try to play it cool on Monday morning as I wander into the office, but when Ryan isn't at his desk on my arrival as usual, my face must give me away. I notice Mimi watching me as I sit down.

"Are you wondering where *Ryan* is?" she teases, raising her eyebrows.

"I was thinking it's unusual that he's not at his desk on time," I reply casually, keeping my voice down.

She grins at me, her eyes twinkling with mischief. "Nice dress."

I'm wearing one of my favorite summer dresses—pale blue with lemons all over it—and I'm hoping to get a bit of color before I leave for Florence on Friday.

"Thanks. I thought it was right for such a sunny day."

"Makes your boobs look good, I see."

"Mimi!" I hiss, glancing round to make sure no one overheard. "That is very inappropriate."

"Got the pins out, too," she remarks, peering over the desk to look at my legs. "Did you fake tan last night after I left?"

"Yes, because it's *sunny*, and I thought it might be nice to be a little bronzed."

"Anyone you're trying to impress?"

I glare at her, but she is unfazed, returning to her typing with an irritatingly smug smile on her lips.

We soon realize that Cosmo is in a foul mood today because he twisted his ankle golfing this weekend, so I pretend to be very busy until his booming voice on the phone to his podiatrist gets too much and Mimi and I both decide we should escape to Roasted.

"I can't stop thinking about what Liam said to you," Mimi admits while we wait for our coffees. "He really still thought you'd write a piece promoting his agency? What planet is that guy on?"

"And a feature on Halo Skewed," I remind her. "I wasn't even going to write one on them in the first place! Ryan was right about him."

Mimi looks intrigued. "Oh?"

"He met Liam at the charity ball, and right away thought he was more interested in the networking opportunities my job provided than in me. He was spot on. I can't believe I didn't see it. It's embarrassing."

"But isn't it sweet that Ryan was looking out for you?" Mimi says, nudging my arm. "I think he really likes you, Harper. And clearly he's a good judge of character."

We take our time strolling back to the office. It's nice to make the most of this warm weather and neither of us is in any rush to get back to our desks.

But when we return, Ryan is there. As soon as I lay eyes on him, I'm flooded with nerves, my stomach turning to mush as I try to walk as normally as possible. It doesn't help that Mimi is watching me like a hawk and will no doubt listen in on any interaction we have.

"Morning," I say brightly as I sit down.

"Morning," he replies, giving me a polite smile before returning his attention to his screen.

It's an unsatisfactory exchange, but I suppose we *are* in the office. The trouble is, Ryan is very good at masking his feelings. I can't decipher if his "morning" was layered with undertones of resentment that I'd abandoned him after that kiss, or whether there was a hint of hope that I might be back on the market.

Or maybe he was just saying "morning" without any kind

of meaning behind it at all and, in fact, he is fully focused on whatever article he's editing.

We can hardly talk about things here. Should I have replied and suggested an exact date and time for our chat? Or should I ask him for a casual drink after work? Am I supposed to wait for *him* to ask *me* for a chat? Who makes the first move here?

I suddenly feel very hot and flustered.

Determined to remain professional, I start thinking about how to begin the Max Sjöberg article. I always like my features to launch with something punchy—a surprising, out-there quote from the subject, or a little-known fact about them that might catch the reader's attention. I lean down to grab my bag and start rummaging about for my notebook.

"Damn it," I whisper when it's nowhere to be found. I start looking around my desk, in case it's hiding under a stack of papers, sending a pot of pens flying onto the floor. I feel tears pricking my eyes. What is wrong with me?

Before I can start picking them up, Ryan has swiveled his chair round and leaned over to help, dropping the pens back into their pot, one by one.

"Thank you," I say, offering him a nervous smile.

"What have you lost?" he asks.

"My notebook. I know it's here somewhere. I remember seeing it this morning, so it's in the office. I got it out when I was going through a feature earlier and then . . . I don't know, I must have put it down somewhere."

"Give me a second," Ryan says, pushing himself up off the chair and walking off.

A minute later, he returns, holding up my notebook triumphantly. My jaw drops.

"Where did you—?"

"It was by the kettle in the kitchen," he explains, looking amused as he passes it over to me and sits back down. "You left it there last week, too, remember? You study it sometimes while you're walking about."

I stare at him in amazement. "I'm impressed by your sleuthing skills."

"It was a lucky guess," he insists, turning back to his work.

Thanking him again, I catch Mimi giving me a pointed look and trying to mouth something at me, but I can't work it out. Eventually she gives up and starts typing quickly on her keyboard. An email from her pops up in my inbox.

He knows you so well, it reads.

Deleting it, I roll my eyes at her and focus on reviewing my notes on Max Sjöberg, but it takes every effort not to smile because I'd been thinking exactly the same thing.

All morning, I pretend to be engrossed in my work when in fact I'm stealthily watching Ryan, mesmerized by the way his fingers swiftly and effortlessly dart around the keyboard as he types, remembering the warmth of his strong hands around my waist, and noticing how when he's reading intently, he rests his right elbow on his desk and presses the knuckle of his forefinger into his lips, his forehead creased in deep concentration. It's an unbelievably sexy pose, magnified by the fact that he has no idea just *how* sexy he looks when he's doing it.

I'm secretly studying his bottom lip when I hear someone calling my name, causing me to jump.

"Harper, it's so rubbish about Artistry! Have you spoken to their agent yet?" Gabby moans.

"Sorry, I've been . . . uh . . . busy," I stammer, trying to bring myself back down to earth. "What are you talking about?"

"*Artistry,*" she emphasizes. "The band? I thought you said a few weeks ago that there might be a reunion tour."

I nod. "That was in the cards, yes."

"Not anymore. Apparently the band had this huge falling-out and they're not speaking. The tour plans have been canceled."

She tilts her head. "I would have thought you'd have been the first to know! I was hoping for the inside scoop."

"Oh! Oh no, that's so . . . I better ring their agent, you're right. I haven't seen any of this yet," I say, fumbling around my desk to find my mouse and, having located it, bringing up Twitter, where I see the news is trending. "Shit. How did I miss this?"

"Like you said, you've been busy," Mimi comments in a sickly sweet tone. "What with your breakup and everything."

Gabby gasps, placing a hand on her heart. "You broke up with Liam? I'm so sorry!"

My face feels like it's on fire as I shoot daggers at Mimi for bringing it up before I was prepared. She doesn't seem the least bit regretful, instead stealing glances at Ryan, who has—it must be noted—looked up from his work.

"Thanks, but I'm fine," I say to Gabby, flustered and squirming in my seat. "It was my decision."

"Still, breakups suck," she states. "Are you really okay?"

"Yes, definitely," I insist. "We weren't right for each other. At all."

"You are so strong. I'm such a mess after breakups! Did he take it well?"

"Um." I think back on Bianca lounging across the sofa in her lacy underwear. "He took it pretty well, yeah."

"If there's anything I can do for you today, please just say," Gabby says, coming over to give me a hug. "In fact, let me go make you a cup of tea."

"You don't need to do that; I'm honestly fine."

"Hot drinks are comforting. I'll be back in a jiffy," she insists, hurrying off.

"She is such a sweetheart," Mimi remarks, watching her go.

"Now I feel bad for giving her all that Max Sjöberg transcribing to do this morning," I admit.

"You broke up with Liam," Ryan says, his eyes fixed on me.

"Yes," I reply, my voice shaking as I meet his gaze.

"Are you all right?" he asks, his voice even.

"Yes," I repeat, not breaking eye contact.

He nods. "Good."

His expression gives nothing away, and he resumes his typing. Biting her lip, Mimi witnesses the exchange and then gives me a baffled, wide-eyed look.

He doesn't seem particularly happy about the news. Which isn't good.

Although, he doesn't seem *unhappy*, either.

Everything he said on Saturday night had led me to think he'd be pleased that Liam and I have broken up. But what if he doesn't like the idea of being a rebound? Or maybe he's still angry at me for leaving so abruptly? Maybe he's having second thoughts now that we're here in the office, and he's realizing it could be unprofessional to embark on a romantic relationship with a colleague? Which is actually a very good point that should be taken into consideration.

That sort of thing does seem less important the more I sneakily obsess over his lips, though.

Can't he show one *ounce* of emotion?! *What are you thinking, Ryan?*

I consider asking if he wants to talk now, but I tell myself it's not the right time or place. And yet sitting next to him with no idea what is going on is *unbearable*.

Gabby's tea turns out to be a lifesaver as it gives me something else to concentrate on. I sip it gratefully, accepting that today is going to be one of those days that I get little to no work done.

"Everyone, I have an announcement!" Mimi declares a little later after receiving a phone call, spinning in her chair so she can address the whole team. "I have just spoken to Sadie, the publicist heading up the Florence press trip this weekend, and she has had a last-minute drop-out and there is a place up for grabs. Thanks to a lovely piece I wrote about another of the hotels on her books recently, she has very kindly offered that space to someone at *Narrative*. We already have the fabulous Harper going on the trip, but now there is room for one more of our journalists. Before you all start showering me in compliments to get the spot—" she holds up her hands as a ripple of excitement spreads through the office "—I am going to make this as fair as possible by putting everyone's name in a hat and pulling one out, and that person will get to go. If you aren't free this weekend or don't want to go, just let me know and I won't put your name in the mix. End of announcement!"

As she swivels back round, I lean across my desk to berate her.

"Why did you offer it to the whole team?" I whisper crossly. "I should have some say in who goes with me on the trip."

"Oh, really, Harper? You think you should decide instead of the travel editor?"

"If you pick Cosmo's name out, then I'm not going."

"Don't be ridiculous; he won't be able to go," she assures me. "His weekends are jam-packed with golfing trips at the moment."

"Don't forget to put my name in, Mimi!" Cosmo calls out from his office, appearing in the doorway and hobbling forward. "How fortunate, the one weekend I don't have any plans. And my foot will be healed by then, I'm certain."

"Of course!" Mimi replies with a fixed smile.

When he retreats back to his desk, I narrow my eyes at her.

"I'm going to *kill* you."

The hours pass, and Ryan and I barely speak.

When Mimi loudly declares that the moment has come for her to pick a name, I've just sent a stiff email to my dad, confirming a date for our dinner in two weeks. I'm not in the best of moods, so if Mimi is about to announce that I'm heading off to Florence with *Cosmo Chambers-Smyth*, I'm going to storm right out of here, go home, climb into bed, and not emerge for a month.

"The moment of truth," Mimi says, relishing her position of power. She swirls her hand around the multiple scraps of paper filling a hat that she borrowed from the fashion cupboard and eventually selects one, holding it above her head for everyone to witness.

"We have a winner!" she declares, before carefully unfolding it. "And the person joining Harper in Florence this weekend will be . . ."

She takes a dramatic pause. I hold my breath and pray: *Not Cosmo, not Cosmo, not Cosmo, anyone but Cos—*

"Ryan!"

Oh, shit.

I'm not going to lie, it's been a strange week.

Ryan and I have *still* not had a chance to have the talk we agreed to. We've both been so busy, and when I finally mustered the courage to suggest an after-work drink, we couldn't seem to coordinate our diaries.

I've been trying not to read into it, but Ryan has also seemed even more tense and serious than usual.

Everyone in the office, of course, finds the Florence trip extremely amusing. As far as they are concerned, Ryan and I don't like each other, so they're all finding it hilarious that we'll be alone on an intimate, luxury trip abroad.

Ryan's quiet and pensive mood made me nervous to approach him about the Max Sjöberg article. I was still trying to figure out the best way of writing the piece together when he suggested we go to a meeting room one afternoon to discuss it.

Once the door was closed behind us, he pulled his chair close to examine what I'd already written on my laptop screen. I could hardly concentrate on a word he was saying, especially when he shifted in his seat and our knees knocked together. He smelled *so good*, all clean with a hint of his woody cologne, not so much that was overpowering, but enough that it made me want to lean in closer. He was wearing the top few buttons of his blue shirt undone, and I had to force myself not to become fixated on the way his Adam's apple moved as he spoke.

Dragging my eyes away from him and looking at the table instead seemed like a safe bet, but I was wrong there because he was resting his arms on it, and with his shirt sleeves rolled up, his strong forearms were on full display.

"This is really good," he said after reading through the document. "Do you want to send it to me and I'll add in some paragraphs about his childhood and his connection to Sweden? Then you can go over those and tweak them however you like."

I tore my eyes away from his forearms and stammered, "Great. That sounds great. Perfect."

He nodded, watching me. "All these years later, we'll have our names together again in the byline."

"Yeah. Who would have thought?"

I smiled and I could see him instantly relax, his expression softening. I was about to ask then and there if we could talk about what happened, but Cosmo barreled in and demanded that Ryan come to his office. The moment was stolen.

Then, that very evening, right before we went home for the day, we got in an argument. I promptly forgot that he smelled really good and had been so lovely about my writing, and I got angry at him for being a prick.

Cosmo, in his infinite wisdom, had decided to let Ryan take charge of the "My Little Luxuries" column, which had been my domain ever since I started at *Narrative*, and had "forgotten" to let me know. When I sent my copy over to art for the next issue, they replied that they already had copy from Ryan.

"That has always been my column!" I cried as Ryan explained

to me the new order of things on Cosmo's behalf—he'd conveniently left early for a dinner. "You can't just take it away from me!"

"Once again, I'm sorry that Cosmo didn't talk to you about this like he promised he would," Ryan replied calmly, trying to keep things civil, blushing as the rest of the team turned to look at us. "But when you think about it, it makes sense that the features editor would do that column."

"It does *not* make sense! It's a *celebrity* every week saying what their little luxuries would be," I countered angrily.

"It's on the weekly round-up double spread that I head up," he responded, growing impatient. "I edit everything else on those pages. My name is literally on the header across the top."

"And my name is at the bottom of the 'My Little Luxuries' column, see?" I grabbed a previous copy of the magazine, flicked to the correct page, and jabbed my finger at it, reading out loud, "as told to Harper Jenkins."

"Harper," he said, rubbing his temples, "I don't understand. You were literally complaining about having to always write this column the other day. Surely you're happy to let someone else take over the hassle of doing it."

"Just because I complain about something, doesn't mean I want you—" I jabbed my finger at him accusingly "—to come along and *steal* it from me in an underhanded and unprofessional manner."

"Cosmo said he would speak to you about it!"

"Well, he didn't! You are both completely out of order!"

"This is ridiculous," he said, his cheeks flushing. "This column bores you to death. You're just angry that *I'm* doing it now!"

"That is *not* true! I've put a lot of work into that column! I've got lots of great names lined up for it, all of the interviews scheduled—"

"That's funny," he interrupted, crossing his arms, "because

I checked the schedule for that column on the server and there were *zero* names listed."

"I don't update the schedule on the server, Ryan," I seethed. "I have it all in my head!"

Closing his eyes, he inhaled deeply through his nose, attempting to regain composure.

"How I schedule things is not even relevant," I continued. "The point is that you and Cosmo made a big change and didn't tell me. I should have been involved in that conversation!"

"You're right, and I'm sorry *again* for that," he said as calmly as he could muster, "but I do also think this column should fall under the remit of the editor of these pages, and, honestly, I thought I was doing you a favor."

"Oh, so you agree with Cosmo, do you?"

"Yes, I do," he stated firmly.

"Well . . . you're both *wrong*."

Turning away from him, I grabbed my bag and stormed out of the office. I was late anyway for the launch of a TV presenter's new self-tanning range.

The next morning, I'd cooled slightly. Over coffee, Mimi and I discussed that, although I should have absolutely been informed, it might be nice to no longer worry about "My Little Luxuries." I often threw it together at the last minute in a whirlwind panic anyway.

When Ryan repeated his apology, I graciously accepted it.

"Thank you, Harper. I really am sorry about you not being told," he said, swiveling to face me in his chair. "I only hope you won't miss it too much."

I noticed he was suppressing a smile as he said this. Glowering at him, I turned my attention back to my screen.

"Oh, and you'll send me over the list of people you have scheduled, yes?" he added.

"I'm sorry?" I replied.

"The celebrities you have scheduled for the column," he explained breezily. "You know, the ones you had lined up in your head."

I noticed Mimi across the way pressing her lips together as she tried not to laugh. He had me and he knew it.

"If you can send those over along with the dates of when you've scheduled them in for an interview," Ryan continued, "I can get in touch to explain I'll be doing the column now. You shouldn't have to deal with all that hassle. You've already gone to all the work of organizing them."

"Yes. Right. Thank you," I said, my cheeks flushing.

I waited a bit before speaking again, my voice slightly higher pitched than I would have liked.

"Actually, Ryan, I think it's best if you just start fresh."

He raised his eyebrows. "Oh? But won't all of those celebrities be annoyed?"

"No, I'll speak to their agents and explain," I said hurriedly, refusing to look at his smug expression.

"Okay, sure. I'll start afresh. *Thank you*, Harper."

We fell into silence, both of us tapping away at our keyboards, and then a few moments later, I stole a glance at him. He was looking at me. As our eyes met, he broke into a knowing smile and I couldn't help but smile back at him. He shook his head at me and we both got back to work.

It really has been a strange week.

⌐⟶

Embroiled in a mixture of excitement and nerves, I've spent a lot of time stressing over what to pack for Florence. My flat is messier than usual—and that's saying something—because I have been trawling through the depths of my wardrobe in the hope of discovering a new collection of holiday clothes, even though I haven't been on holiday in . . . well . . . forever.

On Wednesday evening, in the midst of lobbing shoes across my room in a desperate hunt for a suitable wedge that makes me look elegant but I can also manage to stay upright in, the doorbell rang.

My first, thrilling thought? *Ryan.*

But it was Liam, dropping by to "talk things through" and pick up some of his belongings that he'd left. I told him it wasn't a good time because I was packing for Italy, but he sighed heavily and retorted, "It will never be a good time, Harper," in the voice of an old wizened wizard, so I thought it best to let him in and get it over and done with.

It was much less awkward than the original breakup, largely because it wasn't witnessed by his naked lover, but it was still mildly painful. He felt the need to reassure me that I was a wonderful person and, that having spent some time analyzing what went wrong, he'd come to the conclusion that we were both "too focused on our career paths" right now to "really let someone in."

I dryly pointed out that he'd had no trouble "letting Bianca *in*."

He winced. I regretted it immediately, because even though it was a rather witty comeback, it did prompt him to launch into a detailed explanation about the "purely physical" nature of their relationship—something I very much did *not* need to hear about. But I didn't want things between us to end badly, so I wished him the best. We hugged it out and I ushered him away.

If anything, seeing Liam was confirmation that any feelings for him had well and truly petered out. I needed to use our time in Florence to let Ryan know that, and to work out how he felt about me. That decided, I did loads of online shopping and spent Thursday evening trying on countless outfits and sending pictures of myself to Mimi to gather her opinion on each one.

Bring sexy underwear, she messaged, **just in case.**

I blushed as I read the message. They were already in my bag.

On Friday morning, I wake up to a WhatsApp from Ryan. I sit bolt upright in bed, my heart in my throat as I scroll the preview down to read it:

See you at the airport. Don't forget your passport. x

My face breaks into a wide, goofy, unrestrained grin. It's just so him. Sensible, practical, but also kind of cute because, like Mimi said the other day, he knows me.

And he put a kiss on the end.

I throw my duvet back and swing my legs out of bed, before skipping to the bathroom to shower. I'm well aware that I should be playing it cool, that I should not get my hopes up, and it would be smart to be cautious and pragmatic about what might or might not happen. For goodness' sake, it was one message and it had a kiss on the end. That could mean nothing.

But *screw it.* I'm singing in the shower.

And today, I'm wearing sexy underwear. Just in case.

CHAPTER EIGHTEEN

Ryan smiles when he sees me racing toward him.

I quickly dodge a family of five and try not to trip over the wheelie cases squeaking along behind them.

"Sorry I'm late!" I wheeze as I join the press group waiting in the departures area. "I had a last-minute emergency."

"Oh no! I hope everything is okay?" says a curly-haired woman in alarm.

"Yes, everything is fine now," I assure her.

There's no need to go into the details of said emergency, which was that as I got ready to leave the flat, I suddenly realized in absolute horror that I'd forgotten to shave my legs. I had to cancel the Uber that was already waiting, as the driver was getting grumpy and sending me impatient messages, and then hoist up the blue maxi skirt I was wearing to balance a leg in the sink before doing the other one. I then had to wait ten minutes for another Uber to accept my trip, and by then the traffic was terrible on the way to Gatwick.

"I'm so sorry for holding you up," I say again.

"You're only a few minutes late, it's no problem," the woman says, smiling with impossibly perfect, pearly-white teeth. "I'm Sadie, by the way. It's really nice to meet you—I've heard a lot about you from Mimi."

She introduces me to the small circle of people that will be joining us—two journalists from different travel publications and one from a luxury fashion magazine that is launching a travel section—and I politely say hi to all of them, until she lands on Ryan.

"And of course, you know Ryan," she says as I acknowledge him with a smile, forcing myself to look up into his eyes.

"Right," I say through nervous laughter. "Hi."

"Hi, Harper," he replies, giving nothing away.

"Let's tackle security, shall we?" Sadie suggests before turning on her heel and walking briskly through the airport.

Ryan and I naturally fall into step with one another as we bring up the rear of the group, the other journos forced to make small talk as they try to keep up with Sadie.

"So, did you—" he begins at the same time as I say, "I want to thank—"

"Sorry," I say, blushing. "You go first."

"I was going to check you remembered your passport."

"And I was going to thank you for the reminder."

"I didn't mean to sound bossy."

"I didn't think you sounded bossy."

He nods. "Good."

He still seems tense, and we remain silent until we reach the security queue and he lets me go ahead of him. The only time I see a hint of him relaxing is when we get near the front of the queue and I realize I need to get the liquids out. I plonk my weekend bag on the ground and unzip it, fishing around the crumpled clothes, trying not to send my sexy lingerie flying through the air in the process. As the queue moves forward, I'm forced to awkwardly shuffle along, nudging my bag along with me, my bum in the air as I lean over it.

"Organized as ever," Ryan murmurs behind me, and I can hear that he's smiling.

When we get on the plane, I'm disappointed that I'm not sitting next to him and contemplate trying to bribe the older woman in the seat beside him to switch. But my pride gets the better of me. I'm seated in the row behind, and I spend the two-hour flight studying what I can see of Ryan through the gap in the seats, which is his left ear, a portion of his neck, and the back of his left forearm and elbow.

After spending a little too long daydreaming about kissing that gentle slope of his neck, I force myself to snap out of it and instead open the itinerary that Sadie provided. Today, we'll be relaxing at the hotel, which is, after all, the reason we're here, but tomorrow morning we'll be visiting art galleries and churches and enjoying a wine tour in the afternoon. Reading through, I get a flurry of excitement—it's been ages since I went on holiday. I must remember to bring Mimi back a gift.

I can't stop beaming as we step off the plane into the humid heat of summertime in Italy and spend the mini-bus taxi journey to the hotel gazing out the window in absolute awe of *Firenze*, one of the most beautiful cities I've ever seen. The narrow streets, lined with rustic, warm yellow, red-roofed buildings, are bursting with quirky shops and restaurants, and bustling with pedestrians, and even though I know nothing about architecture, I can tell the sights here are nothing short of spectacular. I'm already itching to explore.

"You've never been?" a voice asks gently.

I tear my eyes from the window to find that Ryan has moved to sit next to me.

"No, this is my first time. How could you tell?"

"Your face," he answers simply, giving me one of his trademark secretive smiles. "You looked . . . in awe."

"I am in awe," I admit. "It's stunning. You've been to Florence?"

"A few times. I love it here. The food is incredible, and wait until you see some of the views over the rooftops of the city. It's really something."

"You'll have to show me some of your favorite spots," I say.

He nods, looking pleased. "I will."

Our hotel is located in a park in the hills just outside the center of the city, and as we drive down a tree-lined avenue and pull up to the villa built into the low hillside—a breathtakingly grand building with a dramatic fountain in the center of the driveway—my jaw drops. There is no chance I'd *ever* be able to afford to stay in a place like this. I really need to make the most of it.

The reception is the epitome of opulence: vast chandeliers hanging from the ceilings, huge gilded mirrors lining the dusty-pink and gold walls, and a vase bursting with white and pink flowers set on the round table in the middle of the room.

"Welcome!" Sadie trills, her delicate sandals clacking across the floor as she comes to stand in front of us. "As I'm sure you can already tell, you are standing in one of the most splendid villas here in the south of the city, built by Baron Cadorna in 1889. Once we've checked in, I'm going to let you settle in your rooms and freshen up from the flight, and then we'll be enjoying a lunch on the terrace, prepared by the excellent chefs of the restaurant here. After lunch, you are free to spend the afternoon relaxing by the outdoor heated pool or enjoying the facilities of the spa before dinner—complimentary, of course. There are also some fabulous walks around the area, if you'd like to explore. Please do ask me first, though, so the hotel staff here can give you a rough guide of where to go. Oh, and I should mention that the bar will be open from—" she checks the time on her phone "—ah! It's open now. Drinks are on the house. I have emailed all of you the full details of the hotel, but please do not hesitate to ask me any questions during your stay here. Right, let's get you to your rooms."

As she goes to sort our keys at reception, I lean toward Ryan, who is standing next to me, busy admiring the surrounding interiors.

"This isn't a dream, right? We really are here."

"I can confirm this is real, Harper."

"I love my job," I whisper, making him chuckle.

⌐⌐⌐⌐⌐

"Can I join you?"

Lying on a sun lounger by the pool, I look up to see Ryan wearing a white linen shirt and navy-blue swimming shorts with a towel over his arm. He's gesturing to the lounger next to me, shielded from the sun by the same umbrella.

"Of course," I say, putting the stapled pages I was reading down on the table next to my ice-cold water that one of the waiters kindly just refreshed for me. "Although there are better ones around the pool if you'd rather be in the sun."

"With this delicate Scandinavian skin? Best not," he says, sitting down and kicking off his flip-flops.

I'm glad I opted for a swimsuit rather than a bikini for this trip, but I still feel very naked in front of Ryan, and as he makes himself comfortable, I quickly check down my front that nothing is out of place and cross one leg over the other, wiggling my toes nervously.

He slides his Ray-Ban Wayfarers off his nose and balances them on top of his head, squinting at my reading material. "Those pages look like work—you're going to get into trouble with Mimi if she hears you've been working on this trip."

"It's not work, but it is related to work. If I tell you what these pages are, will you promise not to tell?"

"My lips are sealed," he whispers conspiratorially.

"Audrey Abbot has been writing her memoirs, and she sent me the first couple of chapters to read through to see what I think."

"Whoa." He grins. "That's amazing."

"I know, right? I feel so honored! And what I've read is brilliant, thank goodness. I can't wait to read the whole thing. She sure has had an interesting life. I never knew she had so many ambitions—she actually always wanted to go into directing, but she was so successful with acting that she stuck with that and then never had the confidence to switch to behind the camera. After The Incident, she decided to give up on that dream altogether. I think she'd be a great director, personally. I'll have to tell her so."

"She must really trust you," Ryan surmises.

"I hope so. Or she knows I'm a writer and an editor and is taking advantage of a free proofreading service before she sends the manuscript through to her publisher."

"Now, that is much too cynical a viewpoint to come out of your lips."

I smile. "You're right. Let's just say she trusts me."

A member of the staff comes gliding over to ask Ryan if he'd like a drink. I've made a mental note that the review of this hotel needs to mention how incredible the service is—everyone is warm and friendly, and so attentive. Lunch was outstanding, and thanks in part to the delicious dry Tuscan white wine that was served throughout the meal, I'm not sure I've ever felt so relaxed.

As if reading my mind, Ryan says, "I feel very lucky that the spot opened up and I was able to come at the last minute. I owe Mimi big time."

"Me too. And I'm so thankful that she pulled your name out the hat and not Cosmo's. Can you imagine if he were here? I bet he'd act as though he knew *everything* about Florence and lecture me the entire time."

Ryan laughs. "I'm pleased I wasn't your last choice, at least."

"Don't be silly," I say, glancing at him. "I'm glad you're here."

He turns his head to look at me before asking in a low, sincere voice, "Are you? Because Harper, I would hate to think that—"

THE LAST WORD

"Ryan," I say, cutting him off, my heart thumping against my chest as he scrutinizes my expression, "I'm really glad that it's you here with me."

He doesn't reply, and I see his throat bob as he swallows. Someone appears to deliver the beer that Ryan ordered, and then we're both distracted by a loud splash that comes from the pool. One of the travel journalists in our group has just arrived, and, spotting us, he gives us an enthusiastic wave and drags a sun lounger over to where we are sitting.

Another moment ruined.

I stay for a while to be polite but eventually leave the pool to go have a nap in my elegant and air-conditioned room before getting ready for dinner. Collapsing on the big squishy white duvet of my bed, I turn on my side and close my eyes, falling asleep in a state of hopeful trepidation, thinking about the elated look on Ryan's face when I told him that I was pleased he was here.

I wear a yellow dress for dinner—it's got spaghetti straps, a fitted bodice with a scoop neckline, and a flowing skirt that swishes satisfactorily around the top of my calves as I walk. I complement it with gold earrings and a pair of wedges that have a delicate gold strap around the ankle, and bold red lipstick. I tie my hair back in a loose ponytail so it's off my neck in the heat, but not too severe around my face. Finally, as recommended by Mimi, I apply some gold highlighter along my collarbones.

Everyone is already sitting around the table in the restaurant when I come downstairs, and they all look up as I enter the room, but Ryan pushes his chair back and jumps to his feet. As I move round the table to take the free chair next to his, I notice Sadie raising her eyebrows at him with undisguised interest as he pulls out my chair for me.

Now that we're all seated, the chef enters the dining room and introduces himself, explaining our menu of local produce, which will begin with a selection of hors d'oeuvres before a starter of squid tagliatelle or Florentine dumplings, followed by a main of slow-cooked lamb with artichokes or spinach ricotta gnocchi, and a dessert of almond and raspberry mousse, each course accompanied with a wine pairing chosen by the hotel's sommelier.

"I'm not sure I'll fit into this dress after this meal," I whisper to Ryan once the chef has finished and left us to it.

He smiles, his eyes flickering down my dress and back up again. "That is a *very* nice dress." He hesitates before quietly adding, "You look beautiful."

I'm so flustered, I don't know what to say, and I'm glad when Sadie asks Ryan what he thinks of the hotel so far, so that I have a moment to gather my thoughts. I feel so aware of him throughout the meal: where our hands are placed on the table, how close our legs are to brushing against each other, how he looks at me after he speaks, as though seeking my approval.

After dinner, we're guided to the poolside bar, which is romantically lit by lamps and candles dotted around the tables. The water is inviting at night, a shimmering magenta-blue thanks to the purple lights set underwater along its walls. We're served the hotel's signature cocktails, and, on top of the wine from dinner, our group is getting tipsier and louder.

Ryan is sitting opposite me now, and I can feel him watching as I fall into conversation with Sadie, who is slurring her words a little as she enthusiastically tells me how much she *adores* Mimi and how she's so *happy* that we've now met after hearing all about me.

After assuring Sadie that she and I are 100 percent good friends now, I announce that I'm heading to bed as it's getting late. The others say good night but don't really acknowledge my departure. I don't notice that Ryan is behind me until I get to the elevator.

"Hey," I say, surprised at his presence, and hold the door for him.

"Hey," he replies, pressing the button to our floor.

We're both facing the shiny silver doors as they slowly close, and stand next to each other in tense silence the whole way up to the third floor. It must only take a few seconds, but standing in the lift so close to him, our fingertips centimeters from brushing against each other, it feels like time stands still.

I keep my eyes fixed ahead on the doors, refusing to glance at him. My heart is thudding so hard against my chest, I'm scared he'll be able to hear it above the soft elevator music.

He allows me to step out first, and I walk toward my room, hyperaware of his soft footsteps behind me. Slowing down as I reach my door, I decide enough is enough and it's time to talk to him properly. I spin round suddenly to face him, but the alcohol and the heels have me a little off balance. He grips my arm and steadies me just in time.

"You okay?" he asks.

"Yes, thanks. Sorry." I take a deep breath. "Ryan, I should say . . . uh . . . well, about last weekend. I'm really sorry for running out on you like that."

"Don't be," he says, his eyes dropping to the floor. "You were doing the right thing."

"I should have broken up with Liam a while ago."

"Harper—"

"No, I need to say this. We've needed to talk all week and—"

"I know and I want to talk about it," he insists, glancing to the lift. "But maybe we should go into a room? Just so it's not so . . . public. Some of the other journos are on this floor, too, and they could come up any minute."

"You're right," I say, realizing that this is a bit of an awkward conversation to have in a hotel corridor. "Come into mine."

He waits patiently as I fumble with the door and then follows me into the bedroom, immediately groaning as he spots the contents of my weekend bag spilling out onto the floor.

"I bet the first thing you do when you arrive at a hotel is unpack your bag and put everything away in the wardrobe," I say, sitting on the edge of the bed and leaning down to undo the straps of my shoes. "Even though we're only here for two days, I bet you've put everything away neatly, hanging it all up or folding it away."

"Of course," he says, sitting down in one of the plush velvet armchairs by the window. "That way I can find everything I've brought with me and nothing is crumpled."

"You know what you need to do, Ryan?"

"What's that?"

"Live a little."

He smiles, sitting back as he rests his elbows on the armrests of the chair. He watches me intently. I stare back and lose myself in his blue eyes. Ryan Jansson is *in my hotel room*. This is dangerous territory. And thrilling.

I swallow the lump in my throat as I take him in. His expression softens, like he understands that I'm really seeing him. His lips twitch as though fighting a smile. I suddenly feel embarrassed for staring and drop my eyes to the ground.

"What did you want to say about last weekend?" he prompts.

I nod and take a deep breath, studying the carpet. "I wanted to tell you that breaking up with Liam was exactly what I had been planning to do. What happened between us may have been a catalyst, but I didn't want you thinking that I'm upset about Liam, because I'm not. I'm glad it's over. And I'm only sorry that . . . well, I'm sorry I hadn't broken up with him ages ago, to be honest."

His brow furrows as he listens. "So, you don't regret what happened last weekend?"

I startle at the idea, jolting my head up to look at him. "Between us? No, I don't regret what happened. At all. Do you?"

"No, Harper," he says, almost looking pained at the question.

He stands abruptly and puts his hands in his pockets, turning away to look out the window.

"You've been acting strange this week," I continue. "I thought you may be cross at me or confused about the kiss."

He shakes his head. "This week has been really painful."

"Why?"

He hesitates and then shrugs. "I didn't know what you were thinking."

"I didn't know what *you* were thinking."

Turning from the window to face me again, he asks, "What *are* you thinking?"

"You first," I insist, jutting out my chin.

"Fine." Agitated, he runs a hand through his hair. "I'm thinking that . . . well, to be honest, the only thing I seem to be able to think about at the moment is you, Harper. I can't get you out of my head. I thought I made this clear eleven years ago, but maybe you didn't believe me or you weren't really listening. You have no idea what you do to me. You're beautiful, but it's so much more than that. I've never been able to talk to anyone the way I can talk to you. Since Adam died, I'd always felt so closed off and alone and irrelevant. Then I met you and—you made everything feel warm and open and *alive*. The world seemed okay again."

I smile up at him.

"You have no idea how amazing you are," he goes on. "Do you realize that everyone adores you? I mean, *everyone*. You're so brilliant at what you do, but it's as though you have no idea just how talented you are. You light up every room you walk into. You somehow turn everything that's gray and orderly into a colorful,

giant jumble. You're like this . . . chaotic, shiny star. I liked you
so much when we were interns. Do you have any idea what that
weekend we spent together meant to me? It was *everything*."

He pauses, exhaling.

Warmth pools in my stomach, and I'm rendered speechless.
No one has ever *seen* me like Ryan clearly does, and I feel a sudden urge to run over and hold him, to be close to him.

He called me a chaotic, shiny star.

My heart might just burst.

"And then I lost you," he continues, agonized, oblivious to
the enamored trance he's put me in. "When I got the job at *The
Correspondence*, I knew our paths were going to cross. I thought
I could handle it; what happened between us was a long time
ago, and at the time, I had a girlfriend. But then seeing you . . .
you acted like you didn't know me, and it wrecked me. All these
feelings came rushing back. I'd already had doubts over the relationship I was in—"

I gasp, clapping a hand over my mouth. "You broke up with
your girlfriend because of *me?* Ryan! We weren't even speaking!"

He shakes his head. "My ex and I were in a bad place. We
were trying to ignore the obvious cracks, but we both knew it was
the end of the road." He hesitates, shrugging. "But I'm not going
to pretend that seeing you again after all those years wasn't some
kind of prompt for me to realize with absolute clarity that I wasn't
with the person I wanted to be with."

My heart is racing and I can't stop myself from smiling. He
looks encouraged by this reaction and continues, his tone filled
with urgency.

"Sitting next to you for the last few months, thinking that you
still can't stand me because of a stupid mistake I made a long
time ago—it was fucking torture. All I've wanted is to pick up
where we left off eleven years ago. And then that kiss last weekend. It gave me . . . hope."

He takes a breath. I grip the edge of the mattress, my knuckles going white.

"Harper," he says, looking at me pleadingly, "kissing you was the best, most incredible thing that's happened to me, because you kissed me back. And I have spent all week wondering how you feel and if there might be hope for us, but telling myself not to get carried away just in case it didn't mean to you what it meant to me. You're fresh out of a breakup and I don't want to be a fleeting fling. I want to be so much more than that to you. So I'm trying not to jump to any conclusions and to show some kind of restraint. But then here you are in . . . *that dress.* Jesus. You need to put me out of my misery. Just tell me what you're thinking. Please."

I stare at him, stunned, trying to process what he's just said. A torrent of bare emotion that was so . . . perfect.

I push myself up off the bed and make my way across the room to stand opposite him. He's breathing heavily, his chest visibly rising beneath his shirt.

"Ryan," I begin, "did you call me . . . a chaotic, shiny star?"

He groans, burying his face in his hands. "God, yes, I did."

"And you call yourself a writer."

"I never claimed to be a good one," he murmurs through his fingers.

I take his hands in mine and lower them, smiling up at him.

"I've been thinking about you all week, too."

He hesitates, his eyes searching mine. "You . . . you have?"

"Yes," I say, reaching forward and placing my hands on his solid chest. "I want this. Whatever this is."

He lets out a sigh and then dips his head to rest his forehead against mine, and we remain still like that for a few seconds, savoring this moment that feels heavy with the anticipation of what's to come.

Gradually, the energy between us shifts. My hands move

down Ryan's chest to his waist and I pull him closer. I tilt my head back, my breath catching in my throat as his lips crush against mine. He kisses me slowly and gently, and I melt into him, my hands reaching up to thread my fingers through his hair, a surge of relief and happiness pulsing through my body that he wants this as much as I do. He kisses me deeper, moving his lips down my jawline, his warm, strong hands moving from my hips to my lower back as I arch against him, my skin tingling beneath his touch. He drops light kisses down the slope of my neck, along my glittering collarbone, nudging the strap of my dress with his lips until it slips off my shoulder.

I'm impatient, suddenly overwhelmed by the urgency of wanting him. He doesn't protest as I start fumbling with the buttons of his shirt, helping me to get it off him altogether, shaking it loose down his arms until it drops on the floor. Pressing my hands against his bare, muscular chest, I guide him toward the bed and he sits down. He reaches for my waist and pulls me down so I straddle him.

His warm hands slide up my thighs, scrunching my dress around my hips, and a low sound emits from his throat as his fingers play along the fabric of my thong. I tip my head back as his lips skim my jaw, and he kisses down to the base of my throat before his hands move to the back of my dress, his fingers finding the zip and slowly, carefully pulling it down. As the bodice of the dress loosens, I pull it over my head and drop it to the floor.

Breathing heavily, he pauses to take a moment to look at me properly, his blue eyes scanning down and back up to meet mine before breaking into a smile that makes my stomach somersault, and any shyness I felt evaporates. Cradling his face in my hands, I dip my head down and give him a slow, deep kiss, and as he responds, my whole body aches for this not to be fleeting.

In one swift move, he lifts me to the side and my breath catches as he eases me down, lying me back on the bed as though

I don't weigh a thing. My legs still locked around his hips, he presses down on top of me. His fingers tangle through my hair as his lips hungrily find mine, his kisses suddenly deeper, more urgent. I sink my nails into the skin of his shoulder blades, and my teeth catch his bottom lip, causing him to let out a small, involuntary groan. I reach down to undo his belt, then his trousers, and he helps me with the task, pushing them down below his hips.

Shifting beneath him, I lift my hand to push his hair back from his forehead so I can look at him properly. I don't want this to be a hazy blur; I want to be able to remember. At my slowing down, I sense him hesitate and my instinctive reaction is to grip him tighter, desperate not to lose this moment, this perfect moment that I suddenly realize I've been longing for. I can feel how much he wants me when he's pressed this close, and I'm aching for him to be closer.

"Do you have a condom?" he asks, his voice ragged, his eyes locked on mine.

I relax, breaking into a smile of relief. "You're telling me you don't carry them around in your pocket on work trips?"

"Funnily enough, no," he chuckles softly, leaning in to graze my neck with his lips.

"Not like you to be so unprepared, Ryan. I must say, I'm a little bit disappointed in you."

"I'll make up for it. And trust me," he says, his warm breath tickling my ear, "it's a good thing that I wasn't prepared for this tonight."

"And why is that?"

He lifts his head again, his face hovering above mine.

"Because if I'd known this was coming, I wouldn't have wasted a moment on anything else," he says simply. "Not the dinner, not the cocktails, not the people. I wouldn't have wasted *one more moment*, Harper."

Goose bumps cover my skin as I gaze up into his eyes. I swallow and then say, "Well it's a good thing that one of us is prepared," and I gesture toward the bathroom.

Ryan smiles and draws away and I take a moment to catch my breath. When he reappears, the sight of his already-disheveled hair; his toned, muscular chest, abs, and arms; his glittering eyes; and his knowing smile does something strange to my chest. My heart flutters and I'm consumed by a surge of dizzying exhilaration as he makes his way back to me.

I can't believe he wants me as much as I want him.

"Are you sure you want to do this?" he checks, leaning over me again, his lips brushing against mine.

"Yes," I say firmly, already arching into him.

No more hesitations. No more pauses. We've waited long enough. I pull his mouth to mine and we kiss so deeply, it sends a series of shivers down my spine. Ryan's hands slip down, over my hip bone and under my thong, and I have just long enough to spare a grateful thought for bringing this sexy underwear on the trip before it's hard to think about anything at all. Something about Ryan's hands on me feels better than it's ever felt with anyone else, and I wonder fleetingly if it's because he knows me so well—this man understands me in every way.

I lose myself beneath his fingers, and it's hard to tell how much time has passed: it feels as though the world has shrunk to the two of us in this bed. When the moment comes to slip on the condom, Ryan's hands tremble as he rips open the foil. I don't think I've ever wanted anything as much as I want him inside me.

When he finally pushes into me, I gasp. He begins slow and sensuous, then moves faster, and it feels so good, I can't believe we've wasted so much time not doing this. It's different than how it was eleven years ago—he's more confident and passionate, I feel less tentative and awkward. I lose myself in the intense pleasure of everything he's doing to me: his light kisses along my cheekbone, his hot shallow breath in my ear, his hands roaming over my body, one clasping my waist, the other dipping under my back to rock me into him.

Breathless, I close my eyes, clutching him.

It all seems so clear now. I never want to let go.

CHAPTER NINETEEN

In the Galleria dell'Accademia, Ryan takes my hand in his and lifts it, kissing my knuckles when no one is looking. At lunch, we sit next to each other and pretend to listen to the conversation while our knees press against each other under the table, sending tingles down my spine. After buying gelato from Mercato Centrale, we hang back while the group meanders through the crowd and he waits until they've turned a corner before wrapping his arm around my waist, pulling me close to him and kissing me, his lips cold and sweet from the ice cream. We have a staring competition during the wine tasting at the vineyard, and I offer him a seductive smile as I swirl the wine around my glass, and later, when we find ourselves alone strolling through the olive trees, split from the group, we kiss with my back against the tree as he whispers into my ear that I'm driving him crazy.

We drift around Florence like we're in a movie montage, grinning from ear to ear, stealing kisses when no one's looking, giggling like teenagers. I don't want to go back to England, where Ryan and I work together and it gets complicated. I want to stay here in Italy and live at a luxury hotel and eat delicious food and drink incredible wine and have mind-blowing sex with Ryan before falling asleep in his arms.

It's perfect here.

And I guess that's part of the problem, the worry niggling at the back of my head when I wake up next to him the morning we're due to fly home. *What happens now?* Are we going to start . . . dating? Is that even allowed when we work together?

It seems ridiculous that Ryan could make me this happy. This is the guy who pushes my buttons like no one else; who humiliated me when I was young and naïve; who lied to me then and could very well be lying to me now.

But this is also the guy who knows I like honey in my tea; who reads all my articles despite often having no idea who the celebrity in question even is; who opens up to me in a way he doesn't around other people; who delivered a baby in the back of a taxi with the jacket of his tux; who looks at me like I have the answers to all of his questions; and who has the kind of eyes that make me forget about saying or doing anything sensible whatsoever.

"Your eyes are so gorgeous," I blurted out to him last night in bed, after sneaking off from the group early again as they celebrated the final night with espresso martinis by the pool.

"You think so?" he said, moving his pillow closer to mine as we faced each other so our noses were almost touching.

"Oh please, don't act as though you haven't been complimented on them your whole life. They haunted me, you know. After I left *The Daily Bulletin*, I couldn't stop thinking about your damn eyes."

"Do you think if I'd mustered the courage to knock on your parents' door after that whole debacle, we might have been able to work it out?" he asked, reaching over to brush my hair away from my face. "If I'd explained that I'd kept the job news to myself because I liked you so much, and I didn't want to lose you—do you think you would have understood?"

"I don't know," I sighed. "I was pretty pissed at you. And very focused on my career. I probably wouldn't have wanted to listen to you."

"But if I'd fought for you a bit harder, things might have turned out so differently."

"I think they've turned out all right," I reasoned. "Maybe it was better that we were brought back together at this time in our lives. We were so young then."

"That's true. Although," he said, a knowing smile spreading across his face, "you haven't exactly made our reunion smooth sailing."

"Me? What about you? Disagreeing with everything I say at work."

"*You* disagree with *me*. Even when I know you think I'm right."

"I would never be so petty."

He gave me a look. "You would absolutely be so petty."

"Says the guy who raced me to the tube after a book event."

"*You* raced *me*." He chuckled. "You hate it when I win anything."

"Only because you do that smile."

"What smile?"

"That mocking smile," I explained. "It's like this very small smirk whenever I argue my point with you or end up making a fool of myself or say something about celebrities. You get this little teasing smile on your face and I want to wipe it right off with cunning words."

He laughed. "You are very cunning. But wait, you think I'm mocking you?" His face turned more serious. "Harper, I have no idea what smile it is exactly that you're talking about, but I can assure you, I'm not teasing you. You just . . . I don't know . . . sometimes you say things and—"

I rolled my eyes. "I *amuse* you."

"Yes! No, wait. Not in a bad way," he fumbled. "As in, I find you fascinating. In a good way! What I'm trying to say is, you make me smile. That's it. And if it looks secretive or that I only do it around you, that proves my point—you're the only person

THE LAST WORD ••• 281

who makes me smile like that." He hesitated. "Am I doing well here or digging myself into a hole?"

"Actually, you're doing pretty good," I said, edging along the pillow to kiss him. "I like the idea of a secretive smile just for me. Better than you snickering at me, which is what I thought you were doing."

"I only snicker at you when you make absurd claims, like that you know things about land mines and that you won that rounders game."

I jolted my head back indignantly. "I *did* win that rounders game!"

"Uh-huh," he said, looping his arm around my waist and pulling me back over, "you keep telling yourself that, but we both know the truth. And anyway, I'm very happy to let you come first in other activities," he added in a low growl, kissing my neck.

It was very hard to argue with him about that.

It's important that whatever this is with Ryan, I don't rush it. Because that's the problem with being abroad; you lose all sense of normalcy and jump headfirst into relationships that crumble the minute the wheels of the plane hit that runway on home soil. Because it's not real life.

Real life is much more complicated, like working side by side and being pitted against each other by Cosmo over features. Moreover, Ryan has clearly built up the idea of me in his head for a long time, and in Florence he experienced the "holiday me," not the "actual me." He's enjoyed sexy black thongs and matching bras and sleeping naked and highlighter across my collarbones. He hasn't had to put up with me dashing out on dinner dates because I've got a VIP call. He hasn't seen the underwear I *actually* wear on a day-to-day basis, which is usually flesh-colored and *never* matching.

Is he still going to be filled with torturous desire sitting next to me when he knows that, under my work clothes, I'm wearing Spanx?

Unlikely.

My mind is racing and I'm tempted to get up and start packing early, just so I have something else to think about, but Ryan stirs next to me and his eyelashes flutter as he slowly wakes up.

I stare wide-eyed back at him.

"Hey," he murmurs, his voice croaky with sleep.

"I don't usually wear matching underwear," I blurt out.

He frowns, squinting at me. "Huh?"

"I think it's important you know that."

"Uh . . . okay, cool." He lifts his head off the pillow, leaning on his elbow. "Are you all right?"

I take a deep breath. I want to stay in the moment, but I also don't want to keep things from him. "Yeah. I've been thinking about what happens when we get back home. Between us, I mean."

"What would you like to happen?" he asks.

"What would *you* like to happen?"

He looks me in the eyes. "I would like to continue this."

"Sleeping together?" I say, knowing that I'm testing him.

"Among other things," he says, positioning his pillow to rest against the headboard and then sitting up, leaning back against it. "I want to take you out on dates. I want to spend real time together, outside of work. As far as I'm concerned, I'm all in. If you would like that?"

I nod slowly. "And what about work?"

"What about it?"

"We'll have to keep it secret, won't we? Everyone would gossip, and it would be horrible. We need to remain *strictly* professional in the office. That's important, Ryan. No special treatment, nothing like that. At work, we're colleagues, nothing else."

Can you *imagine* if Cosmo found out that that Ryan and I were sleeping together? He already has little to no respect for me as it is, but throw in a romantic entanglement with a colleague and he'll consider me a total laughingstock. It's not that I value Cosmo's opinion, but like it or not, he is my boss, and I don't want to push him too far. It's depressing to think that, if word got out, there would be fewer consequences for Ryan than there would be for me. I wish it wasn't that way, but with someone like Cosmo at the helm, there's no doubt in my mind that it would be so. Better not to risk it.

"Okay. Whatever you want." Ryan smiles at me.

"What? You're doing that smile thing again."

"I'm wondering how long you've been stressing over this."

"I'm not stressed. If anyone's the stressed one between us, that's you. I'm the easygoing one."

"Usually," he admits, before shrugging. "And yet here we are, roles reversed. Maybe things have changed now."

"How so?" I ask as he swings his legs out of bed and heads to the bathroom.

"Maybe I'm getting to you, Miss Jenkins," he calls over his shoulder, grinning widely at me before shutting the door behind him.

I sit there in a daze as I hear the sound of the shower turning on. The thing is, he's right.

Despite all my best efforts since he waltzed back into my life, I've fallen head over heels for Ryan Jansson.

And all I can think as I start to pack my suitcase is: *Please don't hurt me again.*

I don't know why I was so worried about coming home.

Everything is going surprisingly well. As far as I can tell, Ryan is still into me, despite my normal daily underwear, and no one at the office has caught on to our secret. Well, except for Mimi, who I obviously told straightaway and is already our biggest fan.

I do need to tell her the truth about my history with Ryan, though. At first, I simply didn't want to talk about it, but now it feels like I'm lying to her.

Dating hasn't been easy for me in the past because I've always felt like I had to choose between romance and my career. But one of the best things about Ryan is that if anyone understands my work ethic, it's him.

We both appreciate the demands of the job—if one of us has to get to an important interview or work through dinner to hit a deadline, it's not an issue. I'm not filled with guilt all the time, nor do I feel the need to justify typing late into the night.

When we tell Cosmo about the Isabella Blossom scoop, including the details of the birth in the back of the taxi, he is so ecstatic that he yells, "CLEAR THE FRONT COVER!" from his office, throwing everyone into utter confusion.

"Ryan, you *genius!*" Cosmo exclaims, standing up from his desk to give him a congratulatory handshake. "They'll be talking about this story for years to come. Ha! One of my journalists delivering a Hollywood actress's baby. You can't make up this shit."

"Harper played the lead role," Ryan presses. "She was the one who—"

"Yes, well done, now off you go and let me know the moment you've got the interview booked in," Cosmo says, ushering us out. "I need to tell the publishers that our sales numbers are going to skyrocket when this hits the stands. We *needed* a win."

"Why?" I ask, concerned by his tone. "Is everything okay?"

He shoots me a patronizing look. "Funnily enough, things aren't hunky-dory in the media industry, Harper. We can't all live in a fairytale land of fluffy celebrities. Behind the scenes we're dealing with a shit storm thanks to that little-known threat called *digital*. Magazines are a dying breed. Sales numbers matter."

"She was only asking if—" Ryan begins, but he is cut off by Cosmo.

"Go on, and get the social media team prepared, I want this to be picked up by every publication in the country, got it? I have to make some phone calls," he concludes, shooing us out.

Ryan seems annoyed at my role being so brazenly overlooked by Cosmo, but I tell him I'm used to it and not to worry. But nonetheless, he insists on cooking me dinner to cheer me up, an offer I eagerly accept. I've really tried hard to keep my flat in good shape since we got back, because I knew the first time Ryan came over, he would enter with a discerning eye. I admit, I'm quite *enjoying* being a tidier person, because I do find things much faster. It is a lot more effort, though, and I can't be perfect—and as soon as Ryan arrives with a bag full of groceries, I notice him clock the ripped cardboard strewn across the sofa. I can tell by his eyes that it's killing him, even though he's pretending not to notice it.

"I had a few book deliveries earlier," I admit as he starts unloading the shopping on the kitchen counter. "I'll put that all in the recycling."

"Glass of wine?" he offers, and I wonder if the cardboard is driving him to drink.

"Yes, please. I need it," I say, leaning against the kitchen counter and watching him look for two glasses in the cupboard before giving up and opening the clean, loaded dishwasher. "My boss was an asshole today."

"Is that right?" he says. "That's terrible. Thank goodness you have a ravishingly handsome colleague to make your day seem that bit better."

"You're right. Mimi is ravishingly handsome."

He chuckles, and as he pours the wine, I move to come

behind him and wrap my arms around his waist. He lets out a contented sigh, turning round to face me.

"Second time in a week you've come here to cook me dinner. I could get used to this." I grin up at him, resting my chin against his chest.

"Yeah? Me too," he says, placing a soft kiss on my lips. He hesitates and smiles against my mouth. "Although, I'd enjoy cooking here a little better if all the crockery was in the right place . . ."

"Are you insulting my kitchen arrangement?"

"It makes no sense to have the plates in a drawer that they don't fit into. Why wouldn't you have plates and bowls all in one place, like a cupboard for example?"

"I like the plates being at reaching distance from the stove."

He frowns. "But only half of them can fit in that drawer."

"I'm only one little person." I shrug. "I don't need six plates available to me on a whim. All I need is one plate waiting for me in that drawer and I'm sorted."

Lifting his eyes to the ceiling in despair, he sighs. "If I open this drawer now, how many plates are going to be in there? Would I be right in guessing there are none because they're all in the dishwasher?"

"You know what you need to do, Ryan?" I say innocently.

"Live a little?" he guesses.

I laugh, releasing him from my embrace and going to open the dishwasher, bending down and passing him two clean plates, before shutting it again. He looks pained.

"Bloody hell," I say, putting my hands on my hips, "you won't start cooking until the dishwasher is unloaded, will you?"

"I'm not proud to admit this, but it puts me startlingly on edge," he grimaces, coming over to help me as I pull the door down again. "And don't get me started on your dishwasher technique. How anything gets cleaned in here when you pile it up in this haphazard way is a miracle."

I let him lecture me on the best way of arranging the cutlery in the dishwasher because it's very nice of him to cook and he looks very sexy when he talks passionately about something, his forehead creased in stern concentration. Florence was great, but I'm discovering that I like the version of us here, too, bickering over plates and bowls, comforting each other after a bad day at work. Small moments with Ryan seem as meaningful as the big ones.

Later, my phone rings, and when I see it's my dad calling, I groan, pushing it away a little too enthusiastically. It flies off the table, clattering onto the floor.

"Whoops," I say, checking that the screen isn't more cracked than it already was.

"Who was that?" Ryan asks curiously.

"My dad. I'll message him later."

"You can call him back now if you want to."

I shoot him a look.

"Or not," he chuckles, recoiling under my glare. "You want to talk about it?"

"What?"

"Your parents," he says gently.

I pause, reaching for my wine and taking a sip for courage. "We haven't seen each other in a while," I say finally. "I think the last time was Easter. It didn't go well. We had a huge row. I don't know why they insist on meeting for dinner. No one has a good time. We should give up. I honestly don't know why we bother."

Ryan listens intently, waiting for me to say more. When I stay silent, he says simply, "Because they're your parents."

"Yeah, well, they wish they weren't," I mutter glumly, picking up my wine again and this time taking a large glug.

He watches me carefully. "You're seeing them for dinner soon, then?"

"Next week."

"Do you want me to come with you?"

I snap my head up to check he's being serious. "What?"

"If you want some moral support, I could come with you," he suggests calmly, looking completely unfazed by the idea.

"Ryan, you don't know what they're like. You do not want to put yourself in this situation, trust me. Avoid at all costs."

"I know that you find it tough to spend time with them, and I want to support you. It doesn't matter to me how the evening goes, as long as you're okay."

I stare at him. Holding my eye contact, he puts his fork down and leans forward, resting his chin in his palm.

"Unless what I've just said has completely freaked you out, in which case, please forget it," he says slowly, scrutinizing my expression. "I get that this is all very new, so if you think it would be inappropriate, then that's absolutely fine. I just don't like the idea of you facing that kind of evening alone, so if you need a friendly face, then I'll be there. That's all." He pauses. "Harper? Are you going to say something? You want me to talk about cutlery arranging in the dishwasher again to make this less awkward?"

"No, no," I say, breaking into a smile. "It's really nice of you to offer. I would like that very much."

His eyes light up and he sits back in relief. "Phew! For a minute there, I thought I was a goner."

"No, I was just processing how lovely you are," I assure him, elated at the idea of not having to face them alone for once. "But if you change your mind, please don't worry."

"I won't," he says confidently.

"Are you sure? Big deal, meeting the parents."

He shrugs. "Not really. You met mine."

"In a professional capacity. To them, I was your colleague."

"My parents aren't idiots, Harper," he says, picking up his fork again and digging into his meal. "They knew exactly who you were to me."

CHAPTER TWENTY

When something starts going wrong in an area of my life, I go into overdrive at work. My job makes me feel in control: I know what I'm doing there, and, with perseverance and focus, I almost always get what I want. If there's someone I want to interview, I'll go to unusual lengths to get them on board; if I want to cover a story, even if Cosmo is against it initially, I'll find another way of packaging it that he'll agree to. It's rare that I lose.

I'm currently on a mission to find out what's going on with Artistry. No one has got the inside scoop yet on the ill-fated reunion tour, so I'm determined it will be me who gets the lowdown.

And the reason I'm putting all my focus into this? Ryan.

Something is off.

Last week, everything was fine, better than fine. Things were *great*. I felt like I was walking around on a cloud, suddenly understanding what people mean when they say how falling for someone can make you delirious. I was infatuated with him, entranced by everything he did.

My heart fluttered when he shot me a secretive smile in the office. I hardly heard a word anyone said in the editorial meetings because I was studying the line of Ryan's sculpted jaw and the perfect slope of his nose and thinking about the softness of his lips, getting shudders of excitement when I imagined kissing him later. I loved that he was stern and serious at work. It amused me that people thought he was quiet and guarded. I enjoyed the way he frowned, his brow tightly furrowed, when he studied the layouts of the magazine. His edits were brilliant. His ideas, astounding. Ryan Jansson was something else and I couldn't quite believe he was mine.

And the secrecy of it all made it even more exciting.

I wasn't sure I'd ever felt like this before—excitable and distracted, vulnerable and open. It was amazing and terrifying at the same time. Usually, I'm able to keep a level head in a relationship, to focus on work and not let myself get carried away like a naïve, lovestruck teenager, but with Ryan, it was different. I *wanted* to get carried away. The world suddenly felt like a beautiful and dizzying place, and that was all down to him. It was madness, but I didn't care.

I realized I might just be falling in love—and when I caught Ryan looking at me in a certain way, I allowed myself to believe he was, too.

Then Monday happened.

Something changed that afternoon. Ryan had a morning of meetings, and then suddenly he was distant, cold, guarded. The longing looks vanished. He could barely meet my eye, even when discussing work-related things. Those secretive smiles that made me weak at the knees were replaced with irritable frowns. I thought he might be having a bad day, so I messaged him asking him if he'd like me to cook for him that night, and when I said cook, I obviously meant order some kind of delicious takeaway. He sent a cold, terse reply that he had to work late. I suggested Tuesday night instead, but that didn't work for him, either. Sorry, he said.

The doubt was immediate, consuming my brain, devouring my heart.

I scrutinized every word I'd said, everything I'd done over the weekend, desperately trying to work out where I'd gone wrong. When I couldn't think of anything that would put him off so abruptly, I put it down to things simply moving too quickly. We'd jumped in headfirst and it was too much; he'd gotten spooked. The Florence bubble had been intense, and now we saw each other every day. Yes, he claimed to have wanted this for a long time, and, yes, he made out as though he was all in and always had been.

But people don't always know what's best for them.

The bubble had officially burst.

We needed some distance and space. I had to embrace his pulling away from me as an opportunity for me to pull away from him.

So, work, as usual, saved me.

In the midst of filling my diary with work events, berating myself for losing my head in the clouds last week and missing some networking opportunities, I remember the Twitter storm over Artistry announcing they had no intention of doing a reunion tour. I try calling their agent, but the person manning their phone is well-rehearsed and, in an admirably polite voice, repeatedly tells me the agent is unable to speak right now.

That evening, while wandering around my bedroom wearing a face mask and trying not to stress over Ryan, I have a brainwave. A few years ago, the lead guitarist, Dylan Knox, took a stab at acting. He had a bit part in a Hollywood film that flopped and, after that, appeared in the pilot of a sitcom that didn't get picked up. Just before the film release, he did an interview with that smarmy journalist Jonathan Cliff. Dylan said he had always wanted to try his hand at acting and he had high hopes, and Jonathan wrote that he could sense that Dylan had what it takes. A few weeks later, Jonathan Cliff tweeted that he'd seen the movie and hoped that Dylan Knox didn't give up his day job.

I go straight to Google and begin searching for the agent who worked with Dylan Knox on his acting career, to see if it was anyone I know. When I see one name in particular come up on my screen, I break into a wide grin.

I set my alarm for 5:55 A.M., 5:57 A.M., 6 A.M., 6:03 A.M., and 6:05 A.M.

I reach The Lark café in Soho at quarter past seven.

I lean against a brick wall and enjoy my flat white in the early morning sunshine, scrolling through social media to make sure I didn't miss any breaking celebrity news overnight.

At half past seven, I spot Shamari walking toward The Lark, her eyes fixed on her phone as she types. Smiling at her promptness, I put my phone away and wait for her to emerge from the café with her coffee in hand.

"Shamari!" I say, bounding up to her and making her jump.

"Harper," she gasps, stopping in her tracks. "You gave me a heart attack!"

"We have got to stop bumping into each other like this. Are you stalking me?"

A smile creeps across her lips. "In twenty minutes, I have a meeting with a particularly difficult, rude, and currently very pissed-off actor who's just been dropped from a project and will be taking his frustration out on me, so you had better get to the part where you tell me what you want, pronto. I need to get to my desk and prepare myself for the torrent of abuse that's coming my way."

"Why was the actor dropped from the project?"

She brushes my question aside with a wave of her hand. "Creative differences."

"I love that phrase. Do you ever get to tell anyone the truth about why an actor is dropped from a film?" I ask, falling into step with her as she speed walks to her office.

"No," she replies. "Now, come on. Who are you after this time?"

"Dylan Knox."

She raises her eyebrows. "Of Artistry? You're barking up the wrong tree, Harper."

"You represented him during his short-lived acting career."

"A lifetime ago."

"Not that long ago," I reason. "Bet you can still contact him and I'll also bet that he's a big fan of yours."

"Why would you think that?" she asks curiously.

"Because *everyone* is a big fan of yours. Even the actor who's going to yell at you this morning."

She breaks into a reluctant smile. "You really live by the phrase 'flattery gets you everywhere,' don't you?"

"Is it getting me somewhere in this instance?"

She gives me a look. "We'll see. Why do you want to speak to him?"

"You know why. The reunion tour that never was. I want to know what happened and whether there might be a chance of fixing it."

She stops and turns to me in disbelief. "You think you might be able to talk to Dylan Knox and persuade him to reunite Artistry for a reunion tour? You're good, Harper, but no one is that good."

"Now, haven't you ever heard the expression 'You won't know until you try'?"

"What makes you think that Artistry might be persuaded by a journalist of all people?"

I shrug. "Because a journalist is very good with words. And words are powerful, Shamari. Anyway, I'm not saying that my goal is to get a world-famous band back together—I simply want to interview him. See if there's any hope."

"I thought you didn't go in for gossip."

"Look, *maybe* it's none of my business why the tour is suddenly off the table, *but* perhaps if they talked about what went wrong, they might iron out their issues. It always helps to talk to someone. I want that someone to be me."

"So, you want me to get in touch with Dylan Knox to see if there's any chance he'll do an interview with you?"

"To discuss the legendary impact that Artistry made—and could still make," I emphasize. "Ask him to consider it. We can talk about whatever he wants. Maybe there's something he wants to say. And you know that I'm a journalist he can trust."

She takes a moment to consider my proposition. "Look, Harper, I know that we managed to get Audrey Abbot on board, but this is a different kettle of fish. She had a play in the works. Dylan Knox doesn't have anything to promote."

"Yet."

She rolls her eyes, but I can tell she's coming round to the idea. "You are a force to be reckoned with, Harper Jenkins. Do you ever let yourself have a social life?"

"Probably as much as you do."

"How's that handsome boyfriend of yours that I met at the charity ball?"

"We broke up."

"Oh no! Why?"

"Creative differences."

She gives me a knowing smile. "All right. I'll let you know if I have time to reach out to Dylan Knox today. I can't promise that he'll listen to me—it's not like we work together anymore. I'm not his agent."

"Last night, I reread that interview he did for *Expression* with Jonathan Cliff. He was so passionate about acting, and you know what? He wasn't bad. The movie was bad. The script was bad. He did well with what he had."

"That's what I told him."

"Maybe this is a good time for you two to reconnect in a professional capacity," I encourage, sensing an opening and going with it. "A second wind for Dylan Knox—a potential reunion tour and perhaps even a brand-new movie role or two? 'If at first you don't succeed' and all that."

I see the wheels turning in her head. "I suppose I might be able to get him a couple of auditions. Artistry have been in the press again recently."

"Everyone loves a comeback," I remind her eagerly.

"Don't they just." She checks her phone. "Shit, I have to go. I'll be in touch—and I'm guessing I'll see you tonight?"

I look at her blankly. "Tonight?"

"The British Silver Screen Awards. I would assume you're going?"

"Oh! Right, yes, of course. That's tonight. See you there."

She nods and pushes the door into her building.

"SHIT!" I cry out once she's out of sight, shocking the commuters passing by.

I completely forgot about the British Silver Screen Awards and didn't bring a change of outfit to the office. Checking the time, I weigh up whether I can head back home, grab a dress and some shoes, and make it to the office for the editorial meeting.

It's impossible.

Well, Cosmo will relish the opportunity to tell me off, which is his favorite thing to do. And he only needs Ryan present in those meetings anyway; it's not like any of my features will be brought up. Starting off toward the tube, I find a new spring in my step, getting that familiar rush of adrenaline that comes when I know I might just land a big scoop.

It's already been a busy morning and it looks to be a hectic day ahead.

Just what I needed. I'll be much too distracted to think about Ryan at all.

Later, Ryan tries to talk to me, but I don't have time, and that's the honest truth.

"Hey, maybe we could go for lunch today?" he suggests when he catches me outside finishing up a phone call.

"Afraid I can't," I say, stepping round him to go back to the office. "I got here too late to take lunch. I'll be eating at my desk."

"How about dinner tonight?" he asks, hurrying to catch up with me.

"I have plans."

"Of course, it's dinner with your parents tonight."

Oh, bollocks.

"Actually, that's been rearranged," I lie, making a mental note to rearrange it. "I have an awards ceremony tonight."

"Ah." He nods. "Hey, did you remember both shoes this time?" he adds, attempting to lighten the tone, but I'm not having any of it.

"Yes," I say matter-of-factly, getting into the lift and pressing the button.

"Harper," he begins as the doors shut and we find ourselves alone, "I'd really like to find some time to talk to you."

"Sorry, Ryan, but today is not a good day," I say, looking straight ahead. "And anyway, you haven't really given me the impression that you've wanted to talk to me at all recently."

I see in the reflection of the silver lift doors that he bows his head, dropping his eyes to the floor. He looks pained, as though he's wrestling with something.

"I know, it's been a bit . . . I've had a lot . . . there's something . . ."

The doors ping open, interrupting him, and I march out, leaving him stumbling over his words.

"Harper, please," he whispers urgently, rushing alongside me. "I need to explain."

"No need to explain," I snap back, holding my head up high.

"If you're going to be hot and cold, I'm not interested. Anyway, I have a very important phone call to make now, so I'll see you later."

"Didn't you just get off a phone call outside?"

"I can make more than one phone call a day, Ryan," I huff, making a sharp turn into an empty meeting room and closing the door behind me.

Looking dejected, he heads back to our desks, while I quickly phone my dad.

"Harper," he says gruffly, "let me guess. You have to cancel."

I wince, shutting my eyes tightly. "Sorry, Dad, I have to go to an awards ceremony tonight."

"You know we all have lives, don't you, Harper?" he snaps. "We all have important events and social occasions to attend, but somehow we're able to maintain a level of decorum, and when we give our word, we stick to it."

"Dad, this was an honest mistake and I'm genuinely sorry," I say as earnestly as possible.

"We were expecting it from you. Hardly a surprise," he grumbles.

"Well, I'm glad I'm such a constant disappointment that letting you down isn't such a big deal," I say impatiently.

"I don't have time for dramatics," he replies dismissively. "Do you want to try to rearrange or is there simply no point?"

Collecting myself, I take a deep breath in an attempt to remain calm and brighten my tone again so we can keep things civil. "How about next week?"

"I'll have to check our calendars and of course liaise with your sister."

"Great, let me know. I can book somewhere."

"I think it's best for you to leave the arranging to us," he counters, his voice laced with disgruntlement.

"Fine," I say briskly, unwilling to take any more stings from him today. "I have to go."

Hanging up, I bury my head in my hands and scream, the sound muffled by my palms. Looking up when I hear a polite knock on the door, I see a group of journalists standing there watching me, waiting to use the meeting room.

"Sorry!" I trill, swinging open the door.

One of the journalists looks at me sympathetically. "Having one of those days?"

"Oh yes," I say, appreciating the smile of solidarity she gives me. "Having one of those days."

⌇

When you're not up for anything, awards ceremonies *really* drag, but once that boring bit is all done with, the mingling afterward is a lot more fun. I decide to let my hair down a bit and take advantage of the free champagne and excellent company, making a beeline for anyone who might make a good profile piece. It's been nice seeing friends in the industry—I've been able to catch up with the publicist of Isabella Blossom's film, Rachael Walker, who told me that Isabella's baby is *divine* and she can't wait until I'm able to come over to get that exclusive, and I also bump into Mae, who arranged the interview with Max Sjöberg.

"So that hot colleague of yours wasn't interested in me, then?" she says after we've done our greeting of two kisses on the cheek. "I did give him my number but I haven't heard anything."

"I didn't realize you'd given him your number," I say, surprised he didn't mention it.

"I was trying to be sexy and confident," she admits with a giggle. "You know, by making the first move. Lot of good it did me."

"Maybe he's playing it cool," I say, taking a swig of champagne. "He's good at that."

"Whatever, I like men to be forward. If they're into me, I want them to let me know. Otherwise I'm not interested. I don't have time for games."

"I will cheers to that!" I exclaim heartily, clinking my glass against hers.

Later, I spot Shamari at a table nearby and head over to slide into the empty seat to her left, disturbing her conversation with a handsome man in his fifties.

"Thank god you came over," she says in a low voice after the man excuses himself and leaves. "I can't for the life of me remember who that person is. He was chatting like we were old friends!"

"He looks familiar. Is he a director?"

"Beats me." She shrugs. "So, how's your night been? How was your table?"

"I was right at the back, sitting on the same table as Jonathan Cliff from *Expression*," I inform her, rolling my eyes. "They always insist on lumping us journalists together."

"The organizers are trying to keep you at arm's length from the talent." Shamari grins. "They don't need any more tears than the awards already cause. Awards are so ridiculous—does anyone actually care? I find these ceremonies so dreary."

"You're only saying that because that sexy client of yours, Julian Newt, didn't win in his newcomer category."

"I'm impressed you remembered his name this time," she chuckles. "And my pushing has got him on your radar, so I'm doing my job. Keep him in mind for an interview."

"You know who I've got in mind for an interview," I prompt hopefully.

"Dylan Knox did not return my phone call today," she says. "But I'll try him again tomorrow, so it's not a lost cause yet. He can be tricky to reach, and now that you've put the idea in my head of him acting again, I have my own interest in getting through to him. Leave it with me and let me see what I can do."

"Thank you, I appreciate it," I say, leaning back and letting out a long sigh.

She watches me carefully. "Long day?"

"It's had its ups and downs."

"I can imagine. I'm really sorry to hear about what's going on with *Narrative*. It's so sad that this is happening with so much print media now, and it happens so quickly, too. Do you know yet if you're safe?"

"Safe?"

"From the redundancies. I heard there's going to be at least two or three at the magazine. You haven't heard anything about your job yet?"

I blink at her. "How . . . how do you know about redundancies at *Narrative*?"

She looks confused. "You know how quickly news like that spreads in this industry, Harper. Nothing is secret for that long. I heard it's going to be this week. Anyway, we're all keeping our fingers crossed at the agency that Cosmo won't be an idiot and will keep your job safe and sound. Although, saying that, if you do find yourself at a loose end, let me know if you'd consider making the switch to the agency side. I could do with someone with your drive on my team."

Her eyes flicker over my shoulder and she plasters a fake smile across her face, wiggling her fingers at someone behind me.

"Shit, I have to go," she says through gritted teeth. "That producer over there is about to start a project that is perfect for Julian Newt. Shame I can't stand her. I'll call you tomorrow, Harper."

"Yeah," I mumble as she gets up, leaving me stranded at the table on my own.

I sit in a daze, too shocked to move. My stomach is in knots and I'm not sure if I might be sick. My surroundings a blur of noise, I force myself up onto my feet and then manage to dodge through the crowds, bursting through the exit of the building and gasping for air. The paparazzi surrounding the exit lift their cameras excitedly and then lower them again once they realize I'm no one important. I stumble and have to balance myself on the shoulder of one of the photographers.

"You all right?" he says as I clutch at my chest, which feels more and more constricted.

"F-fine," I whisper, thanking him and then launching myself into one of the waiting black cabs, desperate to get home to bed where I can lie down and cry.

Because, even though it's too early to say for sure, I think I already know what's coming.

By the end of the week, I'll be out of a job.

CHAPTER TWENTY-ONE

On Thursday morning, we're told that our jobs are at risk. Cosmo holds one-to-one meetings with us all day to talk through our rights, why redundancies are necessary, confirm that anyone in the team could be selected, and ask whether we want to take voluntary redundancy. I almost feel sorry for him—it's a miserable discussion and having it with so many people, one after the other, can't be fun. But then I remember it's Cosmo and any sympathy fizzles away. He's probably secretly delighted that he can make a few cuts.

The mood of the office has never been lower. It's practically silent. And I can't tell if it's a good or a bad thing that Ryan isn't there. He's gone to Wales to interview a couple in their thirties who used to be risk-management specialists at a private bank in London but sacked it all in and left the city to become farmers, for a feature he's writing on the trend of young people swapping urban lives for rural ones. He won't be back until tomorrow.

He also hasn't messaged me, and when I ask Cosmo if Ryan knows what's going on, he says he does with a dismissive wave of his hand. I can't help but notice that Cosmo is fidgeting endlessly while we are talking and can't look me in the eye. He seems flustered and irritated at my questions, as though I'm accusing him of something. His behavior only confirms what I've already guessed.

"You don't know who's going," Mimi says dismally when we've escaped the suffocatingly grim atmosphere of the office that afternoon for a stroll. "It could be anyone."

"Cosmo has never understood my job."

"Travel is hardly a necessity."

"Mimi, *you* don't need to worry. Cosmo just expanded the luxury travel section because it brings in so much paid advertising. Not to mention how popular your pages are because you're so brilliant."

"Same goes for you!"

I give her a look. "You know how Cosmo feels about my role. And since our meeting, I've been analyzing recent events, and something is becoming a little clearer."

She stops to face me. "What?"

"I thought it was strange how Cosmo kept trying to give my features to Ryan—I get that there can be crossover with our roles and sometimes the same topics are of interest to us both, but Cosmo kept trying to palm off what should be obvious celebrity features to him, too. I think he's been testing the waters to see if Ryan can essentially do both our jobs."

Mimi frowns as she considers my theory.

"Think about it. How many magazines have a celebrity editor nowadays? Maybe some of the big women's glossy magazines or gossip blogs, but not publications like *Narrative*. Roles like mine can easily be covered by someone else."

"No one can do your job like you can," she says fiercely, and I feel an overwhelming surge of love for her support.

"Thanks, Mimi, but it's a miracle that I've held onto this job for as long as I have, really. I should be grateful for that, but—" I hesitate, staring at the ground, my voice breaking slightly as I try to hold it together "—I love it so much. I can't imagine doing anything else. It's all I have."

Mimi hugs me and reminds me that we still don't know anything yet. We just have to wait and see.

That night, lying in bed, I come to the conclusion that I can't bear to wait and see much longer. Which is why on Friday afternoon I request a meeting with Cosmo and ask him outright if my job is being made redundant.

"Harper," he begins, startled by my abrupt line of questioning, "we will be announcing the redundancies next week. Everything is still being discussed and prepared, and—"

"But you already know," I interrupt, standing behind the chair opposite his desk, my fingernails digging into the back cushion. "I know that you know. You're just finalizing details at this point. If I'm being made redundant, I'd like to be notified now."

Studying my determined expression, he presses his lips together and then inhales deeply.

"All right," he says gruffly. "I'm sorry, Harper, but I'm afraid you are one of the casualties this round. Although we . . . value you and your hard work for this magazine, we are unable to justify keeping the position of celebrity editor."

I knew it was coming, but it still feels like being punched in the stomach, standing in a glass box and learning that everything I've worked for is slipping from my grasp.

Cosmo clears his throat, making it obvious that he'd rather this conversation finishes sooner than later by checking his watch.

"Anyway, we can have the formal meeting next week to discuss the terms of redundancy and your notice period, and you're welcome to bring someone with you from HR, if you'd like. I must point out that I'm doing you a favor here, giving you the heads-up, simply because you asked, but I'd appreciate it if you didn't tell anyone else on the team quite yet. There are two others who will also be made redundant, and I'll be telling them next week. If people find out that you know, they'll all be banging on the door to find out who else is in trouble, and I'd rather not have that headache today."

He glances at his computer and moves his mouse to click on something.

"I need to deal with this email. Will that be all?"

I don't know how to respond. I'm suddenly too exhausted to speak, so I nod silently and walk out of his office. No one looks up as I emerge. They're all too focused on their work or on their phones. I hear Gabby sniff from her computer and see that her eyes are red and squinty from crying again today. She is a fairly recent hire as the editorial assistant and is therefore convinced that she's going to be the first to go. I wish I could protect her from it, especially when she's only just broken into journalism. I feel so sorry for her, and terrible for myself. I'm cursed with knowing I'm no longer part of this team without being able to share the news with anyone.

Sitting down, I pull myself in toward my desk and stare numbly at my screen. The emails popping up in my inbox seem irrelevant now. I try to picture my life without this job. I can't. It seems impossible. I'll have to start applying elsewhere. The panic begins to bubble through me.

What am I going to do?

"Harper, are you okay?" Mimi asks, peering round her screen. "You don't look so good."

"Yeah, fine, but I've just realized I'm supposed to be . . . at a book launch," I squeak, bile rising in my throat. I reach down for my bag. "I have to go."

"We were all going to go for a drink after work," she says, gesturing to the rest of the team. "Drown our sorrows together, so to speak."

"I really need to be at this launch. It's a big deal. Lots of . . . scandal. Sorry to miss out."

"We'll miss you. Are you sure you're all right?" she checks, concerned.

"Just a bit of a headache. I'll take some ibuprofen on the way," I assure her, logging off and pushing myself up off my chair. "See you."

I don't know if Cosmo notices me leaving as I hurry past his office, but if he does, he doesn't try to stop me. Why should he care now anyway? Standing at the back of the elevator, I blink back tears as reporters from the main paper cram in with me, and I wait impatiently as they file out onto the ground floor, then rush past them to get to the exit.

It's raining. Heavily. It was a clear morning and warm, too, so I haven't brought an umbrella or any kind of jacket with me to work today.

I step out into the rain and begin the walk to the tube, water drops falling freely down my face, dripping off the end of my nose, the wisps of my hair that have fallen loose from my pony-tail plastering against my forehead, my blue shirt beginning to stick to my skin as it dampens. I don't care.

"Harper!"

I'm so focused on putting one foot in front of the other, blinking through the onslaught of rain, that I don't notice Ryan until he's right in front of me, stopping me in my tracks. He peers down at me, holding a large umbrella that he immediately positions over my head.

"What are you doing?" he asks, clearly baffled by my walk in the rain when I'm supposed to be working.

"You're in Wales," I say stupidly, even though he's standing in front of me right here on the pavement in Vauxhall.

"Only until this morning. I've just got the train back. You're soaked! Why don't you have an umbrella?"

"It wasn't raining earlier."

"Where are you going? Do you have an event?"

"Yes," I lie, using the back of my hand to wipe the water off my face. "I have to go."

"Wait, Harper, take this," he says, holding out the handle of the umbrella as I go to step around him.

"No, thanks. I'm fine," I say, pushing it away.

"What's wrong?" He steps back to stand in front of me again. "Something is wrong. Talk to me."

"You heard about the redundancies, didn't you?"

His face falls. "Yes. It's so shit. How is everyone?"

"Not good. Did Cosmo call you yesterday?"

He runs a hand through his hair, and I understand straight-away why he's not answering a very simple question.

"How long have you known?" I ask, looking at him in disbe-lief.

"A few days," he admits quietly.

"A few *days?*" I repeat, bewildered. "Since when?!"

"Monday."

"You've known all week."

Ryan looks pained. "I wanted to tell you. I was desperate to tell you, but I had to be professional. I was under strict instruc-tions that it was confidential information. Even though it killed me, I had to keep it from you. I'm so sorry."

"That's why you've been off with me," I say slowly, putting two and two together. "You could have said something."

"I wasn't allowed to say anything to anyone," he protests.

"Yes, Ryan, but it's *me*. You could have trusted me to keep it to myself! You could have prepared me for this! Instead, you were cold and distant, and I assumed it was all my fault. I had no idea what I'd done wrong. And then when I found out this huge news with the rest of the team, you weren't there and you didn't even message!"

"I didn't want to lie to you," he insists. "I knew I wanted to see you before talking about it."

"Well, you did lie to me. And now I feel like an even bigger idiot than I did before."

"I didn't *want* to know that information, Harper! I didn't want Cosmo to have that meeting with me. I've felt like the biggest fraud the last few days, having to face everyone in the office and act normally with this huge cloud over my head. I wish he hadn't told me a damn thing," he seethes, his eyes flaring with anger.

My blood turns to ice as something else dawns on me.

"Ryan," I begin, my voice weak and shaky, "did you know *who* was being made redundant?"

With a pained expression, he shuts his eyes.

"Oh my god," I say, watching him. "You didn't just know it was coming, you knew that it was coming for *me*. Cosmo told you."

"He didn't tell me straight out," he croaks. "He heavily implied that you were the most at risk. But Harper, I didn't—"

I don't want to hear any more. I don't want to speak to him. I don't want to *look* at him. Pushing past, I march down the road as fast as my legs can carry me without breaking into a full-on run. He keeps calling out my name, hurrying to catch up with me, still trying to hold the umbrella over my head.

"Leave me alone," I cry.

"Please, Harper," he says, trying to grab my arm, but I shake him off.

"Get off me!"

"Can you just listen to me instead of storming off?"

"Why should I listen to you, Ryan?" I yell, turning to face him and throwing up my arms in exasperation. I don't care that I'm shouting in public. I don't care who sees. I'm so tired. "You lied to me! Again! It's history repeating itself!"

"Don't say that, Harper. It's not like that," he insists firmly.

"It's even *raining*. Just like last time! We're in some kind of time loop! I've got fucking déjà vu! Outside the office where we work, my life falling apart, yours perfectly intact. Days of you lying to my face."

"That's not what—"

"I am *such* an idiot. A fucking fool. The kind of person you read about in books and watch in movies who keeps falling for the same bullshit. You'd think I'd learn!"

"Harper—"

"When you got this job, I told myself that I couldn't fall for you again, that I couldn't let myself be taken in by you or let myself be tempted by this weird . . . this weird—" I gesture at myself and then at him "—pull between us. And yet here I am eleven years later in *exactly* the same position! You couldn't make it up!"

"Please, just—"

"Just what, Ryan?" I demand loudly over the noise of the rain. "What would you like me to do? Listen to your side of the story? Trust you? Is that what you want?"

"You have to understand why I couldn't tell you, Harper! I wanted to talk to you. I *hated* that I couldn't say anything. I hated myself for knowing. That's why I had to distance myself from you, because I couldn't bear the idea of not being able to tell you. I wasn't going to make the same mistake as last time and act normal around you with this huge, horrible secret I didn't even want to know! I would have done anything for us not to be colleagues so I could—"

I throw my head back and laugh, the rain pouring freely down my face, my mascara no doubt smudging over my cheeks.

"Well, whaddya know, Ryan? You got your wish! We are officially no longer colleagues. I don't have a job anymore, so there you go. You can wipe your hands of me."

He recoils, stung. Good.

"How can you say that?" he asks me, his cheeks flushing red. "You know how I feel about you."

"What I know is that you lied to me and betrayed me *again*," I say, my voice shaking as I blink back hot tears that threaten to spill over. "And then you made me think that *I* had done something wrong, by essentially ignoring me these last few days. You have no idea how this feels. If I thought I was humiliated last time, it's nothing to how I feel right now. This job was *everything* to me. And now it's gone. You and Cosmo can have a splendid time in your little boys' club, printing whatever the fuck you want to print. I'm no longer the thorn in your sides."

"That's not what it's like," he says, the hand not holding the umbrella clenching into a fist. "I hate how he treats you. I have only ever admired what you do, Harper. For fuck's sake, I know this is a shock, but this job is not everything to you."

I narrow my eyes at him. *"Excuse me?"*

"What I mean is that you are better than this job, Harper," he presses. "You are one of the best journalists I've ever met! Everyone in the industry knows it. I knew it before, but now that I've had the opportunity to see you at work, I'm even more convinced that what you have is an extremely rare talent. You draw the best out of everyone. And you know what? Cosmo has been holding you back. This magazine has been holding you back. I get that being made redundant is scary, but you can do whatever you want now, Harper, and I think that you can do a lot." He sighs. "I appreciate that you probably don't want to hear this from me right now, but I think that this could be a good thing."

I shake my head at him. "You are unbelievable. This isn't a good opportunity, Ryan. This is it. I won't come back from this."

"What are you talking about?"

"My parents were right all along. I shouldn't keep trying at a career that's going nowhere," I admit, trembling.

"You don't mean that," he states. "You're angry and upset. You're in shock. You need to go home and rest. Let me come with you. Let me take you home."

"I do mean it, Ryan," I say, tears streaming down my cheeks as the anger crumbles into hurt. "I'm at the top of my game and I'm still somehow failing. You say that everyone knows how good I am, but look at me. I'm redundant. I'm standing in the rain with you, eleven years after my first big failure, and here I am, a failure once again. I give up."

"So, you've had one setback and now you're giving up?" he huffs impatiently.

"A setback? I've lost my job! It's all I have!"

"It is *not all you have*, Harper," he practically yells, his tone taking me by surprise. "This job is not your be-all and end-all. It's a *job*. It's not who you are."

"That just goes to show you don't know me at all."

I let out an involuntary sob, and he instinctively takes a step toward me, his arm reaching up to my face, but I bat him away, recoiling from him.

"Leave me alone, Ryan. I'm going home."

"Let me come with you," he says softly, his stern expression crumpling. "I don't want you to be on your own. Not when you're like this."

"I want to be alone," I insist.

"Harper," he pleads, "let me—"

"I don't want to have anything to do with you, Ryan," I snap. "This is it. We're done."

His jaw clenches. "Don't say that. Please don't say that."

"I should have learned my lesson last time. You haven't changed. I was naïve to think that I could trust you again."

"You can trust me!" he says, his voice strangled, his eyes glistening. "Harper, I lov—"

"Don't," I instruct coldly, glaring at him. "Whatever this was between us, it's over. For good. I can't be with someone I don't trust. And I will never trust you again, Ryan Jansson."

I turn on my heel and walk away.

He doesn't follow.

CHAPTER TWENTY-TWO

Most of the weekend is spent wallowing in the disaster that is my life.

Friday night was an embarrassing haze of tears, wine, and mini breakdowns—the smallest things toppled me into spirals of despair that concluded with banshee-style wailing sobs. For example, when I couldn't find a clean wine glass, I drank wine from a mug that said WORLD'S BEST WRITER on it—a gift I got in the office Secret Santa a few years ago. This released a torrent of crying. I had no right to drink from that cup. *No right.*

I got into my pajamas as soon as I walked through the door to get out of my rain-soaked clothes—I must have looked a sight on the tube, but I didn't care—and I climbed into bed with a raging headache, without bothering to take off my makeup. On Saturday morning, I catch my reflection in the bathroom mirror and gasp at the state of my face: blotchy, puffy, with shadows of mascara smudged down my cheeks. I feel so drained from the previous day's events that I take my makeup remover back to bed with me, wiping at my eyes from the safety of my duvet.

When Mimi phones, I try my best to sound relatively normal, but she knows me too well.

"Hello?" I answer.

"Oh my god, Harper," she gasps. "What's wrong?"

"Nothing!" I insist, my eyes filling with tears at her voice and my eyes welling with yet more tears. "I'm *fine.*"

"Did something happen with Ryan? I knew something was

off with you yesterday before you left, and then he came into the office and I've never seen him so tense. He looked like he was going to either burst into tears or hit someone in the face. Are you with him now?"

"No," I squeak.

"So you're on your own?"

"Yes."

"I'm coming over," she says firmly, giving me no opportunity to protest.

By the time she arrives, I've forced myself to have a shower and get into fresh pajamas. Mimi is, of course, dressed as though she's going for afternoon tea at The Ritz—in a bright orange sundress. She starts when I open the door. I remember I'm still wearing a face mask that is supposed to hydrate and plump your skin. While I go remove it, she heads to the kitchen to put the kettle on. I plod in a few minutes later to find her washing up a couple of mugs in the sink.

"I've put your dishwasher on," she informs me.

"I meant to do that last night, but I forgot," I sigh, leaning back on the kitchen counter and folding my arms across my chest.

"Tea or coffee?"

"I'm the host. I should be asking you that question."

"Harper, look at you," she says with a sad smile. "You're wearing your pajamas inside out and you have one Miss Piggy slipper on."

"I gave up looking for the other one," I admit. "I think it might be under the bed."

"I'm not sure you're in the right state of mind right now to handle a kettle. So, tea or coffee?"

"Coffee, please. I could use the caffeine."

"You want to tell me what's going on? Knowing you, I'm guessing that whatever this is—" she gestures to my general appearance "—it's not because of a boy."

"You would guess correctly."

She squints her eyes at me, trying to work it out. "Your parents? I know you were due to have dinner with them this week, and that never goes well. But usually you laugh it off."

"I rearranged that dinner for next week. I'm sure fireworks will fly, but you're right, I stopped crying over them a long time ago."

"Is it worry over the redundancies? Because I know it's horrible having that hanging over our heads at the moment, but you can't let yourself get into a state before we have any of the answers."

I look down at the floor. "Mimi, Cosmo already told me."

She looks at me in disbelief. "W-what?"

"I asked him point blank on Friday. I shouldn't have, but I knew that when it came to cutting roles, he would put mine at the forefront. And I was right."

"Oh my god. Harper," she says softly, coming over and wrapping her arms around me. "I'm so sorry. I can't believe it!"

"I can," I reply, my voice muffled in her shoulder. "Cosmo has been looking for an excuse to get rid of me since he took over the magazine. I should have known it was coming."

She pulls back. "Do you know who else—"

"No, I'm sorry," I say, biting my lip. "I don't have a clue about anyone else. And I'm sorry to tell you this now; it's not fair when we don't know who else might go. It's really selfish of me, actually."

She shakes her head. "No, it's not. I'm glad you told me now. And anyway, if it turns out that I'm losing my job next week, too, then at least we'll be going together."

"Right," I say with a weak smile.

"Harper, you know this isn't a reflection on you, right?" she checks, moving away to finish making the coffees. "It's nothing to do with your work. It's because Cosmo doesn't get it! He doesn't get his audience, he doesn't get the magazine—he never bothered to try to understand why your features are so popular and how hard you work to get them. I know you don't want to hear this right now, but honestly? I think you're too good for *Narrative* magazine under his leadership."

"Thanks, Mimi. But it doesn't matter. Obviously the publishers agreed with him."

"Which baffles me!" she exclaims, grabbing a carton of milk from the otherwise empty fridge. "The powers that be care about numbers, right? Subscribers, newsstand sales, digital clicks—the majority of those come from the kind of popular features you head up!"

"Yes, but those features can also be done by Ryan Jansson."

She carries the two mugs of coffee over to the sofa and I follow her, and we sink into the cushions next to each other. I take my mug gratefully, the comforting warmth heating my fingers as I clasp it in my hands.

"Ryan doesn't have your contacts, and he doesn't have your way with people," Mimi points out. "Who else could have gotten Audrey Abbot on our front page but you?"

"Ryan is very good at what he does," I reason. "He'll be able to handle it. Cosmo knows that."

Mimi shoots me a sympathetic look. "Ryan is going to be devastated. He won't have seen this coming."

I smile at the irony. "Oh, he saw it coming before anybody else."

"What do you mean?" she asks, puzzled.

"Cosmo told him about the redundancies at the beginning of the week. I think he likes to see Ryan as his buddy. Anyway, we had a big fight about it yesterday."

"You and Ryan?"

I nod, taking a sip of my coffee. "When he got back to the office. I confronted him about it and he admitted that he'd known for days."

"About the redundancies or about your job specifically?"

"Both. Apparently Cosmo implied I was a goner. Ryan didn't bother to tell me that, though. Instead, he just distanced himself from me so he wouldn't have to lie to my face . . . making me feel like *I* was the one who had done something wrong. Pathetic," I mumble.

"I don't know, Harper," she begins cautiously, "it sounds like Cosmo put him in a horrible position. I doubt he was allowed to tell you anything."

"Of course not, but he still could have," I argue. "He could have trusted me."

"It's not just that, though. I mean, if I were in his shoes, I'm not sure I would have been able to tell you. Breaking your heart like that, when everyone knows how much you love what you do?" She shudders. "It would be so horrible. It's not really his place anyway—even if you are shagging behind the scenes."

"I get that he was being professionally responsible," I huff, irritated that she's speaking sense. "But a warning would have been nice."

"Would it have made any difference?" She tilts her head at me. "Honestly, Harper, if you want my opinion on this, you shouldn't be focusing on who knew what when. You should be taking some time, looking after yourself, and when you're ready, having a think about what you're going to do next. We can look around for other jobs or you could consider going freelance. I bet there are loads of editors out there who would be desperate for you to write for them! There's no harm in reaching out to your contacts."

"And telling them that I've lost my job at *Narrative*? They'll immediately doubt my abilities. I mean, *I* doubt my abilities, so why wouldn't they?"

"No, they won't, Harper. Everyone knows what it's like in this industry. Some of the best journalists in the country have had to go freelance." She gives me a stern look. "You can't let Cosmo make you believe you're not valuable. I won't have it."

I smile at her. "If you get made redundant, I'd say you could hack it as a life coach."

"It's always easier to give advice when you're on the outside of a situation," she says gently. "I know you must be feeling really low. And I'm so sorry."

"Thanks. And thank you for coming round," I say, nudging her leg with my toe.

"Always here for you." She pauses. "So, are you going to speak to Ryan about this? I don't want you throwing away something that has the potential to be really good over Cosmo being a big-mouthed idiot. Ryan is the sensible type, after all. He probably didn't agree with Cosmo telling him that kind of sensitive information and putting him in a position where he couldn't share it with his colleagues. Maybe you can let him off just this once?"

"The thing is, it hasn't been just the once."

She frowns. "What?"

"He's done this before." I exhale slowly. "Mimi, did I ever tell you about the time I interned at *The Daily Bulletin*?"

<hr />

Walking into the office on Monday is like wading through molasses, and then sitting there, acting normal and pretending to do any form of work, is horrific. Even worse, I have to sit next to *him*. At least Ryan has the decency to avoid more contact than absolutely necessary. He seems resigned to the fact that there is no hope for us, personally or professionally, and barely says a word to me. I have to fake a few meetings so I can be out of the office as much as possible, but what is Cosmo going to do if he finds out? Fire me?

When I'm supposed to be at these "meetings," I instead sit in coffee shops and scroll through media jobs, but it feels pointless. My brain is telling me that I need to work in order to, you know, eat and live. But my heart isn't in it and I can't bring myself to open my CV to update it, let alone upload it. When I quietly admit as much to Mimi, she acts as though it's no big deal and says I have to give myself some time to get over the shock.

On Tuesday, Cosmo calls me into his office to discuss my redundancy. He also individually calls in Naomi, the style assistant, and Gabby, the editorial assistant. My heart breaks for them as I watch them emerge from the meeting with downcast expressions.

After receiving lots of hugs, I suggest the three of us go get some air, so we do. We go to Roasted and Gabby cries into the tea that I buy her, and Naomi pats her on the back and says it is going to be okay, even though she doesn't look convinced of that herself. But I assure them that it really *will* be okay. They are smart and brilliant, and once the initial shock has worn off, they will see this as an opportunity to do something new and exciting.

I basically reel off everything you should say to someone in our position.

I can tell they believe it as much as I do. So I conclude with, "To be honest, it's shit. And I'm so sorry this has happened."

They appreciate that a lot more than my little pep talk.

Funnily enough, the office is much more bearable now that everyone knows. We can deal with it and move on, and everyone else in the team can stop worrying about themselves and put all their energy into making us feel better. I haven't paid for my lunch all week, which is a bonus. And Cosmo has been lenient about our notice periods. We only have to do two weeks, including this one, and next week we're allowed to work from home. I thought that revealed he had an ounce of compassion in him, but it turns out he wants to rejig the seating arrangement now that he's losing three members of the team, and he thinks it's better to sort that sooner rather than later, so it's easier if we're out the office.

What a sweetheart.

Still, I'm not complaining. They're throwing us a leaving party at The Old Oak this Friday. Mimi is heading it up and she promises that she's gone all out to make it fun rather than depressing. She also informs me that the main paper has had a round of redundancies this week, too, and they are also throwing a party on the same night, so a strange unspoken competition has emerged between Mimi and someone named Harold, who is heading up the paper's party.

"He thinks he's all that with his mustard-yellow socks, but that man wouldn't know a good finger sandwich if it hit him in the face," she muttered earlier as Harold swanned past.

Mimi has been a lifeline this week. When I've needed a shoulder to cry on, she's been there, and when I've needed a bit of tough love, she's been happy to oblige. She repeats the same sentiments, and they're starting to get through to me: I've been at this magazine so long, stepping away from it seems terrifying, but it's also a new adventure—life is always going to have its twists and turns, and I can't predict them all.

I think the reason I've been so upset is down to the humiliation of being forced out, rather than leaving on my own terms. But maybe I'll be grateful for the push someday.

I try to focus on these optimistic thoughts on Thursday evening as I arrive at the restaurant to meet my parents and sister. Positive vibes only.

The absolute last thing I want to do right now is attend this family dinner.

My confidence is at an all-time low and I know I'll have to take a few punches to the gut over my career, but I can't rearrange again. It's better that I get it over and done with and then hopefully we won't bother each other for another few months.

All I have to do is put on a fake smile, pretend everything is okay, and steer the conversation away from me as much as possible. If I find myself under the spotlight, I'll lie like I've never lied before.

To be honest, the last few days have been so shit, I might as well throw in a dinner with my parents to top it all off.

The three of them are already at the table when I arrive. Dad is in a suit and tie, and Mum is in her signature black from head to toe, wearing a pencil dress and black heels. They always dress in office wear, even at weekends, and everything they own is expensive and tailored. Mum's blond, shoulder-length hair is perfectly coiffed, tucked behind her ears with her pearl earrings on display. Dad is almost fully gray now, and he looks good for it—I may not take after them in any other way, but my parents both have a good head of hair, genes that Juliet and I also inherited.

The thick hair is as far as Juliet and I go when it comes to similarities, and it's not even the same color—she's followed Mum's footsteps and is now a honey blond, which I don't think suits her as much as her natural brown. She has a narrow, angular face and sharp features with striking green eyes and great eyebrows, while I'm a little softer round the edges and unfortunately a victim of the nineties trend for plucking my eyebrows to shit. While I'm stuck there filling my eyebrows in every morning, I imagine Juliet never touches hers.

We all fit our stereotypes perfectly. Them, the sophisticated, brilliant, glacial lawyers. Me, the chaotic, fanciful writer. It's never easy being the odd one out.

"You're late," Dad comments, picking up the menu after an awkward hello, because we're never quite sure how to greet each other. Being family, we civilly attempt a kiss on the cheek, but it's standoffish from both sides. We should probably accept that handshakes would be more appropriate.

"I got stuck at—"

"At work," Mum finishes for me, already topping up her wine.

"Juliet works twelve-hour days, yet she manages to get here on time."

You know, I don't think I've ever had a conversation with my parents that doesn't involve a reminder that Juliet works twelve-hour days?

Juliet remains tight-lipped on the topic, but at least offers me some version of a smile—albeit a small, indifferent one—as I take my seat.

"So, the food looks good," I remark brightly, determined not to engage and instead take the high road. "Have you eaten here before?"

"Yes, last week," Dad replies irritably. "When you didn't come. We didn't want to waste the reservation."

I take the hit, answering brightly, "Then you'll know what to order. How handy! Juliet, could you pass the wine? How is the job, sis?"

"Fine," she replies shortly, pouring me a drink and returning the bottle to its cooling bucket.

I'm impressed by my own self-restraint that I don't down my entire glass straightaway, but I do allow myself two large glugs before I set it back down again.

"Great! You want to expand on your answer at all?"

She scowls at me. "Not really."

"Okay. No problem. Fun chat while it lasted."

Two more gulps of wine are taken. *Positive vibes, positive vibes . . .*

"Juliet has made partner at her firm," Mum announces proudly, beaming at her. "She's done extremely well, considering she's so young."

A blush of pink appears on my sister's cheeks as she stares down at her lap. It's not like her to look so modest about her achievements. She used to tell me all about them the minute I stepped within her vicinity.

"Very impressive, Juliet. Well done," I say dryly.

"It's wonderful news and we should celebrate," Dad announces.

"Dad, it's not news, you've known about it for months," Juliet says, seeming irritated. "And we already celebrated when I came to see you."

"We never tire of celebrating our daughter's success. Not that we're surprised, of course. They really should have made you partner last year with everything you've done for that firm," he says pompously. "But here you are and there are great things to come!"

"I'll toast to that," Mum smiles, raising her glass.

We follow suit, but Juliet shifts uncomfortably under the glare of their attention, glancing at me and then looking quickly away. Maybe she's starting to put herself in my shoes for once and realizes that being in her shadow has always been a bit chilly.

"It's such a shame that Harry couldn't join us for dinner," Mum says, placing her glass down before looking pointedly at me. "You haven't met Juliet's boyfriend, have you, Harper? He's an investment banker, studied at Cambridge. He's very impressive."

"He'd have to be to keep up with Juliet," Dad chuckles. "Not too bad on the squash court, either. Although I taught him a thing or two!"

"And he's so handsome, too," Mum adds.

"He sounds like a catch," I say, studying the menu intently. "Congratulations."

"How are things with you, Harper?" Juliet asks, taking me by surprise. "How's the job? Is there anyone on the scene?"

"I'm single and the job is fine," I say briskly. "Hey, did anyone get the hake last time? Because I'm tempted. And Dad, how's the squash going? Do you still play a lot or just when Juliet's impressive boyfriend is in town?"

My bitterness is overlooked and it's a successful steer of the conversation, prompting Dad to tell us a story about his latest win that he's clearly told several times because it's well-rehearsed and he stops at all the moments that seem to require a laugh.

My determination to ignore any gibes and bat away intrusive questions works right through the starters until our plates are cleared from the table. By then Mum's had enough wine to ignore any willpower to mask her disappointment in me, and I can sense trouble brewing at her first question.

"I read an interesting article the other day about how the evolution of social media has impacted our connection with people in the public eye," she begins. "Thanks to Instagram and the like, celebrities can allow people full access to their lives, so now, media outlets reporting on them are . . . redundant. I wanted your opinion on that, Harper?"

If it was someone else asking, it might have led to a very interesting discussion. But my mum likes to goad. She knows how to get under my skin.

"I think that is probably true in some ways," I answer coolly. "But their social media posts give people a glimpse of what they want you to see. My job is different."

"How?"

"They open up to me about many aspects of their lives. It's not fake or posed—it's a real conversation that touches on their opinions and viewpoints. If you read any of the features I'd written, you'd see they're a little more complex than a social media post," I add sourly.

"I cannot understand why any adults with half a brain are interested in celebrities," Dad sniffs. "I would have thought only teenagers would care about narcissistic pop stars talking about their hair color and who kissed whom. Drivel."

"I don't write drivel," I snap, before desperately trying to pull myself back and taking a deep breath to steady my voice when I continue. "The average age of the readership of *Narrative* is forty-five years old, and the articles are interesting, well-researched pieces."

He snorts. My blood boils. I've tried, but it has been a week. And I am *exhausted*.

"But as a celebrity editor," Mum jumps in, wrinkling her nose, "you're hardly writing well-researched pieces, are you?"

"How would you know?" I ask bluntly. "You've never taken any interest in what I do or what I write. It doesn't matter what you classify as 'serious journalism.' All that should matter to you is that I love what I do. But you don't care about that, do you?"

"Here we go," Dad sighs. "The dramatics. We're trying to have a civilized family dinner."

"I'm standing up for myself. If that's being dramatic, then—"

"Please don't raise your voice, Harper," Dad interrupts, holding up his hand. "All your mother was pointing out is that your role doesn't require the sort of . . . significant journalism that others do. Like my colleague Jasper's son, for example, who is a political reporter. Or that columnist I like who writes about economics. Not fluff pieces."

"My journalism is *significant*," I assert.

But my voice breaks and hot tears prick behind my eyes, threatening to spill over at any moment. They've struck a nerve, but the tears are not of sadness. They're of rage.

You know what? I have had *enough* of people like my parents and sister and Cosmo looking down their nose at me and going out of their way to disparage me. I'm tired of having to prove my worth when I know in my heart that what I do *is* worthy: I tell people's stories. Stories that entertain, inspire, and captivate an audience. When a reader relates to a person I interview, no matter how different their lives might be, they feel less alone.

I won't be told anymore that that's not important.

I've been nothing but polite and decent to my parents tonight;

I've listened to them, I've asked questions about their life. And in return, they've prodded and jabbed, trying to get a rise out of me so they can call me the dramatic one.

It's pathetic. It's embarrassing. I don't need approval from people who can't show any common decency. They can think what they want to think, but I don't have to sit here and let them make me feel small so they can feel superior.

"I have to go," I say, peeling my cloth napkin off my lap and bundling it next to my glass. "Enjoy the rest of your evening."

"What? You can't walk out in the middle of dinner!" Dad declares, while Mum merely swirls her wine in her glass, looking unsurprised at my announcement.

"Yes, I can," I inform him, pushing my chair back. "I don't want to spend any more time in your company. You do nothing but belittle me. I'm not going to be bullied by my family any longer."

"Harper," Dad seethes, his face turning red, "*sit down*."

"And spend the evening listening to you congratulate yourselves and tell me how much of a disappointment I am? No, thanks. I've made the decision to no longer care whether I disappoint you or not. This little get-together has come at one of the lowest ebbs of my life, and actually, that horrifying timing has provided me with the clarity I need to free myself from you. Even though I've been made redundant—yes, there you go, you can dine out on that information, free of charge—and despite not being in a relationship with a Lacoste-wearing, big-earning Ken doll, I feel sorry for *you*."

I point my finger at each of them accusingly to hammer in my point.

"How boring if everyone met your approval and your approval only," I continue confidently. "The world would have no differences, no color, no fun. Are you even happy? Are you *really* happy? Because if you were, I don't understand why you'd want to bring me down all the time. Ever since I decided to branch out from your idea of success, you have gone out of your way to make me feel like a failure. How does that saying go? 'Misery loves company.' Well, you three can go ahead and enjoy these family dinners without me, I really don't care anymore. I thought that I'd be able to make you proud one day, but Ryan was right all those years ago when he said I should do it for myself. I'm proud because at least I have the guts to follow my own path in the face of your contempt and ridicule. So, in conclusion, screw all of you."

Mum and Dad stare at me in utter shock at my outburst.

Picking up my bag from under the seat, I get to my feet.

"Harper," Juliet pipes up, her face crumpling, "wait, please, I need to say something. I—"

"You're just as bad as them, you know," I say with disgust, cutting her off. "You've never had my back or attempted to stand up for me, even when they were being downright nasty. You're my big sister, and you never once reached out. I'm really not interested in anything *any* of you have to say."

Leaving them in silence, I walk out of the restaurant with a smile on my face.

I feel lighter than I've felt all week.

CHAPTER TWENTY-THREE

I'm watching old episodes of *Modern Family* when the doorbell goes. Moving my laptop off my stomach, where it's been balanced so that I can pretend to myself that I'm doing some form of work, I go to the door, wondering whether I unconsciously ordered another takeaway.

Working from home has been both liberating and suffocating: I've enjoyed the freedom of wearing tracksuit bottoms and my Miss Piggy slippers all day, but I've also felt slovenly and useless, trapped in my flat with no one to talk to but the orchid I bought at Sainsbury's on a whim the other day. I've named him Bud and he is a pleasant, if somewhat minimal, conversationalist.

Most of my industry contacts are now aware of my redundancy. I spent Monday sending emails to all the agents and PR reps I could think of and received a torrent of support in reply. I thought it would make me upset, but actually it was nice to read their opinions on the matter. Almost all of them pitched me clients to interview on a freelance basis, which was promising—I suppose I could book some in to write up and shop around to publications until I find a new position.

The rest of the week has been spent wrapping things at *Narrative*, including telling the agents and managers of the interviewees that I was leaving, which was mildly embarrassing. The worst was telling Isabella Blossom. I sent her an email with her film publicist, Rachael, cc'd in, saying that I understood if she'd rather Ryan do the interview now, since I probably wouldn't be at the magazine by the time we could arrange to come see her and the baby. Rachael quickly replied saying how amazing I was at my job and how sorry she was to hear about the redundancy, before concluding that she and Isabella would be in touch regarding the interview.

Leaving *Narrative* has also meant compiling a handover file for Ryan, so he can stay up to speed on any features that are currently in the works. His request for a spreadsheet of interviews and dates has not been fulfilled because such a document does not exist. When I emailed to tell him that, I imagined him reading it with his secretive smile. The one he used when my chaos amused him.

I doubt he smiles like that now.

Whenever Ryan's name has popped in my inbox, my heart has leaped into my throat, but he's only matched the formal tone of my original email. Which is to be expected. He's following my lead, and I did say some things during our rain-drenched spat that must have hit home. Ryan is the kind of guy who would respect my request for him to leave me alone. He'd believe me when I tell him that I won't trust him again.

Still, I find myself toying with the idea of calling him—or, in more desperate moments, showing up at his door. After my outburst at dinner with my parents, I realized that he was the one who gave me the courage to speak my mind. If he had been there, I think he would have been proud of me.

But then I think about how I wracked my brain for days wondering what I did wrong, how I threw myself into work thinking at least I could excel in that area of my life, and my cheeks grow hot with humiliation. My pride can't quite forgive him. Besides, I don't have time to be thinking about matters of the heart. I need to get back on my own two feet first. I need to focus on *me*.

As firm as I am about this decision, I still wonder every time the doorbell rings. Which is why, when I pause *Modern Family*, I have a teensy flutter of hope that it might be Ryan standing on the other side of the door, holding a bouquet of flowers, begging me to take him back.

It's not him. It's not a Deliveroo driver, either (who would have been equally welcome).

"Hi," Juliet says sheepishly.

I'm so stunned to see my sister that I don't say anything at first, staring at her open-mouthed. I wonder if I'm hallucinating, that maybe the three Nobbly Bobbly ice creams I've ingested today have gone to my head. For one thing, my sister has never been to my flat before. I don't know if she's even been south of the river before, let alone ventured as far as Brixton. And for another, it's 2 P.M. on a Thursday, which means she should be in an office somewhere yelling at people on the phone or taking important clients out for lunch in The Savoy. She definitely shouldn't be at my door wearing jeans.

Oh my god, she really is wearing *jeans*. I haven't seen her in casual wear since she was, like, ten. And that's not even an exaggeration: Juliet was one of those kids who became conscious of her style early on and would select adorable little outfits with Mum that involved buckle shoes and bows in her hair. I preferred the oversized T-shirt and shorts look, an outfit that would be dirty within roughly two minutes of me throwing it on. I was literally made to star in laundry detergent adverts.

Juliet clears her throat expectantly.

"S-sorry, hi," I stammer. "What are you doing here? It is Thursday, right? Is it Thursday? Have I missed a couple of days and it's the weekend?"

"No, it's Thursday," she confirms. "Sorry to show up unannounced like this. Can I come in?"

Part of me would like to say no and slam the door in her face.

I haven't spoken to any of my family since the dinner last week. I wasn't expecting them to contact me after the way I spoke to them, and as I made clear at the time, that was fine by me.

But there must be a reason she's made the journey here, and somehow manners and curiosity override my feelings of anger.

Standing back to let her in, I watch as she treads carefully into the flat.

"Do I need to take my shoes off?" she asks, gesturing at her designer pumps.

I suppress a laugh. "Uh, no. You're fine."

She nods and shuffles in, standing awkwardly in the kitchen while I shut the door. She takes a good look around. It's currently not the tidiest of homes, but it's definitely not as bad as it's been.

"Would you like a drink?" I offer.

"Thanks, that would be lovely. Do you have any herbal teas?"

"Peppermint."

"Perfect, thank you," she says as I go to fill up the kettle. "This is a nice flat."

"Thanks. A little smaller than yours, I imagine."

"It's much more homey than mine," she says carefully. "It has character."

I snort. "One way of describing it."

Reaching for two mugs and the box of peppermint tea bags out the cupboard, I set them down on the counter. She watches on in silence, clutching her handbag.

"You can sit down if you'd like," I say, gesturing to the kitchen table. "Or on the sofa if you'd prefer."

"Here's fine," she replies, pulling out the chair and perching on the edge.

Even the way we sit is completely different. Juliet looks regal, sitting up straight, shoulders back, chest out, chin up.

The kettle signals that it's boiled, and I pour the water into the mugs. I don't really want a peppermint tea right now, but I'm going to need something to distract my hands with, and it might as well be a mug.

"Do you leave the teabag in?" I ask.

"Yes, thank you."

"Me too," I say, although I'm not sure why she'd be interested.

I set the two mugs down and sit at the opposite side of the table. She thanks me and then falls silent again, her eyes darting about nervously.

"Juliet," I begin, too inquisitive to remain polite any longer, "what exactly are you doing here?"

She nods as though she's been waiting for me to ask and needed the prompt.

"I wanted to check you were okay after what happened last week. And . . . I wanted to apologize, too," she says, looking me right in the eye.

I raise my eyebrows. "Really?"

"Yes. I need to apologize for a few things, actually. But mostly, I'm sorry for not standing up for you. Mum and Dad . . . they shouldn't say the things they do. I feel terrible about how they speak to you, and I wanted you to know that."

I stare at her. Completely taken aback by the apology, I'm suspicious that this is some kind of trick somehow. That she's going to reach into her handbag and bring out a custard pie to throw in my face before roaring with laughter and shrieking, "AS IF!"

She looks as though she means it, though. And there's no sign of a custard pie anywhere. But it's still too sudden and random for me to be convinced.

"I know it's too little too late," she continues, recognizing the confusion in my expression. "But I wanted to say it anyway. It's important to say it, according to my therapist."

"You're seeing a therapist?"

"For a few months now. The best thing I ever did." Looking down at the table, she taps the handle of the mug. "I speak about you a lot. And Mum and Dad. But a lot about you."

"Really? I'm surprised I feature at all," I say, unable to mask the bitterness.

"You do. Heavily." She lifts the mug to her lips to blow on it and I notice she's shaking.

"So, you came here to apologize," I check.

"Not just that," she says hurriedly, putting the tea back down. "I also wanted to let you know that I thought what you did at the dinner last week was extremely brave. Brave and inspirational. It inspired me."

I narrow my eyes at her. "Did you come here to take the piss out of me?"

"No!" she insists, panicked. "I'm being serious. I swear."

"What I said at the dinner *inspired* you?"

"Yes," she says, nodding vigorously. "It inspired me to tell Mum and Dad the truth, which is what I did after you left. I told them that I quit my job five months ago."

My jaw drops to the floor. "You *what?*"

"I know." She gives me a faint smile, as though she can't quite believe it herself. "Right after they offered me partner at the firm. I've been unemployed and lying to everyone this whole time."

"You quit your job? Why?"

"Because I was miserable," she says with a shrug, her eyes brightening. "And I'm so much happier now. I mean, I'm not *happy* as such. I'm still working out what I want to do. But I hated my job. I hated the pressure and the stress and the fact that I worked all hours of the day but didn't get any fulfillment. When I told Mum and Dad that I'd been offered partner, they kept saying this was what I'd been working for—that's when it hit me. I'd got to where I wanted to be and I was even more miserable than before. So I turned down the firm's offer and quit."

I don't know what to say. I'm stunned into silence.

"Oh, and I broke up with Harry weeks ago," she adds before taking a sip of her tea. "I've been too scared to tell Mum because I know she adored him, but I told them that at the dinner, too, after you left. Harry is a great guy for someone else, but not for me. I think he was a bit relieved when I called it off, to be honest."

"Juliet," I say, my brain scrambling for words, "this is a lot of information to process."

"I know. You're taking it a lot better than Mum and Dad. They weren't very happy."

I grimace at the thought. "I can imagine."

"Dad said I was obviously confused and had had a little blip, but that he was sure the firm would take me back if I explained." She sighs. "I told him I wasn't ever going back and he threw his napkin down on the table in protest."

"Scandalous."

She hesitates, adding quietly, "Mum couldn't even look at me. She said she hoped I knew that I was sabotaging my life. I left after that."

I stare at her, impressed. "Have you heard from them since?"

"Dad has left a few voicemails that have covered a range of emotions. In some, he's attempted to be understanding, saying he knows the pressure of the job can be a lot, but that he's certain I can find my way through and get back on track. Others have been full of yelling." She lets out a heavy sigh. "I'm going to give it some time before I respond."

"That's a good idea. Let the dust settle."

"I can't imagine what it's been like for you," she says, looking pained and shaking her head. "Dealing with them all this time."

"I'm used to their disappointment," I assure her with a shrug.

"I've resented them for a long time," she admits, bringing her eyes up to look at me again. "Therapy has helped me realize that. I've been so focused on pleasing them and living up to their expectations that I forgot what it was like to make myself happy. I got used to shutting myself off from any feelings of joy. All I focused on was maintaining their approval. Along the way I lost myself. And I lost you, too."

I hesitate. "Yeah, well, we've never been on the same page."

"I want that to change," she says fiercely. "I know that I've been a terrible sister to you, Harper, and I know that we're different. But I would like to repair whatever relationship we're able to salvage. Or build a completely new one. It's a lot to ask and I know you . . . you might not be interested, but it's important that you know how much I want to make things better between us. You don't have to decide now. You can take your time. But that's the main reason I'm here today."

She's looking at me so earnestly that I feel overwhelmed with a mixture of emotions. I've been so angry at her for so long and felt so distant from her that the idea of finding common ground when we're in our thirties seems delusional and futile. But I also find myself grappling with feelings of compassion toward her. Maybe, for the first time ever, I understand her a little better.

"I had no idea that you were unhappy," I say eventually. "I thought you had the perfect life."

Her expression clouds over. "Trust me, I didn't. I don't. Looks can be deceiving."

"But why do you want to build a relationship with me now, when you've never wanted to before? You didn't even notice me before now."

"That's not true," she says firmly. "Yes, I've been wrapped up in my own life, but the thing is, Harper, I've always been envious of you."

"Envious of me?"

She nods, frowning. "You had the guts to stand up to Mum and Dad and tell them who you are and what you wanted. I had no idea who I was, really. I was so jealous of the freedom you created for yourself. And then being around you only amplified the guilt I felt over letting Mom and Dad be so horrible to you while allowing them to fawn all over me. I was too scared to let them down because then . . . then they'd treat me . . ."

"The same way they treated me," I conclude for her.

She nods, her eyes welling up. "Exactly. I've been so cowardly. I'm sorry, Harper."

I press my lips together, blinking back tears.

"What you said at dinner, you were right. They are bullies, and I've enabled them," she continues. "I want to thank you, because it's you who finally helped me find the courage to be honest with them. For the first time. And I don't know if they'll ever get over it, but I do feel much better now they know the truth. It's like a weight has been lifted and I can finally move forward. So even if you decide that you don't want me in your life, I'm always going to be grateful to you for that, Harper."

We fall into silence. I consider what she's said and try to work out where to go from here.

"I'm proud of you," I say finally, surprising myself but meaning it.

She inhales sharply, her knuckles whitening as she grips her mug.

"What you've done—quitting your job, going to therapy, telling our parents the truth—all of that is stuff you should be proud of," I say. "And . . . I would like to take some steps to repairing our relationship. I've always thought it would be fun to have a sister."

Tears stream down her cheeks.

"That means a lot, Harper. Thank you."

"Thank *you* for coming here to talk to me. Can't have been easy navigating South London," I say playfully.

"It is a strange new world," she grins, opening her handbag to pluck out a tissue and dab her eyes. She takes a moment to regain composure, drinking some tea before giving me a sympathetic look. "I'm really sorry about your job, Harper. I know you loved it."

"Thanks. It's been a bit rubbish. But my friend Mimi threw a great leaving party last Friday that involved a piñata with my boss's face on it. I got to smack the shit out of him."

"I take it he didn't attend the party."

"He had a bowling tournament."

She laughs. "By the way, I read your Audrey Abbot interview."

"Yeah?"

"It was brilliant." She hesitates. "Someone who pulled themselves up from the ground, dusted themselves off, and made it through. She's iconic."

"She is. Wait until you read her memoirs. Talk about ups and downs, she's been through it all," I inform her proudly.

"I've been listening to this great podcast recently about failure and how it can mold you into being the best version of yourself, and how you can use it to build your success. Everyone you've admired has failed at some point, or felt like they were failing. There are famous guests on it every week talking about their failures and how they got to where they are now. You should listen to it. Not that being made redundant is a failure, but it might help to give you a new perspective on things. It's helped me, anyway."

"Sounds interesting. I'll give it a try."

"If anyone can pull themselves up, it's you," she says simply.

I glance down at the table. "I don't know about that."

"I do," she replies without hesitation, forcing me to look back up at her. "Change is scary, but sometimes being forced out of your comfort zone is necessary. This could be the best thing that ever happened to you."

"You're not the first person to tell me that. A few others have said the same thing."

"Maybe we're on to something."

I smile and offer her another drink. She accepts and I suggest making us honey tea. It turns out she loves it, too, but only has it on the weekends as a treat. We agree to make an exception for today.

"After all, neither of us has a job." She shrugs. "So I guess every day is a weekend."

Now that we've had the difficult conversation and we've cried and laughed, something in the air between us has lifted. We relax, moving away from the heavy topics. Talking about the honey tea Mum would make us when we were sick encourages us to reminisce about our childhood, bringing up memories that the other may have forgotten. It's cathartic to remember the happier times we shared, before life got in the way and things were expected of us.

We hug when she leaves and she holds on a little tighter and for a little longer than I'm expecting. She tells me she'll message some dates that we could do lunch. I shut the door behind her and feel lighter, something within me beginning to heal.

I return to my laptop to see very few emails have landed in my inbox while I've been busy having a heart-to-heart with my long-lost sister, and I'm just about to slump back on the sofa when my phone rings. I check the caller ID—it's Isabella Blossom.

"Harper, hi," she says when I pick up. "How are you?"

"I'm good," I reply, hearing the baby gurgling in the background. "How are *you*? How's mum life?"

"I'm so sorry about your job," she says, ignoring my question. "I hope you haven't been too upset about it."

"Taking it all in my stride," I assure her as I head toward the freezer to have my fourth Nobbly Bobbly and wondering whether it's acceptable to speak to a Hollywood A-lister on the phone while eating an ice cream.

"Listen, I've spoken to Rachael and she agreed—I want you to have the exclusive about me and the baby."

"That's so lovely of you, but I'll have to check with Cosmo that he's happy for me to write it when I don't technically—"

"No, Harper," she interrupts. "I promised the exclusive to *you*. Not the magazine."

I shut the freezer door and straighten. "Huh?"

"It's in your hands what you do with the interview, although maybe run it past me and Rachael first. I know you have impeccable taste with publications, and I do trust you, but there are a couple of magazines out there I'd rather didn't get it, based on past run-ins I've had with them. But the point is, it's your article, no one else's. We can do this however you want, as long as I'm speaking to you."

Something sparks in my brain. An idea. A *good* idea. And a lot of the credit for it goes to Juliet. I lean against my fridge, phone against my ear, my brain suddenly whirring with possibilities.

"Harper, are you there?" Isabella prompts. "Have I lost you?"

"I'm here," I assure her. "But I think . . . I might have an idea that I'd like to discuss with you about how to make this work."

"Yeah? Okay, great! Are you free tomorrow?"

"Tomorrow works perfectly."

"Wonderful. I can't wait to see you. I know that you'll write the perfect article."

"That's the thing," I say, a smile spreading across my face. "I don't think I'll be writing anything at all."

CHAPTER TWENTY-FOUR

I needed a lot of help setting up the podcast. Mimi came over at the weekend and we brainstormed the format it would take and all the equipment I'd need. I was nervous to tell her my idea: that maybe as well as doing some freelance writing, I could launch a celebrity podcast. She thought it was genius and offered her help right away with getting it off the ground. I already knew all the right people and I believed that enough of them trusted me to be a part of it at the beginning, then hopefully it would grow a big enough audience for others to gain interest and put their clients forward for it when they had something to promote. I would essentially be doing what I love—talking to those in the public eye and hearing their stories—without having to fight Cosmo for the front page. I would have to learn how to edit in an entirely new way, but I was ready for the challenge.

I floated the idea to Isabella Blossom when I visited her beautiful West London town house on Friday and she agreed without hesitation to be my first guest. She finally disclosed the full name of the baby to me in strictest confidence, having done an extraordinary job of keeping it from the press so far: Ryan Daryl Harper Blossom.

"Daryl after my dad, and I couldn't not name him after the two people who delivered him into this world," she said with a grin, gazing down at him as he slept cradled in my arms. "Do you think Ryan will mind?"

"I think he'll be very touched," I whispered, my eyes prickling with tears.

"Good." She smiled. "I could tell he has a gentle soul, your Ryan. I liked him."

I nodded and the conversation moved on. I know she only said "your Ryan" to differentiate from *her* Ryan, but the phrasing still stung.

A couple of days later, when the equipment had all arrived and I'd gotten the software sorted, I returned to Isabella's house and we recorded the pilot episode of *What You Don't Know*, which the blurb describes as "the brand-new podcast where your favorite celebrities sit down with host Harper Jenkins to cover everything you think you know about their careers and personal lives—and a few things you don't, including what they've learned along the way and where they're headed next."

Isabella gave a fantastic interview, and I knew as soon as we'd finished that, whether or not the podcast would be successful, this particular episode was going to be a hit. We were in hysterics as she discussed the details of the birth and we recalled the poor taxi driver's reaction. But when she talked about the trials of single parenthood and how scared she was, I got a lump in my throat. She described feeling like she had no idea what she was doing—crying tears of despair one minute because baby Ryan wasn't sleeping well and tears of happiness the next simply because he smiled—and I knew listeners would find themselves easily relating to this Hollywood star whose life might have otherwise seemed a million worlds apart.

We also talked about her career and the pressure she'd felt when she was starting out to look a certain way and be a certain way. She was both critical of the industry and adoring of it, acknowledging the important changes it was making in how it treated women and minorities and what more needed to be done, while also describing how she fell in love with making movies and the magic of slipping into a character.

It was interesting, it was sad, it was happy, it was real.

It was a *lot* of editing.

But so worth it. After Mimi listened to it, she gave me a giant hug—and when she told me I'd done something special, I could feel it in my bones.

That gave me the boost of confidence I needed to start spreading the word. I wanted to record a few episodes before launching so I wasn't scrambling once we were live. I contacted agents to pitch my new venture, carefully noting that the pilot episode was an exclusive interview with Isabella Blossom, and I had excellent responses straightaway. Shamari called me the same day saying she had a great lineup of guests for me.

"Let me guess, that sexy up-and-coming actor Julian Newt?" I said, smiling into the phone.

"He is fascinating, Harper, and can talk about starring alongside Audrey Abbot in the play. Not just that, but—hot-off-the-press news—he's landed the lead role in another romantic Netflix movie. A London high-flyer whose distant aunt leaves her a pub in her will moves to the tiny village in the countryside where it's located and falls for the brooding local guy who works behind the bar. You know it's going to be a hit."

"I have no doubt."

"Let me send you some of the interviews he's done for others. He's a funny guy, full of personality, *and* he has some great stories about breaking into the business. Plus, he's got some interesting views on pressures on men in the industry, too."

I rolled my eyes and smiled. "Okay, send the articles over and I'll give them a read."

"Excellent!" she exclaimed. "And to thank you for that, I would also like to suggest Dylan Knox of Artistry fame for your consideration."

I almost dropped the phone. "W-what?"

"Oh yes, Harper, you heard that right." She chuckled, sounding very pleased with herself. "I persuaded him to talk to you for the magazine, but I will let him know that the podcast will be better. I imagine that's more his style anyway. He does like the sound of his own voice."

"Dylan Knox will be on my podcast?"

"We'll have to go over the questions, Harper," she informed me sternly, "because he won't go into the recent fallout with the band and why the reunion tour got pulled. Saying that, I will reveal to you—*strictly* off the record—that they are back in discussions. If you're lucky, by the time you record, he might be able to reveal some news about it on your podcast. But more importantly, it looks like he's about to land a role in a big prison-drama TV show, and it would seem he's had a fresh boost of confidence in his acting abilities . . . largely thanks to me, of course. I think it might work out this time. Sometimes you just need the right role at the right time, as I said to him."

"Shamari, how can I ever thank you?" I said, gripping the phone.

"You can keep giving my fabulous clients publicity on your podcast," she replied matter-of-factly. "It's always been a two-way street, darling. And you know I can't resist your charm and the way you stalk me on my coffee runs. Anyway, I must dash. One of those fabulous clients I mentioned has just turned up at the office, and judging by her evil glares through my glass door, I'm about to get a bollocking about putting her up for a gigantic flop. I'll email you to arrange dates for recording! Bye now!"

Dizzy with excitement, I hung up the phone and started dancing around my kitchen floor. Thanks to Shamari, I managed to record two more episodes in quick succession, and then Isabella Blossom contacted me to say it was time to release the podcast—she was worried one of her untrustworthy acquaintances had gotten details of the birth story and was going to blab to the press.

It was now or never.

The day the podcast goes live and Isabella's episode becomes available, it's an instant hit. I knew she was going to go down well, but I had *no* idea the episode would take off like this. I'm astonished by the response, sitting at home on my laptop, watching the number of downloads shoot through the roof, scrolling through the mentions on social media. The story of Isabella giving birth in a taxi goes viral—people *love* it. They love her. And they love me. I suddenly gain hundreds of new Instagram followers and the inbox I'd set up specifically for the podcast explodes with guest requests and pitches.

Isabella and my podcast are all over the showbiz headlines, and the attention gets even more frenzied when I post that the next episode will be an interview with Dylan Knox of Artistry.

I sit alone in the flat, letting it all sink in. My phone vibrates with messages and calls from friends congratulating me. A huge bouquet of flowers arrives from Isabella and Ryan Blossom. Another bouquet of flowers is delivered, and I laugh as I read the message attached to it from Juliet. SCREW MUM AND DAD, it reads. YOU DID IT FOR YOURSELF.

And then I get a message that I'd been hoping for, but not expecting. A WhatsApp from Ryan. *My* Ryan:

I knew you could do it. This is just the beginning.

Congratulations x

That night, Mimi and I go out for a *very* boozy dinner. It's nowhere fancy, one of our favorite places in Brixton Village where you have to queue for ages and then sit on a makeshift chair of stacked wooden crates and drink wine from tumblers. When we're done eating, we're moved on quickly by the staff, who are trying to get the queue down as much as possible, and head to a cocktail bar a few doors down where we continue to drink from tumblers, but this time sitting on a wooden bench.

"A toast to you!" Mimi declares, holding up her glass. "Harper Jenkins, who has turned redundancy into an absolute triumph!"

I laugh, knocking my glass against hers. "It's still early."

"The podcast is already a smash and you've released one episode. *One*. Everyone already knows that it's here to stay," she tells me. "They were all talking about it in the office today. Your ears must have been burning."

"Really?" I say nonchalantly, like it's no big deal. "What were people saying?"

"How amazing it is and how you're going to be famous."

I wave that off with my hand. "No thanks."

"You're going to be like this host extraordinaire. One day, you'll have a show like Graham Norton, I just know it."

I burst out laughing. "Okay, that's a stretch, but I appreciate your belief in me."

"Oh, and you should have seen Cosmo. Ha!" Her eyes widen with glee. "He knows he's made a big mistake. At first he was up in arms about you getting the Isabella Blossom exclusive, kept shouting that it was the magazine's, but Ryan set him straight on that one, reminding him that Isabella entered into no such contract with *Narrative*. Then when he realized that Ryan was right, he switched tactics and became your biggest fan. The response you've got, the interaction online—he's already scrambling about, trying to work out a way to get you to write for the magazine again. He's desperately trying to capitalize on your popularity. Did you see all the posts from the magazine's social media today about the Max Sjöberg piece that you and Ryan wrote? It was in the magazine over the weekend."

I blush, thinking about the Manchester trip. "I saw it."

"Cosmo has been yelling about making sure your name is included in every post we put up on socials. Apparently, the powers that be are not happy about the fact they've just let go of their star journalist. You really have made them sorry."

"I wish I was the kind of person who could be mature about this, but I'm not." I grin. "Hearing that makes me *very* happy."

"May they rue the day."

"Absolutely."

"Ryan is very proud of you."

I snap my head up. She smiles into her drink, pleased at my reaction to her comment.

"He said something to you?" I ask eagerly.

"He said something to *everyone*," she informs me. "You're one of the most talented journalists he's ever met, and he had no doubt that you'd be a success. He said he knew that the moment he met you."

Nodding, I look down at the table.

"He also told me the moment he met you was when he fell head over heels for you," she continues casually.

"*What?* He said that in front of everyone?"

"Have you met Ryan? Of course not," she snorts. "He told me that back before you went to Florence."

"Wait, what? I'm confused."

"Before the press trip to Florence, Ryan confessed his love for you," she says. "It was very sweet. He made me promise not to tell you, though. He said you likely already knew, but you would probably be embarrassed about me knowing. So I kept schtum."

"But . . . why would he tell you that?" I ask, aghast.

"He had to tell me so that we could concoct our little plan for the two of you to end up on the press trip together." She sighs, setting her glass down. "You didn't really think you ended up on that trip together by coincidence, did you?"

"But . . . you pulled his name out of the hat. I saw you! We all saw you!" My brain is clouded by alcohol, but I distinctly remember there being multiple pieces of paper in that hat.

"That was all down to me being a genius magician," she declares proudly. "I'll let you in on the secret behind that clever trick. Every piece of paper in the hat had 'Ryan' written on it. Sneaky, right? It was a bit mean on the other members of the team, but I'll make sure they get nice press trips at some point. You know I'm fair about these things, usually."

"Mimi," I say, reaching out and gripping her arm, "please explain to me how and why this all happened."

"It's very simple. I made the announcement about there being a spare place on the Florence weekend, and Ryan asked if he could have a word, so off we went for a coffee and he told me about his feelings for you and offered to do whatever work that I needed doing if I gave him the place on the trip. He said he'd work weekends, evenings, whatever. But I'm an old romantic, so I said that wasn't necessary. I knew how you felt about him— everyone knew how you felt about each other—and, considering the hot kiss you'd had in his flat and how flustered you'd gotten composing that message to him after breaking up with Liam, I thought it would be a gentle nudge in the right direction for you both. And I was right."

"You never . . . I didn't . . . Wait, what do you mean everyone knew how we felt? You're not talking about . . . you don't mean people in the office *knew*?"

She cackles with laughter. "Jesus, Harper, the way you two look at each other? Nothing has ever been more obvious. From the very first week that Ryan started at the magazine, the art team had a bet on how long it would take you to end up together."

"The art team had *what*?"

"Nobody won. It took you two idiots a bit longer than they were expecting. If only they knew the whole story and that it actually took you more than ten years to work it out."

"I don't understand," I say, shaking my head. "We were always fighting."

"Undeniable chemistry."

"Everyone knew we hated each other."

"Everyone knew you loved each other."

I blink at her.

I haven't said it out loud, but the moment she says it, I know she's right. I do love him. Deflating, I close my eyes. It could be the cocktails speaking, but it suddenly feels that no matter what's happened between us, it doesn't matter, because I was wrong. I can trust Ryan. I do trust him.

More than anything, I don't want to be without him.

"I said some horrible things to him. What do I do?" I whimper, opening my eyes and looking at Mimi pleadingly.

"You're Harper Jenkins. You'll think of a way to get what you want." She smiles. "You always do."

When I stumble home that night, it hits me.

I set my alarm for 5:55 A.M., 5:57 A.M., 6 A.M., 6:03 A.M., and 6:05 A.M.

CHAPTER TWENTY-FIVE

I'm at Roasted by quarter past seven.

I nervously hang around outside for a bit, remembering why I don't like getting to places early, because you have time to think about things and I'm already feeling sick to my stomach as it is. That is partly down to the hangover from last night and such an early start this morning, but it's mostly because of what I know I have to do. Pacing by the door, I join the queue at half past, glancing back over my shoulder every few seconds, terrified that I'll get the timing wrong and this won't work.

When my coffees are ready, I grab them and linger by the door again. My calculations have paid off, though. At exactly seven forty, Ryan comes into sight, walking from the tube station, his hands in his pockets, his jaw set, his eyes fixed on the ground a few paces ahead of him. He wasn't lying when he used to say how early he got to the office every day.

I exhale shakily and, steeling myself, I march over to stand in his way.

He stops and looks up. His eyes widen with disbelief.

"Harper!"

"Hey."

We stare at each other for a moment, taking the other one in.

"What are you doing here?" he asks, his forehead creasing like it does when he's confused about something and is trying to find the solution.

"I got you a mocha," I say, holding it out for him. "I know you like those."

He takes the cup from me and raises his eyebrows as he reads the name written in black marker across the side.

"This is for Parker."

"I purposefully said Parker this time," I confess. "It seemed easier."

He nods. "Thanks."

"I wanted to give you a mocha and also an apology," I say hurriedly, desperate to get this out before I lose my nerve. "The day I lost my job, I said a lot of things . . . angry things, and I was upset and hurt and you didn't deserve it. So, I wanted to say sorry."

He looks surprised. "Oh."

"I've been thinking about everything and how it was unfair of me to explode at you like that," I ramble, "especially when I'd been the one in Florence telling you that I wanted to keep things professional at work. Cosmo put you in a difficult position, and as upset as I was, I shouldn't have taken it out on you. I'm sorry."

He hesitates. "Right. Thank you."

"You're welcome."

We both stand there awkwardly.

"I'm sorry, too," he says eventually, frowning. "For not telling you."

"I know." I nod. "You already told me that."

More silence.

"Congratulations on the podcast," he says. "It's incredible."

"Thanks! And thank you for your message. That was really nice of you."

"Of course."

This is *excruciating*. I didn't think it was going to go like this. I didn't know how it was going to go, but I didn't think there would be so many awkward pauses. There's a gulf between us, and I have no idea how to close it.

The only thing I can think to do is follow Ryan's lead from Florence. Time to bare it all.

"Okay, here goes," I say out loud, psyching myself up and looking into those piercing blue eyes that make my heart thud so hard, it rings in my ears. "Ryan, since you started working with me at *Narrative*, I—"

"Harper!"

The last voice I would like to hear right now is Cosmo's, but of course he's barreling over to us, beaming at me like an old friend.

"What are you doing here?" he asks, stopping beside us before checking his watch and letting out a forced laugh. "The one time you're early for work and you don't work here anymore. Classic!"

"Hi, Cosmo," I say warily. "I'm here to . . . uh . . . see Ryan."

"Fantastic! I hope you're in discussions to work on another piece for us. Any ideas you have, send them over to Ryan here—" he slaps Ryan on the back, causing him to flinch "—and I'm sure we can get them in, no problem!"

"I'm quite busy now, so—"

"Oh yes, the podcast. Excellent stuff. Any freelance features, though, send them our way. We pay competitively, as you know, and we could use some celebrity angles." He sees someone behind me and grimaces. "I have to go. Rebecca is over there and we have a publishers meeting in a minute. Nice to see you, Harper, and remember, we'd love to have you writing for us again. Name your price."

He scurries off toward a smartly dressed woman standing by the building who waves him over, a stern expression on her face.

"I can't *believe* him," I utter, watching him go.

"He's a piece of work," Ryan agrees, looking irritated.

"He really is. They need to give you his job. ASAP."

The corners of his lips twitch. "What were you saying before he interrupted? Since I started working with you at *Narrative*," he prompts, his gaze fixed on me.

"Yes, that was it. Okay, since you started working with me at *Narrative*, I have had certain feelings toward you. Strong ones," I admit, my cheeks burning. "At first, I thought they were feelings of dislike because, you know, we clashed quite a bit and you're a nightmare for someone like me to work with and because of our history—it was a big jumble of irritation in my head."

"Okay," he says slowly.

"But then I realized, they weren't feelings of dislike, they were the opposite," I explain nervously. "You said that you were crazy about me, right from the start. Well, I think I've been crazy about you, too. And I *know* I'm crazy about you now. I have missed you so much. When everything was awful, I wanted you there. And now that everything's finally looking up, I want you there. I want you all the time, to be there through everything. You're the most thoughtful, lovely, best person I've ever met." I hesitate, before adding, "And I love you."

Because, hey, might as well be completely honest.

His lips part in surprise. He's about to say something when that most unwelcome of voices comes booming at us once again.

"Ryan!" Cosmo calls out, approaching us speedily. "Sorry to interrupt, but Rebecca would like you to join us in the meeting as well. I've said you're busy talking to one of our *star* freelance writers—" he winks at me "—but she's insisting. She wants to know about the . . . direction of the magazine."

"I can't," Ryan says firmly. "We're in the middle of an important conversation."

"Ah, I'm afraid I have to insist," Cosmo presses, sucking a stream of air in through his teeth. "Perhaps Harper would be happy to rearrange. In fact, how about we take you for lunch, Harper, eh? We can discuss fresh ideas!"

"That's okay, thanks," I say, horrified, before turning to Ryan with an encouraging smile. "You should go. Don't worry about it."

"No, we were . . . we need to talk," he says, his eyes wide with panic.

"It's fine, honestly. This meeting sounds important for the magazine; you shouldn't miss it. We can talk later."

"But—"

"It's okay," I assure him. "Go ahead."

He looks visibly distressed, but Cosmo doesn't notice.

"There you go, we'll rearrange. Come on, Ryan, can't keep them waiting."

"Harper, we'll . . . we'll talk," Ryan promises as Cosmo urges him to go.

"Yeah."

They head toward the building, and I turn to see Ryan glancing over his shoulder at me. I suddenly remember something important.

"Ryan!" I call out after him, and he immediately stops and waits as I hurry over to him, Cosmo nervously holding up a finger to Rebecca, who is standing by the door, pointedly tapping her watch. I hold out the tote bag that's been hanging off my shoulder this whole time.

"Here," I say, giving it to Ryan. "Almost forgot. This is for you. Good luck in your meeting."

"How lovely, a gift!" Cosmo declares, before taking Ryan's elbow and leading him away. "Thank you, Harper, and speak soon to sort that lunch."

I turn around and start making my way home.

He doesn't call me. Or message me. The whole day. *Zilch.*

I told him I *loved* him! Does he think I do that every day?! I certainly do not! And he thinks it's acceptable behavior to leave someone in the lurch after they've poured out their heart? *Well.* I guess that shows what kind of person he is after all.

I'm not messaging him, obviously. I've already said my piece. I get that it was quite a lot to throw at him before eight o'clock in the morning, but he's had the entire day to think on it and get back to me, and I haven't heard a peep out of him. I'm not expecting him to say it back or anything. I get that we had a big falling-out and maybe he's still cross or maybe he thinks we had our chance—twice—and it didn't work then, so it's not going to now. That's *fine.*

But he still needs to acknowledge what I said.

I've been trying to stay busy so I don't check my phone every few seconds, but that's not easy when you've launched a highly successful podcast and your phone is buzzing all the time with emails and notifications. Every time it goes off, I grab for it, desperate for his name to come up on the screen, and you know what? It's never him.

No amount of work can distract me from thinking about this morning and the butterflies dancing around in my stomach. Not hearing from him can't be good news, though, can it? Surely, he'd have been in touch by now if he felt the same. Instead, he's probably writing an essay in his notes app, trying to work out a way to let me down gently.

It did occur to me that I have a mole inside the office in the form of Mimi, so I could ask how he's behaving to try to work out what's going on, but I was too embarrassed to tell her what I said to him. If I haven't heard from him by the end of today, then I will call her and explain everything and she can give me some advice on what to do.

For now, it's just me in this.

Tucking my phone under my pillow so I can't look at it anymore this evening, I come to the disappointing conclusion that I *could* tidy up. It's a drastic idea, but I can blare music while I do it so my thoughts are drowned out and it *will* take a long time, which is exactly what I need.

As I start the soul-destroying job of unloading and then reloading the dishwasher to a motivating playlist of Queen's greatest hits playing from YouTube on the TV, I start to understand why people recommend cleaning as you go along. There is a mountain of work ahead of me tonight. Singing along to "Radio Ga Ga" as I scrub the sink, I praise myself on throwing myself into being a responsible adult tonight and cleaning the house rather than seeing if anyone was around to go for a drink.

I stop what I'm doing as I realize that seeing if anyone was around to go for a drink would have been a much better idea and I'm a complete idiot.

My doorbell rings. That will be the delivery of some new books I ordered this week.

But it's not. It's Ryan.

"Hi," he says, his eyes immediately landing on the bottle of surface cleaner and the cloth I'm holding. "Are you *cleaning?*"

"Yes," I reply defensively. "What are you doing here?"

"I wanted to finish our chat from earlier. May I come in?"

"You've taken your time getting back to me. You said we'd talk, and then I didn't hear from you all day."

"I'm sorry, but I thought it best to talk in person about this."

"How did you know I was going to be in?"

"I took my chances."

"You could have messaged so I knew you'd be coming over," I point out indignantly.

"I did!" he protests.

"No, you did not!" I say, aghast at the very *cheek* of it.

He rolls his eyes. "Check your phone."

"I've been checking it."

He sighs. "Can I please come in? I'd really like to talk to you in the flat rather than in the doorway."

"Fine," I say, taking a step back.

He wanders in with the tote bag I gave him this morning slung round his shoulder, admiring the lack of usual clutter covering the table, the clean counters, and the shiny sink. Queen is still playing at a high volume and "Crazy Little Thing Called Love" has come on. It takes me a while to locate the remote to turn it down a bit.

"You really messaged me?" I ask him.

"Yes."

Leaving him in the kitchen, I head to the bedroom and reach under the pillow for my phone. Looking at the messages, I find a string of them from Ryan. He must have sent them just after I hid my phone from myself. Typical.

The first one is him asking if he can come over after work, followed by practically an essay. I take a moment to read it before joining him in the kitchen:

Harper, I owe you an apology for how I handled the days leading up to your redundancy. I'm so sorry. I need you to know that all I wanted was to protect us and I hated the idea of hurting you. I wanted to do things differently this time round . . . I couldn't act normal with this knowledge hanging over my head. That's what I did last time and I lost you. I figured I was doing the best thing by staying distant until you were informed and we could talk it all through, but I realize now that avoiding you hurt you even more . . . and it ended up hurting us even more, too. I wish I

356 •••KATY BIRCHALL

could go back in time and change my behavior, but
since I can't, please know that I am truly sorry and
will do everything in my power to make it up to you,
if you'll let me.

After everything you said this morning, I'm really
hoping you will let me.

I'm on my way to you now Xxx

I read his messages a few times, taking it all in, and then,
composing myself, return to find him waiting for me in the
kitchen.

"The place looks great," he comments.

"You messaged an hour ago," I note, putting my phone on
the table. "That still means you left me waiting all day to hear
from you."

"I'm sorry, Harper, I had so many meetings, and I was trying
to figure out what to say to you on the phone and I knew I had to
apologize properly, so I rambled on in a WhatsApp before realizing it would be better to come see you in person. But I should
have worked that out sooner and messaged you earlier. It's just—
the office is pretty stressful at the moment, now that we're three
people down. I don't know how we're going to make it work."

I cross my arms. "I'm not sure I have that much sympathy for
you there."

"Right." He nods. "Anyway, about this morning."

He puts the bag on the table and slides out the gift I gave him.
It's the Max Sjöberg article we wrote together, and it's framed. I
didn't have time to get it done properly. I put it together in a
rush last night after I got back from dinner with Mimi. I had
to search around all my pictures in the flat to find a frame that
would fit the article. I found a black one that used to house a very

pretty print I bought from the Saturday market in Herne Hill and swapped the article into it.

"Thank you for this," Ryan says, holding it out and gazing down at it. "Our second ever byline together. I'll have to hang it next to our first. I would say that maybe there will be plenty more to come, but I'm not so sure of that, now that you're a famous podcast host."

I look down modestly. "I've only done one episode."

"And it's already top of the charts. I wouldn't expect anything less," he says, putting the frame down on the table. "I'm sorry that Cosmo interrupted us this morning and that I had to go to that meeting. I thought about quitting on the spot just so I'd have the chance to go after you."

I raise my eyebrows at him. "That would have been an extreme action."

"Some moments deserve extreme action," he states firmly.

"I wouldn't have approved," I say, unable to stop a smile. "If you were going to quit all along, then the least you could have done was accepted voluntary redundancy and let me keep my position there."

A smile plays along his lips.

"And if that had happened, you would have been under Cosmo's repressive rule for even longer, and you have suffered that long enough. Look what you can achieve when you do your own thing."

I shrug. "Maybe it has worked out for the better."

"*Maybe?*" He chuckles, his expression softening as he relaxes into the smile. "You're on the edge of something big, Harper. That much is clear."

"I hope so. I guess we'll see."

He stares at me intently. "Did you mean what you said this morning?"

"About you being a nightmare for someone like me to work with? Yes."

"I already knew about that bit," he says, rolling his eyes. "For the record, you're a much worse colleague. Do you know how annoying it is to work with an editor who doesn't keep a schedule of publication dates for their features?"

I tap the side of my head. "I don't need a schedule. It's all up here."

"It's not up there," he says matter-of-factly. "You had no idea when any of your articles were coming out. And let's not get started on those email chains I asked you to forward to me before you left."

"As I told you, my inbox must have swallowed them. There must have been a technical glitch," I proclaim innocently.

He gives me a knowing look. "You couldn't find them because you never file any of your emails into folders and your inbox is flooded with thousands of unread messages."

"My inbox is organized in the way that I prefer it, Ryan. I know who I'm talking to and where I need to be at all times."

"You forgot about the dinner with your parents, didn't you? The night you had that awards ceremony that you'd *also* obviously forgotten about."

"Maybe." I eye him suspiciously. "How did you know?"

"Because," he begins, a smile creeping across his lips, "I *know* you."

I swallow, melting under his doting gaze. "I guess you do."

"I do. And I love everything about you."

"You do?" I whisper, hardly daring to breathe.

"Yes," he says softer, moving slowly toward me. "Everything. Even the things that drive me up the wall. Your messiness, your infuriating organizational style, your shocking timekeeping skills, your stubborn inability to back down whenever we argue."

"You know me. I like to have the last word," I say, as he stops right in front of me.

He pauses, waiting for me to lift my head and bring my eyes

up to meet his. "Harper, I love you. And I'm never going to lose you again."

Cupping my face in his soft, warm hands, he leans down and kisses me.

And as I kiss him back, pulling him closer toward me, I can't help but smile against his mouth. Because at last we agree on something.

EPILOGUE

R yan is getting impatient.

He's trying not to, but I know that I'm wearing him down because the lines on his forehead are getting deeper, and every time I fly past him in a whirlwind of stress, he watches me with narrowing eyes.

"Harper," he growls, his phone vibrating in his hand, "the driver is going to cancel the trip unless we leave the house *now*."

"Just tell him we'll be one more minute!"

"I already told him that three minutes ago."

"Tell him again."

He sighs, rubbing his forehead. "Is there anything I can do to help speed up this process?"

"Yes, you can leave me be and go tell the Uber driver we'll be one more minute."

Muttering something inaudible under his breath, he leaves the flat with his bag in tow and, while I locate my phone charger in a plug in the sitting room, I hear the muffled sound of their conversation through the windows. Darting into the bedroom, I throw my charger into the wheelie case that Ryan bought me a few months ago when the shoulder strap on my old weekend bag broke and he couldn't handle the fact that I happily tied a knot in the strap and carried on using the bag.

I hear the front door open as Ryan returns, and I'm just about to zip up my bag when I remember I haven't packed my wedges. I find one lurking at the bottom of my wardrobe, but the other one has somehow disappeared. Holding the one I have safely in my hand so I don't lose that one, too, during the search—a pickle I've been known to get myself into before—I get on my knees and start tearing through the bottom of both sides of the wardrobe, sending shoes flying in all directions.

"Are you looking for this?" Ryan says behind me.

I turn round to see him standing by the bed, the missing shoe dangling from his forefinger by the ankle strap.

"You found it!" I exclaim brightly, jumping to my feet and taking it from him before squishing the pair of shoes into my case. "Where was it?"

"Under the bed, where all your missing shoes can be located. If you didn't kick your shoes off and then leave them wherever they land, fewer might end up lost under there."

"You have been extremely helpful, thank you," I say, shutting my case and leaning forward on top of it to do up the zip. "I am officially ready to go."

"Finally," he says with a grin, lifting the case off the bed and making several unnecessary remarks about how heavy it is as he lugs it to the car waiting outside while I lock up.

A few months after we declared our love for each other, Ryan moved into my flat. It was quite fast, but we figured we'd known each other long enough, and the constant trekking between North and South London was getting tiresome. Although Ryan's flat was much nicer than mine, I really didn't want to live in North London again, so Ryan agreed that he'd relocate south of the river. It's a bit of a squeeze with two of us, but Ryan's so tidy, there's not too much encroaching. We're currently in the market for somewhere to buy—Ryan insists it has to be a two-bedroom, even if that means moving farther out, because he says that my mess is making him go gray early and he wants my wardrobe in a separate room to our bedroom.

I am much tidier now that I live with a cleanliness dictator. One pot out of place in the kitchen and I suffer lectures for a week. I've been banned altogether from attempting to load the dishwasher, which, I won't lie, is fine by me.

On the way to the airport, I smile to myself at Ryan double-checking he's got our passports, even though he's checked several times since we set off.

"What?" he asks, when he catches me smirking.

"Nothing. I'm excited for Stockholm."

"Me too," he says happily, reaching over to squeeze my hand, his thumb brushing lightly over the top of the diamond ring sitting on my left hand.

Three weeks ago, Ryan suggested a picnic in Greenwich Park. I thought it was a random but lovely idea and didn't think anything else about it. It seemed a bit strange that he wanted to go in the evening, but he said that way, it wouldn't be too crowded.

Once we got there, I was happy to sit anywhere there was a space and dig into the food he'd placed very carefully in a hamper, something I gleefully took the piss out of him for (my picnic style is to buy food on the way and throw it haphazardly in a shopping bag). But Ryan insisted we keep walking to the very top of the hill, and it took me a while to realize that he was aiming for the exact spot we'd sat in many years ago, two interns at the start of their career, looking out at the view of the city.

When we'd sat down on the blanket he'd brought with him (adorable; I usually plonked myself on my jacket or put up with the grass), he pulled out a bottle of champagne and cracked it open, pouring us both a glass. It didn't even click then. I just thought he was being a bit extra. But then he said that he'd chosen this spot specifically because it was, he considers, where we had our sort-of first date and the moment when, thanks to our almost first kiss, he was filled with hope that he might have a chance with me, the girl he knew with certainty he would always love.

He got a box out of his pocket, and it felt like the rest of the world disappeared as he swiftly maneuvered from sitting on the blanket to being on one knee in front of me.

It was the easiest answer I've ever had to give.

Mimi helped him pick the ring, he revealed, and she and Katya were the first people I called to tell the news the next day. They screamed with joy as though it was a *huge* surprise, and Mimi immediately set about planning a celebratory dinner for us. Being my best friend and Ryan's colleague—not to mention, instrumental in getting us together in Florence—she is maid of honor and is not taking those duties lightly. We're thinking of doing a small wedding abroad and she emails me at least three or four times a week with different location ideas and beautiful venues.

Florence is the leading contender.

After telling Mimi the news, next we video-called Ryan's parents to let them know, and they started jumping up and down. Poor Sully had no idea what was going on and burst into celebratory zoomies, bounding across the sofas and knocking over a lamp.

The Stockholm trip was their idea, as Fredrik wanted to introduce me to his side of the family. Ryan and I are going for a full week where we'll spend the first few days just us so we have some time alone and he can show me around the city—strictly no working allowed during this period (his rule)—and then the last few days, his parents are coming to join us and we'll meet the family. I'm nervous because I want to impress them, but if they're anything like Fredrik, I know I won't have to worry. I've never felt so welcome anywhere as I do when we go to visit them in Manchester.

I've finally got the family I always wanted.

Things with Juliet are going well, and she's much more a part of my life now. It took us a while to get into a rhythm, starting with lunches and dinners here and there, getting to know each other once again. We had a lot of years to catch up on. She's thrilled about our engagement and has met Ryan a few times, which means a lot to me. Having found a job in advertising, she's much more at ease when we meet up. Her body language and facial expressions are noticeably warmer than ever before.

Mum and Dad are a work in progress for both of us. Juliet is intent on making it work with them, while I'm happier to let it go. But she keeps saying "family is family," and at Christmas we all agreed to our first gathering since that summer dinner where everything fell apart. Not that it had ever really been together in the first place.

The dinner was stilted and forced and I was so grateful to have Ryan with me. Somehow it helped having someone from outside the family present, and, as I should have guessed, my parents took to him. They had obviously Googled him before the dinner, and some of his pieces had impressed them—they made a point of bringing up certain topics that he'd written about and asking him questions about them.

They even admitted that my podcast was a success, despite "not being into that sort of thing." Ryan took great pains to tell them how the first series had topped the charts and been nominated for several awards at the time, two of which—"Best New Podcast" and "Best Arts and Culture Podcast"—I went on to win. My parents listened to Ryan's raving about my achievements and politely wished me luck.

Their effort toward Ryan was, Juliet believes, their version of an olive branch. This was further confirmed in her mind when Dad emailed us both afterward to thank Juliet for organizing the "pleasant" evening and suggest scheduling the next date for dinner with us and Ryan. But we still haven't spoken about what I said that night, and they still haven't apologized for anything. I've accepted that they never will.

Juliet is hopeful, though, that things will improve, for herself as much as for me. They still haven't shown much of an interest in her job and continue to make disparaging comments about her career pivot, which I know hurts her. I'm still not sure whether we'll invite them to the wedding. But whatever happens with my parents, I'll be okay. I have Mimi and I got my sister back. And now I have Ryan.

I have all I need.

Not to mention, work is going very well. The podcast continues to soar and I have incredible guests lined up for the third series, including Audrey Abbot, who will be speaking to me about her soon-to-be-released memoirs and promoting the new London show she's directing—an all-female production of *Much Ado About Nothing* at the National Theatre. I'm still writing, too, on a freelance basis now. I've written a lot for Rakhee at *Sleek* and have formed some excellent relationships with the editors of other leading publications—my work has been published in *Vogue,* and I've just filed my first piece for *TIME* magazine. I have turned down any commissions from Cosmo Chambers-Smyth at *Narrative,* although word on the street is that he won't be there much longer if the publishers have their way. I have a feeling I know who the next editor might be, although the candidate I have in mind will have to juggle his new responsibilities with meeting the demands of the book deal he recently clinched.

I have no doubt he can handle it.

The success of the podcast undoubtedly gave me a confidence boost, but I've also been working on another project that I'm pretty excited about. After leaving the constraints of the powers that be at *Narrative* and finally shrugging off the burdensome weight of my parents' opinion, I realized that my work could help others aspiring to careers that might seem out of reach. So I set about planning and editing a book that will be a collection of stories from women in the arts—it's a labor of love and will take a while to collate. I'm selecting and interviewing women from all walks of life working in varying cultural endeavors—film, TV, theater, music, publishing, galleries—and with all types of job titles, whether they're stars of the show or unsung heroes behind the scenes. Once I interview them about how they got to where they are, what challenges they overcame, and what advice they'd give to others hoping to follow in their footsteps, I write up their chapter in the first-person narrative, doing my best to capture their voice. I've already tested the waters with publishers and several have come back to request a meeting to discuss its potential. A couple of them have already expressed their hopes that it could even be a series.

I hate for Ryan and Mimi to have been right all along, but it turns out that the redundancy was a shake-up that helped me after all—I'm proud of what I'm doing and I'm excited for whatever comes next.

When we arrive at the airport, Ryan screenshots my boarding pass and sends it to me so I have it on my phone to go through the barriers to join the security queue. Wheeling my case behind me, I get the pass up on my phone and then stop in my tracks.

"Hang on. The flight isn't until midday."

"Yes, that's right," he replies coolly, encouraging me to carry on walking.

"You said it was at eleven."

He smiles smugly. "I did."

"Why did you say that?"

"To get you out of the house on time."

"Ryan!" I look at him incredulously. "You lied to me!"

"I told a little white lie to make sure we got to the airport early, which is what you're supposed to do before an international flight," he explains without a hint of remorse. "If the flight was really at eleven, then we'd only be here an hour and fifteen minutes before takeoff, which is much too late."

"That is the perfect amount of time!" I argue.

"The airline recommends two hours."

I throw my hands up in the air. "Who arrives at the airport two hours before their flight?"

"Smart, organized, happy people. We'll have no stress or rushing getting to the gate. We can enjoy a drink beforehand. This is the way to do it, trust me," he says cheerily, strolling toward security.

"I can't believe this," I grumble, stomping behind him and dragging my bag behind me. "You made me rush around getting ready this morning for no reason!"

"We both know you would have still been rushing around getting ready this morning, even if you'd had the extra hour. Nothing would have been different."

"That is not true! I would have had a luxurious time getting things packed," I counter.

"Now you can have a luxurious time waltzing around the terminal with no panic about missing the flight."

"That's the last time you'll fool me. From now on, I'm in charge of booking flights so there won't be any chance of you pulling the wool over my eyes again."

He sighs, turning back to stop me and wrapping his hands around my waist.

"I think from our Prague experience we both know that it's not a good idea for you to take charge of travel plans, wouldn't you agree?"

I blush at the memory, before stubbornly saying, "I still maintain that the hotel got the dates of our stay wrong, not me."

"No question." He grins, dipping his head and kissing me on the cheek. "Even though your booking confirmation stated the same dates the hotel had, it makes much more sense that they were somehow at fault."

I exhale as his lips brush along my cheekbone, sinking into him as he holds me close. It's very difficult to argue with him when he does this. My brain is compromised and my line of thinking becomes scrambled due to the fluttering deep within my stomach.

"All right," I say, unable to fight a smile, "you can be in charge of travel plans. But I get to be in charge of travel snacks."

"That seems fair," he murmurs against my skin, his hands pressed against the small of my back so that I arch into him as his lips make their way to mine. He kisses me, a long, deep kiss that drowns out the hubbub of the airport surrounding us, before pressing his forehead against mine and giving me one of those knowing smiles of his.

"I thought you wanted to get through security for a luxurious couple of hours waltzing around the terminal," I say, closing my eyes and grinning.

"No rush," he says, finding my hands and threading his fingers through mine. "We have all the time in the world."

I don't usually let Ryan have the last word. But as he leans in for another kiss, I decide that I might just let him have this one.

ACKNOWLEDGMENTS

Huge thanks to my wonderful editors, Kim and Sarah, for your creativity, guidance, and excellent senses of humor. Working on this book with you both was, as ever, so much fun, and I'm very grateful to you for believing in Harper and Ryan. You're the best, thank you.

Thank you to Amy, Olivia, Jenny, Rebecca, Drue, Marissa, Kejana, Mary, and the talented teams at Hodder & Stoughton and St. Martin's Press. Thank you for everything you've done to make my book ten times better than it was and for getting it out into the world.

Thanks to my fabulous agent, Lauren; to the amazing Justine, Julie, and Paul, who stepped in to help with this project; and to everyone at Bell Lomax Moreton for always cheering me on.

To my family and friends, thank you for your continued encouragement—I couldn't do any of this without you. Special thanks to Ben for your unwavering support and for making me hot chocolate to keep me going through late nights writing, and to my loyal and loving dog, Bon, who snoozes at my feet while I work and never fails to put a smile on my face.

And, finally, a huge thank-you to everyone who takes the time to read my books. I write stories like this one in the hope of bringing some joy to your day and making you laugh, so fingers crossed it does just that.

ABOUT THE AUTHOR

Imogen Forte

KATY BIRCHALL is the author of *The Last Word*, *The Wedding Season*, and *The Secret Bridesmaid* as well as numerous books for young readers. The former deputy features editor for *Country Life* magazine, she is also a freelance journalist. She lives in London with her husband, Ben, and their corgi-cross rescue dog, Bono.